"Please raise y[...]

The driver could sh[...] could move, probab[...] could reach him, and then finish off the job with bare hands if there was no choice. But in the next moment, two ground scooters pulled out of the darkness, each of them containing two human riders. None of them seemed to be armed, but then one of them slid a hand into his jacket pocket. Two muffled pops, an eruption of scorching cloth, and two explosive bullets ripped into the driver's side.

The impact flung him sideways, but he didn't drop the pulser. He was actually trying to turn and fire at his killer when the strength went out of him. He wavered, braced for a moment on a tripod of tail and legs, then fell on his side with blood covering belly and muzzle.

Davidson had a moment of relief that the driver was no longer a menace, then another muzzle rose, and another finger squeezed a trigger. This time darts stitched Davidson's chest. He felt the sharp stabs, then numbness spreading around them, and gagged. As he went to his knees, another dart stabbed his neck. He was vaguely aware of falling facedown on the road, but after that it was all blackness.

STARCRUISER SHENANDOAH

4

VAIN COMMAND

ROLAND J. GREEN

A ROC BOOK

ROC
Published by the Penguin Group
Penguin Books USA Inc., 375 Hudson Street,
New York, New York 10014, U.S.A.
Penguin Books Ltd, 27 Wrights Lane,
London W8 5TZ, England
Penguin Books Australia Ltd, Ringwood,
Victoria, Australia
Penguin Books Canada Ltd, 10 Alcorn Avenue,
Toronto, Ontario, Canada M4V 3B2
Penguin Books (N.Z.) Ltd, 182–190 Wairau Road,
Auckland 10, New Zealand

Penguin Books Ltd, Registered Offices:
Harmondsworth, Middlesex, England

First published by Roc, an imprint of New American Library,
a division of Penguin Books USA Inc.

First Printing, October, 1992
10 9 8 7 6 5 4 3 2 1

 REGISTERED TRADEMARK—MARCA REGISTRADA

PRINTED IN THE UNITED STATES OF AMERICA

Principal Characters

A. Humans

Marshal Emilio BANFI: Retired Federation officer, resident on Linuk'h.

Admiral of the Fleet Wilhelmina BAUMANN, U.F.N.: Commander-in-chief, United Federation Navy.

Captain Pavel BOGDANOV, U.F.N.: Commanding officer, U.F.S. *Shenandoah*.

Ursula BOLL: Wife of Nikolai Sergeyevich Komarov; Federation Intelligence agent.

Commander Joseph BRONSTEIN, U.F.N.: Commanding officer, U.F.S. *Powell*.

Leo BUTKUS: Boatswain, R.M.S. *Somtow Nosavan*.

Commander Jacqueline CHARBON, U.F.N.: Executive officer, U.F.S. *Shenandoah*.

Colonel Malcolm DAVIDSON: Caledonian (British Union) Army officer, aide to Marshal Banfi.

Sergeant Juan ESTEVA: Security & Intelligence NCO for Candice Shore's LI company and the commanding officer's bodyguard.

Commander Herman FRANKE, U.F.N.: Federation Naval Intelligence officer, initially assigned to Victoria.

Commander Shintaro FUJITA, U.F.N.: Chief engineer, U.F.S. *Shenandoah*.

Jeremiah GIST: President, Planetary Republic of Victoria.

Nikolai Sergeyevich KOMAROV: Artist and Federation agent residing on Linak'h under the name Oleg Govorov. Candice Shore's father.

Rear Admiral Sho KUWAHARA, U.F.N.: Staff officer at Forces Command, Charlemagne.

Commodore Rose LIDDELL, U.F.N.: Flag officer commanding the Linak'h squadron; pennant in *Shenandoah*.

Charles V. LONGMAN: Chief engineer, R.M.S. *Somtow Nosavan*.

Lieutenant Commander Brian MAHONEY, U.F.N.: Communications watch officer aboard *Shenandoah*.

Joanna MARDER: Captain, R.M.S. *Somtow Nosavan*.

Major Lucretia MORLEY: Federation Military Police officer, assigned to the same intelligence mission on Victoria as Commander Franke.

First Lieutenant Olga NALYVKINA: Federation Army officer, assigned as Marshal Banfi's personal pilot.

Colonel Liew NIEG: Federation Army Intelligence officer, assigned to Linak'h.

Lieutenant General Alys PARKINSON: Commander-in-chief, Defense Forces of the Planetary Republic of Victoria.

Carlos RUBIROSA: Governor-General of the Federation Territory, Linak'h.

Major Candice SHORES: Commanding officer, *Shenandoah*'s embarked Light Infantry company.

Sergeant First Class Jan SKLARINSKY: Sniper in *Shenandoah* LI company.

First Lieutenant Brigitte TACHIN: Division officer, Weapons Department, *Shenandoah*.

Major General Joachim TANZ: Commanding general, Linak'h Command.

Lieutenant Commander Gordon UHLIG: Observer from *Shenandoah*, assigned to U.F.N. *Powell*.

Lieutenant Commander Elayne ZHENG: Electronic warfare officer in the 879th Squadron (Heavy Attack).

B. Nonhumans

Fleet Commander Eimo su-ANKRAI: Baernoi; former commander of the Seventh Training Squadron off Victoria.

Emt DESDAI: Ptercha'a; representative and agent of Payaral Na'an.

Ship Commander First Class Brokeh su-IRZIM: Baernoi; Inquirer, assigned to Linak'h.

Ship Commander First Class Zhapso su-LAL: Baernoi; Inquirer, assigned to Linak'h.

The LIDESSOUF twins, Kalidessouf and Solidessouf:

Baernoi; elite Assault Force veterans, assigned to the Inquiry mission on Linak'h under Rahbad Sarlin.

Payaral NA'AN: Merishi; head of the trade mission on Victoria.

Ship Commander First Class Rahbad SARLIN: Baernoi; veteran field agent of the Special Projects branch of the Office of Inquiry, assigned to Linak'h.

Fleet Commander F'Zoar su-WEIGHO: Baernoi; retired but still influential Fleet officer. Patron of su-Irzim and Zeg.

Ship Commander Second Class Behdan ZEG: Baernoi; Special Projects field officer, half brother of Rahbad Sarlin.

Glossary

AD: Air Defense.

Administration: Ptercha'a government within the Federation Territory on Linak'h.

Alliance: Freeworld States Alliance, principal human rival to the United Federation of Starworlds.

Antahli: Leading minority nationality in the Khudrigate of Baer.

Baernoi: Sapient humanoid race, highly militarized, whose remote ancestors resembled Terran pigs. Refer to themselves as "the People."

BEU: Battalion expeditionary unit; smallest self-contained Federation ground forces unit, built around a rifle battalion.

Blue & Gold: An officer militantly loyal to the Navy.

Blue Death: Large pelagic predator native to planet Farsi.

C-cubed: Command, control, communications.

Charlemagne: Capital planet of the Federation and site of Forces Command.

Climb: Merishi term for a subspace transition.

Coordination: The major Ptercha'a state on Linak'h.

COS: Chief of staff.

E&E: Escape and evasion.

EI: Electronic intercept/intelligence.

Emergence: Appearance of a starship after a Jump; is detectable at interplanetary distances.

EMP: Electromagnetic pulse.

EVA: Extravehicular activity.

fmyl: High-protein vegetable, a staple Ptercha'a crop.

goldtusk: Derogatory Baernoi term for an idle aristocrat.

Great Khudr: Military leader who united the planet Baer under Syrodhi leadership.

House: Merishi mercantile association within which membership is hereditary.

Hufen: Capital city of the Governance of the Merishi Territory on Linak'h.

IFF: Identification friend/foe.

ihksohn: Ptercha'a term for a matchmaker.

Inquiry: Baernoi term for Intelligence.

inward-eating: Baernoi term for a condition equivalent to stomach ulcers.

JAG: Judge Advocate General.

Jump: Interstellar transition through subspace. A micro-Jump is a subspace transition within a planetary system.

koayass: Ornamental shade tree, native to Merish but highly popular among the Ptercha'a.

Merishi: Humanoid sapient race, evolved from climbing omnivorous reptiles; ruthless and far-flung traders. Refer to themselves as "the Folk," and are called "Scaleskins" by both Baernoi and humans.

nest-free: Merishi term for being of legally adult age.

Och'zem: Ptercha'a capital of the Administration of the Federation Territory.

OECZ: Outward edge of the combat zone.

okugh: Potent Merishi distilled spirit, about 130 proof.

OOW: Officer of the watch.

PE & D: Planetary Exploration and Development.

Petzas: Nearest major Baernoi planet to Linak'h; Petzas-Din (Petzas, the City) is the capital.

Ptercha'a: Humanoid sapient race with strongly feline characteristics, first encountered by humans when serving as mercenaries for the Merishi. They call themselves "the Hunters," and are called "Catmen" (human), "Furrics" or more formally "Servants in War" (Merishi), and "Furfolk" (Baernoi).

R.M.S.: Registered Merchant Ship.

SAR: Search and Rescue.

Scaleskins: Derogatory term used by both Baernoi and humans for the Merishi.

Security: When capitalized, the Merishi's term for their armed forces.

SFO: Supporting fires observer.

sgai: Spicy fruit-based after-dinner Merishi drink, nonalcoholic.

skrin: Small, voracious predator, native to mountain regions of Baer.

SSW: Squad support weapon; long-range crew-served infantry weapon firing solid and explosive projectiles.

Syrodhi: Dominant nationality among the Baernoi.

TI: Training instructor.

TOAD: Temporary out-of-area duty.

TO & E: Table of Organization and Equipment.

True Speech (also "Language"): Ptercha'a term for their native language.

Tuskers: Derogatory human term for the Baernoi, who have nonvestigial tusks.

U.F.N.: United Federation Navy.

uhrim: A staple of the Baernoi diet, a tuber resembling the sweet potato.

uys: Fortified fermented Baernoi beverage, resembling sherry.

watch: Baernoi unit of time, equivalent to 5.2 hours. The Baernoi day is divided into five watches.

XO: Executive officer.

z'dok: Merishi obscenity borrowed by the Ptercha'a: one who defecates in another's nest.

Prologue

Linak'h:

The snowleaf trees across the stream cast only a single shadow on the burnt-gold sand of the bank and the rippling green of the water. Their pale leaves also rippled.

Rahbad Sarlin had fieldcraft enough to not break freeze. He also knew what had happened, without needing to look up. The clouds had veiled the Yellow Father, leaving only the Red Child in Linak'h's sky.

The ruddy twilight would give the Lidessouf twins visual cover for their crossing of the stream. A good rainy night would be even better, but this spring's rains had been dismally scant in the Territories of the Old Continent of Linak'h. One whose kin farmed broad lands on Kythas and did his drinking in the farmers' beerhouses, Rahbad Sarlin had been uneasy over this even before he left on this mission.

He hid this from the team, however. Solidessouf and Kalidessouf were city-bred; Virik ihn Petzas might have been born anywhere on the planet he had incorporated in his name, but had gone straight from a city orphanage to the Army. All three were Assault Force veterans—the "Death Commandos" of so many tales the Smallteeth used to frighten children and recruits.

None cared to follow a leader who fretted about something that could not affect their mission and about which he could do nothing.

All three might be right. Sarlin willed his attention away from a growing itch under his left ear, felt a flying insect explore his right tusk, and left the weather of Linak'h and all other worlds to the Sky Lord.

The snowmelt at least was feeding the stream. It ran shoulder-high to one of the People, ear-high to the average soldier of the Furfolk. How high it would come on a Scaleskin, Sarlin never expected to see— the Merishi hated to immerse themselves in water. Icy snowmelt water flowing fast from the mountains could be death to them.

The faintest of sounds, a few fallen needles giving under the weight of a foot, told Sarlin of Virik ihn Petzas's return. The scar-seamed Guide froze against a tree whose name Sarlin did not know, but which blended perfectly with the old warrior's clothing and skin cream.

Without turning his head and barely moving his lips, he reported. The twins were across the stream, with all the essential equipment.

"The rocket too?"

"Yes." The tone was nearly insubordinate. What the Guide muttered afterward would surely have been so, if Sarlin had heard it clearly. He judged it a good time to be partly deaf, although his hearing was in fact remarkably perfect for one of sixty. He would not have presumed to lead this field mission himself otherwise.

Virik did not believe in the miniature rockets as message-carriers. He might not believe in the existence of the mission's space support. He certainly doubted the support's willingness to violate Scaleskin or Smalltooth territory to retrieve what might not be vital information.

Sarlin believed in the rockets, having used them successfully on missions before the twins were born. He also felt that the support would come.

"Those we seek can trace the rockets quickly enough only by detectable means," he had said—it seemed five or six times. "Perhaps detectable from orbit, certainly from our surveillance lifters. Our quarry has made a great effort to hide himself. Why abandon it, when *he* cannot know what intelligence the rocket carries?"

Virik ihn Petzas had grunted. The twins at least had been silent and met his eyes, but Rahbad Sarlin was not Assault Force and Virik was. Their politeness fell short of belief.

In half a watch, they would at least know who was right. Sarlin had been on Linak'h long enough to read time by the suns in daylight and the stars by night, but he could see his watch without breaking freeze. Certainly no more than half a watch, unless their estimate of the enemy camp's location was hopelessly off.

It seemed not merely half a watch but half a day before Virik moved. Sarlin took his cue from the Guide, shifting to free the radio. Already voice-coded for "Receive," it merely purred softly. Twice a faint crackle of atmospheric electricity broke into the purr.

Then the homing beacon of the rocket came on the air. The sharp whine, like a hundred skrins imitating the ritual keen, made Sarlin wince even as he sought a direction. He'd just found that the beacon came from across the stream when Virik moved again, this time with little regard for the freeze.

"They're in trouble!" the Guide said. "Something

set off the beacon by accident. They never launched the pox-rotted rocket!" Gracious in victory or perhaps only too concerned for the twins, he said no more, but only unslung the sniper's quickgun from his back. Then he pulled a twenty-round magazine from his ammunition pouch and put it ready to hand.

Sarlin followed the Guide's lead, complete to putting the magazine with the latch upright, so that no dirt or needles would keep it from seating. They had ten magazines of mixed explosive and incendiary rounds apiece, not much for a serious fight and useless against heavy armor, but then neither was in their plans—

The drone of fast-firing Smalltooth pulsers was sudden but unmistakable to trained ears. Without a word or a gesture, the two People rolled apart and began crawling. When they stopped, they were out of sight of each other and out of hearing unless they shouted.

The radio would be enough for battle codes, however, If they needed more or if the enemy could fix and launch on field-radio codes, their situation was graver than Sarlin would allow it to be without evidence.

The evidence came almost with Sarlin's next breath. The twins burst from the snowleafs and plunged down the bank of the stream. Spray leaped as they dove in, half running, half swimming, Solidessouf in the lead. Even half submerged, he showed blood and an empty harness where the rocket had been.

Virik shouted something that was neither battle code nor the language of the People. The twins both ducked under, and Virik let fly with his weapon. Incendiary and explosive rounds both started fires, the fires raised a veil of smoke on the far bank, and the twins finished their crossing behind the veil.

An enemy on the flank, however, found a clear target. Sarlin heard pulsers droning again, this time punctuated with the thumps of grenades being launched and vicious flat cracks as they exploded.

The twins lunged up the bank and dove under cover to either side of Sarlin. They were drenched and dripping, Solidessouf was still bleeding, and both were shaking with rage.

"The filth-weaned rocket caught fire!" Kalidessouf growled, as he checked the barrel of his launcher for water. "That had them right on to us faster than you can spit out bad beer!"

In spite of his wounds, the other twin seemed calmer. He saw Sarlin's confusion, pulled out a tube of wound spray, and began squirting his cuts while he explained.

They had reached the perimeter of the camp about when they expected it, but encountered much more activity. From a purely visual estimate, it seemed that this was what they were looking for—a camp where mercenaries and agents were trained to serve the Merishi, mostly against the humans but possibly against the People as well.

Rather than risk detection by penetrating farther, they recorded their intelligence where they were. Scaleskins, Furfolk, and Smallteeth were all there, with the Scaleskins apparently in command if anybody was.

Then, still undetected, they withdrew to launch the rocket, faithfully obeying orders and thereby nearly ruining the mission. The rocket misfired, and by a freak of electronics the misfire started the homing beacon.

Solidessouf tried to turn off the beacon, and the rocket exploded—"more in my arse than in my face, the Lords be thanked!" he said—which alerted the camp. The twins ran, and thought they had kept out of visual contact with their pursuers even though there'd been a good deal of random firing.

"You have a backup copy of the data?" Sarlin asked.

This drew pitying looks from both twins. "We used the backup for the rocket. *We* have the primary. Don't they teach you that in Special Projects?" Kalidessouf said, with an exaggerated Court accent.

Sarlin was about to suggest that they needed him as a marksman rather than a mimic when Solidessouf raised both thumbs for silence. They all heard it then—the splash as a body hit the stream, followed by a new burst of firing, pulsers and a single quickgun dueling across the water.

"If they're on Virik's flank, we'll be on theirs," Solidessouf said. He snapped the sight/guidance tube up into firing position and slipped down toward the bank.

"Stay under cover," Sarlin hissed. "We want to leave them confused about who probed them."

"If it doesn't mean abandoning Virik, we will," Kalidessouf said. He crawled in the other direction, also fitting his launcher for long-range work.

Sarlin barely had time to wonder what they would call "abandoning Virik" when the twins opened fire. Their fire raised a curtain of spray across the stream and toppled two standing figures from the far bank. Another figure—Sarlin thought it was Furfolk—tried to use the spray for cover. He seemed almost across the stream when he threw up his arms and toppled backward into the water.

Four thumps, and four grenades flew across the stream to bracket Virik's position. Sarlin shut his ears to the explosions, knew he would hear no unworthy cries, but doubted that he would hear Virik again. That last shot at the river-crosser had given away the Guide's position.

Two—Smallteeth, Sarlin thought—immediately plunged into the stream. One of them died from a head shot. The other reached the bank before one of the twins put a round through something explosive on the human's belt. He not only died but disintegrated.

The rain of fragments seemed to discourage further stream-crossers. At the same time, Sarlin saw movement in the undergrowth opposite him. Before the mover could get a proper sight line or even a good look at the twins, Sarlin had sprayed the area with half a magazine. Smoke and screams floated out of it, and the twins needed no orders to come leaping up the bank into cover.

"Solidessouf, you're hurt. Take the data and move out. Kalidessouf, you and I are going to retrieve Virik's body."

That was Assault Force custom, so the order finally gained Sarlin willing obedience from the twins. It was also the standard procedure of Special Projects, when you wanted an opponent to remain ignorant of who had been asking questions— and in this case, taking a toll—of his people.

"Where do we hide him?" Kalidessouf asked.

"There's an overhang on the north side of that ravine we crossed, about a tenth-march back."

"That won't give us time to bury him."

"We can't risk being overtaken by carrying him farther than that. Besides, who said anything about burying? I'll wire some of our explosive rounds into a charge and bring the whole overhang down on him. It's loaded with rocks, so I doubt if they'll bother digging it out."

Solidessouf nodded. "There's a big cluster of wizard's-tool that commands all the approaches to the overhang. I'll take position there and use battle code if anyone gets there before you do."

Both twins now looked at him almost with respect instead of mere politeness and obedience to superior rank. Sarlin nodded. This was not the time to add that he also had graduated from the Assault Force Advanced Field Demolitions course, because it was the best offered among the People.

He would let them take their own time about forgiving him for the rocket and for Virik's death. Then they would find their way to a beerhall and drink to the Guide's memory, and after that be ready for another mission together.

Unless his colleagues from the Fleet thought this mission had learned everything necessary—and Rahbad Sarlin knew that Fleet Inquirers would be that easily satisfied on the day the Great Khudr rose from his grave!

One

Charlemagne:

Rear Admiral Sho Kuwahara was a rarity among the staff at Federation Forces Command: he commuted from the suburbs of Europa. Not just an outlying section of the Federal District, either—Bennington was clear outside the District, in Geneva County.

His wife, Fumiko, had not objected to leaving her position with her family's business and packing herself and their daughter, Hanae, all the way from Akhito to Charlemagne. She had balked at living in the flag quarters at Fort Montgomery, and promised to cover the difference between Kuwahara's quarters allowance and the lease of a decent home outside the District.

Since her share of the profits from her family's firm slightly exceeded Kuwahara's salary, Fumiko's offer had some substance to it. Hanae cast a further vote in favor of staying away from the city and close to the ski and hiking trails.

"This isn't the Eastern Limb on Yamato," Kuwahara pointed out, in a mild dissent. "Europa may have two million people, but it has its share of green space. I don't think there's a Satsuma Circle within ten kloms of the river."

"That is because the subsoil won't support one,"

21

Hanae replied. She had an annoying habit of alternating between bursts of all-consuming research on what currently interested her and bursts of enthusiasm for nothing except hiking or skiing, frequently with the current best male friend. The prospect of the move to Charlemagne brought on a research fit devoted to the Starworlds' capital planet and particularly the Federal District.

The Kuwaharas ended with a four-bedroom house five minutes by foot from the Bennington train station and ten minutes from its lifter pad. This morning Kuwahara had planned to lift in. After staying up late digesting the file on the dual-sovereignty planets, he had hoped to turn over most of the morning's work to the second watch and sleep late.

Unfortunately Admiral Joshi was down with something that wasn't responding fast enough to the antivirals, and Admiral Harlow was on leave attending her daughter's wedding. This left one less than the legal minimum of flag officers for handling some of the business Kuwahara wanted to delegate.

So there was nothing to do but get up early enough to eat a solid breakfast, discover that a blizzard was delaying lifter commuting, and slog through the snow to the railroad station. The warmth of the train nearly put Kuwahara to sleep before the caffeine began filtering through his system, but for the first time his luck was good. He was alert and aware by the time the train announced, "Forces Command."

Even flag officers did not wisely face Admiral of the Fleet Wilhelmina Baumann ("Chilly Willi" or *die Kaiserin* when she was out of hearing) on an empty stomach or with a cloudy mind, and when they knew why she wanted to see them. When all one had was an assortment of mutually exclusive and somewhat ed-

ucated guesses, one ideally needed a few days' medita-
tion and prayer as well.

Charlemagne:

As a Forces Command watch CO, Kuwahara rated a
princely suite of three rooms, with a deputy, two secre-
taries, an aide, and an orderly. All of them had beaten
their admiral to work, and Kuwahara thought that at
least the deputy and the aide were trying not to grin.

He also realized that if they had been grinning, he
would have taken skin and maybe flesh off their bones.
A mysterious summons from Baumann shouldn't be
making him *that* edgy, even if such visits had been
known to terminate careers.

"Good morning, Admiral," the deputy said. She
handed him a sealed note, hand-addressed in writing
Kuwahara recognized.

In his office, Kuwahara poured himself a cup of tea
and opened the note.

> Sho,
>
> I suggest that we meet for our little talk over
> lunch, in my quarters. Try to leave a clean desk
> in your office when you come.
>
> W. Baumann

Kuwahara was glad that no one could see his expression. "Leave a clean desk" was a command the
Empress often gave to officers about to be reassigned
to penal colonies, and not always as staff either. On

the other hand, she had a strict rule about never chopping anybody off in quarters or at social functions.

Reassignment, probably. Punishment, almost certainly not. And a whole morning to work on that desk.

"Intercom, Station Two."

The computer put him through to his deputy. "LaVerne," Kuwahara said, "give me the priorities on our leftovers."

"Well, the coffee is pretty good, but I don't trust the chocolate, and we had to toss the—"

"I will toss you in another minute, Captain. Baumann's having me to lunch—*to*, not *for*—and we need to push."

"Aye aye, Admiral." Kuwahara's screen beeped plaintively, and began scrolling at speed-reading rate a depressingly long list of unfinished business.

Charlemagne:

By noon the depression and most of the list were gone. Kuwahara actually had time to shower and change his uniform, always prudent when calling on the Empress. (No one willing to talk could confirm or deny that she slept in uniform-cut pajamas with her awards embroidered on them, but the rumor persisted.)

Baumann's quarters were an eight-room penthouse on the roof of Courcy Tower. Courcy had been as traditional a residence for Navy flag officers as Claremont for the Army or Barbarossa for Services, and in fact was linked to Forces Command Tower by a tube at the thirtieth level.

The Navy chief saved Kuwahara all the elevator and tube time. Her personal lifter under robot control picked him up on the Forces pad, bounced him through the wind and the snow to the Courcy Tower pad, and turned him over to the steward.

"Good afternoon, Admiral," the steward said. Kuwahara remembered his name as Naran Singh, a senior cook in the mess aboard Baumann's flagship when she fought and won the Federation's single fleet action against the Baernoi. He looked too young to be retired, but then a Force commander-in-chief was actually allowed a domestic servant, or even two, from the active-duty roster.

"Good afternoon, Chief," Kuwahara said. He handed his overcoat to the steward, then brushed snowflakes off his uniform. Wind-hurled snow had crept through unsealed openings even in the ten meters between the lifter and the door.

"The admiral is in the lounge," the steward said. "What do you want to drink?"

"Tea."

"Western or Asian style?"

"Whatever's handiest, as long as it's hot."

The steward smiled, "Are you joining the Decentralists, Admiral?"

"I suppose the Federation could choose a capital with milder winters if it had to start over again. But Europa has five hundred years of tradition behind it. Besides, the shipping charges for dividing up the monuments alone would bankrupt the government!"

The lounge door slid open, and Kuwahara came to attention as a tall woman in undress blues rose from a couch across the room beyond.

"Come on in, Sho, and Chief, don't listen to this effete gentleman. Two of the Pied Noir '97."

"Aye aye, ma'am."

Kuwahara stepped through the door as it closed,

feeling more than usually like a discipline case called before the school director.

Charlemagne:

Unlike Captain—no, she was a commodore now—Rose Liddell of *Shenandoah*, Admiral Baumann couldn't set people at ease simply by coming into a room. With her height, chiseled beauty, and display of ribbons, she looked too inherently formidable.

Fortunately being a watch CO gave Kuwahara direct access to Baumann, and he'd learned that her reputation for vivisecting captains before breakfast was largely unjustified. (A mild disappointment, too—Kuwahara had encountered at least three captains at Forces Command who deserved such treatment.)

Previous acquaintance, mutual respect, and the excellent Pied Noir sherry had both officers at ease before lunch arrived. The broiled Firelands bluefish, salad, and lemon mousse improved matters further. By the time Naran Singh produced Japanese-style tea for Kuwahara and coffee for Baumann, Kuwahara was ready to attend his own court-martial in a relatively tolerant frame of mind.

They took their second cups to the study, with its wall of pictures recording Baumann's forty years in the Navy and its case of golf trophies recording her other great passion. Baumann took a lounger, stretched her long legs out on a hassock, and fixed him with what he hoped was a friendly stare.

"So. What do you think of the dual-sovereignty situation now?"

Nobody ever helped himself with Baumann by giving a vague answer. Unfortunately, Kuwahara loathed false precision, even if it meant sounding too cautious. One answer met both his requirements and Baumann's. It was even true.

"If the Federation had been as sloppy about handling anything else as we've been about dual-sovereignty planets, there'd be riots in the streets and nasty remarks in the history books."

Baumann gave one of her rare grins. Kuwahara felt better, which was not the same as relaxed. "Also possibly an Alliance twice as strong," she said. "In fact, I think the Alliance is the key to the problem."

"I can't see a war with the Alliance over fewer than thirty second-rate planets," Kuwahara said.

"Neither can I," Baumann said. "But I wasn't thinking of the future. I was thinking that even during the Hive Wars, the Federation could have anticipated that something like the Alliance would emerge. Then any subplanetary government that wanted off-planet help would have someplace to go, as it hadn't before. Lack of imagination, to say the least."

To Baumann, "lack of imagination" was a crime nearly on a level with child-molesting or floating fraudulent bonds.

"They didn't anticipate the Baernoi, either," Kuwahara added.

"No, but again, it was something they should have allowed for. I admit that we knew a lot less about the range of nonhuman sophonts the Universe could throw up, two centuries ago. But nobody seems to have allowed for a race like the Tuskers."

What was it that a previous Navy C-in-C had said about the Baernoi? Oh, yes. " 'Impossible to buy off and too tough to beat down,' " Kuwahara quoted.

"Exactly. Especially with the Alliance ready to take advantage of the situation if we're stupid enough to try the second option. And now we have the Merishi developing a militaristic streak, just to make sure we *never* get any sleep."

Kuwahara nodded politely, now sure that he faced a new assignment and impatient to just this side of rudeness to learn what it would be. Probably something that drew on his experience at Victoria, one of the classic dual-sovereignty muddles.

There the Alliance and the Federation had divided up a chilly, dusty little world and more or less kept the peace until some of the frontier settlers in Federation territory decided to rebel. They set up an independent government rather than joining the Alliance, but matters still went rapidly from bad to worse.

Humans contributed their share of folly, including a willingness to fusion-bomb civilians, but both Merishi and Baernoi gave various sets of humans both lethal weapons and motives for using them. In the end Victoria was intact, united, and temporarily at peace, and some of both the Baernoi and Merishi were cooperating with Federation Intelligence to undo their compatriots' injudicious plotting.

However, Alliance Field Intelligence, the source of more trouble than anyone else, got off nearly free. (Except possibly for what its own Navy would do to it, and Kuwahara did not have a need-to-know for progress in that area—if any.) Also, it was obvious that not all the Merishi would always be content to sublimate their competitive urges into underbidding humans for shipping contracts.

Well, it would be another blunder to assume that Merishi gratitude for human help during the Hive Wars would mold their whole culture and their internal politics to the end of time. But Kuwahara could have wished that the Merishi had chosen some other time to experiment with militarism.

He ran this proposition past Baumann, and she nodded vigorously. "I like the word 'experiment.' I think the Merishi are testing our responses, and how we respond will make a difference in the success of their new military."

She raised her voice. "File Linak'h, please."

A picture of *Centurion*, Baumann's first command, slid aside to reveal a screen. The chairs swiveled until both admirals were facing the screen, which now displayed a map of a remarkably Earthlike planet.

Kuwahara watched the file scroll by, although it said very little he hadn't known already. Linak'h hadn't been in the dual-sovereignty file, but as chief of staff to the Eleventh Fleet, Kuwahara had dealt with it several times.

One of the remotest but most prosperous Ptercha'a colonies, it held about thirty million of the Catpeople under the planetary government (or Coordination) and quite a few more in four Territories assigned to non-Ptercha'a races. These Territories were originally dirtside R&R sites for the spacemen of the four major space powers, Federation, Alliance, Baernoi, and Merishi, taking advantage of the planet's general habitability, scenery, and fresh food.

Over the years, those Territories became states in miniature. The Alliance Territory was the most miniature; they sent few settlers and most of those probably part-timers for Field Intelligence. The Merishi traded on their long relationship with the Ptercha'a to allow tight rule of their own territory, but also sent few settlers.

The Baernoi had not had time to send many settlers, and might never do so. It was an article of faith among humans that no Tusker would ever understand the Catpeople—a faith that Kuwahara personally did not share, even if he did not care to proclaim himself a heretic in public.

This left the Federation's Territory, two thousand kilometers deep and eight hundred wide, with a human population running into six figures and a Ptercha'a population running into seven. Seventy years ago the Federation had turned over virtually all government of the Territory to the Ptercha'a Administration, leaving only a small enclave (the Zone) on the coast where humans were not subject to local law. Living in the enclave was *not* a point in any human's favor, either.

"What is the problem with Linak'h?" Kuwahara asked. "When I was with Eleventh Fleet, most of the senior officers felt that the Navy could get from the Coordination anything we were getting from the Territory. So the only problem was those settlers who weren't willing to live under Ptercha'a law."

"We embarrassed the other three Territories," Baumann said. "The Alliance didn't like it when we abandoned extraterritorial rights. Neither did the Merishi, although that was kept fairly quiet at the time. The Hive War was still too fresh in everybody's mind to risk a public brawl."

"But now it would split the Ptercha'a off from the Merishi, right?" Kuwahara said.

Baumann frowned. "Is that a guess, or have you been talking to Social Conservatives?"

"I avoid politicians like mite-fever, Admiral. It was a guess."

"A damned good one, though. We might just be able to do that, and the Merishi military revival would lose a lot of its potential recruits. The Merishi can put as good a Navy as anybody into space, but as ground fighters they have too much to learn."

Baumann killed the screen. "Anyway, that is in the hands of the politicians, whichever way they decide. The Navy's problem is a little closer to what we handle.

"First, there's a suspicion that the Merishi are exporting spies and mercenaries into human space from a base on Linak'h. In their Territory, but probably with the Coordination's support or at least tolerance.

"Second, some of these Merishi mercs seem to be raiding into the Federation Territory. Small-scale operations, probably training exercises, with the raiders pretending to be outlaws. But it's hurting trade, and people are getting killed.

"The third problem is that the Tuskers seem to be taking an interest in the planet. We have reliable IDs on several senior Inquiry and Special Projects officers operating out of the Baernoi Territory. One of them is our old friend from Victoria, Rahbad Sarlin."

"How reliable?"

"A-4."

Kuwahara translated mentally: an extremely reliable source, nearly certain of Sarlin's identity. He also frowned.

It seemed to him that he and some of the other Victoria hands could have been brought in earlier. If a regular assignment was out of the question, why not at least a need-to-know so they could access current intelligence and possibly use their experience to provide input the pure Intelligence types might not otherwise obtain?

He decided to wait and see if that question would be answered without being asked. The Empress didn't outline a problem over lunch without asking you to participate in the solution, or at least not often enough to matter.

"I want to hide our interest in Linak'h under a dust screen of a study group to handle the whole dual-sovereignty problem," Baumann said. "As of the end of your watch on Friday, you are relieved of your watch CO duties and appointed chief of the study group."

Kuwahara could not even pretend to be surprised, and he did not have to feign a mixture of pleasure and annoyance. It was a responsible and important job, for which he was highly qualified. It also meant visibility to a wide range of both military and civilian potentates, who could carry away with them indelible impressions of Sho Kuwahara that might equally end or enhance his career.

"Aren't you going to thank me?" Baumann asked, with a just-discernible edge in her voice.

"I'm grateful, of course, Admiral, but are you sure I won't be a Tusker in a turnip patch?"

"You'll have a reasonably free hand with recruiting, up to your authorized limit. I anticipate you'll have about ten officers and six senior chiefs, with a generous space and facilities allowance. As long as you don't strip your present watch, you can line up all the diplomats you need, if you think you can't play soft police yourself."

"I'm better at being the hard one."

"So a number of people have noticed," Baumann said. "Which is one reason I'm picking you, apart from your Victoria experience and your being available here."

"Admiral, I don't think I'm tracking you."

Baumann refilled both cups and frowned. "The Eleventh Zone Intelligence Division did a thorough interrogation of the prisoners on Victoria. Rumor is that they talked fairly freely, in return for promises of immunity or at least reduced sentences.

"None of them have showed up anyplace you'd expect them to. I'd like to believe it's just the Witness Protection Division of the JAG's office finally beginning to work. But there are other possibilities."

Such as "shot while trying to except," being allowed to actually escape, or at best being transported to such distant planets that nobody who wanted to learn more than the mercenaries had already told would ever find them.

"Neither has their intelligence—at least to hear Flicr Vallee tell it. It's been two Standard years since we wound things upon Victoria. Something's missing."

"Something could also be staying undercover, to stay out of the hands of the politicians. I seem to recall reading that the Consensual Democrats and the Socialist Laborites were both taking up the dual-sovereignty issue."

"Are you implying that John Schatz would deny Forces Command vital intelligence to undercut politicians?" Baumann made them sound lower than Tuskers on her scale of esteem, which Kuwahara knew was largely an act put on for his benefit. Baumann was skilled if not comfortable with politicians, and seemed to have him typed as the rough, tough combat spacer.

He didn't try to keep the annoyance out of his voice when he replied. "I would not insult Admiral Schatz that way."

"Good. And I've known Flier Vallee for ten years. She wouldn't play games for the politicos' benefit either. Also, I had an analysis of the political statements on the issue run a few days ago. There's no sign of any security breaches."

"So if the intelligence went somewhere, it wasn't to the politicians?"

"Exactly. And I want *you* to find out where it went, what it was, why it vanished, and who made it vanish."

Which meant, in spite of any fine phrases the Empress might deploy to mask it, an internal-security job. Or to be even ruder, spying on his fellow officers, in a matter that might end with resignations or even criminal charges.

Kuwahara wondered briefly if Baumann really thought him naive enough to overlook that little fact. No point in raising the question, however: if she had, he'd been insulted in a way that meant either ignoring it or refusing the study group. If she hadn't—maybe she thought he was a good ninja, which had ramifications he hardly wanted to think about.

"I accept," Kuwahara said. "On one condition." That word dropped the temperature of the room five degrees and the Empress's eyes resembled cobalt lasers, but Kuwahara pressed on.

"I and at least two other people on the study group have clearances, needs-to-know, and everything else for *all* intelligence on Linak'h and the other planets covered by our charter. If we have a retired Marshal running a shadow command op on Petard—"

Baumann started at that phrase, but covered it so quickly Kuwahara knew she would be alert to any probing. Instead she nodded.

"That will mean a big Command Secret file. Are you sure you want to tie up the resources for one?"

"I'm just implementing your suggestion. The best way to hide critical intelligence is in a pile of noncritical intelligence."

Baumann smiled, restoring all the lost warmth. At least she could see the humor in one of her own maxims being turned around and trained to bite her. She stood up, with a grace so casual that one practically had to use slow-motion film to recognize it.

"Good luck, Sho. And by the way, your acting third star returns with this assignment."

At least he was considered worth high-priced bribes, Kuwahara thought as Naran Singh escorted him out. Off Victoria, he'd been too junior as a rear admiral for his acting vice admiral's rank to be made permanent. Now he had two and a half years' seniority with two stars. If he made a success of the study group with a temporary third star, it would become permanent. And the job might even be considered a four-star one, in which case—

No, Ambition *after* mission, as the saying ran. And before either, telling Fumiko that the time of seven-day weeks and fourteen-hour days had finally arrived.

Charlemagne:

Kuwahara explained his new assignment in the bath that night. At some point in its two-hundred-year history, the house had acquired a genuine Japanese-style *ofuro*, and a shared bath was part of the Kuwaharas' nighttime ritual.

Fumiko lay back in the steaming water, her long black hair with only highlights of gray floating about her head like the petals of an exotic water flower. Then she settled on the underwater seat and looked at her husband so appraisingly that he began to wonder if he'd left something out.

"That means you will be needing quarters in town," she said. "Will you be leasing privately or using a flag suite?"

"I'll wait and see what the security requirements are likely to be," Kuwahara said. "We may also recruit a flag rank who already has secure quarters near Forces Command, in which case they can provide the local base."

Fumiko smiled. "I see I will not have the traditional opportunity to furnish the husband's city apartment, complete with a carefully chosen mistress."

"I distrust your taste in young women, honorable wife."

"Then I must atone for this lapse, honorable husband." She managed to get out the last phrase with a straight face before breaking into laughter. She also managed a bow that parodied traditional deference, and at the same time displayed a figure that had survived twenty-six years of marriage and two children without any changes that would have made Kuwahara look elsewhere.

Charlemagne:

Kuwahara was late to his office the next morning, and found that his deputies had the situation well in hand. Everything that didn't need his approval had been acted on, a farewell party was already being planned, and a Dual-Sovereignty File was open in his Command Secret/Eyes-Only data storage.

He spent the rest of the morning and half the afternoon orienting himself on the expanded data. When he left he understood why the Empress had started at the phrase "retired Marshal."

For whatever reason, there *was* a retired Marshal of the Federation on Linak'h, Emilio Banfi, a roughhewn old groundpounder who was more of a legend than even a Marshal of the Federation had to be. He was also nearly a hundred and twenty Standard, so it was long odds against his being intended to command anything more than his bodyguards and servants.

The file held two other items of interest to Kuwahara. One was a copy of a joint order from the four C-in-Cs, directing the Eleventh War Zone at its discretion to initiate a limited program of reinforcements to Linak'h.

The Federation presence on Linak'h consisted at the moment of one light cruiser and one converted merchant vessel acting as an orbital depot. On the ground stood one Regular battalion, several Reserve supporting units of company strength, and assorted Militia raised by the human population of the Territory and subject to both human and Ptercha'a law.

"Limited reinforcements" was a necessary phrase, to avoid accusations of provocation in both Senate and Chamber of Deputies. If it really described what was going to be sent, it meant adding zero to zero, the kind of vain command that killed good soldiers without either honor or results.

Kuwahara decided that his study group would make its first priority an evaluation of the forces requirements for the dual-sovereignty planets, under various interpretations of the nonprovocation agreements. (He remembered at least five, and the lawyers were still arguing over whether Victoria had created a sixth.)

The problem was so absorbing that Kuwahara was eating lunch at his desk when he saw a flagged bit of new intelligence come up. It concerned Rahbad Sarlin, who it seemed had been positively identified, to A-5 level—the picture had just arrived.

So had a new bit of intelligence about the Tuskers' formidable Special Projects field agent. Shortly after being positively ID'd, he had completely vanished.

Two

Aboard U.F.S. *Shenandoah*, off Schneeheim:

U.F.S. *Shenandoah* swung in a circular four-hun-
dred-kilometer orbit above the aptly named world of
Schneeheim. At this point of the orbit, all Commodore Rose Liddell could see was the planet's northern
glacial zone, blazing white where it wasn't spotted
with clouds.

Silhouetted against the whiteness was the dark
shape of the Honan-registered Free Technician ship
Emerald Dragon. Silhouetted against the screen on
the far side of the table was *Emerald Dragon*'s Captain Mesu.

"Your hospitality justifies its reputation," Captain
Mesu said. He was a small, heavyset man, with a head
so bald that Liddell doubted the condition was natural, and a dozen varieties of Asian in his ancestry.

"Your contribution to it was beyond price," Liddell
replied. That was not only appropriate to Mesu's code
of etiquette, it was the literal truth. Liddell's hospitality budge was robust; her hospitality supplies were
not. Schneeheim local products were limited in vari-
ety, and not even the most lavish hospitality budget
could afford its imports.

On the other hand, *Emerald Dragon* had come out

to Schneeheim on a Navy charter straight from three successive stops at planets where they gave food and drink to visiting ships. Captain Mesu wasn't worried about lack of supplies; he was worried about lack of storage space. A bit of judicious negotiating, to prevent either party's seeming too eager, and not only Captain Liddell's but her whole ship's larders had all the nonration supplies they could use.

Have to arrange some sort of Ship's Fund activity, she noted. *Exhibition bouts of unarmed combat, treasure hunts, things like that.*

Most of the crew wouldn't have a lot of stellars to spare, after their dirtside leaves on Schneeheim, and the fund had already been tapped for a couple of charitable contributions right after the ship hit orbit. If the contributions had generated enough Schneeheimer goodwill, maybe they would offer a facility to hold the exhibition bouts dirtside?

Check the files, and also with Major Shores, when she brings her people up from their exercises.

Captain Mesu returned from the buffet with his plate reloaded, mostly with deviled Kaloris eggs and vegetarian sausage. Liddell's steward, CPO Jensen, was dirtside, probably actually doing some shopping, and half the ship's complement of robots was aboard *Emerald Dragon* being overhauled, so even in flag quarters meals were largely self-service.

"You are gracious, but it is well known that no food is good enough to survive bad cooks," Mesu said. "Yours may ship aboard *Emerald Dragon* any time you wish to release them."

"I'll have Personnel check the records to see if any are taking their discharge during this refit," Liddell said. "But I should warn you. They may sign aboard

Dragon just to avoid having to wait on Schneeheim for another ship out."

Mesu looked back at the display and shivered. "One can understand such reasoning. If they meet their contract obligations, they can go where they please afterward."

Liddell herself didn't much care whether she saw Schneeheim or not, beyond the necessary courtesies expected from any visiting Federation flag officer. It was half glaciated and the rest frigid much of the year; its being inhabited at all was a monument to the human spirit or proof that the human itchy foot could lead to strange worlds indeed.

However, to her crew it was dirtside, after six months of operations and two months without setting foot outside their ship. Besides, there was no place aboard *Shen* now for anyone not working on the refit.

The same six months of continuous operations that had made Schneeheim look so attractive to *Shenandoah*'s crew had also made this "Assisted Self-Refit" necessary. Newly commissioned for the Victoria crisis, *Shenandoah* had taken no damage there that made a real overhaul necessary. But she'd been rushed back into service after nearly a century in orbital reserve, then rushed out to Victoria when the situation began to need a capital ship.

A correct decision, but one that had left a good many minor faults uncorrected, and not given her two features of more recent battle cruisers. One was a direct link between the carrying racks for her embarked attacker squadron, so that she could launch the forty-meter craft at the same rate as a carrier. The other was Light Infantry quarters with their own airlock and link to the shuttles.

Neither had mattered at Victoria. The 879th Attacker Squadron had spent most of its time based dirt-side, moving dirt in support of some of the most confused and messy ground fighting Rose Liddell never wanted to be close to again. The ship's Light Infantry detachment had been two lieutenants commanding forty NCOs and privates, parceled out for security duty both aboard ship and as part of the landing parties *Shenandoah* kept being called on to provide.

Now the 879th had spent the past six months intensively training in antiship work, which needed a space base and quick-launch capabilities in that base. The Light Infantry were now a full company of more than 120 of the Federation's elite troops, fully suited and commanded by Candice Shores, with a below-zone promotion to major under her belt and the good prospect of stars in her future.

Equipped as she would be in another ten days (assuming the refit stayed on schedule), and with a couple of light cruisers, a scout, and a courier or two, *Shenandoah* would be capable of independent operations as long as her supplies, ammunition, and crew's endurance permitted. She could raid, fight in space or from space, land her own small ground force, escort ships carrying larger ones, and generally shift the balance of forces toward the Federation in quite a few places.

The fire-brigade concept was too venerable for Rose Liddell not to recognize what was intended for her ship and people. Her knowledge of history also told her that how effective a fire brigade was depended heavily on correctly assessing the size of the fire.

The door chimed. "Come in," Liddell called. She wished she could sound more cheerful. It could hardly be someone with a case of nerves over something minor, not if he or she was coming in person and after what happened to the last offender.

"Good evening, Commodore." *Shenandoah*'s CO, Captain Pavel Bogdanov, loomed in the doorway, his full two meters of height at attention.

"Captain Mesu, if you will excuse me briefly for a matter concerning my squadron . . ." She did not add "urgent" to the description, although if Pavel was bringing the message himself it could hardly be anything else.

"Of course," *Emerald Dragon*'s captain pulled out Liddell's chair as she rose. "My own tender is at your disposal, if necessary."

"Thank you."

It had better not be necessary. Half of *Shenandoah*'s crew might be taking turns dirtside, because storage, repairs, or *Emerald Dragon*'s work gangs had taken their quarters. The ship might be quivering half of any given twenty-four hours, as she had seldom done except during low-altitude maneuvers at Victoria. The air might hold strange and by no means exotic smells that all the circulating and scrubbing could not remove.

But she was still a commissioned ship of the Navy of the United Federation of Starworlds. The weapons, power, and life-support watches, the computer and ammunition security, and the duty shuttle would be maintained. If they weren't, the person responsible would badly *need* a place aboard *Emerald Dragon*.

Aboard U.F.S. *Shenandoah*, off Schneeheim:

Commander Shintaro Fujita, *Shenandoah*'s chief engineer, ducked as a slung crate sailed past on the overhead cableway, narrowly missing his head. He winced as the crate failed to make the next turn in the passageway and slammed against a bulkhead. He ducked again at the volley of Chinese curses flying down the passage after the errant crate.

The work gang from *Emerald Dragon* was still picking up the pieces when the security watchstander at Engineering Control saluted Fujita. "All quiet?" he asked.

"Inside, yes."

"Good." Fujita slipped through the half-open door, then let the big plug hatch swing shut behind him. This was one of the Stern Sphere's strength bulkheads, as tough as the main shell, with hatches intended to be as strong as the bulkhead itself. It felt good to have that much metal and ceramic between him and the work crews from *Emerald Dragon*, who were undoubtedly doing a fine job with the refit and only *seemed* intent on wrecking *Shenandoah* and killing themselves into the bargain.

Inside Engineering Control the work noises were shut out and nobody there was making any. The four watchstanders sat with the relaxed intentness of experienced Engineering chiefs, as one might expect when they had fifty-three Standard years' service among them. The security backups were as intent but less relaxed; they looked as if they wanted power cutters rather than wad projectors on their belts.

Major Shores had offered Fujita a squad of Light Infantry for Engineering security, after it got around that the *Emerald Dragon* people would be staying out of the Engineering spaces. Fujita was tempted, particularly after people began showing up at odd hours, usually when there was work to be done but without any intention of helping with it.

"A squad of my people could have them retreating in five minutes," Shores said. "I don't want to square off with the crew this early in the cruise unless I have to, but part of my job is making it easier for you to do yours."

For that remark alone Fujita would have awarded Major Shores a medal. Not all Light Infantryman were as cooperative in shipboard routine, to say the least.

Instead he'd merely bowed and thanked her. "We will guard our own street, I think," he'd said, and then mentioned this proposition to a few of his key chiefs. The trespassers started thinning out the next day, and vanished entirely the day after that. Fujita recalled seeing what might have been bruises on one or two of the more notorious trespassers, but there were lots of sharp projections aboard *Shenandoah,* more than usual now during the overhaul. There were also things that officers were not meant to know.

Fujita went over to the urn bolted to the bulkhead to the left of his folddown desk. A cup popped out of the socket and brown steaming liquid gurgled into it. He raised it, gulped, then gasped.

"Coffee!" he said, when he had his mouth clear.

"Sorry, Commander," the senior watchstander said. "We sent for some tea when the dispenser ran empty, but they said they were out."

"Who are 'they'?" Fujita said. His tone promised a dreadful fate for the unknown source of coffee.

"The overhaul supply coordinator," another chief said. "Most of Supplies went dirtside after they loaded from *Dragon,* so we had to go to the OSC, and she didn't know her way around *Shen.*"

"There's probably plenty of tea aboard," a third watchstander said, with an optimism Fujita thought unsuited to the occasion. "But it's probably all inaccessible until they get through with the Light Infantry quarters."

"No doubt," Fujita said heavily. He felt like retreating to his quarters and hoping that the refit would be done when he woke up, but knew this was impossible. Also, he would be both leaving his post and running the gauntlet of the work crews, and he could not face both at once with only coffee in his stomach.

"I forgive the coffee," he said. "Did anyone think to order hot chocolate?"

"Ah, I've got a couple of bars in my locker —" one of the security people began. She had to be older than the sixteen Standard she looked, but was probably young enough to have a sweet tooth.

"Then may I ask you to sacrifice one?"

"Aye aye, sir."

She left, and everyone looked at Fujita. He grinned. "I am about to demonstrate field-expedient hot chocolate, if someone will adjust the hot-water feed. . . ."

The chiefs couldn't leave their seats, but the security people nearly fell over each other to produce a cup of hot water.

Schneeheim:

One whole wall of the Waalfisch Hotel's main lobby showed a glacier calving off icebergs. While the reception desk checked them in, Lieutenant Commander Brian Mahoney and First Lieutenant Brigitte Tachin watched the spectacle of chunks of ice larger than *Shenandoah* plunging five hundred meters into the sea. Sometimes a second would topple on top of the first one. Once they saw the second shatter like a bomb, except that each fragment was larger than an attacker.

The display was silent, except for a distant piping that Mahoney thought might be simulated wind.

"Either that, or there's a leak in the hotel's weather barrier," Tachin said.

Mahoney shuddered. "If the barrier goes, I'm going back up to *Shen*."

Tachin slipped a hand through her companion's arm. "What, no courage in the face of danger?"

"That's not danger, that's just the indignity of being too cold to keep your mind on what you're doing." He saw her flush slightly. "I had enough of that as a boy."

"Enough of what? The cold, or what one must keep one's mind on when one is doing it?"

Mahoney was saved the trouble of an exasperated reply by a beeping robot with their bags and room cards. It led the way to the elevator, then down the fifth-floor hall to their room.

"Brian," Tachin said when they were alone, "you are *not* going back to the ship until our four days are up. When was the last time we had dirtside leave together?"

It had been during *Shenandoah*'s post-Victoria inspection, when Riftwell Dockyard more or less bodily ejected the ship's whole crew. Both Tachin and Mahoney were Critical Technical Personnel for the first half of the job, which meant the TOQ aboard Dockyard while the ship was uninhabitable. After that they had a few days on-planet—at the height of a Riftwell summer, when you really could fry eggs on the sidewalk (although you might not want to try eating them afterward).

"There was that day on Scandia, above the Eriksfjord."

"That was a *pass, mon vieux,* not leave."

"It was also your favorite fantasy come to life."

She smiled at pleasant memories. "Not my favorite. The dream only came once, as I told you."

"You did better than that," he said, cupping her chin in one hand and drawing her against him with the other. More than two years into their relationship, he no longer had to be so careful about the protective gestures that came naturally when he was twenty-five cems taller and fifteen kilos heavier.

"The company was excellent," she said into his shirt. It was checked flanax, and she began to nuzzle at the closure with her teeth as her hands crept around to the back of his trousers. "After you recovered from your plunge in the stream, at least."

"I haven't been in a pond this time," he said.

"No." She was an expert at the tantalizing torture of almost but not quite groping him. "Also, I learned that beds are better than flower-filled meadows."

"The bed is behind you, Brigitte."

Her eagerness he put down to three weeks of neither privacy nor free time aboard ship, but if he hadn't shared it, he might have thought it a challenge rather than an opportunity.

Aboard attacker Gold One, 879th Squadron, Schneeheim:

The White Bear Mountains floated up in Elayne Zheng's display as Gold One of the 879th Attacker Squadron made a sweeping turn over their southern foothills. Then the other three attackers of Gold Flight were turning in their leader's wake, their signatures blurring slightly as they presented constantly changing aspects to Zheng's sensor suite.

A moment later all four attackers were sliding south parallel to the five-thousand-meter summits of the range. It was avalanche season in the White Bears— it seemed to Zheng that it was avalanche season somewhere on Schneeheim every part of the year—so they were holding well below Mach One.

At that pace it would take them another twenty minutes to reach the exercise area where Candice Shores's Light Infantry were jumping off. But lately Elayne Zheng seemed to have lots of time to waste. If she hadn't, she'd have been snug in a hut in the Grauenfels, using up her leave in the best way possible.

She had to admit that it was more her fault than not that she wasn't there. She had casually assumed Kurt would be free and interested, and turned up at his door to find him not just affiliated but married. Full legal and Christian rites, too, and to a woman who was clearly one-man and one-way. She didn't mind sharing a sauna or putting up Elayne in the guest room, but any other sharing was plainly out of her envelope.

Being more of a lady than most of her friends would have admitted under torture, Elayne didn't ask for what she wasn't going to get. She accepted the sauna, dinner, bed, and breakfast, and was back at the shuttle field for the flight to *Shen* by midafternoon the next day.

Fortunately they had plenty of work that she could do. She'd been an enlisted electronics technician for ten years before she qualified as an attacker EWO, and could still troubleshoot a wide range of equipment. It also helped that she could court, flatter, criticize, or if necessary curse *Emerald Dragon*'s people in both Universal Sinic and Old Cantonese dialect.

This prevented boredom and led to several offers which Zheng regretted having to refuse. Both regulations and common sense precluded on-board fraternization with the visitors, at least at the early stages of the refit.

She finally rejoined the Gold One crew fifteen days into the refit. Playing target for the Schneeheim Defense Force was only slightly more interesting than overload-testing toilet sensors, but it added to her flight hours and kept her around attacker crews, her own kind of people.

Now they were into the first day of a planned four days of exercises with Candy Shores's Light Infantry, and that was going to be *fun*.

"Weather report," the navigator said, and it came up on all four crew displays. Northeast winds up to 130 km/h above three thousand, from just north of the exercise area on up to the Amundsen Gulf.

The pilot and flight leader nodded. "Change course to three twenty-five," he said. Golds Two, Three, and Four acknowledged, and in front of Zheng the four sparks marking the flight swung onto a course that would take them farther west. Now they would come up on the exercise area from the west rather than the east, heading into the wind.

The attacker retained its mass, even when the lift field had reduced its three hundred tons to the effective weight of a soap bubble. It also retained the considerable cross section of any object forty meters long and ten in diameter. The combination made handling the bird in high winds and high mountains no job to be taken casually.

Without waiting for orders, Zheng ran checks on the computer's memory of all the Light Infantry signatures the sensors would pick up today. There'd be more of them than before; today the LI's were working out in deep glacier territory, using full armor.

"Gold Three, status check on your medpack," the flight leader called.

"Complete as of ten minutes ago, Gold One. The SAR team is suiting up."

"Good job."

Zheng split-screened her display, with real-time visual on the top half. Great Mother, would she hate to go down in this icy wilderness. Even looking at the icefalls and the plumes of snow whipping five kloms long from the higher peaks made her shiver.

"Greenbud Leader to Gold One. Greenbud Leader to Gold One. Can you read me, Gold One?"

Static and what sounded like wind blurred Candice Shores's voice but left it recognizable. "Gold One here, Greenbud Leader. We read you four by four. Our ETA is now twelve minutes, thirty-five seconds. Mark!"

"We'll be watching for you, Gold Flight. Mind if we test our suit scanners?"

"No need to ask, Greenbud." The flight leader sounded peevish.

Zheng grinned. Lieutenant Commander Shauli was a good man at the controls, but not one hundred percent comfortable with deviations from plan. That wouldn't help him make commander, so he tried to hide it—but hiding something like that from Candy Shores during a long cruise was harder than getting an interest-free loan from a Scaleskin!

Again without waiting for orders, Zheng switched on her passive sensors. It wouldn't hurt anybody to have a recording of how well suits in active-scan mode showed up in glacier territory. It might even make Shauli easier to live with.

Schneeheim:

Major Candice Shores tested the footing, then stepped out from between the two sheltering rocks and down into the icefall. It had no name, like most features around here. Schneeheim had two million people, with a mostly uninhabitable land area larger than Earth's. Mountains large enough to make good climbing and glaciers larger than any on her native Quetzalcoatl more often than not had nothing but coordinates to label them.

The command group filed on to the icefall behind her, spreading out alternately to the left and right. Except for Sergeant Esteva, most of them moved cautiously, still not completely at home on ice even with the crampons *Dragon*'s metal shop had made for them.

"Two minutes, ten seconds for command group movement," Shores whispered into her recorder.

A helmet clinked against hers, and a soft voice pierced the wind. "Too slow?" With helmets in contact and no radio, the others couldn't overhear her and Esteva.

"A bit. But this is the first time on the ice in low light and high wind." Unsaid was the promise to imitate the wrath of God if the people didn't improve with practice.

Shores lit off her heads-up display, the basic one that showed the XO's and platoon leaders' beacons. It came up, but blurred, as if by a low-grade EMP or jamming.

"Yariv, all-hands sensor check."

"On the way." The company com sergeant started the remote test of each suit's active sensors, ordered turned on ten minutes ago. Shores's clock showed four minutes gone when Yariv came back on the air.

"Two out, most of the rest not coming in too good."

"Diagnostic check on the two out."

"On the way." That took thirty seconds. "Other indicators nominal. Ah—the two out are in Fourth Platoon."

Shores muttered under her breath. Fourth Platoon's maintenance was just a little below standard, and the platoon leader had a weakness for staging "simulated equipment failures" on top of that, usually without consulting her superiors. There were worse vices, but not many, most especially in a high-hazard environment.

"We can settle that account later," Shores said. She shifted to the attacker frequency. "Greenbud Leader to Gold One. Are you doing a jamming test against our active sensors? If so, I'd appreciate your stopping it."

She didn't feel as polite toward Shauli as her phrasing implied, but knew he had a thin skin. Provoking him to push the matter upstairs would waste time, particularly when *Shen*'s communications might be impaired by short crew, interference, or systems down for maintenance.

"Negative on the jamming, Greenbud," the reply came. "I think you may have a trickle left over from that solar flare. Do you want a metwatch check?"

That would mean owing Shauli a favor. Not letting him do it would mean either doing it herself, with com gear that might not reach if atmospheric interference was getting heavy, or carrying out an exercise in a high-hazard area with impaired communications.

Lost time the first way, maybe lost people the other, and she refused to risk either because she thought Shauli was a grumbler's behind!

"Clear on the check. We can still start the exercise if you'll leave your SAR bird on station."

"We can do better than that, Greenbud. How about three?"

"No problem with that, Gold One."

A sonic boom slammed across the icefall as one of the attackers leaped into sight in a supersonic climb. As it climbed, all its visual signals flared on.

"Show-off," muttered Esteva. "That boom could have tumbled ice blocks or opened crevices."

"Let's be nice, Sergeant," Shores said. "If Shauli thinks he's been generous, why spoil his mood?"

She still ran an all-hands status check before letting the company jump off. Nobody reported ice trouble, so she gave the visual signal, a green flare.

As if the skies themselves were replying, auroral waves glowed in the shadows to the northwest. Green and purple, crimson and gold, they cascaded from nowhere to nowhere, like a waterfall of light a thousand kloms long.

The report from Gold One confirming a final-stage flare was superfluous.

Aboard U.F.S. *Shenandoah*, off Schneeheim:

It took Commodore Liddell one minute to read the message, another minute to memorize it, and two more to discuss it with Pavel Bogdanov. Then they waited a minute more before return to the flag suite.

"That may keep Mesu from becoming suspicious," she said.

"Mesu will be suspicious anyway, Commodore," Bogdanov said. "The word you want is 'cooperative.' Perhaps you should look in a mirror before you go in."

That took another two minutes, but Pavel was right. He usually was, which was more than Liddell could have said of any of her lovers. But then with Pavel Bogdanov duty was a much stronger motive than sex for learning how another's mind worked.

Probably the same could be said of her, although not as loudly. At fifty-six Standard she was probably set in that pattern, too—although the face in the mirror could have claimed forty-five without being questioned. She'd struck a weight balance that rounded her rather small features, concealing the sharpness of chin, jaw, and nose, and letting the eyes that were her best feature dominate.

The eyes also looked harassed, even trapped. She spent another minute breathing deeply, thought that the worst of the look had passed, then rejoined Bogdanov.

Mesu rose to greet them. "I trust that the news is not bad, or that if it is I and my people may assist?"

"It's not great, and you can help a lot," Liddell said. "Pavel?"

"How fast can you complete all the Priority One items and have us ready for space? Priorities are safety and reliability. Habitability is not a factor."

Mesu frowned, then bowed. "If I may update my data . . . ? I arrived late and your excellent hospitality made me forget this duty until now." He'd been five minutes late at most, but the flattery was expected, and anyway he probably needed time to organize his thoughts too.

Mesu plugged his belt computer into the terminal and Liddell gave him the voice code for the cleared version of the progress report. On a flag-suite terminal, that took longer to come up than the secret one, but Mesu undoubtedly knew that. If he was going to be gentleman enough not to claim exemption from security procedures, Liddell would not put temptation in his way.

"Four days, ten hours Standard," Mesu said finally. "This means much overtime and leaving your ship rather dirty."

Liddell avoided looking at Bogdanov. She knew the choice the old Pavel Bogdanov would have made. She awaited with interest the new one's decision.

"If we bring our people back, without regard to habitability, and you dock *Emerald Dragon* to reduce transit time, how long?"

"We would need a minimum of an hour to undock."

"We can guarantee two hours' warning minimum." Liddell nodded in confirmation. There were no Baernoi or Alliance ships off Schneeheim, and only one Merishi freighter. *Shen* would also have four attackers and her light cruiser companion *Donnerberg* on high patrol at all times.

"Excellent," Mesu said. "Your crew would, I presume, clean up as fast as my people vacated spaces?"

"That, and do as much of the Priority Two and Three work as we could without interfering with yours."

Mesu's calculations went faster this time. "Six days, twenty hours. This is assuming that your people start returning tomorrow before oh seven hundred and are all back and on duty by twenty hundred."

"Do it that way," Bogdanov said, with a wintry smile.

"At your service, ma'am, sir," Mesu said. "I suppose my security bond requires that I discourage curiosity among my people?"

"Yes, but we'll be polite if you don't. They won't learn anything, and nobody has started a war."

"I would hope that our work may make *Shenandoah* able to prevent one. With your permission, ma'am?"

Mesu bowed himself out. Liddell sat down and toyed with an empty glass. Was that their mission off Linak'h? Both Intelligence and the media had put various suspicions about the planet into plain words, but that could be just neither of them liking a planet divided among five powers and four races. Liddell wasn't sure that didn't stretch her enthusiasm to its limits too.

At least Eleventh Fleet was still in good hands. Admiral Schatz's orders to proceed to a rendezvous off Wendigo and then to Linak'h would let them complete most of the overhaul without exhausting the crew. Schatz's orders—and Pavel Bogdanov's.

Shen's people would be working their tails off for five days, hot-bunking when they slept and eating rations instead of food. But when the ship left orbit, she would be clean and habitable. They might even have a split duty-free day—half of the crew able to relax for twelve hours.

Bogdanov broke into her optimism. "What about our LIs?"

"They can finish their exercises, because the LI quarters won't be ready for at least three more days. But they'll have to do without attackers for anything except SAR. We'll need to pull the fliers up tonight, let them rest, then start them chasing down our people dirtside."

"Cut the orders, Pavel, with a copy to *Donnerberg*. Then can I offer you some cream sherry, or would you rather be observant and stick with tea?"

"I think Commander Fujita will be happier if I do not swill tea while he must go without. The sherry, by all means."

Three

Victoria:

Councillor Payaral Na'an contemplated the Space Security watch leader squatting on the cushions opposite
him. The leader could hardly be much older than
Na'an, in spite of his high rank—the human equivalent
would be a commander in their Space Security Forces,
or *Navy*.

But there were paths to high rank at early ages
other than the one Na'an's birth had allowed him to
follow. This a merchant of the Folk must always remember, even when dealing with his own race and
more so when dealing with others.

The robot glided forward on its cushion of air. Its
top opened to display a cold jug and two glasses.

"Apricot juice?" the leader said. "You have adopted
that—human custom?"

The leader's tone and the hesitation before using
the word "human" irritated Na'an. However, good
relations with the Security Service were essential to
his work on Victoria. Even if this watch leader was
only a transient—and about this Na'an would inquire—security closed ranks against offense to any of
its members.

"I did not expect that your business here today was

to question me about the human customs I have been obliged to adopt in order to do business with them," Na'an said. He used for "do business" the phrase that implied filthy and degrading work done out of a sense of obligation.

The leader appeared satisfied. Na'an had not expected otherwise. The Security Service seemed of late to be attracting more and more cultural particularists, who wished to ignore several hundred years of relations between the humans and the Folk. It was not the much-debated "cult of gratitude" that kept Na'an from that faction; it was mere good sense.

"My mission here is to inquire about your provisions for the *Somtow Nosavan*," the leader said. He appeared to be either refusing the juice or waiting for Na'an to admit the inferior position by pouring it out for him.

Na'an signaled the robot to do the pouring. Done without spills, this took long enough for the councillor to frame another tactful reply.

"The phrase has many meanings, and you probably do not wish me to guess at which one you use," he said. "We have certainly found it worthwhile to be among the investors in the purchase and operation of the ship."

" 'Worthwhile' also holds many meanings," the leader said, sipping his juice. "Do you mean it in the sense of 'profitable'?"

"If I could tell at this point in the venture's history whether it will be profitable or not, I would be prescient. If I develop that art, I will found my own House, not invest in ventures aboard old human-manned ships."

The leader smiled enough to show that he had a sense of humor but kept it within his cave. "Then the ship is fully crewed?"

"For the voyage it is making, yes."

"Refresh my memory. They are going to Linak'h, which is only a single Climb, with a cargo of components from the abandoned Dockyard."

"Your memory needs no refreshment that I can offer it. That is correct."

"What of other voyages beyond Linak'h?"

Payaral Na'an decided that he did not want more precision on that matter. Indeed, why ask for what he did not need? That the Folk had dealings with planets the humans would rather not acknowledge was no secret.

"For such a voyage, they might well need a few additional hands, as well as handling robots for other kinds of cargo. Much would depend on where they were going, and on the number of passengers on each additional leg of the voyage."

"The life support is deficient?" the leader asked. Na'an thought he recognized eagerness, which might have several explanations if it existed. None of those explanations pleased him.

His pleasure, however, was not an issue here. At least not now. It was otherwise with good relations toward his human trading partners. There he had obligations toward his House and his own reputation.

"I think *Nosavan* is nearly ready to depart. It would be late for them to change their voyage plans now, still later for them to take aboard new hands. If those new hands were of the Folk or the Servants—"

"They would be human."

Na'an read the meaning clearly. There were survivors of the humans in the service of the Folk who had played such a large part in the Victoria Wars. One or more of these survivors was still on Victoria, or otherwise available to the leader.

"They would also be in some danger, if your presence here on Victoria were known."

"How so?"

"New volunteers for *Nosavan* so soon after your ship's arrival would seem an odd coincidence. Some of the humans might refuse to believe it a coincidence at all."

"Any ones in particular?"

"Too many to silence."

"Do you take me for a fool, planning murders?"

"If you were, I would call you one to your face."

The leader's face showed extreme distaste for Na'an's presence. It was a sentiment returned in full. The councillor hoped he would not have to summon any of his armed Servants to deal with his visitor. Their action would reach the human media. Their laying claws on a cultural particularist might reach the nearest Folk court—although a Security watch leader could hardly be so foolish as to protest against Servants in War doing their duty to their sworn master.

The danger of confrontation ebbed. Na'an decided on a placating gesture. He had other resources if it failed, more if it succeeded.

"I offer as much cooperation as will be useful to you in this matter of a crew for *Nosavan*. It will not be enough to make the humans suspicious, nor violate obligations to my House."

"I cannot quarrel with that. Have you details to offer?"

Na'an had been a quick thinker since his earliest years of nest-freedom. Now he used that ability to improvise a scheme that brought a genuine smile to the leader's face.

"And these Servants you send—they will of course obey those sent by Security?"

"My Servants are loyal. Even a human may command their obedience, if he identified himself properly."

"The proper identification will be provided."

"I rejoice that you command such resources."

"The Folk will profit much from them, I agree. I believe that you and your House will do likewise."

They finished the juice, to find that it had given them an appetite. The councillor was careful to serve only Folk dishes, except for another jug of apricot juice.

The leader refused to stay for the seedcakes and hot sgai, but did not rush the departure ritual. Na'an showed him out personally, conscious of his staff watching, and wishing that they might lack either sight or curiosity.

He would not provide the human Intelligence leaders with a recording of this meeting, except under extraordinary circumstances. One of those circumstances might be distorted rumors of what had happened reaching the humans, and making Payaral Na'an sound more vicious or more stupid than he thought himself capable of being.

At least he could send the message to *Nosavan* and interview Emt Desdai without watchers or listeners!

Aboard R.M.S. *Somtow Nosavan*, off Victoria:

"Charlie," Joanna Marder said.

At the Engineering display at the rear of the bridge, Charles Longman didn't stir. Marder repeated the name, louder. No response.

"Mr. Longman! Report to the Bridge!" The order raised echoes on the half-stripped Bridge deck and brought Longman leaping out of his seat. He promptly stumbled and caught himself on his hands, missing sprained wrists only because the gravity was on one-third to speed the cargo handling.

"Foot gone to sleep again, Mr. Longman?"

"I guess so, Jo—aye aye, ma'am."

It would not take many more parodies of Navy manners to make her believe it was a mistake, shipping Charlie Longman aboard *Nosavan* as chief engineer. He had a new license, he could handle everything except the heavy repairs that would end *Nosavan*'s career on the spot (particularly if that spot was light-years from the nearest inhabited planet), and he was still good in bed.

Damned good. Marder wondered. Had she substituted addiction to Charlie for addiction to alcohol? She'd stayed sober since they started sharing a bed, but she'd never spent so much time in a shared bed either.

If she was addicted to Charlie, was she fit to take a shuttle up to orbit, let alone *Nosavan* forty-eight light-years to Linak'h?

And if she started worrying herself to a nub over the question, she would certainly be even less fit than she had been, however fit that was. *Try to remember that there are two Charlies, both good but in different ways, and maybe you'll be all right.*

"Sorry, Mr. Longman."

"No problem, Captain. Ah—Jo, I was just trying to hook the Engineering display into the external pickup. We'll be passing over the farm in about five minutes."

Marder looked at her watch. He was right, damn him! When he wasn't drugged with chemicals or sexual satiation, Charlie had an almost inborn time sense.

"Why didn't you tell me?"

"You didn't ask." That was almost insubordinate but not nearly a pout. Ignoring it seemed the best way to handle it.

The main display flickered, then steadied on the planetscape passing below. Gray sand, yellow sand, brown sand and rock, gray gravel, a thread of stream, a ruddy slash of canyon across more grayness, then a rolling plain of hills instead of dunes, with lights glowing in the dawn—

"There?"

Marder nodded. She wanted to close stinging eyes, but the farm would be gone in seconds anyway. She focused on the tiny green dot of the organics plant, then it was gone.

Instead of closing her eyes, she put her hands over them. She heard Longman's footsteps approaching, then felt his hands on the back of her neck, an amazingly soothing touch for someone like Charlie—unless you remembered how graceful he was, moving when he didn't think he was being watched, or when he'd forgotten about watchers because his mind (and other things) were on you—

"Thanks, Charlie."

"It was home for a while, but we're both star people, aren't we?"

"Not like Paul. The spaceborn really deserve the name."

Charlie said nothing. He was surprisingly free of any jealousy of Paul Leray, who'd been Marder's lover when he was captain and she XO of the Alliance heavy cruiser *Audacious*. Possibly it was the way Leray had died, with his ship and crew at the hands of Merishi and Merishi-employed madmen. Possibly it was the abuse and snobbery Paul had suffered as a spaceborn. It might be hard for Charlie to be jealous of a hero or a victim.

Then again, Charlie just might be growing up, for all the outward signs to the contrary, and the likelihood that he was growing into something that his family of Federation admirals might not approve.

"Wonder if 'Reesa and Lucco have decided to make it official yet?" she mused.

"I'm as curious how Karl's courtship of that boy two farms over is going. The last I heard, the father felt he was rushing it."

"Is it the father being old-fashioned, or is Karl getting sloppy?"

"Karl's lonely," Longman said. "I mean, he came close to trying me once, and this *after* you and I had been awake and noisy all night. He'll be lonelier still if we stay in space and Lucco and 'Reesa pair off."

"Lucco and 'Reesa will be lonely if they don't," Marder said. She couldn't really wish that anyone suffer at the farm, not after how the year and a bit there had healed all of them—a widow, three people who'd lost lovers, and an ex-Navy officer in dire need of a home where he could grow up.

The lights of Port Harriet passed below, and then *Nosavan* was out over the sea. By straining both eyes and imagination, Marder thought she could make out ship wakes and even whitecaps. It probably was rough off Port Harriet this time of year—

The com alarm chimed softly (a soft alarm for regular use had been one of Charlie's custom features). "Play on all Bridge positions," she commanded.

The switchover sent a few digital readouts wavering, but that was no worse than you could expect with venerable wiring like *Nosavan*'s. If the ship hadn't been built for the last Hive War, she'd certainly been built by a shipyard still suffering from its effects.

They both listened to the message with dawning interest, and ended up looking at each other.

"So we're getting the four extra hands we needed?" Marder said. "Since when has Payaral Na'an gone into the body-broker business?"

"Crew registry," Longman said, with elaborate pomposity. Then he shrugged. "How the Hades should I know?"

"It might help to learn."

"Aye aye, Jo. And while I'm at it, shall I try to learn if he can come up with more cargo-handling robots? I can fix two of the ones we have if I can be in two places at once or use—"

"No chemicals, Charlie." The sharpness in her voice startled her. It also startled one of the crew—Butkus his name was—who'd just stepped into the compartment with a tray.

"Sorry, Mr. Butkus. We were having a little argument about cargo limits. Do you have any experience in handling chemical containers?"

Butkus had some, and was willing to talk about it. By the time they'd all exchanged notes, the tray was empty and the tense moment defused. Longman held Marder's eyes for a moment after Butkus left, then turned back to a properly tuned Engineering console.

One day at a time, Marder thought. *One day at a time.*

Victoria:

The Ptercha'a (Payaral Na'an preferred that term for the Servants in War) who used the name Emt Desdai laid his ears back. His ruff and orange facial fur did not stand up, however, and his tail remained motionless.

He was annoyed rather than angry, and possibly not at Payaral Na'an. However, it would do no harm to ask, since Desdai's grievance was perhaps one Na'an could ease.

"I ask pardon for offense given without intent," Na'an said. He used High Merishi. Desdai had as fluent a command of it as a Ptercha'a's vocal apparatus allowed. It was one reason why he had been valuable in Na'an's service and was now going aboard *Nosavan*.

"No offense has been given," Desdai said. He spread his hands, palms upward, and flicked an imaginary speck of dust off the chair with his tail. "However, I am left in ignorance on one matter.

"Will your House protect any whose welfare I value if Security takes offense at the game we play against them?"

Na'an had some time before decided to tell Emt Desdai only the truth, so his reply was quick. "Only to this extent: that a pledge made by someone in my position should not be dishonored."

"Certain kin and friends may face worse than dishonor from Security if that is all you can pledge."

This was the first time Desdai had spoken of kin or friends, who were not mentioned in any file on him Na'an had seen. It was almost certain that he had some, however, possibly recently discovered or acquired. Ptercha'a paired off by preference, and went kinless only in an emergency or in madness. Serving Payaral Na'an and in due course the trade mission to Victoria was not an emergency, and Desdai had shown no signs of madness by normal Ptercha'a standards.

"I do not doubt that. What would you accept?"

The bargaining that followed would have lasted

until lunchtime if both had not been aware that the electronic shielding of Na'an's office might have leaks. Also, common organic devices (eyes and ears) could see how long they spent together, and pass on this knowledge to potential enemies.

In the end, what Emt Desdai accepted was a large transfer of Na'an's personal funds to an account to which three named Ptercha'a would be given access in the event of his death. Desdai would be responsible for informing them of this promise; Na'an for transferring the money and making sure that the account was proof against Security.

That used to be something any of the Folk could do before they were nest-free. With Security climbing everywhere with open jaws, it might no longer be so simple. But Na'an was sure that one of his House could still do an adequate job.

"It seems to me that you have in all but law persuaded me to pay in advance for work not yet done and dangers not yet faced," Na'an said.

The Ptercha'a laughed. "If we are agreed that the dangers exist, it is enough. To tell the truth, if the dangers did not exist, I might ask even more for myself, for taking to space at my age."

"You are no closer to the preserver's couch than I am," Na'an said. That was not entirely flattery. Desdai was nearly halfway through his normal life span, but he was so fit and vigorous, even for a Ptercha'a, that it was hard to remember.

"Perhaps I am distant from the preserver's couch," Desdai said. "But I am also distant from the years when I was a scout for Legion Four-One. I need one more good fight before I am ready to lie down on the elders' couch and sing to the children!"

In private, Na'an and Desdai gripped forearms as

equals. Then Desdai made the traditional deep bow, tail curled between his legs and ears drooping, that signified a blood oath to serve to the death.

The gesture moved Na'an enough to leave him speechless, but not mindless. Racing through his thoughts was the question: *service until whose death?*

Four

Linak'h:

Brokeh su-Irzim cut back his roadrider's power as he headed up into the Byrkoot Hills. There was less traffic but also less road, twisting like a mating serpent as it rose from the valley. The children from the Ptercha'a villages were also bolder about playing by or even on the road.

Of course, su-Irzim knew that he could always give up his roadrider, at least while he was on Linak'h. Indeed, the Territorial Governor had stopped just short of ordering him to do so when he unpacked.

"The dignity of a ship commander of the first class is too great for a roadrider," that wrinkled goldtusk had said. "The Furfolk place some value on the dignity of our commanders. You should also consider that you may reach even higher rank."

Brokeh su-Irzim doubted that. Beyond his present rank came the squadron and Fleet ranks, and no one was ever promoted to them while on Inquiry duty like his on Linak'h. Few associated as he had become with Inquiry work ever reached them at all, and certainly none who did not spend their time closer to the seats of power. Baer itself by preference, certainly at least some place like Petzas or Moykus.

At least neither promotion nor any other reward or punishment was in the goldtusk's gift!

Anger at the old one's presumption faded in su-Irzim as the road curved along the edge of the gorge leading to Dewi's Falls. Rain had been scant of late; the falls themselves were only a silvery trickle over the night-hued stones at the head of the gorge.

The gorge itself was as fine a sight as ever, already shrouding itself in the evening mists. Those mists reminded su-Irzim that he should not stop to admire the scenery. This road was no place to be found after dark, not with its bends, its dropoffs sometimes on both sides, and the occasional adolescent Ptercha'a who wanted to test courage or match wits against one of the People.

The roadrider's whine swelled above the call of the night flyers and the mating rootcarvers, as su-Irzim fed the power again.

Linak'h:

The waning of the Yellow Father left only the Red Child's glow from below the mountainous horizon to give light. Su-Irzim needed his headlights before he was halfway to the crest, and felt the mist crawling up out of the gorge after him as if it was a living thing with an appetite.

Too much imagination, he reminded himself. But was too much imagination for one serving with the Fleet enough for an Inquirer working puzzles with three pieces out of every four missing or misshapen? He had not understood before he came to Linak'h what now seemed as self-evident as the need of life for air—an Inquirer might hold a commander's rank, but he heard on the wind a rather different set of trumpets.

Now there was no wind, only the mist rising straight up, to be parted by the headlights where they struck but everywhere else veil the land. Su-Irzim decided to rely less on speed and more on the headlights, even if that took more time. The mist was more than a veil. It also left the road slick, usually in places where long-dead trees or jagged stones waited to spit or shatter a fallen rider.

The commander was a tenth-watch behind his schedule when he reached the house. As he reached the crest he was sure he heard the whine of a lifter, then knew he saw the pad lights going on. They had gone off by the time he slowed before the gate and held up his ID for the scanner.

"Welcome back, Commander," came the voice of the housemaster, Senior Engine Technician Fygos Dravin. "Any trouble on the road?"

"Just the mist," su-Irzim said. He thought Dravin sounded uneasy. He also thought he heard the sound of the sector-defense turret rifle slowly training. It had been located so carefully that even somebody who knew where to look for it could miss it from where su-Irzim stood. Dravin did not let his dislike of the "Furwads" (as he always called the Ptercha'a) blind him to their military skill, and the house was the better defended for it.

"All right. Come in quietly, and try to park without any lights."

That was unusual enough that su-Irzim was about to ask why. Then he heard the scanner shift over to distant mode, the intercom die, and the gate begin to swing open. If he didn't want to be left standing on the road trying to raise Dravin again, he had best obey what was an order in all but name.

One thing had not changed. Fygos Dravin had no respect to spare for any section, company, or ship commander. Squadron and Fleet commanders got at least basic Fleet courtesy, most of the time.

Su-Irzim wheeled the roadrider through the gate as it began to close. The metal grille slapped the rear tire hard. He pushed his roadrider to the garage, which he could have done not only without lights but without sight, locked the power and steering, locked the door, and stepped out into the night.

By then his eyes had fully adjusted to the dimness that was all the Red Child gave this far north this early in the year. He saw that both pad and roads had fresh scars, which meant not only activity but a need to rebake the dirt. (Or forget about the dirt, dig it out, and lay in gravel, which compacted and drained naturally; was it time to raise that issue again?)

A door hissed open. The doorway was dark, but su-Irzim recognized the silhouette.

"Warm greetings, Zhapso. Forgive my lateness—"

"Rahbad Sarlin has returned."

"You did not tell me?"

"The lifter maintained silence all the way to land-ing—"

"The lifter I saw and heard from the road?"

"—and by the time we knew it had Sarlin aboard, we had no secure communication with you."

Zhapso su-Lal's orthodoxy in procedures was rigid. Su-Irzim would have despaired of him if the other Inquirer had not been able to enjoy the company of Ptercha'a and tolerate the veiled insubordination of Fygos Dravin. His imagination and creativity were carefully hidden, but they were there.

"I am here."

"So you are, and it would be sad if you were not." Su-Lal seemed to frown, then lowered his voice. "The lifter you mentioned—it brought beer and ale for all and company for the Lidessouf twins."

Female company, of course. "Enough so that there will be drink even after Virik—"

The frown turned into a harsh mask. "They buried Virik in the Scaleskin Territory. The twins will not be with us tonight."

Thinking of the kind of bond that joined them to Virik, who had known them since they were recruits, su-Irzim found no fault with that. He also found his own news, that the Consolidationists had apparently won the Diet elections, to be rather tepid.

"There has to be enough to drink to Virik's memory," su-Irzim said.

"There will be," su-Lal said. "His memory, and the memory of those dead but not yet given knowledge of the fact."

It was the first time in years that this common scrap of the Great Khudr's poetry had held any power to move Brokeh su-Irzim.

Linak'h:

The twins seemed to prefer ale, and left their seniors with the beer. Quite a lot of that went down while the three Inquiry commanders watched the recording of Sarlin's debriefing, then the twins'. Although he must have quenched one thirst, Sarlin seemed to have developed a fresh one, and drank level with his companions.

By the time the recordings were done it was nearly

the Newday watch, and su-Irzim had visited the bath chamber three times. When he returned from the fourth trip, Dravin had brought another keg and a tray of sausages, smoked fish, and cheese.

"That the last?" Sarlin asked, pointing at the keg.

"Afraid so, Commander. Unless you want to broach the one saved for the twins."

"The Lords forbid such a thing."

"Don't know about the Lords, Commander." It sounded as if some of the missing beer hadn't reached the twins, but there was much said about the unwisdom of looking too closely at good servants, and su-Irzim had found most of it true.

"The twins won't forgive it, though." Dravin belched. "Their wenches won't, neither. Never saw three such stout ones. Wrestle any of them with pleasure, any night, and let them win gladly."

He belched again. "So go and see if the twins have left anything of their friends, and ask," Sarlin said. "Go, and leave us." Su-Irzim heard anger crackling just below the surface cheer, although the beer he had drunk was more than enough normally to fuddle his hearing.

Dravin had a much harder head and had drunk rather less. He heard, obeyed, and vanished.

"The lifter pilot was a big-snouted Consolidationist," Sarlin said. "So if that was your news from town, Brokeh, call it something else."

"They haven't actually won an outright majority," su-Irzim said. "They still have to rule by a coalition with the Minority Collective and the Lords' Way Party. That—"

"—won't make a bugfart's worth of difference," Sarlin said—or rather, growled, like a Ptercha'a frustrated in a rutting mood. "The Lords' Wayfarers and the Consies have been like *this*"—he held thumb and midfinger about a bug's wing apart, and held both steady as well—"since before I was born. Will they come apart, just to give us easy sleep at night?"

No one could be drunk enough to ignore the venom in Sarlin's voice.

"It might not be so serious as that," su-Lal said, in more measured tones than somebody who had drunk so much beer ought to be able to use. "The party's stated *goals* are to consolidate the administration of all the People's planets for greater strength. But they have been stating those since before *I* was born—and I am somewhat past being a green youth, even if Commander Sarlin often doubts it."

"Since when have you behaved like—?" Sarlin began.

Brokeh su-Irzim strangled a groan at birth. One who had spent much time on the road and then heard bad news over much beer should not have to play peacemaker. However, it was either him or no one, and either a peacemaker or a breach in their ranks and the failure of the mission.

Failure was unthinkable, when the ground patrol had confirmed their worst suspicions. Correction: most of their worst suspicions. There might be some reason for Scaleskins, Smallteeth, and Ptercha'a all working together to train mercenaries that made this enterprise of small concern to the People's Inquirers.

And the Great Khudr might rise from his grave, to repudiate all his work and that of his descendants.

"We need not insult one another to be frank," su-Irzim said. He stretched out in his chair, kicked off his boots, and held out his mug for a refill like a goldtusk in a comedy awaiting service.

His companions now formed a common front, to

imply that his ancestry was irregular, his habits dubious, and his destination likely to be one even a drunkard should fear. By the time they had begun to laugh, su-Irzim knew the latest crisis was past.

"What bothers me is the Consolidationist victory coming at the same time as we stumble on this—camp, or whatever you want to call it," Sarlin said. He looked deep into his empty mug, apparently without finding anything in it to ease his mind. So he eased his thirst instead, set the mug down, wiped foam from his lips with the back of his hand, and sighed.

"We can delay sending the full report at least a hundredwatch," su-Lal said. "After all, we have been complaining of limited resources since we were here."

"What makes you think that was an excuse?" Sarlin grunted. "I know you've done no Inquiry work in the field, but even you should know that—"

"We've been put on sadly short rations?" Su-Lal actually bared his tusks, but it was a mock challenge that neither drunkard nor Lords' Party fanatic could mistake for a real one. Sarlin merely clapped both hands over his scarred nose, a similar parody of the classic gesture of a patron displeased with an artist's performance.

"Compared to what we ought to have, our ribs are showing," Sarlin muttered. "Do you know *that*?"

"I know it, and I suspect that some of those who will be receiving our report know it as well. If we delay sending the report as long as possible, then say that we would have sent it sooner with the resources to obtain confirmation . . ."

When they served together aboard Eimo su-Ankrai's flagship *Nightwind* off Victoria, su-Irzim had known su-Lal to spin out such a ponderous analysis for a quarter-watch. Did enough beer make him briefer rather than longer, as it did most?

If so, then the mission's beer consumption was about to rise sharply. Su-Irzim had a moment's pleasant fantasy, sketching the design of a trailer that would tow bchind a roadrider and carry four or even six kegs of beer.

However, shaking any beer or ale worth drinking in such a manner would most likely send the kegs into orbit halfway through the journey. Reluctantly, su-Irzim turned his mug bottom upward, for an end to his evening's drinking and a monument to absent friends, and leaned back to listen to the two real Inquiry professionals spin their scheme.

Both of them had forgotten more about how to manipulate other Inquirers all the way up to Fleet level than su-Irzim had ever learned. That was plainly forging a bond between them that su-Irzim prayed might prevent further quarrels.

If the Lords had any further attention to spare for his prayers, he would offer up one more. That was that no one in Inquiry with strong Consolidationist leanings (he mentioned Rahbad Sarlin's half brother Behdan Zeg by name) learn about this scheme.

Then the mission would no longer be starved. It would be executed on the spot, as Lord Petzas was by the Formit's gunner, and something much better supplied and much more closely watched put in its place.

That would most likely tell the People more about what was happening on Linak'h. It would surely tell humans worth their pay that the People were more than casually interested in the planet. Then the same sort of race to commit resources to intervention would begin, without any time for voices of wisdom to suggest that perhaps this race ought not to be entered in the first place!

Victoria had been bad enough, with the factions of only one race offering themselves to service with others. With three races and four Khudrigates all bargaining like merchants in a shop-alley, the confusion alone would be enough to slay seasoned warriors from inward-eating or heart failure, before the actual fighting began.

Five

Aboard R.M.S. *Somtow Nosavan,* off Victoria:

Joanna Marder watched as Victoria Dockyard drifted toward the center of the navigational display. It wasn't a pretty sight, scarred by its conversion from an asteroid and further scarred by losing much of its equipment to *Nosavan*'s cargo. But it was as good a benchmark as any.

"Benchmark for acceleration initiation coming up— *mark*!" Marder said. She didn't need to use the intercom; *Nosavan*'s Bridge was small enough that six people crowded it, and a whisper carried as much authority as anyone needed.

At the Helm console, Butkus (newly appointed Boatswain) looked to Charlie Longman. Charlie nodded; the Engineering readings came up on the Helm displays.

"Power nominal, shield generator warmed, life support nominal . . ." The litany ran through the eight functions that spacemen nearly worshiped.

The last, "computer on-line and nominal," came in Anglic overlaid with accents of both Ptercha'a and several varieties of Merishi. Emt Desdai had been until six days ago number-two man in the Merishi trade mission's computer-maintenance section. A sudden need to carry a message to kin on Linak'h had him working his passage aboard *Nosavan,* with right to sign regular articles if his business was concluded before *Nosavan* departed Linak'h.

"Speak up," Butkus growled. That got a sharp look from Charlie, but no more. She had spoken to him about his landing on Butkus over the man's dislike of Ptercha'a, which she didn't like but hoped to smother rather than disintegrate.

"Elayne Zheng's been mad at the Ptercha'a for twenty years over her uncle's death on Agamemnon," she remembered Charlie saying. "Butkus hasn't half her brains. How much do you want to bet we'll have to blow him up anyway?"

"I'll blow you up if you ever say that where he can hear it," Marder snapped. "A good helmsman and a good computer chief are equally hard to come by. Possibly harder than good engineers."

Which was why she'd signed on three more humans for Engineering at the same time as Desdai. The check of their records had to be cursory, but they had all passed what could be made in the time available, and all seemed to be settling in well enough.

"What about good men?"

"Charlie, in that capacity nobody could be harder than you," she'd said. "But this is a professional situation."

"Oh?"

She understood then and now the skepticism. They were going to have to separate ship's business and pillow talk, and sooner rather than later. After Linak'h, maybe—that was a three-week round trip at most, plus time for cargo handling.

"Computer on-line and nominal," Emt Desdai repeated, then for good measure held both hands over his head in the traditional visual signal. Those hands were distorted by a set of adapter gloves, idiot versions of power armor that let Merishi, Ptercha'a, and human each use the others' tools, controls, and keyboards.

Several others aboard *Nosavan* had adapter gear of one sort or another, including Charlie. *Nosavan* was human-built, but too long in service. Somewhere along the way, one refit had included a set of so-called Universal Devices, supposed to be equally usable by all three races.

To Marder, the usability was about as real as the friendship among the three. If the budget had allowed for it, she would have bought adapter gear for all eighteen of *Nosavan*'s crew. However, they'd had to borrow cargo handlers from the *Glen of Dyfri,* Na'an's own charter, to get their load up, aboard, and secured.

That cost money. It also cost time, partly because of Charlie's insistence on scanning the cargo to make sure it was reasonably free of espionage devices or bombs. He would have scanned the passengers if that had been legal, and Marder was quite sure that some of what he'd done to their baggage wasn't. However, if they never found out and *Nosavan* wasn't hijacked, dishonors would be about even.

Dockyard was beginning to waver now. This close to a planet, you could stabilize a ship by playing off drive against gravity only so long—less than an hour, even for a warship in top shape. For *Nosavan,* the time was measured in minutes.

"Engage drive."

"Drive engaged."

Marder waited until Dockyard began moving on the

screen and the numbers began moving on her display. Then she said softly:

"Drive, one-third ahead."

It was amazing how fast Dockyard vanished from the main screen. A shift to a rear view showed Victoria slowly falling away, the north polar cap already visible and the lights on the night side creeping into sight on the eastern limb.

Marder slid as far down in her command chair as the harness would allow. She felt a surge of release that had nothing in common with the sexual kind, but was nearly as satisfying.

She was back in space, and in command. Could you be not spaceborn, and still find space a more natural environment for you than most planets?

Charlemagne:

"I relieve you, Admiral."

Sho Kuwahara returned Captain Lena Ropuski's salute and stepped aside for her to sit down behind the desk. It was a tight fit, made tighter by the fact that Captain Ropuski was nearly as tall as Kuwahara's meter seventy-six and if anything broader through the torso.

Ropuski sat down, logged herself in as officer of the watch, and leaned back. The twelfth duty watch in the career of the Naval Command Dual-Sovereignty Study Group was officially underway.

Twelve watches, four days in registration (instead of being commissioned, study groups were registered, a procedure that to Kuwahara seemed more appropriate to confidential publications or exotic diseases). Several hundred hours' work put in. Previously unknown facts learned about at least five planets by every one of the ten officers and eight enlisted people on the roster—and there were thirty planets in their jurisdiction, or whatever the technical term was.

(Kuwahara had considered himself a trained staff officer until the study group assignment landed on him. He was now discovering arcane and obscure facets of staff work faster than he was facts about dual-sovereignty planets.)

And very little done about Linak'h, except learning that the reinforcements were on the way, detailed TO&E to follow by secure means later.

(Dilemma of high commands, as old as interstellar flight: high-capacity communications slow, low-capacity communications faster, *nothing* instantaneous. Minimum turnaround time about two Standard days, except under special conditions. This gave would-be micromanagers ulcers and sometimes drove them out of military service, but they weren't the only victims.)

"Anything I should know about, Admiral?" Ropuski asked.

"Nothing came up on my watch," Kuwahara said. He sidled around the end of the desk and poured himself a cup of tea from the dispenser. The cleaning robot prodded him in the back as it approached to change the tanks and lay out snacks for the second watch.

"I won't mind if it stays that way," Ropuski said. She was a fuller-figured Slavic variant on Admiral Baumann's basic design, not surprising in someone who was genuine Jaghellion military aristocracy (four COs of the Vistula Wing, among other distinguished ancestors). "I also won't mind if we get some help from the Army."

"Baumann's negotiating," Kuwahara said. Privately

he thought the study group could have waited until it was a joint undertaking from the beginning. Warned in advance, the Army might take its time, hold out for a high price, send people it didn't want, organize a spy ring, or all of these.

"I hope she can negotiate us some more space," Ropuski said. She picked up a crumpled cup from under the desk, aimed it at the robot's trash receiver, and let fly. It hit precisely on target; years away from the controls of an attacker, Ropuski had a reputation as a viciously competitive handball player. "I'd as soon have that as Army help."

Kuwahara felt moderately guilty. Two of the three senior officers in the group were on TOAD assignments to Monticello and had no families. Living in quarters, they could take the second and third watches and let Kuwahara live a normal commuting life.

Descended from a long line of the winners in the Bad Manners Wars, Kuwahara hardly believed in the archaic concept of "face." He believed absolutely in a CO's obligations to his crew, and was conscious of not fulfilling all of them in the matter of working space.

Unfortunately, there was such a thing as too much austerity in staffing and equipping Forces Command. Kuwahara shared the conventional pride in a "lean, mean" central headquarters, but knew it was at least partly an illusion. There wasn't all that much one could *do* from Charlemagne or even the Zone Command planets; work had to be done well at the corps or task force level if it was going to get done at all.

But it had not been necessary to reduce the allotment of space, personnel, and facilities for temporary operations like the study group to their present level. Nor to give what seemed like a good part of what was left to the representatives of various academic research bodies. The Kishi Institute was all right, and others had to be admitted or there would be questions in both Federation houses, but why the Columbia College of Peace Studies, in the name of every Higher Power?

The tea did not improve Kuwahara's disposition, but at least it quenched his thirst. Good tea, too; they were certainly getting full service support. He'd had one experience with having to turn enlisted personnel into servants because the officers were working twenty hours a day and there was nobody else allowed to do the job. He refused to contemplate, let alone endure, another.

The tight quarters also made them a small, easily secured target, in the event that they ended up on somebody's list. Kuwahara had seen nothing to suggest this possibility, but the group was new, animosities on a dozen dual-sovereignty planets were old, and calling something "unlikely" was a notorious temptation to Fate.

Aboard U.F.S. *Shenandoah*, the Schneeheim system:

Thirteen hours out of Schneeheim, any excuse for Commodore Liddell's hovering over Bogdanov or anyone else had long since vanished. She decided it was time to do the same. She hadn't slept in eighteen hours or bathed in half again as long, and meals had been snatched on the fly.

Her standing (or mostly, sitting) command watch had given Pavel the same twelve hours off duty as the rest of *Shen*'s people, and he'd needed it far more than she had. It also reassured her that she hadn't lost the ability to think of one ship even if she wore the star that might give her power over anywhere from four to fifteen.

But it had tired her out. It also drew sparks from Commander Charbon. Jackie Charbon had moved up to exec of *Shenandoah* when Bogdanov became CO; nothing else about her had changed. Liddell had searched for a year for some aspect of the job where Charbon could sublimate her martinet urges, the way Pavel had worked off his with shiphandling.

Unfortunately, she was still searching, and even bringing Pavel tactfully into the search hadn't provided a solution. Now Liddell faced the prospect of independent command, where her flag would become a serious matter, and misplaced officers aboard even her flagship would have to work out their own destinies.

She *had* to be tired and hungry, if independent command as a commodore was doing nothing but make her worry about the running of her old ship. She hoped it was nothing worse; she had handled a few cases where it had been, during her three years as Eleventh Fleet's deputy chief of staff for personnel.

Shower, Rose, and now!

Tired as she was, she would not have minded having someone to shower with, if nothing more. The nearest man she'd ever been on those terms with, however, was thirty-one light-years away on Riftwell, and reaffiliated the last time she'd heard of him. (She wondered how the affiliate would cope with a bigamous relationship to the Riftwell base hospital's neurosurgery department.)

Anyway, water conservation was in effect. With the LI and the 879th both embarked, *Shen*'s complement was pushing the capacity of even her large water tanks and high-powered recyclers. To leave a margin for emergencies and accidents, everybody was on the "wet down, soap up, rinse off, and don't cheat on your rinsing time even if your back tells you to!" routine.

It was almost indecent to take that kind of shower with anyone else.

Aboard U.F.S. *Shenandoah,* the Schneeheim system:

Candice Shores subvocalized a Command Diary entry:

"1720. Schneeheim Orbital Departure + 15.36. The planet no longer shows a visible disk except under higher magnification than we are receiving in the LI company office."

That was all she could honestly say, and even that sounded querulous, but she'd be cursed if she was going to erase it. Maybe picking away at Commander Charbon's refusal to give the LI CO a department head's office as well as department head status would get somewhere.

Of course, Charbon had no choice with the status. Regulations said the senior officer of any assigned Army detachment ranked as a department head, right up there with Engineering, Weapons, Navigation, Medical, and so on.

They didn't say what that meant in practical terms, of space, priorities for training and computer time, and a whole bunch of other things. After half a year aboard *Shen,* Shores still hadn't decided if the XO didn't like LI or was shoving LI aside to hide the fact that she wasn't as good in her new job as she'd been in her old one.

Since the situation never got more than annoying, and not always that to the enlisted people, Shores had been prepared to let it ride. But she hoped Linak'h meant a dirtside deployment long enough to let them get the taste of Jacqueline Charbon's style of ship management out of their mouths!

She turned back to the screen. It showed nothing but stars now, and some of those kept winking in and out as asteroids passed in front of them. The Schneeheim system's asteroid belt ran rather large to the barrel, which made for easy navigation around it and might make for profitable mining if the planet ever provided a market. Since its two million people met all their copper requirements from one mine that required six people on each shift, the day of rich asteroid miners hailing from the Schneeheim system was clearly a long way off.

It was, if one stopped to think, rather amazing. Here she was, launched on a *voyage among the stars,* something that pre-starflight humanity had regarded as an act approaching the divine (if the historical novelists had it right, which she doubted). In practice, it was about as interesting as spading up the compost heap in the spring, to see what the winter might have left.

It was less interesting than spading up the neighbor's compost heap had been, those last two years before she and her father both left home in different directions. For one thing, the neighbor's compost heap came equipped with the neighbor's son, Raul, and she wondered if all the time they'd put in on the vegetable garden had helped make the parting more amicable.

(It was the only amicable parting she could remember from those years.)

The door signal lit up and the chime began pulsing. An open-door office helped morale, and dirtside it was possible. Aboard a ship under acceleration through an asteroid belt, safety regs outweighed morale considerations.

"Come in."

It was Juan Esteva. Bodyguard and corporal in her Scout company on Victoria, he'd been a sergeant by the end of the campaign. He'd also doubled in under-cover intelligence work for Major (now Colonel) Liew Nieg, but he'd been out of that for a year. When Shores's company was being put together, the beer-vine sent him word that it had a vacancy for a buck sergeant.

The only problem was in making him the company top. Buck sergeant just wouldn't cut it in that job, with six or seven other NCOs senior to him. So they compromised on a good second-best—Security & Intelligence NCO. If this had raised any questions, Juan had handled them himself, without leaving any visible injuries on the questioners.

"*Hola,* Major. *Que tal?*"

"*Mucho de nada.*"

"That bad, hunh?" He toed the door shut and sat down.

"What brings you here?"

"See how you were doing?"

"Besides bored? Try again, Juan."

"Okay. I've been getting questions about how you are when it comes down hard and heavy."

"What kind of questions? No names, please."

"Well, one name you should know. The top's been real straight on this matter. Said as far as she was concerned, I could tell them to go bounce themselves. You'd done fine on Victoria, the Pocket Pistol didn't make aides out of mite-brains, and you didn't win your course prize in a planetary lottery. But if I wanted to check it out with you, that was also fine as far as she was concerned."

"Four cheers for the top." Esther Timberlake was one reason Esteva wasn't the company top. Shores might have pushed him into the slot over Timberlake's predecessor, who was overage, overweight, and underbrained for heavy LI work. Timberlake had twenty-two years and three campaigns under her belt, and no fat on her there or between her ears.

"I don't blame them, Juan. Anybody who doesn't know me could mistake me for somebody with a bad case of promotion fever. They're not always good news when you hit combat."

"Victoria should take care of that."

"For the old Vics, but how many of those do we have? You, me, Timberlake, and six others. Like I said, anyone who doesn't know me . . ."

Which I sometimes think includes myself. In less than three years she'd been one of the real heroes of the Victoria campaign, aide to Frieda Hentsch during the Pocket Pistol's first year as CG, Eleventh Army, and first in her class at the Eleventh Zone's Intermediate Staff Course. To others, it might add up to a future of stars or a dangerously aggressive combat leader. In her own eyes, it didn't add up so neatly.

Esteva kept a compassionate silence until Shores reached into her desk and pulled out a flask of rum. As she poured two cups, she said, "You can tell anyone who wants to plumb my depths—"

"Is that the phrase you want?"

"May mites infest my armor if I lie."

Esteva looked resigned. "So plumbing your depths—?"

"Is out. Also I didn't sleep with the Pocket Pistol."

Rumors to the contrary, Frieda Hentsch seemed to have a strong celibate streak in her. Given all the handicaps she'd overcome on her way to four stars, this hardly surprised Shores. Hentsch's penchant for good-looking aides and staff juniors of both sexes seemed to be a method of decorating her office, although one of her pilots had been so congenial that Shores had tripped him (or he her—it hadn't mattered in the end).

"Anything else?"

She wanted to suggest that the gossips could spend their time training, or if they wanted to worry, worry about themselves and their mates. Forty percent of the company were first-termers, some with barely the minimum two years needed to qualify for LI. Of the five platoon commanders, three were new and the XO was a captain who apparently didn't have a vocation for that rank like Nate Abelsohn on Victoria.

No way to send that message through Juan, though. Not Timberlake, either. Beyond a certain point, bracing officers could not be left to the sergeants. The old lady had to pull her weight—or land it on lieutenants who got too far out of line, if it came to that.

The cups were full now—almost overflowing, in fact. Shores trickled half of Esteva's back into the bottle. She wanted to leave hers intact, but those expressive Latin eyes—a lot like Raul's, when she came to think about it—were saying things she didn't want to hear as they studied the cup.

She trickled her rum back too, then hoisted her cup.

"To the *Shenandoah* Company!"

Linak'h:

The two converted gunships slipped through the Ka'amfi Pass at their usual treetop altitude. In the backseat of the leader, Marshal Emilio Banfi noted with undimmed eyes and memory changes in the vegetation, the slopes a klom to either side, the Ka'amfi River alternately crawling along and boiling through rapids—

The two pilots simultaneously juggled lift, shrouded propellers, and aerodynamic control surfaces to swing the gunships into a sharp turn. Banfi could now look down on the other gunship. In the backseat, Colonel Davidson wore his usual expression of grim determination. Sergeant Major Kinski's face was invisible, but he was probably grinning.

Banfi decided that if Davidson didn't stop looking martyred every time they rode the gunships, he was going for a ride with Lieutenant Nalyvkina. That should teach him that he was well off with Kinski!

The propellers went into reverse and the gunships came out of their turns, both descending and slowing rapidly. They both flared out just above the Chura Hunt landing pad, and the propellers stopped in time to avoid kicking up dust.

Just as well. The Chura Hunt Warband was already drawn up for the Marshal's inspection. No, not quite. Two laggards were still running down the path across the *fmyl* fields, fully equipped and moving with the speed of desperation. A human Olympic runner might have kept pace with them, thanks to their twenty-kilo loads.

Banfi waited until Nalyvkina had secured the controls, climbed out, and lowered the steps. Leaps from cockpits were a thing of his long-gone youth. Now babying himself meant not merely dignity but survival.

Banfi pretended not to notice the two latecomers dashing into their positions, one in the rear rank, one in the front. The Warband leader shouted "Attention" in both Anglic and the True Tongue; both pilots snapped to attention along with the Warband.

Not much had changed since the last inspection thirty days ago. Not much did change, in these Hunt Warbands, and not much would unless the Administration back in Och'zem either increased its appropriations for them or allowed them to buy directly from humans.

Banfi hoped it would be the former. He didn't want to add to his workload the task of inspecting human arms merchants eager to overcharge Warbands for undersized weapons shipments. Not to mention the question of wanting a firm commitment from the Territorial Administration to let its people defend themselves against the Planetary Coordination.

Hopes tomorrow, inspection today. Banfi tried to look all-seeing but not unforgiving, firm but not intolerant. Ptercha'a for much of his life had told him that he succeeded, which either made him a skilled actor or them the politest race in the known universe.

He stopped before one four-leader, with the name "Tskun Igan" embroidered on his sleeveless tunic. Igan had to be from Dezowny Flatlands stock, with that pale amber fur and eyes the color of rubies. He was a bit short for a Dezownyer—no more than a meter seventy—but beautifully groomed and with more muscles than even the average Ptercha'a's cult of fitness could produce. He had to weigh at least sixty-five kilos, and his tail was one of the longest Banfi had ever seen in a lifetime of keeping company with Ptercha'a.

Apart from tunic, shorts, and ankle and wrist braces, he carried the pack he was now turning out for Banfi's inspection, a bullpup-style rifle firing caseless explosive-propelled slugs, ammunition and medical pouches, a canteen, helmet, and ankle boots, and a natural-leather harness to carry everything.

The turned-out pack revealed a change of clothing, extra boots and helmet liner, a computing laser sight for the rifle, two days' rations (pressed meat and *fmyl* bars and hard candy), toiletries (he had a brand-new claw-trimmer), repair kits for weapons, pack, and helmet, and a small embroidered bag of personal possessions. From the way it bulged, one of the possessions was a fair-sized print book.

"How does the world treat you, Leader Igan?" Banfi asked. "You look better than when I last was here." Banfi spoke True Speech even though any leader had to speak Commercial Merishi.

Banfi had never subscribed to the belief that the Ptercha'a preferred the more intelligible *lingua franca* of all three races to their own tongue, mangled as it was when spoken by an unaugmented human. Again, his experience had led him to believe that either he was right or the Ptercha'a were unbelievably tolerant.

"The Skyfather has blessed me twice," Igan replied. "My parasites have departed, thanks to the medicine. Also, I have been chosen as a pair-mate."

"Nira—what is her family name?"

"Ohn'kh," Igan said. "The grooming you praise is her work."

"So it is proclaimed, eh? Something in the way of a pairing gift may be coming your way, if I have any money left after I pay my taxes."

One of the rites of betrothal among the Ptercha'a was the couple's thoroughly grooming each other's fur, with tongue and claws as well as more modern techniques. It usually led to their first sexual encounter immediately afterward.

The Warband smiled; a few laughed out loud. Taxes were not a burden in the Territory, but Banfi had never encountered a sane member of any race who actually enjoyed paying them, or was unhappy to learn that the mighty (like Host Leader Banfi) had to pay until it hurt just like them.

Banfi continued his inspection with the heavy weapons, two crewed launchers that would not have been out of place in an arsenal of the Starworld Revolution, four SSWs of an obsolete model (but if it could kill you, was it obsolete?), and the command center. It could be loaded aboard the Hunt's lifter or either groundcar, or broken down into four man-portable packs.

Not heavy armament for fifty Ptercha'a, practically the whole adult population of the Chura Hunt. But clearly well maintained at least, and the Hunt's firing test last year ran up a score in the nineties. Two firing tests a year would really help, but the ammunition bill for that was something the Administration hadn't yet been prepared to meet.

Banfi took the salute of the Warband leader, then he and his companions returned the salute as the Warband wheeled about and paraded back to their homes. Only a few children too young for service and one elderly woman with a bobbed tail and almost hairless ears were not back at work when the two gunships lifted off.

Colonel Davidson was both right and wrong, Banfi reflected. He was right in saying that these Hunt Warbands would not offer much resistance to a determined thrust by the Coordination's crack legions. None at all if they used their air assets, only a little more if they were groundbound.

But that would be fighting the campaign on the Coordination's terms. Davidson was wrong in assuming that the Warbands would do that, even if they were ordered to. And if they were ordered to fight guerilla-style, their knowledge of the land and their fieldcraft and personal weapons, with the skies overhead friendly and the Administration's troops of both races ready to strike once the Coordination's spearheads had been herded into killing zones . . .

Which reminded Banfi to check the communications log. When he had a choice between doing paperwork and eating breakfast before a five-hundred-klom flight, he now ate breakfast. The word that Federation reinforcements were on the way to Linak'h was nearly a week old. Maybe there was something new, such as details on what those reinforcements might be.

Six

Petzas:

On this clear night, the window of the private room gave a startling view over the rooftops of Petzas-Din. Fleet Commander (Retired) F'zoar su-Weigho could even with his dimmed eyes see the pad lights atop every tower all the way to the shore. He thought he could see the lights of the pleasure strips there.

With a little imagination, he thought he could even see the white foam curls on the surf beating against the seawall. They had to be there; nothing but a fierce wind could make a night on the Crawler Deep Coast so clear.

He turned back from the view and ordered the shutters closed. They slid shut behind him as he sat down again at his table. It was almost empty, except for two glasses and the third bottle of uys, which itself was almost empty. Much of that bottle and its two predecessors had to be inside his dinner companion, Fleet Commander Eimo su-Ankrai.

The other commander did not show the effects, however, although he had never had su-Weigho's reputation for a head resistant to any amount of beer, ale, uys, or strongwater. He was a trifle flushed, his eyes had sunk perhaps a nail's thickness farther into his wrinkled face, and when he raised his ears to greet his companion they rose at noticeably different angles. That was all. Perhaps su-Ankrai had decided to wait until he was past sixty to begin a reputation as a mighty partygoer.

Or perhaps it was only a more than usually serious matter that had led to this invitation at the Night of Deep Club. Su-Weigho was inclined that way, and not only because of the Consolidationist victory.

The Night of Deep Club had, for most of its existence, which was only twenty Petzas years less than People settlement of the planet itself, enjoyed a unique privilege. As in the legendary Burrows of Hyml, it was strictly forbidden to eavesdrop on conversations here, physically or otherwise.

Any Inquirers worth their pay could note down who met whom when at the club, and decide if that justified eavesdropping elsewhere. But anyone who violated the rule against doing it on the premises was in serious social trouble, and sometimes more professional trouble than a wise Lawbound courted.

Su-Weigho reached across the table for the bottle and filled the two glasses, drop by drop in alternation, until they each held within a hair's length the same amount of uys. Then he raised his glass.

"To a swift answer to our quest."

Confusion did not make su-Ankrai forget his manners; Ptercha'a tortures could not have done that. He emptied his glass in one gulp, ceremoniously licked his lips and patted his stomach, then shrugged.

"Is my secret out, then?"

"That you have a problem which requires my assistance? That is hardly a secret. The nature of the problem, however—"

"Behdan Zeg."

"Has he finally been arrested for molesting the unlawfully young?"

"You jest, I hope."

Su-Weigho did not, at least not entirely. Suspicions in plenty of that and other offenses had trailed Zeg like a marshdweller's stink for many years. Proof, however, had always been lacking.

"I do jest. Is the matter so serious that you would rather I not?"

"Judge for yourself," su-Ankrai said harshly. "It is intended to send Behdan Zeg to Linak'h."

Su-Weigho was moved enough to knock over his glass with a spasm of his left hand. If the person responsible for that witling's idea had been present, the Fleet commander would have seized the bottle in his right hand and rearranged the culprit's features and possibly cranial aspects as well.

"I did not think Zeg was a Consolidationist," su-Weigho said, in measured tones.

"He isn't. Or at least he only makes mouth-noises pleasing to Consolidationists. Sufficiently so, I judge, that they will hide his unpleasing habits from the Lords' Party faithful."

Su-Weigho briefly wished for another bottle, or at least another full glass. In the two hundred watches since the Consolidationist victory became official and binding on all worlds of the Khudrigate, there had been a good many posts handed to otherwise marginally competent Consolidationist faithful. To do them justice, these were not the most critical posts, and contrary to expectations there had been no mass purge of non-Consolidationists who held such posts.

At least not yet. That the Consolidationists were not now utter fools did not prove they would not become such in time. For su-Weigho, it had long been an axiom that most elected officials were fools whose folly had merely yet to be exposed.

Whoever had conceived the idea of sending Behdan Zeg to Linak'h at this time had just exposed himself, and in a manner that would have set street boys giggling madly.

Su-Weigho leaned back in his chair. Its back joints were not as flexible as his, and the front legs came off the rug. He recovered balance before he lost dignity, and crossed his arms on the table.

"You look ready to put your tusks at my throat," su-Ankrai said.

"At somebody's, yes," su-Weigho said. "Do you have any names?"

Su-Ankrai gave with undeniable reluctance a list of five. "Any or all of them could have their reasons to wish Zeg on Linak'h," he concluded, "and these are only the ones I am sure of."

Su-Weigho's head seemed to have gained half an ingot. He propped it up with one hand under his chin and stared past his companion into chaos.

Plainly, Behdan Zeg could be on his way to Linak'h with at least two different objectives. He could be going to sabotage the Inquiry mission there, if only by his mere presence and disagreeable temper. It could also hardly be a secret that he and Rahbad Sarlin were half brothers, and that "mutual detestation" was not too strong a term for what they felt toward each other. (Sarlin would of course avenge Zeg's blood if it was shed by another, but su-Weigho wondered if the elder would also be punishing the offense of not letting him shed it himself.)

Or perhaps Zeg, who was undeniably a skilled if ruthless field agent, was going to strengthen the mission, but in a particular way. He would take command of other field agents already in place in the People's Territory on Linak'h, probably without the knowledge of the Inquiry mission, and use them independently.

That also had to be opposed. It was too soon to decide what the People ought to do about the Merishi-sponsored training of human spies and mercenaries on Linak'h. It was not too soon to keep the People's Inquirers on Linak'h from working against each other, until *no* decision could be implemented when the time for one came!

So—how to keep Behdan Zeg at a safe distance from Linak'h? (Allowing for the fact that with Zeg, a safe distance meant the next stellar cluster, if not the seventh or eighth galaxy toward the edge of the universe.)

Or would Behdan Zeg be safer on Linak'h, with a known location and capabilities that could be monitored by three Inquirers all his equals or superiors? Considering the rumor that su-Weigho had also heard about his dining companion—

"Are you being offered a new command as well?"

"Yes. Commander of the Petzas Area Fleet Reinforcement Operations. I will be ground-based, but I will definitely have ships under my command." Su-Ankrai's face and voice both lightened as he spoke.

Su-Weigho did not blame him. Though he was a Syrodh of high rank and old family, with ancestors who had served under the Great Khudr, the Victoria episode had not been to his professional credit. He had stood no more than an even chance of ever being sent on active duty again.

Now he had a new command, even if it was one often given to a Fleet commander second class or even a squadron leader first class. He could move ships, order supplies, load those supplies aboard ships . . .

"If you will help me, I think we can make the best solution doing the will of the Consolidationists or their minions."

The uys was possibly beginning to hit; su-Ankrai stared in bemusement. "I mean sending Behdan Zeg to Linak'h. But not just him. Send a ship that will be under the control of the Inquirers already there, loaded with everything they can possibly need, including cases of uys and strongwater. If Zeg complains, send him aboard the ship, in luxurious quarters, with a female companion of suitable age, and promise that he too will have a ship at his orders once the situation on Linak'h has been assessed."

"Bribe the skrin's-get until he chokes on it?" Definitely the uys was working fast; su-Ankrai seldom used such language.

"Of course. We can certainly afford it. More than we can either a quarrel with the Consolidationists or having Zeg roaming about hungry and ready to devour the first member of the present team he encounters."

Su-Weigho smiled. "If your authority extends to chartering ships, and the vessel is available, why not our old Victoria friend *Perfumed Wind*? Captain ihr Sular knows this kind of work, the Inquiry team knows her, she is certainly able to handle a marsh-dweller like Zeg—"

A grunt and snort from su-Ankrai interrupted su-Weigho. He looked up, expecting a protest from the other, that *Perfumed Wind* would be a major piece of evidence for the Federation's Inquirers about the nature of the People's interest in Linak'h. Su-Weigho agreed that it would, but skill sometimes outweighed stealth, and if the Smallteeth's Inquirers had already identified Rahbad Sarlin anyway . . .

Su-Weigho received no such answer from his companion. Instead he saw the other Fleet commander sliding gracefully out of his chair, to vanish under the table. A thud and, a moment later, a snore floated up from the depths.

Su-Weigho pressed the call for attendants and also for his own lifter. Robots were more discreet than human attendants in most places, but not in the Night of Deep Club. Having a Fleet commander hauled to a guest room by robots as if he were a faulty climate-control unit lacked dignity.

Su-Ankrai was gone in moments. Su-Weigho remained seated, until he was sure that his own efforts to rise would not end with a loss of balance and dignity. As he walked with exquisite care toward the door, he had two hopes.

One was that his legs would uphold him as long as needed. The other was that su-Ankrai would remember tomorrow morning, through the ache in his head and the howling desert in his mouth, what he had promised the night before.

Charlemagne:

Several displays in the study group's office were lit up like the Combat Center of a light cruiser in action. However, Commander Thuy assured Kuwahara that everything was being handled adequately.

"Except for this," he said, handing a message form to the admiral.

The message would have been too short to upset anyone who didn't know that the Empress's shortest messages meant the worst of tempers. The words "Come now" had on occasion led fairly directly to a court-martial.

This one at least included the phrase "The Admiral of the Fleet's compliments to Vice Admiral Kuwahara" before the imperative summons to the Presence. Kuwahara brushed his teeth, decided after a look in the mirror that the rest of his person and uniform would past muster, and began the trek to Baumann's office.

The office staff didn't look away from him as he passed through the successive lines of defense, from receptionist to secretary to junior aide to senior aide. By the time he was outside the Inner Sanctum, though, he sensed a number of pairs of eyes firmly targeted on his back.

"Come in, Sho," Baumann called. Neither words nor tone carried much except the simple order, which Kuwahara prudently obeyed.

The tone changed the moment the door was closed. The C-in-C's face took on the expression that had inspired the nickname "Chilly Willi," and she waved one long-fingered hand at a display.

Kuwahara read the contents of the display, trying not to look either amused or bewildered. Either would have been an appropriate reaction.

The display was simply the long-promised TO&E of the reinforcements on their way to Linak'h. A battle cruiser with an embarked company-strength LI detachment and an attacker squadron and a light cruiser from Schneeheim. A squadron of light cruisers escorting transports with a battalion expeditionary unit and reinforcements for the existing garrison on Linak'h, already in transit, to rendezvous with the battle cruiser en route. Loading at Riftwell, two more transports with equipment for the garrison, including light attackers, ammunition, hardened satellites, and the usual grocery list of things snatched off the shelves when a distant garrison shouted for help.

The source of the trouble, if any, had to be the battle cruiser. She was *Shenandoah,* flying Rose Liddell's pennant.

Amusement and bewilderment remained as Kuwahara looked back at Baumann. The first twinges of a migraine joined them. Baumann's stare remained fixed and the temperature in the office several degrees below Kuwahara's comfort range.

"Why *Shen*?" Kuwahara asked. Baumann nodded. "May I sit down?"

Baumann's head jerked in what Kuwahara chose to interpret as a nod. He pulled up a chair and relaxed— or rather, assumed a more relaxed posture. He was *not* going to do serious business with Baumann while sitting braced like a first-week officer trainee in the mess hall!

"I don't think there's any impropriety involved," he said. "Schatz would not be giving Liddell this chance without complete belief in her professional qualifications. Of course, my knowledge of Admiral Schatz may cover different areas from yours—"

"We *did* bounce a few times, if that is what you're trying to get at," Baumann snapped. "But that was, oh, something like twenty-two years ago. You are a much better judge of John Schatz as an admiral."

"Then I think he sent *Shenandoah* because she still has a majority of Victoria veterans aboard, who have this kind of situation—not mastered, precisely, but for whom it isn't a Great Unknown."

"I'll concede that point. I'll even concede it may be an advantage. But there's a disadvantage too."

"Telling everybody the extent and nature of our interest in Linak'h?"

"Precisely. What I want to know is why Schatz didn't consider *that* factor."

It would be true but tactless to point out that Schatz was retiring in a few more months, at the end of his command of Eleventh Fleet. He had no desire to spend years maneuvering for succession to Baumann in the corridors of Charlemagne. In fact, his last letter to Kuwahara had contained a picture of a retirement home he was planning to build—by chance, on the planet after which the battle cruiser in question was named.

"He probably did," Kuwahara said. "In fact, I am sure he did."

Baumann's reply needed no words: "Why?"

Kuwahara's reply to that needed both words and thought. Also, he realized, some risk-taking—and not risking petty funds, either. He could be kissing farewell to his third star, although probably not to the study group. (The Empress was sometimes punitive; she was hardly ever petty; she never disrupted an important job simply to get back at somebody.)

"I'll defer to those with superior knowledge of how the Baernoi think," Kuwahara said, letting each word fall like a drop of water in the traditional water torture. "But it seems to me that a case could be made that they sent Rahbad Sarlin deliberately. They wanted to indicate to *us* that they saw Linak'h as the source of the trouble on Victoria. Possibly the source of trouble on other planets too, but certainly Victoria."

"So Schatz, knowing this, decided that *Shenandoah* would carry the same message back?"

Kuwahara nodded, less tense but not yet at ease. He was offering an analysis of Baernoi behavior to someone who had a degree in Baernoi Cultural Analysis. Someone who had used her knowledge of the Tuskers to plan the battle and pursuit that had probably prevented the first human-Baernoi war. Someone who was widely regarded as *the* expert on fighting Baernoi, among all the high-level decision-makers on Charlemagne.

Someone who might also have begun to believe her own media coverage on the subject. That would not be surprising. The Empress had won a single fleet action, and was now sitting in a chair that had been occupied by men and women who'd won six or seven (or in one case, ten). If she felt a few insecurities that the media could soothe, she would be no more than human.

She could also be tempted to micromanage subordinates who didn't go along with her notions about the Baernoi, and run head-on into the dimensions of the Federation, the laws of physics, and the customs of the Forces for centuries.

"I've heard worse ideas," Baumann said, after a long silence. "I don't mean your theory about Schatz. I mean the notion of sending the same message to the Tuskers that they're sending to us."

She straightened further, if that was possible. "There's also another message that *Shen* will carry, maybe better than another ship and flag officer. We are taking dual-sovereignty situations *seriously*!"

Kuwahara smiled. "Might I ask who is supposed to receive that message, besides the Baernoi?"

"You can ask," Baumann said, returning the smile. "Let's just say by way of an answer—the dual-sovereignty situation is one where there's been a lot of sloppiness over the past two generations. If the message reaches any of the people who've been behind that sloppiness, it can't hurt."

It did not take Kuwahara's experience on the study group to tell him that this was a considerable understatement.

Seven

Linak'h:

"Good night, sir," the cloakroom attendant said. It actually came out sounding like "Gat noyt, zar," but Davidson had learned to tune out the accents and awkward constructions from most Ptercha'a attempts to speak Anglic.

His birthworld of Caledonia had attracted the British Union's largest resident population at Ptercha'a. In spite of the jokes, this gave a Caledonian an advantage in learning the True Speech. That knowledge of Ptercha'a had been crucial for Davidson's appointment as Marshal Banfi's aide; he was not sure whether that made it a blessing or a curse.

"Good night, Leader," Colonel Davidson replied, draping his dress cloak around his shoulders and checking the hang in the mirror. The attendant's title came from his rank in the Warband of his native Hunt, which he had not seen on more than the annual duty visit for fifteen Lanak'h years. However, he still drilled with the restaurant's Warband even if he had not sworn into it, so using the rank was according to custom.

Davidson stepped out onto the veranda and knew immediately that the wind was up. The banners on the gatehouse of the drill field now stood out nearly straight from the poles, and dust stung his eyes. He pulled his goggles down over his eyes and decided to call a taxi rather than wait for one of the lifters from the Marshal's compound.

It was at least the hundredth time he'd wished that the Marshal had the sense to live at least in Och'zem, if not in the Federation Zone. He'd stopped mentioning it after the tenth time, and after the third time the Marshal tore him off a strip that made anything he'd ever heard from a drill sergeant sound like a nesting mother bird cooing to her hatchlings.

The weather there was better for flying, the roads better for ground vehicles, and communications both official and personal were a good deal more secure. That last point wasn't so important as long as the Marshal held only a sort of shadow post in the Federation military, permanent active duty or not. If that shadow was ever told to turn solid—

He must have hailed a taxi by telepathy. There it was, an elderly but well-maintained dual-drive three-wheeler.

"Where to, sir?"

The driver was Ptercha'a and spoke better Anglic than the attendant. "Marshal Banfi's. You know the address?"

"Of course. Who does not?" (It was really "Oo dez knout?") You are of his Warband?"

Davidson responded to that bit of excess curiosity with a curt nod and climbed in. The driver cut in the fans and the cab skated off down the road on the ten-centimeter cushion of air.

It was thirteen kloms of mostly level road and three more in the hills to the Marshal's compound. Before they were halfway to the hills the crosswinds made the driver throw up his hands in disgust and cut the fans.

"No extra fare, sir, for the extra time. I think it better we both get there, not to the bottom of the river."

Since the New Bridge was visibly swaying in the gusts as they crossed it, Davidson couldn't argue the point.

Just short of the hills, the driver cocked his head, checked his displays, then cut power. "Excuse me, sir. I do not like the sound of the front wheel bearing."

The driver climbed out and knelt in the windy darkness, a spectral figure lit yellow on one side by the headlights and red on the other by the interior lighting. Davidson hoped it was nothing serious; it would be a long and chilly walk home, and a time-consuming process even to wait for a repair lifter to battle through the winds.

Ten minutes, fifteen, twenty. The driver seemed to be trying the same thing over and over again, or at least almost the same thing. Davidson was already impatient; now suspicion began to creep in.

Davidson climbed out, and the wind promptly took charge of his cloak. He fought it back under control and knelt beside the driver.

As he did, the driver drew a snub pulser from inside his tunic and pointed it at Davidson's stomach.

"Please raise your hands, Colonel. Thank you," he added, as Davidson gave precedence to survival over heroism. The driver could shoot before Davidson could move, probably hit before Davidson could reach him, and then finish off the job with bare hands if there was no choice. In comparable gravity, Ptercha'a reflexes were about one-third faster than human; unarmed combat against one could be either embarrassing or suicidal, depending on the Ptercha'a's motives.

Davidson suspected that the driver had something more than embarrassment in mind for him.

In the next moment, suspicion hardened, as two ground scooters purred out of the darkness and drew up on either side of the taxi. Each of them had two human riders, all four wearing coveralls and helmets. None of them seemed to be armed, and Davidson wondered if they could possibly be on his side or at least not on the side of the pulser-waving Ptercha'a.

The driver, however, bowed his head at their approach, without pointing the muzzle away from Davidson. Then one of the newcomers slid a hand into his jacket pocket. Two muffled pops, an eruption of scorched cloth, and two explosive bullets ripped into the Ptercha'a's side.

The impact flung him sideways, but he didn't drop the pulser. He was actually trying to turn and fire at his killer when the strength went out of him. He wavered, braced for a moment on a tripod of tail and legs, then fell on his side with blood covering belly and muzzle.

Davidson had one moment of relief, that the driver was no longer a menace, then a longer moment of guilt at owing his life to such cold-blooded killers. Their saving him wasn't going to keep him from testifying at their trial, although he'd better keep even that *thought* hidden until he was out of their hands if he wanted to live—

Another muzzle rose, and another finger squeezed a trigger. This time it was darts that stitched Davidson's chest. He felt the sharp stabs, then the numbness spreading around them, and gagged. As he went to his knees, another dart stabbed his neck. He was vaguely aware of falling facedown on the road, but after that it was all blackness.

Linak'h:

Into the blackness, dim sensations intruded. Davidson thought he was being pulled into a heavier ground vehicle, then from it into something that moved like a lifter. He heard what sounded like voices, all speaking human languages but two or three different ones, and most of the voices were men.

He had a clearer memory of a spray injection, a clearer memory still of someone looking at him from a range of only centimeters. Someone with a small, neat-featured brown face that could have belonged to either sex.

Still clearer was the memory of being loaded either back into the lifter or into another one. Then there was another period of blackness, and when that ended it ended in what Davidson knew must be waking up.

Not that it was going to do him much good. He was in the backseat of a four-passenger general-purpose lifter. His hands and ankles were both locked in restraining bars, and there was an armed man—at least it looked male—in the seat beside him.

In the front seats the pilot and copilot were busy guiding the lifter swiftly through the darkness. It had to be cloudy; the blackness outside was so complete that Davidson couldn't even judge the altitude, let alone recognize the kind of terrain below.

No, the blackness wasn't quite complete. Off to port rode the dim lights of another lifter. As Davidson's eyes adjusted to the darkness, he thought it was a slightly larger version of their own, with a rear cargo door. He also saw that both his pilot and copilot were armed—something from either Steurmann or Rykov & Adler—although come to think of it, R&A built a lot of Steurmann designs under license—

"Hey, he's awake," muttered Davidson's companion.

"Congratulations," the pilot said. Her voice sounded female. "You aren't going anywhere now. If you don't try to go anywhere once we land, you'll be all right."

"Like your Ptercha'a pawn?" Davidson said. Either the drug was still working on his inhibitors or else it had wiped out his patience with verbal manure.

"That furball got in the way," the pilot said. "What do you expect?"

"Now just a goddam minute—" the backseater muttered. Muttering seemed to be his normal tone. Davidson wondered if his speech or his mind was defective. Better either than defective ethics like the pilot's, though.

"Not a second!" the pilot snapped. "If he was smart enough to work for us, he was smart enough to know what he'd get turning us in. If the Ptercha'a were really dumb, why bother wiping them out?"

Davidson's inhibitors were in no better shape than before. Only the restrains kept him from reaching for the pilot with intent to maim—severely, painfully, and preferably fatally. The backseater saw the passion and jabbed something sharp into Davidson's ribs.

"This won't kill you, Colonel, but it might make you think again."

Davidson knew that he could think until the heat death of the universe without altering his intentions toward the pilot. But right now he had intentions without ability. He slumped back in his seat.

As he did, the pilot turned the lifter onto a new course. The copilot sat up to make some adjustments to an unfamiliar type of laser rangefinder on the top of the control panel, and Davidson saw his face briefly reflected in the windshield.

If Davidson's memory was worth anything at all, it was the same small, neat face he had seen bending close over him. The hand making the adjustments was also small, but male and not so neat—it had the sinews and cording of a martial-arts adept.

Its fingers were also moving, in a pattern that made no sense for adjusting the rangefinder. But there was something familiar about the pattern nonetheless—

Very familiar. Standard Federation covert code.

FRIEND. DO NOT MOVE UNTIL I SIGNAL.

That was the message. Davidson wondered what the "friend" expected him to do. Outside was still nothing but darkness, broken only by the faint glow from the other lifter. They might have been light-years inside a dark nebula, for all the evidence he could find of any reality outside the two lifters.

They must be well out into the wilderness, but that didn't mean such a long trip, not on Linak'h. Thirty million and some-odd sapient beings spread over a land area larger than Earth's meant that a hundred kilometers beyond the frontier of settlement, the land might never have known a sapient visitor. As for lights, landing pads, law-enforcement authorities, and other luxuries, they might as well have been on Aphrodite.

The copilot might only be proclaiming himself a friend, but that was more than anybody else had done tonight. Davidson was prepared to give the man the benefit of the doubt—not as much of a dilemma as one might think, if the alternative was suicide or submission to armed and homicidal captors.

Linak'h:

It seemed to Davidson that a millennium passed before anything happened to break the monotonous flight through the darkness.

Or maybe longer. He began to wonder if perhaps the two lifters hadn't passed not only beyond the frontier of settlement but beyond the frontier of time, into a place where it was always now and would be now forever and ever, with neither past nor future.

He reminded himself of some of the basic points of his course in Terrorism and Counterterrorism, where the Caledonians also taught their officers how to be terrorist hostages—"for fun and profit," the instructor had said.

One thing the man came down on heavily: don't let yourself get disoriented, in either time or space. That's half the battle to the kidnappers right there.

What the man hadn't said was how to stay oriented when you were flying through the intestines of the Great Galactic Serpent, which had swallowed the planet you thought you were on when you were kidnapped in your previous incarnation as a Macedonian hoplite—or had the Macedonians used hoplites?

Davidson smiled. The ability to laugh at yourself was another thing you were supposed to retain, since it wasn't always safe to laugh at your captors and there often wasn't anything to laugh about in your situation.

Then he stopped smiling, because the copilot pulled something out of a pocket with his *left* hand and jammed it hard into the pilot's side. She sat bolt upright, opened her mouth, let out a gasp, and then stayed sitting that way, hands half raised toward the controls.

The copilot was turning toward Davidson when

the backseat kidnapper realized that something was wrong. His hand shot up toward his breast pocket.

Davidson slammed the top of his skull against the man's cheek, and writhed over him so that his shoulder was pinning the man's hand to his chest. Then something went *phut-thwock*, the man under Davidson jerked and filled the cabin with unmistakable stenches, and something that the colonel told himself was not the man's brains spattered everywhere.

The copilot reached over the back of his seat, and Davidson could suddenly hold up his hands and move them freely. Or as freely as the stabbing pain of circulation returning to his wrists would let him, at any rate. Once the stabs had returned to prickles, he was able to take the locking tab and free his own ankles.

Meanwhile, the lifter was swinging in gentle circles in the sky. The glow of the other lifter's lights showed that they were trying to stay with Davidson's, and at the same time keep their distance.

The copilot muttered something rude in a language Davidson didn't understand. He bent over to hear better.

"Never mind that," the copilot said briskly. "Look under your seats. There's a pulser launcher there with a mixed case of ammo. Tell me if it's a model you can use."

Davidson was a small-arms expert and felt relief at being finally invited back into territory he knew better than counterterrorism. However, he felt that this was the wrong time to boast.

He pulled out the launcher, and by the light of the control-panel displays recognized a Steurmann 1012Z. "I can handle this."

"Good. I'm going to pretend a radio failure, and let our friends close to naked-ear hailing distance."

"What about lasers?"

"Too visible, and anyway these birds don't have anything trainable. If they do turn bow-on to use their rangefinder, though, just pop the window and aim between the eyes."

It took the ritual of inserting magazines, activating feeds, and adjusting sights to take the taste of the copilot's tone out of Davidson's mouth. By the time he was ready, the other lifter was unmistakably closer.

Davidson peered past the shoulder of the dead pilot at the distance display. Three hundred twelve kilometers on this flight, which could mean a little over an hour for this kind of lifter. More than enough to take them so far into the wilderness that it would be a long walk out.

"Heads up," the copilot said. "They will be in easy range any moment . . ."

For Davidson they had never been out of easy range, but again he decided silence would be best, particularly since the pulser was about to make his case for him.

The other lifter yawed, presenting its right side to Davidson. The copilot slapped a plate, the left-side windows of their lifter dropped, and Davidson let fly without even bothering to stick the muzzle outside the hull.

Pulser slugs were enough against unarmored windows; 22mm grenades would smash armored ones. Davidson had loaded both elements of his weapon and had both set to fire on one trigger.

The right side of the other lifter became a display of sparks, flames, smoke, and flying fragments. Some of the fragments looked as if they had begun as part of human beings. The lifter yawed again, this time swinging away so that its rear door was toward Davidson.

It stopped yawing as he put a grenade through a fan, sending blades flying. Some of them flew clear to Davidson's lifter. One stopped with a meat-cleaver sound in the dead pilot's left temple. The copilot used the same unknown language as rudely as before.

Then two armed people sitting with their backs against a pile of crates raised what looked like hunting rifles. Davidson smashed both of them back against the crates with a burst of slugs, then the slug magazine ran empty. He groped for a refill, couldn't find one, raised his weapon again, and ignored a shout from the copilot as he squeezed the trigger.

The blast as the ammunition in the other lifter exploded was vented in more directions than out the rear door. Otherwise Davidson's lifter would have dropped out of the sky along with its victim. Flames streamed from every opening in the other lifter as it tipped over on its nose, wobbled on a last remnant of lift power, then plummeted straight down.

As it fell it lit up a winding silvery-green river with tree-grown bluffs on either side. It dropped below the level of the bluffs, showing striated rocks with foam curling past them. Then it struck the water, which set off another explosion. By the time the cloud of smoke, spray, and steam dissipated, the lifter had vanished completely.

"I should have warned you about that," the copilot said. He might have been passing judgment on an inferior brand of whiskey.

"About what? And who the devil are you, anyway?" Davidson snapped. He could contain his enthusiasm for being ordered about by total strangers, even if they knew their business well enough to save his life.

"I'll tell you who when we're someplace where there's no danger of your being recaptured," the copilot said. "I gave you the antidote for the flattener in a trifle of a hurry, and I think I overdid it. When that happens, it can produce euphoria or overaggressiveness."

"Overaggressiveness?" Davidson said, as if it were a word in a language he understood but did not speak well. He wanted to laugh. He'd just been in his first battle, and he was being called overaggressive.

He wanted to laugh so badly that the cold realization of drugs at work leaped up and slapped him in the face. He not only wanted to laugh, he didn't want to stop.

"Is it euphoria to prefer being alive?" he asked, forcing himself to speak precisely.

"Not as long as it doesn't interfere with your staying that way," the copilot said, and turned back to the controls.

Linak'h:

The copilot stayed at the controls another ten minutes, keeping the lifter low and slow. Davidson didn't mind the slow. He wasn't so sure about the low, not when the running lights were all off and even then he could see treetops that missed scraping the lifter's belly by meters if that much.

Finally the copilot slowed the lifter to just barely steerageway. "Are you jump-trained?"

"The New Inverness Rifles are LI," Davidson said. He knew he sounded thin-skinned, but then he was feeling somewhat that way. After all, this had been his first combat. He might have overkilled the other lifter, but he hadn't frozen either, sitting around with his thumb up his arse until either the copilot did all the work or the enemy replied effectively.

"All right. Check in the cargo compartment. There should be a rack on the left side with some padded chutes. Find two that don't show any signs of damage, put one on, and give me the other."

"Why not just land?"

"Because I don't know if—the people we want to evade are plugged into the SAR satellite data net. If they are, and that lifter you blew up was spotted from orbit, they'll have too good an idea of where to start looking for us already. I do *not* want to give them any additional help."

Davidson liked neither what the man said nor what he implied, but couldn't see any alternative. If they jumped while the lifter was high and then popped their chutes at minimum altitude, the lifter would register blatantly on any hostile radar. The departure of its occupants might not.

Even if the enemy—Davidson found it easy to use the term, now that the situation had "combat" written all over it—chased the autopiloted lifter to the end of its flight and suspected something when they found the wreckage, where would they start looking? Davidson and the copilot could be anywhere on a flight path several hundred kloms long, and several hours' hiking to either side of it in forest that was mostly temperate-zone triple-canopy.

"I have no problem with your plan," Davidson said.

He did have some problem with the parachutes, which were only bagged rather than encapsulated, and had no readouts or even safety-inspection seals. But this was far out into the wilderness of a planet that itself was a long way from the centers of civilization. You used what came to hand and hoped you didn't as a result come to a premature end.

By the time Davidson had his chute on, the copilot had the automatic controls set for course, speed, and altitude. He also had disabled the radio equipment, so that nothing but actually boarding the lifter would let anyone gain control of it.

Then he pulled on his own chute. By the time he'd finished that, the altimeter was rising at an alarming rate. Davidson told himself that the barometric altimeter (radar or laser ones gave off detectable emissions) told only the altitude above sea level, not above the ground that here was approaching two thousand meters, if the map display was right. He was not going to jump four thousand meters into a yawning black abyss. It only felt that way.

"Move it," the copilot said, with the brusque manner of jumpmasters since the days of fixed-wing aircraft. "We don't want to come down more than a day from the Braigh'n River."

"That's in the Merishi Territory, isn't it?"

"Give the man a passing grade on his geography test." The copilot slapped a plate and all four doors blew off. The sudden gust of wind took the pilot's body with it, and a moment later the copilot followed it.

Davidson was almost as much alarmed at being alone with the mangled rearseater as he was at the thought of being separated from the copilot. He tightened the strap holding the pulser across his chest with one hand, hurled himself out into space, and started counting.

"One thousand, two thousand, three thousand—"

From two thousand meters, a ten-count would take

you off most radars, a fifteen-count would take you off the rest, and a twenty-count risked spattering you on rocks or impaling you on trees. Davidson was up to sixteen when a yell came out of the darkness almost at his feet.

"Pull it, you idiot!"

So he pulled, and somewhat to his surprise the canopy opened. It only felt as if his teeth were jarred loose and the contents of his groin irreparably damaged. The canopy had time to sway three times, then branches slapped Davidson's face, clutched at his clothes, bent under his weight, and finally snagged his canopy and brought him to rest.

The treetops blocked out the sky and the wind drowned out the sound of the lifter fading in the distance. He didn't need eyes or ears to see a small figure standing below him in the pale green glow of a survival light. Quite a way below, too. Davidson judged that he was a good fifteen meters above the ground, a drop that could break bones even if he landed up to his neck in needles.

"Watch out," the copilot said. The same *phut* made Davidson shudder, but instead of a skull disintegrating, a line soared up and caught in the parachute webbing. Davidson tested it; his fingers identified three-ply survival cord. He carefully tied his end into the harness while the copilot tied the ground end to a bush. Even more carefully, Davidson tightened all his straps, flaps, and fastenings.

Then he called softly:

"Look out below!"

—and swung onto the line to begin his descent.

He began it with care, ended it with a sprawl on ground that was deep enough in needles, leaves, and dogfern creeper to cushion even the clumsiest landing.

The pulser left bruises across ribs and one shoulder but took less damage than it inflicted.

"I hope you've something besides rope on you," Davidson said, brushing himself off. "You didn't mention a survival kit, and you didn't give me time to look for one."

"The lifter had a basic one, but it was not what I would have chosen myself," the copilot said. He popped the weight off the upper end of the cord and rewound the rest as it floated down to the ground. "Pity about having to leave your chute, but it's camouflaged, and there's at least one layer of canopy over it. They'll find it eventually, but probably not soon enough to help them."

"Who are 'they'?" Davidson asked. "Or is that another question you'll answer when I'm not in danger of recapture?" He emphasized the word "I," and not entirely out of sarcasm. He had the distinct impression that the copilot had in some manner and for reasons of his own cut off his own retreat, and had to either evade or die. Davidson apparently had some hostage value that might keep him alive at least long enough for interrogation.

Considering the methods those interrogators might use, Davidson wasn't entirely sure he was better off than his companion.

"You assume correctly," the copilot said. "My own kit is limited to personal weapons and what I could hide in my boots, helmet, and vest, but it has its uses. Fishing line, for one thing, also hooks, wire saw, fire-tabs—it will hold no surprises for you, if you've had E&E training."

Davidson was tempted to remind the other again about the New Inverness Rifles being LI. But he had the feeling that the man here was Ranger or the equivalent, and that mere LI officers did not impress him that much. Besides, without the other Davidson might still be literally turning in the wind, or lying on the ground hoping that he would be recaptured before hypothermia from a cold night or gangrene from a broken leg killed him.

"Anything I can carry?" he asked.

The copilot handed him his parachute, which he had somehow managed to bundle into a package almost as compact as the original while talking with Davidson. Davidson hooked it to his harness, then unslung his rifle and held it in the alert-travel position.

He thought he saw the copilot nod approval before the smaller man took point and led the way into the night.

Linak'h:

They reached what the copilot said was a tributary of the Braigh'n River even before Red Dawn. To Davidson's surprise, they took a short breather, munched ration bars that would have satisfied any reasonable definition of mortifying the flesh, and started off upstream.

"Downstream leads us past too many Merishi settlements," the copilot said. "Upstream leads us to the headwaters. Then a short jog over the ridge above the spring where it starts, and we'll be on our way downhill. The Braigh'n loops back to the northwest, and that stretch is pretty nearly uninhabited. We can hail a lift without every lumber camp and boat landing knowing it."

If he'd been reported missing and SAR efforts already launched, every lumber camp and boat landing would already be on the lookout for Colonel Malcolm Davidson. Not wanting to contact any of these suggested that he might have disappeared without anybody raising the alarm—at least not yet.

Somebody in the Federation's chain of command on Linak'h was courting trouble, however. Marshal Banfi was very senior, very patient, very willing to abide by the regulations that limited his authority in spite of his rank—and totally unwilling to be jerked around more than once or twice before he became as easy to placate as a runaway antimatter feed.

If Davidson's companion was responsible for any part of the failure to inform Banfi, vengeance for his bad manners would descend on him without the colonel having to lift a finger. The satisfaction of this thought kept Davidson on his feet and on the move until noon, let him consider another couple of ration bars fit for human consumption, and even kept him moving all the way up to the crest of the hills in the bend of the Braigh'n.

He knew that downhill wasn't as much easier than uphill as novices in the field believed. For one thing, a steep downhill slope, bad footing, and fatigue added up to a fatally easy invitation to lose your balance. By Murphy's Law, balance always went just above a fatally high drop, too.

But rest, rations, and cold water from a mountain spring were a good starter set for the last leg. That was one good thing about Linak'h—most of its wilderness water sources had no detectable pollution. You could stick your head in a spring like this and guzzle.

Davidson had just finished doing that and was wringing water out of his beard when he saw the copilot signaling for silence. A moment later the whine of the approaching lifter was loud enough for the colonel to hear it over the gurgle of the spring.

Both men had a trained eye for cover. Davidson's mind and muscles both screamed at the thought of more huddling on hard rock, but he was behind the nearest boulder only seconds after the copilot. By then the lifter was in sight.

The copilot pulled out a compact monocular and handed it to Davidson. "That's a regular SAR machine, but disguises aren't impossible. Study the cockpit and see if you recognize anybody."

"Why?"

"Just do it."

Davidson gripped the monocular until his knuckles turned white, the plastic casing gave, and the urge to shove it down his companion's throat passed. Then he obeyed.

A familiar tanned face peered out of the cockpit, framed by glossy black hair. With a ten-magnification, Davidson could even recognize Olga Nalyvkina's shade of lip gloss. He also thought she'd been crying.

"That's one of Marshal Banfi's staff pilots in the lifter," Davidson said, in measured tones. "You must have been out of contact with civilization for some time, to—not know the SAR people." He thought that was more tactful if less true than "to behave like a Tusker with a skinful of *uys*."

"Good." The copilot's pistol sprang into his hand and a red flare trailed smoke across the sky over the ridge. Then the copilot seemed to reach the top of the boulder in a single bound, without using his hands, and waved frantically.

Davidson only heard the note of the lifter's fans change as it turned and descended toward them. His legs had finally gone on strike and he sat slumped against the boulder, his pulser across his lap.

"Oh, I am forgetting my manners," the copilot said, leaping down with the same improbable skill he'd used going up. "I promised an introduction. I am Colonel Liew Nieg, Federation Intelligence."

It was not entirely fatigue that made Davidson's mouth gape and stay open. It was the inward sound of a great many things falling into place.

Then he smiled, for the first time that day. If Marshal Banfi had been denied a need-to-know about the activities of somebody of Nieg's stature, on the kind of matter that would have brought him to Linak'h, the old man would not be pleased. When Banfi was displeased, the first six or seven people he could plausibly blame for his displeasure usually felt something even worse.

"Vengeance is mine, saith the Lord," but Marshal Banfi would be an adequate substitute until the Lord had time for Linak'h.

Eight

Linak'h:

Oleg Govorov (he had to make an effort to think of himself by any other name) was in his studio when the com alarm rang. Or at least he heard a noise that sounded like the alarm. Since he wasn't expecting any calls, he went back to his sketchbook and displays. Now what *would* Queen Victoria I of England have worn, if full regalia had allowed women to wear pants—trousers, as they'd called them then—?

"Oleg! Can you come here, please?"

Ursula sounded impatient. With a muttered oath, Govorov froze the display, slammed the sketchbook down on his table hard enough to scatter color sticks halfway to the door, and stamped out.

"What is—oh?"

Instead of being in the steam bath off the study, Ursula was sitting at the communications console, water beading on her bare skin. She was entirely nude, except for a look compounding irritation, weariness, and surprise.

"You'll catch cold, Ursl."

"Much you care, Polar Bear, or you wouldn't have carefully picked up my robe after I went into the bath."

"Did I? I'm sorry. I must have forgotten that you were in there."

"I'm quite sure you did." Some of the irritation left her face and voice. "You were on your way to the studio. One of these days a kilometer-deep canyon will open in your path when you are going to the studio, and you will fall into it."

"If I do, don't call SAR."

"What am I supposed to do then? There isn't that much rope in the house."

Govorov sat down on the threadbare carpet and put a hand on his wife's bare thigh. She gently plucked it away.

"The alarm went off because our traffic-control scan picked up mention of an Emergence."

"In clear?"

"As far as mentioning it, yes. Reception wasn't perfect, but I think they also said something about multiship. So I switched to the military frequencies. The volume of messages is up, but all coded."

Govorov slipped into lotus position. "I wonder. Davidson's kidnapping and rescue, and these new ships. If they're Federation, they might be connected."

"What makes you think they're Federation?"

"Little dove, how many people besides the Federation have sent more than one ship at a time to this planet since we have been here?"

"I don't remember."

"I do. The Baernoi once, the Merishi once, the Alliance never."

"*Ech.* Why can you remember that sort of thing and then forget I might need my robe?"

"Maybe because starships do not look so good without robes as you do."

"Flatterer. But would you please get that robe now?"

"I know of another way to warm you up."

She looked down. "So I see." She looked at the hall; the children's bedroom doors were both tightly shut. She looked down again, and this time she did more than look.

Ten minutes of happiness on the couch left them both as warm as if they'd been in the steam bath. Another ten minutes and the couch was damp.

"This could go on until we both cry for mercy—"

"Was that mercy you wanted a minute ago?" Govorov said, softly biting the lobe of Ursula's right ear.

"Whatever. But I want to finish the bath, and I think you need one too. There's paint in your beard."

"There's some on your breast, too."

"Whose fault is that?"

"The woman tempted me."

She wriggled close against him, licked sweat off his shoulder, then traced a path with her lips down across his chest until he twined his fingers into her hair and let her finish what she'd begun.

The bath nearly sent Govorov straight off to sleep, and even the vigorous strokes of the birch branches brought him only partway back to awareness. It wasn't until they plunged into the cold pool that his wits began shaking off the weight of creative problems, sex, and steam.

Even then they came up with more questions than answers. The incoming ships were almost certainly Federation. The trouble with bandits raiding Federation territory had been going on long enough and seriously enough for that kind of response.

And Davidson's abortive kidnapping would have been the appropriate response, for anyone with advanced knowledge of the ships' coming *and* a certain lack of substance between the ears. Govorov didn't like to think about the first kind of person, and not really about the second kind either, except that he knew the Brothers of the Woods (pretentious title!) too well to have any illusions.

(The Brothers were actually half a dozen different factions, drawn from at least two different races, and they changed constantly. But at any given time during the last few years, there had always been at least one faction capable of something like the attempt on Davidson.)

A lifter droned past, no more than a klom or two to the south and flying so low and slow that Govorov stiffened. Was it going to circle or even land?

So far this not-yet-crisis had produced only not-yet-threats. The worst was a pair of messages, one that might be interpreted to imply advanced knowledge of the Davidson kidnapping, the other from Davidson's rescuer.

(The man was as secretive as ever, but the timing and contents made any other source impossible. At least Govorov would have been able to receive Davidson if the man had appeared with the proper codes, and in shape to need no more than Govorov's somewhat rusty medical skills.)

"Not yet." He'd been saying the words like an incantation, ever since Sophia was born, more loudly since Peter came along. So far they'd worked. His paradise bought by his art and his value to all factions on Linak'h (or at least all the factions who had approached him—the Baernoi probably just hadn't found time to make an offer) was free of serpents.

Now the gate was creaking as someone battered at

it. How long before they battered it down? And what colors would the serpent wear when it crawled through?

He reached for Ursula, and felt her trembling from more than the water of the spring-fed cold plunge.

Linak'h:

"I've been examined by Dr. Feinberg. Surely you aren't questioning her qualifications, are you?"

The name at least bought Colonel Davidson a moment of silence from the face on the screen. He went on, now earnestly rather than angrily. Left to himself, he would have tanned this clown's hide for a sporran, but actions that in the ancient Highlands had led to blood feud could still make trouble for innocent bystanders.

Not that either the Marshal or Olga Nalyvkina wouldn't be happy to take up the fight if Linak'h Command Med HQ declared one. But they had better things to do with their time.

"She is not a specialist in posttraumatic stress disorder, particularly accompanied by severe physical deprivation," the screened face said.

By an act of pure will, Davidson refused to let outrage strike him speechless. That would simply give Colonel Nardesian a chance to question Feinberg's qualifications, or do something else equally idiotic.

"What—what sort of—*severe* physical deprivation are you talking about?" He was too outraged not to stammer. "The drugs were out of my system within a few hours. I was picked up within one Standard day of being kidnapped. In fact, by twenty-three hundred on the day of my rescue I'd finished a four-course dinner, half a bottle of wine, and a workout followed by a steam bath. Deprivation, my arse!"

"The interaction of the wine with residual drug traces deserves—"

"Examination? Then Dr. Feinberg can come back, and you don't have to waste your time on me unless she thinks I need hospitalization. Even then, she might not refer me to Territorial General. She's also licensed for St. Jude's—"

The screen blanked. Davidson's last sight was of Colonel Nardesian struggling for control, the way he himself had been a few minutes ago.

From behind came the sound of applause. Davidson jumped up as if his chair had sprouted thorns and whirled, to see Marshal Banfi, Lieutenant Nalyvkina, Sergeant Major Kinski, Corporal al-Mansur, and both the domestic and guard Ptercha'a. The humans were applauding; the Ptercha'a were either applauding in human style or using their own ritual, which was holding their tails in a high curve and raising both hands over their heads.

Davidson flushed, glowered, and bowed. Banfi returned the bow, then swept one of his eloquent looks across the spectators. Except for the Marshal and the lieutenant, the room was empty in seconds.

A robot rolled in, with two covered trays and its cooler in the middle loaded with bottles and chilled glasses. Davidson poured himself a cup of coffee, added a shot of brandy, and let Nalyvkina play waitress with a plate of smoked fish, eggs, sausages, and what the cook insisted on calling "scones." They would have cost any Caledonian restaurant owner his customers if not his license, but once you got used to them they were filling, if not precisely tasty.

Three healthy appetites emptied the robot quickly

and sent it back to the kitchen for refills. Marshal Banfi flicked the cap off a bottle of homebrew and handed Davidson a long message form.

"Our copy of the TO&E of what's coming in," he said.

"Took them long enough to decode and pass it on, too," the lieutenant said around a mouthful of scone. She wiped butter off her exquisite chin. "I wonder if they thought we didn't pick up the Emergence signals three nights ago, just like everybody else with the right equipment."

"Do them this much justice," Davidson said, picking the skeleton out of a smoked fish and tossing it in the disposal. "They're probably running around in circles, trying to get everything ready for the newcomers."

"Or trying to hide under the rugs everything that would prove how little they have been doing until now," Nalyvkina said. She pushed a lock of dark hair away from her forehead. The lock now glistened with butter, but the movement was so elegant that Davidson wouldn't have stopped it if he could.

"Yes, let's do them justice," Banfi said, politely asserting his rank. "Our situation only slipped beyond local resources in the past few months, and that was in *our* estimate. What their estimate was, I don't know."

"You ought to have been told," Nalyvkina persisted.

"Indeed, and I will find a time to tell them that," Banfi said. "But if they came to their estimate even a month later than we did, they acted as quickly as reasonable officers might be expected to. What I do not like so much is what has been sent out."

Davidson read the TO&E in the light of that cryptic remark, and it remained cryptic to the end. A battle cruiser—*Shenandoah,* of Victoria fame—five light cruisers, two scouts, three courier ships, and four transports. *Shen* carried an embarked attacker squadron and a company-strength LI detachment. Two of the transports carried a mass of supplies and individual reinforcements for units already on Linak'h, everything from the Regular battalion and its supporting units down to the Environmental Monitoring Service and probably the Young Pioneers and the Scouts! The other two transports carried a BEU, built around the Fifth Battalion of 222 Brigade—

"Fifth Battalion?" he said. Banfi nodded. Davidson swung around to the console and called up the current file on 222 Brigade. It was part of III Corps, Eleventh Army, and normally based on Agamemnon. It hadn't been in action since the Agamemnon incident twenty-three years before, and it had no organic LI battalion.

"Why is everybody looking so gloomy?" Nalyvkina inquired. "A battalion is a battalion is a battalion, unless it's LI, isn't it?"

"Oh, ye fliers of little knowledge," Banfi said, rolling his eyes dramatically at the ceiling. "Forgive her, oh Lord, for she knows not what she has put her foot into."

Nalyvkina glared and made an elaborate charade of scraping something off one of her polished flying boots. "So I am but an ignorant flier. Tell me, exalted mudfeet, what am I missing?"

"A five-battalion brigade with no LI is a second-wave force, designed to move onto a secure planet, or at least a secured LZ," Davidson said. "If they're Regulars they can still be good. But they're likely to be a bit slow in reacting to highly fluid situations, and less proficient at guerrilla warfare than at set-piece combat."

One could see the implications of this sinking in as Nalyvkina's elfin face grew suddenly sober. She reached out a hand, and Davidson resisted the temptation to hold it. Instead, he put a glass in it, then poured beer.

"Or would you rather have something stronger?"

"No. Not if I'm going to be flying before dinner."

"What makes you think you will be?"

"Because Kinski said he was going to be working with the techs on the modulator of Devil One. The ETA on our new friends is only five days." She smiled, teeth gleaming white in her tanned face. "I think the Great Human Fathers are not the only ones who want to make a good appearance when the visitors arrive."

Davidson did not add the obvious, that it was almost impossible for the lieutenant to make anything else. "With your permission, Marshal, Colonel?" she said.

Banfi nodded. When the door closed behind Nalyvkina, the old soldier switched the console to scan, watched for indicators of any penetration of the net or physical placement of eavesdropping devices, then cut it off after everything turned up negative.

"Something else, that I'd rather not have talked about until we know what to make of it," he said. He loaded a third plateful, even though the sausages were cold and the eggs beginning to congeal into something the consistency of blasting putty.

Davidson's stomach winced at the sight, but his mind overrode the reflex. If you'd eaten rations or lived off the land for twenty years in the days when Banfi was beginning his career, the time of hardscrabble soldiering when your CO might be a radiation-sterilized veteran of the Third Hive War, you were either dead or capable of digesting titanium capsules of concentrated toxics.

"What's that, Marshal?"

"The BEU CO is Colonel Barbara Hogg."

"Any Baernoi in her ancestry?"

"It's spelled with two g's and its not funny. She's very senior—overage for the rank, in fact, unless she chose to freeze, and I happen to know that she didn't. She's also not one of the Hentschmen."

"So?"

Banfi's look would have curdled the eggs if they hadn't been that way already. Davidson thought it made the coffee quiver in the pot.

"She's not one of the Pocket Pistol's rounds, and she's facing involuntary retirement. Two powerful motives for taking unnecessary risks to look good, and only one substandard battalion to take them with. Or maybe not substandard, but one requiring time to be made fit for the situation on Linak'h, time an over-eager CO might not allow it."

"How senior is Hogg?"

"Senior to everybody around except you, me, and the Dancer."

Major General Tanz, the CG of Linak'h Command, was the classic example of the lazy but intelligent officer who was supposed to make the best kind of commander. Davidson thought personally that he had too much laziness to let his intelligence pull its weight, but this hadn't done any harm so far. Colonel Goerke, ground CO of Linak'h Command, had so far justified everybody's trust as an administrator and field commander, even if he didn't like Ptercha'a.

"Don't lose any sleep over it until I order you to," Banfi said, scraping the last of the egg onto a pseudo-scone. "Even then, the first thing I'll do is pay a little visit to Tanz." He shook his head, in response to Davidson's unspoken question. "I'm not going to pull rank. The chain of command around here is tangled enough. But Tanz's not such a fool that he won't listen to a friendly warning from a Marshal. If that's enough to make him keep Goerke and Hogg pulling together—"

The incoming message alarm broke into their review of the newly complicated internal politics of Linak'h Command. They both tried not to be the first to fidget as the message ran through the decoder and came up on the display.

Banfi grunted, then signaled for the robot to clear away the dishes. "A courier-ship signal, probably Baernoi," he mused. Then in a brisk, interrogative tone that would have been rude used to a human:

"Query: probability of Baernoi origin?"

Computers couldn't hesitate or try to cover their reputations in the event of a mistake. The people lurking at the other end of the net had human vices. It was five minutes before the answer came back:

"Ninety-one percent plus or minus four point two three . . ." to seven decimal places, or at least that was when Banfi turned off the console again, by kicking it sharply near the power plug.

"*Diavolo!*" he said. "Our Tusker friends must be very concerned about informing someone on this planet of a major development. It can't be the Diet elections; they've already been announced. Are they sending reinforcements?"

"If they do, they'll have to tell us as well," Davidson pointed out. "The nonprovocation protocols—"

"I piss on the nonprovocation protocols," Banfi said. "Go back and read them again, Colonel Davidson. That's an order, by the way. It seems to me that you need to learn just how much the Tuskers can send to a planet like Linak'h without having to tell anybody, including their own Fleet commanders! I'd bet my burial fund that they've read the protocols more recently than you have!"

Davidson saluted. There was nothing more to do when the Marshal fell into one of these moods, except observe the most formal military courtesy until he climbed out again.

Linak'h:

Rahbad Sarlin and the twins were swimming in the stream behind the house when they saw the light on Sarlin's belt unit blinking. He made an obscene gesture at it, then dove, trying to reach the bottom of the stream.

Both depth and width made this stretch of the stream safe for swimming. Sarlin touched bottom, then rolled over on his back to gaze up at the dappled surface. He must be a good thirteen paces down.

The breath in his lungs still held all the way to the surface, and when he broke into the air his breathing was controlled. Not bad for one of his years—but his pleasure vanished swiftly when he saw the light still blinking.

This time he addressed harsh words to the water, where the twins had vanished again, and swam toward the bank. As he reached it, the light went off. A moment later the balcony door opened. Fygos Dravin stepped out on the balcony, locked a portable sensor pack to the railing, and crouched beside it. His sight-equipped quickgun leaned in one corner.

Now the back door of the compound opened and Senior Code Specialist Lyka ihr Zeyem came hurrying down the hill. She carried a message block and wore a disagreeable expression.

"I thought something worse than a bathing party had happened to you, Commander," she said. "This has just arrived."

Sarlin looked at the block's security and code symbols and nodded. Something like this would have been sent coded all the way from the courier ship to the house's receiver. Specialist ihr Zeyem must have put in a good tenth-watch running it through the main computer, then found its intended recipient unavailable.

"Apologies," Sarlin said, and took the block. A moment later he let it fall. He wanted to throw it into the stream and ask ihr Zeyem to swear that she had never received it.

That, however, would not save him any trouble. It would only make more for others, who would have no time to prepare for the coming of Behdan Zeg.

Shouting and cursing seemed no less productive, and more satisfying. Sarlin let out a stream of curses that by right ought to have killed fish and reversed the flow of the stream. They did make Dravin stare in admiration and ihr Zeyem take a few steps backward, staring at something else.

Sarlin picked up a flat stone and tried to skip it across the stream. It not only sank, it nearly hit Solidessouf as he surfaced. Sarlin ground his teeth, gripped a small boulder half sunk in the earth of the bank, and was trying to wrestle it free when Kalidessouf surfaced right behind him and tripped him.

For a moment the ignominious tumble nose-first into the mud left Sarlin more furious than ever. Then sanity returned, enough to make him realize that he must be both frightening and mystifying everyone in sight.

He rose, washed his face with handfuls of water, and retrieved the block.

"Behdan Zeg is coming to Linak'h."

The twins looked at each other. "Are they sending him to help us or sabotage us?"

That question eased the rest of Sarlin's rage. The twins at least were no strangers to his half brother's reputation. Ihr Zeyem was less well informed. She was looking back and forth between Sarlin and the twins, as if unsure who had gone mad.

"Specialist, sit down and listen to these warriors on the subject of my half brother," Sarlin said. "Don't believe everything they tell you, of course."

"That warning is quite superfluous," ihr Zeyem said, but Sarlin thought a smile was hovering just to one side of her face.

"We swear by the Most Holy Lord to tell no lies," Solidessouf said.

"Do you swear to tell the whole truth as well?" ihr Zeyem replied. In spite of the twins' insatiable appetite for women, they had never given ihr Zeyem or the other female staff of the outpost any difficulty. That the woman be willing was their strictest law, and also that she could freely choose either or both of them (even if they preferred that she find both of them worth her attention).

As the twins' reputation went ahead of them, sometimes by entire light-years, they had yet to find any shortage of willing partners. Sarlin had a small bet on with su-Irzim that they would eventually charm ihr Zeyem, but expected that she would also give them plenty of exercise with a good long chase.

Sarlin toweled himself dry, then pulled on his coverall, tucked the block inside the towel, and walked back to the house. He wasn't surprised to find Brokeh su-Irzim waiting on the terrace.

"Forgive the uproar. This was not just bad news, it will be a personal problem."

Su-Irzim also understood what weight the name Behdan Zeg carried, as trouble for the mission. He suggested that they go inside and have a beer, in the secured study. Sarlin was not sure that his restored good temper would survive much beer, but saw no purpose in sulking in his room the rest of the day.

"It may be mixed news rather than bad news," su-Irzim said, after they were well into the first jug. "I cannot imagine that they are sending him out alone."

"No. He has few followers, and hardly any friends."

"So the others who come will be coming to us, even if they are Consolidationist allies." Su-Irzim clearly wanted to use some other word than "allies," but thought it imprudent, even in this secure space. "That should mean money and equipment as well. Or at least authorization to draw on local resources, which not even our beloved Territorial Administrator can ignore."

"Optimism is distorting your judgment, if you think the Administrator cannot find some way of ignoring anything short of the Yellow Father going nova," Sarlin growled.

"If we cannot obtain it appropriately, there are other methods."

Sarlin stared. "What would your Fleet colleague say about that?"

"He would say that you are a corrupting influence on honest Inquirers," su-Irzim replied, and refilled his mug.

Sarlin grinned. It did no harm that Brokeh su-Irzim was developing a wide streak of unorthodoxy. If he had not needed it before, he would certainly need it to cope with both Smalltooth reinforcements and Behdan Zeg.

"You are probably right," Sarlin conceded. "I cannot imagine that unless the whole Office of Inquiry has gone mad, they are sending out Zeg in ignorance of his reputation. They may be ignorant of the human reinforcements, but that will give us an excuse to keep the mission in passive mode for—oh, until the nature of the human mission becomes a trifle more obvious."

"We, of course, will be the judges of when that takes place?"

"Of course." Sarlin decided that his good mood could survive more beer. Part of it came from what they had already discussed, part from something even su-Irzim was not yet open-minded enough to consider.

The Inquirers of the Smallteeth would be hard on the tails of their Fleet reinforcements, if indeed they were not already present in force. (There were mysteries about the kidnapping and escape of Colonel Davidson that Sarlin would have given his left tusk to see answered.)

Many Inquirers roaming about the same limited territory risked accidental encounters, even exchanges of fire. It would be tragic if Behdan Zeg did not pull his head down fast enough in one of those exchanges, but then how recently had he been in a combat zone?

Aboard R.M.S. *Somtow Nosavan*, in the Linak'h system:

Somtow Nosavan didn't have the massive display tanks of Navy warships' Combat Centers. However, she did have two good men, one human and one Ptercha'a, who liked to burrow into unknown machinery. They did it for the same reason hardcore PE&D people went walkabout—to see what they could stumble on—and just as often came out with something either strange, valuable, or both.

Eight days out of Victoria, only seven hours from Linak'h, *Nosavan*'s radar was scanning the Federation squadron also cruising toward the Ptercha'a planet. Joanna Marder had no trouble interpreting the assortment of blips, blobs, and splotches on the main screen, but most of the rest of the crew weren't so trained.

But Charlie Longman and Emt Desdai had in their burrowings found a way to link radar, main computer, the intercom, and the graphics programs of the entertainment memory in sequence. Now in every screen aboard *Nosavan* the Federation task force floated like ships in a game, easily interpreted even without Charlie's patter.

"—big one is of course the battle cruiser. *Shenandoah*'s my old ship, for those of you who don't know."

Marder rolled her eyes. If there was anyone aboard *Nosavan* who didn't know most of the details of Charlie's life before he met her, she wanted them off the ship at Linak'h. They were either too deaf or too reclusive to be safe crew.

"You'll also see a cruiser and some of the light ships out in front, on junk watch. The other cruisers are englobing the transports, and a couple of attackers are flying close to *Shen*. If she has to launch buses, they'll be ready to take control of them when she blacks down or shields.

"Then out beyond where we can see them will be lots more attackers. If something really comes down hard, we'll see the transports running like Hades for Linak'h and everybody else spreading out into a big globe with *Shen* at the center. That way she can fire outward, everybody else can fire inward, no friendlies will get hit—but anybody penetrating the globe will be hit and *fried*."

Marder heard and saw Charlie drinking water and clearing his throat. "We'll probably be in radar contact with the task force most of the rest of the way to Linak'h. Commodore Rosie's picking the most junk-free route in for almost the same reason we are. She wants her attackers out and free, and they don't have shields or too much hull protection. We could survive a rock that would take one of them—"

On both the modified display and the radar repeater, the task force was changing formation. *Shenandoah* was slowing hard; the signature of her drive field showed that plainly. The transports were accelerating, skimming past the battle cruiser and her attackers so close that Marder held her breath. She knew the separation distance must be at least a couple of hundred kloms, but it looked like the thickness of the hull paint from out here, and anyway larger separations than that hadn't prevented space-to-space collisions.

"Communications!" she called. "Passive listening watch on Navy frequencies. We don't want them to catch us eavesdropping, but I don't want them buzzing us without notice either."

Communications acknowledged, but the displays and Marder's memories of Federation tactics gave her the answer before radio intercepts did. Somewhere astern of the task force—somewhere astern of *Nosavan,* come to think of it—was an unidentified contact. One that had remained unidentified after all the standard scans, signature evaluations, sensor readings, and IFF queries.

The process of trying to identify the unidentified had just been accelerated. Which meant that the same thing was going to happen to quite a few ships in the task force in the next few minutes. Some of them would be accelerating right through the same patch of space as *Nosavan*.

"Alert One," Marder said, and pressed the button for the alarm. Since virtually everybody was on duty already, all she heard was a few curses, a cup slamming down, and two or three pairs of feet running.

"Communications, record everything you pick up on the listening watch until I tell you to stop. Mr. Longman, I need to speak to you."

In the passage outside the Bridge, they embraced briefly. Marder hadn't planned this, until she saw the tears in Charlie's eyes.

"Homesick?"

"A little. No, I guess more than a little. God, *Shen* looks beautiful."

"Maybe we can help her, too. Have you edited the recordings we made of our contacts?"

"Outbound, yes. Not since the Jump, though."

"Start editing, and do what you can to enhance that ghost contact two days ago."

"That uses enough computer capacity to show up on Emt's board."

"I'll suggest to Citizen Desdai the wisdom of keeping his whiskers out of your business. When you've finished the editing and enhancing, make an extra copy of the recording and put it in my safe. Put an antitamper guard on it too."

"We're out of them."

"The issue ones, yes. But didn't you and Emt spend some of those spare hours jury-rigging a few?"

"You don't want me to leave the charge in?"

"No." Spontaneously, she hugged him again. "Charlie,

I'd miss you if you were arrested for accidentally blowing up somebody from *Shen*."

Aboard U.F.S. *Shenandoah*, in the Linak'h system:

Rank Hath Its Privileges is ancient military wisdom, and even sometimes the truth. For Rose Liddell, the privileges of her rank included not conning *Shenandoah* through the complex maneuvers of the task force, as it tried to surprise their trailer into a revealing move.

Instead, she left the job to Pavel Bogdanov, who was better at shiphandling anyway and enjoyed it more than anything else he could do with his clothes on. Her job was to sit in the flag chair in Combat Center, stare at a display tank raising more questions than it answered, and occasionally glower around the two-deck-high compartment to remind everybody of her presence.

That plus the occasional order for maneuvering other ships wasn't really enough to occupy her for three hours. It took that long before Liddell decided that the unidentified ship was going to stay that way, regardless of what the task group did. She'd suspected it was going to come out that way an hour earlier.

Space is large. Ships are small. One that is shouting for attention sometimes gets overlooked, as any history of space accidents can tell even a cursory reader. One that is trying to imitate a hole in space can take a formidable toll of nerves and time with nothing to show for it, if the senior pursuer has no judgment about when to stop looking for the unfindable.

Rose Liddell had judgment; after three hours the

task force resumed its previous formation, course, and speed. She sent a revised ETA to Linak'h, ordered a close monitoring of *Somtow Nosavan,* and retired to her quarters.

She couldn't get to sleep, however, so she had a snack sent up and began roughing out a revised plan for her ships' first few days in orbit. Intruders meant Alert Three at all times and priority to getting the troops and supplies unloaded. (Priority in getting them sheltered and hardened would help, but that was up to Tanz and the Governor-General.) No duty-free time, no dirtside liberty or leave, and only minimal intership visiting until that was done.

Maybe she could ease off while they were checking and if necessary reinforcing the satellite network? Maybe, but if her crews weren't needed around-the-clock, then all the dirtside VIPs would assume that she also was a lady of leisure.

No. The first four days after they hit orbit would be strictly work. But check the hospitality supplies, just in case somebody too important to completely ignore wanted to come *up.*

Nine

Linak'h:

Commodore Liddell reflected that possibly the view from Governor-General Rubirosa's office window affected his view of the world. If one saw two hundred meters of barracks, drill grounds, lifter pads, and garages for both lifters and ground vehicles, it might lead to some kind of deprivation syndrome in almost anybody. In Carlos Rubirosa's case, it seemed to have deprived him of a sense of proportion.

"Five days before you came down!" he snapped. "Five entire Standard days. Even now, meeting me here, you cannot promise to accept all the invitations I have assembled for you."

For Rubirosa's glare, Liddell returned her blandest and most maternal smile. Lieutenant Mahoney, acting as her aide, kept a straight face with some difficulty. She thought she heard a snort of strangled laughter to the left, which meant that Major General Joachim Tanz wasn't succeeding even that well.

"Your Excellency," Liddell said, "I appreciate your concern at the squadron's getting off on the wrong foot with the local leadership. I'm the last person around to ignore their value to civil-military relations.

"But we didn't expect to arrive in the wake of two

events. Neither of them is necessarily serious, but together they add up to new variables in our situation. One was that courier-ship message, in a Baernoi code."

"A Baernoi code we cannot read," Tanz put in. His voice was light, even high for someone of his build, although he was not tall.

"Exactly. One of the codes the Baernoi use for highly critical intelligence. Since we know that one of their best Special Projects people is on Linak'h already, odds are that it was orders or information or both to him. I don't know how much you have been told about Rahbad Sarlin's reputation, but I invite General Tanz to take the floor if you need to learn more."

Rubirosa shrugged. "I am not such a fool as to underestimate an opponent through ignorance, Commodore. Please have the courtesy to remember this in the future."

The concepts of "courtesy" and "Rubirosa" had so far seemed mutually exclusive, but Liddell knew that too much was at stake to ignore that advice.

"The other problem was our unidentified tail on the way in. You may remember from the Victoria campaign that a similar incident on the way in from the Jump point turned out to be rather significant for future developments."

"Did you identify the ship?"

"No," Liddell conceded reluctantly. "At least no positive identification. The ship did not use her active sensors after she came under detection. She simply ran, too fast for us to learn much about her except that she is very fast."

"That covers a good deal of territory," Rubirosa said. It was the most sensible remark Liddell had heard so far. "What about one of those new Merishi cruisers, the *Fireflower* class?"

"As I said, we have no positive identification, and speed alone isn't conclusive." She sensed something behind the question. "Why do you ask?"

"Because the Alliance Territory to the north of us is largely a Navy preserve. You would know more of the details than I would, but my impression is that the Freeworld States Navy is not cooperating with the Merishi to any great extent at the moment."

Rubirosa was definitely shrewder than he had seemed, apart from having a gift for understatement. If the Alliance Territory was Navy-run, they would be looking for any safe opportunity to pay the Scaleskins back for the squadron destroyed off Victoria thanks to Merishi cooperation with human terrorists. The actual fusion bombs had been Baernoi, of course, but they would never have destroyed Alliance ships without Merishi blundering.

"Your impression is correct," Liddell said. "However, I am going to keep my ships looking in all directions at once for a few more days, at least."

"That will increase the sense of crisis, unless you make the social tour," Rubirosa said. "I am not saying that there is no crisis, you understand. I merely suggest that making people so nervous that they become trigger-happy is easily avoided."

Liddell's estimate of the Governor-General's intelligence dropped back a notch. If he thought her attendance at a series of diplomatic bunfights would really do anything except give terrorists a series of irresistible targets, he needed a brain scan and perhaps some neural regen.

However, a compromise had popped over the horizon a few hours ago, just as she was boarding the shuttle for landing. She hadn't been aware at the time that it would be needed as a compromise, but now that she was here—

"I've received an invitation from Marshal Banfi," Liddell said. "He described it as a get-acquainted party. He—"

"Banfi has no official status!" Rubirosa snapped. Any pretense of calm completely vanished.

"Your Excellency, I think we should hear Commodore Liddell out," General Tanz said. Liddell had seldom heard anyone speak with less expression or more inward meaning in his voice.

She had to avoid playing Tanz and Rubirosa against each other. Whichever she won to her side, the other could block outright, or at least sabotage. She also had to avoid driving them into a common front by too openly courting Marshal Banfi.

With Rubirosa it was prestige—not being thought fit to handle his job. With Tanz it was something more understandable but potentially even more serious. Any encouragement to Banfi to put himself back in the chain of command risked Tanz's freedom of action, even his command authority.

Major generals did not ignore Marshals. Nobody did, in fact. If the Federation had added an Eleventh Commandment, that was probably it.

"Why don't we try a cooperative approach?" Liddell suggested, using the tone she had practiced on Admiral Schatz when he needed soothing over some unreasonable transfer or body-snatch. "Banfi is certainly someone important enough to be worth meeting. But if he's outside the normal chains of command and protocol, nobody can be offended by my meeting him first."

"Probably not," Rubirosa said. "But meeting anybody else there will not count. You still have to do the official rounds."

Fine. After I've picked the brains of all the people Banfi will invite, I can spend the next month murmuring platitudes at parties.

"I'll promise that, if you'll promise a complete update on the situation here. If my staying away from parties is going to cause mass panic, things must have deteriorated beyond even the attempt on Colonel Davidson."

"That's enough deterioration for me," Tanz said. "It's also enough to make Banfi's party a security problem, if half the people he's likely to invite show up. A half-platoon raid could behead all four Territories and start a war besides."

"I can suggest a solution for that, if you'll put it before Marshal Banfi," Liddell suggested. "The three requirements for security personnel at an event like this are invulnerability, high-capacity sensors, and mobility.

"Suppose we use *Shen*'s Light Infantry detachment?"

"In suits?"

"Some, at least. It would help if they were partnered with Banfi's own staff and some of Tanz's people. Together, they should raise the threshold of strength any terrorists have to generate a lot higher."

Rubirosa and Tanz looked at each other, then nodded as if both heads were on a single neck. *And why not? If it works, it spreads the credit. If it doesn't, it spreads the blame.*

Not to mention that the Linak'h outlaws would now have to carry their assault through two hundred assorted Regulars, both LI and "mob-job," as well as Banfi's staff and possibly armed guests with their own bodyguards. If they could do that, then there *was* an escalating crisis on the planet and the sooner they found out the better.

Linak'h:

Candice Shores's view from the room assigned the squadron's Ground Patrol was better than anything the Governor-General had. The room was in a Military Police station, twenty meters from the border of the Federation Zone instead of two hundred meters inside the Secure Area.

The transparent armorplast of the window was proof against any weapon your average drunk or prankster of any age or race could bring to bear on it. The scars and gouges showed that. These same traces didn't block a fine view across the Och'zem Valley, alternating strips of wild forest, terraced commercial flower gardens, and private villas for the wealthier Ptercha'a and those humans who chose to live outside the Zone.

The rooftops of the city itself sprouted from beyond the last strip of trees, mostly snowleaf and adapted Gulbrandtsen's birch, one of the Catmen's favorite trees. (Shores knew she shouldn't use that term for the Ptercha'a, but she understood how it had originally come into existence as a term of praise. Ptercha'a grace of movement was impossible to associate with anything except felines.)

None of the rooftops sprouted very high, except one miniature Satsuma Circle that rose about five stories in the center of town. But then Och'zem didn't need to rise high. Its fifty thousand Ptercha'a and twenty thousand humans sprawled over more area than the half million of Ciudad San Leonardo, the metropolis of Candice Shores's girlhood on Quetzalcoatl.

She couldn't quarrel with the scenery, the hosts, or their hospitality. The problem was her being here at all, even though she had arrived strictly by regulation.

It was a regulation that a LI detachment of the size of *Shen*'s was an "autonomous formation." That gave her department head status, so up to that point she didn't complain.

However, autonomy had its price. One of these was the obligation to contribute a contingent to the Ground Patrol, supplementing the MPs. A small one, two officers and six NCOs or enlisted men, but not less than eight bodies, two of them commissioned.

There was the sticking point. Shores's outfit had seasoned NCOs, if not to burn, then at least to spare for Ground Patrol. Officers were another matter. Out of the six besides herself, she trusted only two for top duty as GPO. And one of these was the maintenance officer, newly commissioned after twenty-three years of enlisted service and up to his hairy black ears in keeping the suits cranking smoothly!

She had faced this situation before. Faced it, and solved it by substituting reliable sergeants for some of the officers. This substitution was against regulations, but three times out of four it was winked at.

This was the fourth time. Colonel Goerke, Linak'h Ground Force CO, wanted *officers*. No substitutes accepted—commissions or nothing. The BEU CO, Colonel Hogg, was senior to Goerke, but so far she hadn't said a bouncing word about Goerke's edict. Shores also knew perfectly well that it would be a mistake to bypass Goerke and appeal to Hogg, let alone Tanz. That would raise from zero to three the number of people seriously angry with her and likely to make her troops suffer for it.

Well, maybe she had somehow stepped in it where Goerke was concerned. She didn't entirely believe the story that the Ptercha'a and local humans needed to be impressed (translate: intimidated) by an officer.

But she would learn the truth when it was ready to be learned. Meanwhile, she could at least see that most of the experienced NCOs were dirtside, supervising the field-orientation and suit-adaptation exercises, leaving the old lady free to wear a chair instead of armor.

Which reminded her, there was the company's first commendation since reaching Linak'h to be written out. Lance Corporal Doyle (no relation to *the* Doyle, she suspected) had used his training, his head, and a few unorthodox tricks on a drop from an underwing pod to save not only his own arse but his suit. The MO had endorsed a commendation, saying that Doyle's quick thinking had saved a minimum of forty-one hours of extra repair time on the suit, and as none of his people had more than two hands and one head this was an occasion for gratitude at least.

Doyle would have the gratitude in time; his name now headed the liberty roster. However, it would be another week before anybody got any liberty, and besides, commendations were public.

The MO wasn't as good with words as he was with tools; his draft of the commendation was going to need editing. Shores had the text displayed on her portable's screen when an understated knock sounded at the door.

Whoever it was knew the etiquette: if the reply to your knock is printable, come in. The newcomer was a thirtyish sergeant first class, a wiry dark woman who looked rather like a taller and less Asian version of Elayne Zheng.

She also looked like someone Candice Shores hadn't forgotten in the years since he died on Victoria. Corporal Pete Sklarinsky, sheltered under Juan Esteva's wing until he started getting his act together, only to die in one of the stupidest incidents of the whole campaign. Sklarinsky was one of the people Shores would have cheerfully given all her Victoria awards and promotions to bring back—and now that she thought of it, either Sklarinsky himself or Juan had mentioned that Pete had a sister in the Army. . . .

The first-class wore no name badge. In fact, what she wore hardly deserved the name of a uniform. There was explanation if not excuse for this, however. One of the badges she did wear on her pullover sweater with its odd pattern of reinforcements was a Master Sniper badge.

"Good morning, Sergeant," Shores said, returning a salute that hadn't been given. "I think I had your brother in Scout Company on Victoria."

The sergeant smiled, a slow smile that was neither sensual nor sleepy, just unconcerned. Then she looked down at her sweater.

"Sorry, Captain. I guess I owe it to Pete to start off better." She casually dropped her shoulder bag to the floor, stripped off her sweater (she wore nothing under it), then pulled a shirt out of the bag and jerked it on.

This time Shores stood to return the salute. The nametag read "J. Sklarinsky," and the shirt showed that she was not only a Master Sniper but a Master Jumper, LI, Scout, and TI-qualified, and a Zone All-Weapons Marksmanship Gold Medalist.

"Sit down, Sergeant. What's the J for? Your brother

mentioned you, but my memory's not what it was. The rarefied atmosphere of field grade, I suppose."

"Jan," Sklarinsky said. Again that slow smile. Shores returned it. She began to understand why Jan Sklarinsky hadn't been busted to recruit third class for her lack of military courtesy, and it wasn't entirely because of her shooting skills. A lot of officers didn't know how to handle snipers, particularly female ones; most could be disarmed by a sergeant who made lack of military courtesy a private joke between her and the officer. (Shores would place a considerable bet that when the occasion required, Sklarinsky turned out looking like a recruiting poster and her saluting and snapping-to generated sonic booms.)

"Pete thought a lot of you," Sklarinsky said quietly. "So when I heard you were coming to Linak'h, I cleared it with the sergeant major and drew up an application." She reached into the shoulder bag and pulled out a complete card and printout of her file, plus a request for transfer.

Shores skimmed the printout. It backed up all the badges and then some. So why the request for transfer?

"I thought I would see more action with your company," Sklarinsky said. "Also—Pete said you had the *baraka*."

Baraka. An old Arabic word for a special kind of good luck, transmitted to the Federation by way of the French Foreign Legion. The kind of good luck that lets a commander win, and keep her people alive in the process.

Shores looked at her desk, unable to meet Jan Sklarinsky's eyes for a moment. *Damned if I know what kind of good luck it is, to get your brother killed by letting him go first into a lifter full of half-dead and half-crazy rebel wounded.*

"Action," Shores said. She pronounced it as a Merishi would have pronounced *kheblass* ("incapable of climbing"), one of their worst obscenities. "Really? You should know we're not understrength in snipers, and I haven't heard the Linak'h garrison's LI people kept up their suit qualifications."

"I did, and the battalion's overstrength in snipers. The top's not too unhappy to share the wealth."

"I suppose not. What about Goerke? I'm not going to poach, you understand, even if you can wipe out a whole Death Commando Force single-handed."

Shores immediately regretted that remark, and not only because sarcasm to juniors was bad leadership. It wiped the smile off Sklarinsky's face, and what took its place came on very quickly and was neither warm nor tolerant. It might have contained a prayer for patience with officers who didn't know when they'd stepped in it, but that was all.

"Goerke wanted somebody else as Force Sniper."

"Somebody less qualified?"

"That's a matter of opinion. I don't think I spent my time on the ranges playing with myself, but neither did Laval."

That name rang small alarms in Shores's mind. After a moment's ringing, even a major's memory was equal to reconstructing the crime. Or what Jan Sklarinsky and others saw as a crime.

Goerke was technically competent, but as much driver as leader. He didn't want too many arguments from people who had direct access to him—as the Force Sniper would. So from his point of view, it made sense to have Laval in the slot, even over the objections of his top and of other NCOs all down the line who preferred Sklarinsky.

Shores stared at Sklarinsky until the sergeant noticed it.

"I'm not two-way, ma'am," she said formally.

"I wasn't looking at a frat partner. I was looking at the answer to a prayer." *If Goerke realizes that I've done him a big favor by taking over Sklarinsky.* And if the colonel was grateful enough for that favor to listen to—she wouldn't call it "reason," rather "an alternative view"—on the subject of letting NCOs handle officer duties in the Ground Patrol slots . . .

Shores stood up and held out her hand. "Barring some extremely bad luck, welcome to *Shenandoah* Detachment. You have your own weapon?"

This time, the answering smile was absolutely predatory.

"I do know something about snipers, believe me," Shores added. "I also know something about colonels with a territorial sense."

Shores put her signature and code on Sklarinsky's file. "We still have to be clear with Goerke, but that's my fight, not yours. Take this down to—would the best way of processing you be Juan Esteva, by any chance?"

This time Sklarinsky grinned. "The best. Not necessarily the fastest. We have a lot to catch up on."

Shores's answering smile wasn't entirely free of envy. Clearly Juan and Jan weren't going to suffer from their CO's problem of involuntary celibacy, at least not for long.

"Just remember that you both need to be back in full-dress uniform, fit for duty, by seventeen hundred tomorrow. I've been conscripted for security and aide duty at Marshal Banfi's brawl tomorrow night, and that's when we have to ship out."

Shores had been right; when Jan Sklarinsky wanted

to deliver a smart salute, it was precise to fourteen decimal places.

Linak'h:

The houses in this area nestled so far under the trees that with both primaries below the horizon, the darkness in the street was nearly complete. Or it would have been complete, to a human or a Merishi without night-vision devices that might have revealed their purpose.

To one of the Hunters, even one so long city-dwelling (and on dreary Victoria) as Emt Desdai, there was light enough to read by.

Desdai had nothing to read and no time for such amusements in any case. Each night since he came down from *Somtow Nosavan* six days ago, his work had been a little closer to the edge of the law. It had not stepped over, or placed him in danger from anyone except those bold enough to fight Payaral Na'an's House. (The number of those was not trivial, but no Hunt ever took place outside the reach of Fortune.)

Tonight, Desdai's work took him into a land where even Payaral Na'an could not protect him, and where indeed the master might not wish to. Desdai considered this only natural; in Na'an's position he also would consider such matters disloyalty deserving punishment.

The shadows between an earth-banked house and its sheltering koayass, arching higher than usual, came slowly alive.

Desdai held up empty hands, then brushed them three times along his crest, fingers interwoven and claws just touching his fur. The leader of the group replied with the same gesture, then recited four lines of "The Highest Hunt."

Desdai gave the proper reply: the first two and last two lines of the same poem. He felt the fur prickle along his spine at the last words:

"—hunt the free home for all, among the very stars."

The Confraternity's use of the poem was no coincidence.

"Welcome, Confrere," the leader of the group said. Desdai could count only two companions, neither of them armed, but did not doubt that the shadows hid guards armed with silent weapons. This area had not become informally barred to unescorted humans or Merishi without developing a proper self-defense band.

"You have knowledge for me?" He used the most formal of the five Hunter words for "knowledge," the one that meant facts able to save or doom a whole tribe. This was not inaccurate, if one considered *Somtow Nosavan* his adopted tribe.

"Questions, first. Or a question. Are your people curious about how fast their old cargo has been unloaded and the new one found?"

Desdai considered that question for long enough to create impatience. "I thought you understood the human tongues," the other said sharply.

"I do. But not all messages are put into words with them, any more than with us."

"I know that."

"Then do not—then I urge upon you honorably to consider that you may be mistaken in thinking that my hearing their words tells me everything."

"So tell me what you *do* understand."

"They are grateful for the quick unloading, and assume that your master has found a buyer sooner than expected. As to the cargo, they are also grateful for that, but wish it was not so much of it bulk foodstuffs.

They understand why there might be need for it, but the profit is low and the ship is not entirely suitable for carrying it."

"Is the problem safety or spoilage?"

"More spoilage than safety, although grain dust has been known to explode. But the Longman seems to be confident that he can prevent that."

"From what one hears, he is confident about a great many things, including his power to please his woman the captain every time he beds her."

Emt Desdai made the gesture conveying a refusal to discuss a matter out of concern for taboos. The other smiled.

"As you—as they wish. Very well. This is what we must tell you. There are rumors that there will be danger at the Supreme Leader's festival tomorrow night. Danger to the Hunters, less because we are the target of the violence than because we may be made to appear responsible for it."

"May I expect to learn more?"

"If we ourselves learn more in time to send it safely to you, you may. Otherwise we will do our best by having trusted people in position to help our friends or hurt our enemies."

"As soon as you can tell the one from the other, that is."

The other gave a short barking laugh. "Anyone would think you had been born into the Confraternity."

It was against Confraternity etiquette to praise a Master. However, truth was truth.

"In the service of Payaral Na'an's House, as I and my father and his father have all been, one learns much besides what they are willing to teach." He suspected that Na'an at least was giving him much knowledge deliberately, and some that Security would not be happy to see in a Hunter's brain, but there truth gave way to etiquette.

Then both truth and etiquette gave way to an opportunity, as plainly scented as any prey.

"There is passenger space available on *Nosavan*, you know."

"We do. What of it?"

"Merely that some of those who fight tomorrow may find themselves unwelcome on Linak'h the day after tomorrow. Suppose I arrange a way for them to speak to me, about passage aboard *Nosavan*?"

"You are traveling far from any settled spacefields, Confrere."

"Also far from Linak'h, and there may be many for whom that is enough, or indeed necessary."

"Agreed." The Confraternity leader's ears went back. "Letting those who brand our people with blood-shame escape is not to my liking."

"Who spoke of letting them escape?" Desdai said. Then, seeing that he had the other's attention as never before, he went on.

"The guilty will leave Linak'h. I do not promise where they will land. Also, if some of our own people, even those who do not *need* to flee . . ." He stiffened his tail, then struck it three times on the ground and drew his left hand across his throat.

"You will have a dirty ship when this is done," the other said. He spoke in a tone of disapproval that made it plain to Desdai he had once been a spacefarer, for whom a starship was next kin to a temple, profaned by bloodshed even if it was the blood of enemies.

"Yes, and the Hunters will have fewer enemies," Desdai said. He did not repeat the gesture with tail and hand; even in the shadows, the faces told him that the message had reached them the first time.

Linak'h:

"Christ and his saints," Brian Mahoney half said, half breathed.

Candice Shores had just entered the Governor-General's reception room, where the official delegation to Banfi's party was assembling. Commodore Liddell was in one corner, with a glass in one hand and the fingers of the free hand moving in one of her peculiarly eloquent gestures.

The eloquence, Mahoney was sure, came from the strength of Liddell's opinion on the subject, not from the contents of the glass. Faced with a gathering like this, Liddell was as rigid an abstainer as Bogdanov— even when there were no rumors of terrorist activity floating around the night's events.

Now Candice Shores and her personal bodyguard of two sergeants were joining the gathering, and suddenly terrorism seemed merely a word. Brigitte followed Mahoney's gaze and nodded, then whispered as they both saluted:

"Yes. If the idea of the warrior goddess had not been invented before, anyone who saw her tonight would think of it now."

Shores did not have a particularly spectacular array of decorations and badges. Juan Esteva nearly matched hers, and the other sergeant, someone Mahoney hadn't seen before, had more than either. She also had a look in her eyes that Mahoney knew he should recognize but for a moment couldn't.

Then memory cooperated. *Sniper.*

"Good evening, Brian, Brigitte. You know Sergeant Esteva. I'd like to introduce Sergeant Sklarinsky, on temporary transfer from Linak'h Command."

A look passed between the two NCOs, behind Shores's back. It was one Mahoney had no difficult remembering, because he had benefited from it so often. Two NCOs were agreeing to keep their mouths shut about an officer's shading the truth in a good cause.

"Juan, Jan. Could one of you check our lifter assignments, and the other try and scare a drink out of the steward? No, make that drinks. I wonder how long our Navy friends have been standing here drying out?"

Shores raised her voice a little higher than her rank might seem to allow, much higher than Mahoney would have dared. Her call started two human servants, a Ptercha'a, and three robots toward the group. One of the robots abandoned a full colonel of Militia, who opened his mouth to protest, then closed it instead and silently applauded. Before Mahoney could say a word, he found a filled plate in one hand and a glass that definitely held something stronger than Liddell's juice in the other.

Candy—you could now think of her by that name without cringing—smiled. It was a disarming smile, which turned her from an angel of death waiting to go to work to a tall, rather attractive woman who set off her dress whites as effectively as they did her.

"I know there's going to be plenty of food at Banfi's," Shores said. "I saw a manifest for one of the lifters going out. But I don't know how much time we working swine will have to enjoy the goodies."

The drink was a potent one, but didn't take any of Mahoney's attention. After all, Candy had been an aide herself, and not on this highly informal basis. A solid Standard year jumping through hoops for the

Pocket Pistol would teach the aide business to anyone capable of learning.

"Remember, more aides have been lost through indigestion than through court-martials or fraternization," Shores said. Mahoney noticed that she had both hands empty, and bulges hinting of at least two sidearms and a knife as well as body armor under the blazing white tunic.

She lowered her voice. "But don't let that make you careless. If there are two of you, work as a team and always have one of you watching your flag officer." She nodded toward Liddell, who was looking around the reception room.

"The flag officer should never have to wonder where you or anything you can—" Shores began.

Then the Governor-General and Major General Tanz walked in—really walked, not marching, and without a flourish of trumpets and a roll of drums even though Rubirosa carried himself like one who expected them.

"Heads up, people," Shores whispered. "Once more into the breach, and all that sort of thing." Her smile this time was an impish girl's.

"I for one will be happy when this is over," Brigitte said. "Then it will be once more out of the breeches!" She also looked impish, as she saw Mahoney's blush.

Ten

Linak'h:

High above Marshal Banfi's estate, the lights of lifters on security patrol sparkled in the twilight, red, green, and gold. Higher still, the fading remnant of light from the Yellow Father gleamed on the mirror-finished hull of an attacker on the same mission. The trees on the hills visible from the terrace cut off Colonel Davidson's view of the suited LI sentries posted on each crest, but he could tune in on their periodic reports with his lightweight command radio.

From the attacker crew down to the Ptercha'a guards in the subbasement, more than two hundred armed beings were guarding the Marshal's party. That did not include the reserves not actually on or above the estate, such as a platoon of Light Infantry, suited up and loaded aboard attackers, or the Special Branch and Tactical Emergency police teams on alert in both human Zone and Ptercha'a Administration police stations.

Colonel Davidson ran the TO&E of the security force through his mind once again, failing as before to find much comfort in it. He also could not console himself much with the knowledge that once Banfi decided to go ahead with the party, no power on Linak'h

could have really held him back. Nor was it much help
to realize that since this function, like the Marshal,
was only semiofficial, most military and political bodies were represented by the second or third being from
the top.

Somebody could pop a suitcase fuser or even missile
the party from orbit, and the planet of Linak'h would
be able to go to war almost as efficiently as it would
have before a hundred high-placed functionaries were
turned into radioactive ash. Malcolm Davidson did not
find this thought terribly consoling, either.

"May our meeting please," a Ptercha'a voice said
from close behind Davidson. The colonel turned and
saluted. The Ptercha'a assistant military attaché's rank
was equivalent to brigadier general, and Banfi was
ruthless about imposing full military courtesy in all
dealings with the Ptercha'a.

"I have been pleased. Tell me how I may please
you." When he first learned the True Speech, it had
taken Davidson several weeks before he could utter
the most formal Ptercha'a greetings with a straight
face; they sounded rather like a proposition. However, practice and an adaptation took away that sensa-
tion. (Davidson doubted that the Ptercha'a were really
as tolerant of mangled human pronunciation of their
language as Banfi thought. Or if they were, it was
limited to cases like Banfi, where a combat record—
commanding Ptercha'a, too—compelled respect that
outweighed any lapses of manners.)

Warband Second Leader Fomin zar Yayn shrugged.
A Ptercha'a shrug involved not only the long supple
arms but the tail and the round ears, and looked to the
uninitiated as if the shrugger were having a seizure.

"I hope at least I have given no offense," Davidson
said. It was not just diplomacy, looking for opportuni-

ties to do zar Yayn a favor. The Ptercha'a general had done everybody a favor by refusing to be accompanied by his own bodyguard. As everybody had been looking to the Coordination for a lead in the matter, his willingness to trust Federation security imposed the same obligation on everybody else.

Without zar Yayn's example, personal bodyguards and security forces might have descended on the party like the Hivers on Bourbon. The result might have been confusion rather than destruction, but complete of its kind. The absence of the well-intentioned and badly trained and the presence of a functional chain of command had already reduced tension and might save lives.

"You have not," zar Yayn said. "But unless I read you wrongly, you are not at ease. Are your responsibilities then so great that you cannot even admire the women, let alone seek a pairing mate?"

Davidson smiled. "You speak with more zeal than even the usual Hunter, which does honor to your mate." Zar Yayn had married half a Linak'h year before, to the owner of a small lumbering business in the Coordination, a widow with one son by her first husband.

"She has done honor to me," zar Yayn said. "We expect a child of our own during the winter."

"Great honor indeed," Davidson said, genuinely impressed. A Ptercha'a widow or widower might and often did remarry, but only a minority chose to have children by the second spouse if they had any by the first one. The Ptercha'a laws of inheritance, orders of magnitude more complex than Davidson could understand, apparently had something to do with this.

"So I am settled. What of you?"

Davidson could tell that zar Yayn was going to play

with him, as much as any Ptercha'a ever made a joke
of pair-mating. Their famous sense of humor fell short
in that area.

"I am of an age where I may pair, but am not
bound to, by rank, law, custom, or family obligation,"
Davidson said.

"Well enough. But consider the opportunities. There
is the Marshal's warflier—"

"By our custom, too young."

"There is the shipleader, talking with the Marshal."

"Commodore Liddell is too old to bear children."

"She has never been paired, either?" Davidson
shook his head. "Your ships gain, your blood loses.
The choice is yours. But what of her, in the white?
She is fine to look at, even in the eyes of a Hunter."

Several people had told Davidson that it was easy
to recognize Major Shores, one of the heroes of Victoria and now *Shenandoah*'s LI CO. They said she was
a meter eighty, was dark-haired, and moved like a
Ptercha'a. Davidson agreed, and now he'd heard that
opinion confirmed by one of the Hunters.

"Do the Hunters court on duty?"

"Ah, there is a problem I too have faced. A pity I
have no Warband under me. I could relieve you from
duty for a while."

"Indeed, but had you brought a Warband you would
have insulted my leader, saying that those who follow him cannot keep his own house safe."

Davidson kept his tone light, but hoped zar Yayn
was not under pressure from the Coordination to
expand their mission's size or activity in the Territories. Or if he was, that it was only one of the several
factions there. (At times, the term "Coordination"
seemed embarrassingly ironic for the government of
the major Ptercha'a state on Linak'h.)

"May my claws grow blunt if I dishonor the Marshal." That was a subtle apology—blunt claws were less than teeth, but using the human title was a higher honor than the Ptercha'a alternatives of "Great Warband Leader" or "Supreme Leader."

"I wish that they stay sharp," Davidson replied. "We may yet find new enemies to face together."

That was certain. What was not so certain was that the enemies would be as easy to recognize as the Hive People.

The two officers went through the rituals of parting. Davidson drifted past the door to the atrium as Marshal Banfi and Commodore Liddell passed out of it, but did not speak to either. He'd inspected the main hall and the terrace; the atrium could wait until he'd visited the landing pad and the tents on the lawn.

Linak'h:

Marshal Banfi let Commodore Liddell help him to a seat on a bench in the atrium. He still managed grace in sitting down, if not agility, and the cane seemed more ornamental than necessary.

"A man knows he is getting old when a flag officer gives him her arm," Banfi said. "So be it. No shame, either, when it is the arm of the hero of Victoria."

Liddell was glad the atrium was lit only by the underwater lights in the pool. She was too cursed senior to blush, and it wasn't the gallantry that made her do it, either. Banfi was not only a Marshal, he was one of the more plain-spoken men ever to carry a baton. What he said, he meant.

"There are more of those arms that you would find in a clan of K'thressh," Liddell replied. "If I was awarding prizes for work on Victoria, both Admiral Kuwahara and Major Shores would have bigger ones than I."

"Perhaps," Banfi said. "At least I would listen to arguments on that point. All three of you knew when to make a decision, even if not always what decision to make."

"Acting for the sake of action has been known to kill people," Liddell said. She did not want to argue with a man who had commanded a field army before she was born. But she wanted to draw Banfi out, if she could do so without lies or disrespect. One did not find oneself sitting with a Marshal of the Federation every day, let alone one in a mood to play mentor.

"There you make a common mistake," Banfi said. "It's so common and so easy that I wouldn't say anything, except that it also gets people killed."

He folded both hands across one knee. Liddell saw that the left hand was scarred and the right hand missing the last joint of the fourth finger. She wondered how many other scars Banfi's legendary thirteen wounds had left under the undress general's uniform with the Marshal's cloak flung rather than put on over it. Banfi did not seem to believe in regens or even cosmetic repairs.

"What is the mistake?"

"Equating *acting* with *attacking*. Attacking has its advantages—it forces your opponent to react. But it isn't a universal solution. Standing still, on the other hand, is almost always bad."

"Even when we can detect from orbit a single soldier taking a leak?"

"Even so. A moving target is harder to hit and its intentions harder to predict. That's a function of the way the sapient brain operates, and electronics haven't changed it. Keep your people moving faster than your enemy's thoughts, and you can limit the damage even if you can't win."

Liddell did not point out the obvious—that this only worked if your own mind moved faster than the enemy's. That was something that Banfi had always been able to take for granted. Would she be able to pass even once the test of battle that he had survived a dozen times? In spite of what he said, Victoria had not been that kind of challenge. At her level at least there'd been hours, even days, to decide what to do.

A miniature flower boat drifted up to the edge of the pool. No one was swimming in it tonight; a chilly spell had set in, and besides, too many different standards of swimming etiquette were represented under one roof. When people who thought bathing suits were an insult to their fitness met people who thought nudity was an offense to the Higher Powers, keeping the peace meant closing the pool.

Banfi leaned over, with more limberness than Liddell had expected, and plucked a flower from the boat. She was ready to grip his arm if he threatened to topple into the pool, but he straightened up, with a grunt but without her help.

"I should have asked them to put roses in the boat, in honor of you," Banfi said. He pulled a bondstick from his tunic pocket and fastened the top to the stem of the white flower, the bottom to Liddell's tunic. Then he surveyed his work.

"I have adorned you, though not as much as you have adorned my house with your presence. Now I fear that duty calls." Banfi nodded toward the far entrance, where Colonel Goerke was silhouetted against the lights of the hall.

Liddell rose and saluted, so determined not to be in Banfi's way that she came within two steps of falling backward into the pool.

Linak'h:

Candice Shores kept her distance from Banfi's meeting with Colonel Goerke. If it led to anything she needed to know, she would have to trust Goerke to pass it on. The official chain of command led from Goerke in two directions, one to her for the Federation forces and the other to Davidson for the local guards, Ptercha'a and human.

Just as well, too. Colonel Goerke didn't have a lot of use for "Catmen," and kept this hidden just enough to let him do his duty. Davidson spoke Ptercha'a, seemed to get on famously with them, and also had the Marshal's confidence. She decided to find some occasion to meet with Davidson and discuss the care and feeding of friendly Ptercha'a, and if it turned into a social occasion when business was done, there were worse men around.

Goerke was coming away from the Marshal now, and not even looking in Shores's direction. No reason there *should* be anything she needed to know right now, although she wondered about the informal chain of command that had to coexist beside the official one. Banfi no doubt stood at the head of it, Davidson in the middle, and several humans and Ptercha'a who might hold no official title at the end.

She certainly wasn't going to learn anything about it from Goerke, that was for certain. Goerke would probably take a harem of Ptercha'a women if it would get Banfi off Linak'h!

Time to eat, Candy. Your stomach is beginning to suck blood from your brain and it's turning you into a worrywart.

The food was served buffet-style. Shores found herself in line between a Merishi who was filling a plate with what looked like (and probably were) fried worms, and three humans she didn't know, except that one of them was in Alliance Army uniform.

She dipped and spooned and skewered until her plate was full, picking what looked like dishes compatible with all three races' digestions and hoping that she'd succeeded. Eggs, vegetables, and rolls went down with everybody, and the barbecued meat the Ptercha'a devoured by the kilo was fine with any human except a vegetarian. (At least as prepared for a multispecies buffet—on their native turf, Ptercha'a barbecue was spiced enough to give humans ulcers.) For the Baernoi, all you needed was quantity, both in food and liquor—they were the smallest group here but each ate enough for three of any others, and they had the highest tolerance for ethanol.

Shores had her plate filled quickly, took a glass filled with something fruity and bland from the nonalcoholic table, and drifted toward the art gallery. It was a slow drift; the hall was crowded and she was glad her duty status freed her from wearing a sword. She didn't mind looking like an animated statue from a museum; she did mind adding to the traffic problems.

The art gallery was opposite the stairs to the second floor. Shores briefly inspected the sentries posted there, two LI, two Linak'h Command, and two of the house security detail, one human and one Ptercha'a. All looked alert and discreetly armed, and together they could probably block the stairs simply by linking arms and kicking the shins of anyone who tried to come through them.

Even a Marshal's salary wouldn't pay for shipping much original artwork to Linak'h, so Banfi had compromised with high-quality reproductions from offplanet and a selection of local artists representing all three races. Shores was examining a Baernoi carving that subtly turned a snowleaf root into something whose eroticism crossed all the barriers of race when she saw Colonel Davidson come into the gallery.

"Can I get you anything?"

"A guidebook on how to deal with Ptercha'a."

He smiled. "I'd have to write it first. Would you take a fresh glass now, and an introduction to Leader zar Yayn later?"

"The military attaché? Certainly."

"If you want to greet him by his full title, it means 'Diplomatic Speaking Delegate for the Great Warband of the Coordination of Linak'h.' "

"How does that go in the True Speech?" She used the Ptercha'a word, and Davidson's smile broadened.

"You have a good accent."

"I'm a polyglot by necessity. Anglic, Hispanic, Russian, some Universal Slavic, and enough Commercial Merishi to know I don't want to talk to Ptercha'a in it."

"With that attitude, you will have zar Yayn playing *ihksohn* every time he sees us."

"Pair-mating?"

"He's a respectable married officer now. Of course pair-mating."

Shores tried to look shy, with, she suspected, no more success than usual. "Colonel, this is so sudden." They both laughed, and Davidson took her glass.

"I'll be back in a minute, or as soon after that as

the crowd lets me. Meanwhile, you may want to see the mythological scenes down at the far end. They were done by a local artist who lives out somewhere in the woods, but there's nothing naive about them."

Shores nodded, her curiosity aroused. Her father had read to her aloud from a book of Greek and Roman myths when she was five, and she'd never forgotten some of the stories.

There was one of the scarier ones—the Titans piling up mountains to storm the home of the gods on Mount Olympus. The Titans looked human with a flavor of Baernoi, the gods looked half terrifying, half frightened, and the colors jumped out at you even though the technique was simply paint on fibercloth.

Then there was something from Hindu mythology, the ascent of the Prophet Mohammed and right next to it the ascension of the Mother of Christ, then something Shores didn't remotely recognize, although the style looked vaguely familiar. Next to that a deep-layer, somebody being rescued from a monster—

Recognition froze her to the spot. It was deep-layered recognition, like the work. She recognized the subject—it was the Greek hero Perseus rescuing the Princess Andromeda from sacrifice to the sea dragon, using the head of the Gorgon Medusa whom he had slain to turn the dragon into stone.

She recognized the dragon—it was a reworked Farsi Blue Death. She recognized the rocks where Andromeda (a Noreuropean-looking nude blonde) was chained—they'd been her favorite swimming place during summers on Bonita Bay.

She recognized Medusa's face, frozen as thoroughly as one of her victims by Perseus's sword, caught forever in the moment when the knowledge that she had met her match sank through the snakes into her brain. It was the face of Candice's mother, Catherine Shores.

She knew without looking who Perseus would be— then looked, and saw that she had guessed wrong. Perseus was herself, at about seventeen, when she'd reached her full height but could still pass for a boy. A little artistic license here—Perseus's brief tunic could never have concealed even the modest frontage Shores had at seventeen, but the face was hers, and so was the hair and the coloring and some of the muscles (soccer, running, and swimming kept everything she had in top shape).

The work had no signature and no label. She looked along the classical section. None of the others did, either. She spun around, putting out a hand to regain her balance, and nearly punched Colonel Davidson in the stomach.

"Something wrong, Major?"

"That—the myth scenes. Who's the artist? There's no signature—"

"He doesn't sign his work, although he doesn't exactly keep his identity a secret either. He's a Bogatyrik who calls himself Oleg Govorov. As I said, he lives way out in the forest, with a wife about your age even though he's seventy Standard at least."

"I—his work impresses me. I'd like to visit his studio, if I could."

This sudden upthrusting of artistic interest raised Davidson's eyebrows and made him pull his ginger-colored beard. "He's practically a recluse. I'd rather deal with a Merishi House over a ship charter than with him over a visit. Besides, anybody in uniform has twice as much trouble, partly from him and partly from the Merishi. He's over in their Territory, not far from—"

Davidson turned, and Shores turned with him. They bumped shoulders, then sprang apart as if the touch had burned, but it was only to draw their sidearms. They'd both heard the shouts from the hall, and the thrumming of a pulser on rapid-fire.

Then the shouts turned to screams on the one hand, war cries on the other, and the sound of smashing windows drowned out the thrum of the pulsers. Both officers ran toward the hall.

Davidson ran with a grim face and his mind apparently empty of every thought except duty. Shores wasn't smiling either, but one word sounded in her mind louder than the gunfire.

Father.

It was a plea, a prayer, a message, a greeting, a prayer for help—as it had been during the ten years when the man was light-years away, instead of suddenly on the same planet

Eleven

Linak'h:

Colonel Nieg was operating undercover tonight more out of concern for his own side than to confuse potential enemies. Anyone sufficiently determined to attack the party wasn't going to care if the caterer's chief of security was the Great Khudr in disguise.

However, Colonel Goerke would care greatly if Marshal Banfi's unofficial chain of command was out in the open tonight. It ran from the Marshal on a bifurcate course, one fork to Nieg and his motley collection of operatives, the other to Davidson and his security people.

The Linak'h Command chief of Intelligence knew about it, and General Tanz had guessed enough to rein in his curiosity about the rest. Goerke, Rubirosa, and a number of other large and sensitive egos were totally blanked out as far as Nieg was concerned, which would not improve their dispositions or his status if they ever learned the truth.

Tonight he'd been planning first to see that the caterers' men worked hard (he might need this cover again); second to see that no terrorists crashed the party to disrupt or destroy; third to evaluate the *Shenandoah* party for a need-to-know about his operations.

Commodore Liddell would be a valuable addition,

if she could be approached in such a way that she didn't have to refuse outright. Quite rightly, she would place high value on good relations with both the Marshal and the official authorities on Linak'h; she might not be able to find a path that let her deal with Nieg and still maintain them.

Candice Shores was more promising, particularly since she'd be dirtside more often. Nieg hoped it was his memory of her unorthodox and agile mind, not of her magnificent body, that caused him to put her on his private short list.

He was, in any case, looking forward to their reunion, although with a firm intention to stay out of bed until the professional business had been settled to both parties' mutual satisfaction. Successful negotiations frequently improved the sex; the reverse was less often true.

For the first half of the evening, Nieg spent most of his time upstairs, working on objectives one and three. By 2145 he was satisfied that he'd done as much as necessary on both, and went downstairs.

It was 2147 when he heard the shooting and cries from upstairs. In ten seconds he was on his way up stairs; in another ten he'd reversed his course and was sprinting along the central passage of the basement.

A serving robot had rolled out of the elevator and was trundling down the passage toward a yellow-painted door. There was the house's central control, for lights, life support, elevators, and security. It was manned and guarded, but the robot had to be a rolling bomb—

Nieg dropped to his knees and snatched out his Yamaha ripper. No time to unfold the shoulder stock; he took a two-handed grip and aimed the fat barrel.

A ghastly scream echoed around the basement, two doors flew open and disgorged Ptercha'a and humans, and suddenly Nieg couldn't shoot for fear of hitting people who might be on either side or none. He thought he recognized one of his own Ptercha'a operatives, but in the tangle of leaping bodies and flashing limbs he wasn't sure.

Two Ptercha'a met in midair, with another scream tearing from both throats. Ptercha'a died in grim silence; they fought with the howls of beings from some particularly horrific Nether Region.

They also fought with a speed that no human could match and few human eyes could follow. Nieg knew he could do nothing if one of the Ptercha'a was a comrade, except confuse the man, maybe enough to cost him victory and life. Then it would be just as well that Nieg would be the victor's next victim; it would save his operative's kin the trouble of blood feud, if they honored that custom.

The Ptercha'a leaped again, landing grappled and rolling. The other spectators had decided that they were in the wrong place at the wrong time. They hadn't closed the doors all the way, but they were out of Nieg's line of fire. He dove to the floor, banging his elbows but not spoiling his aim.

Two explosive rounds took off the robot's left-side wheels. A third punched through the casing, but fortunately set off no secondary explosions. The robot began to squeal, wobble, and trail smoke and blue sparks.

Then one of the Ptercha'a lay still, blood pouring from a torn throat and a thigh slit from groin to knee. The other rose, pulled off his claw-augments, and smiled at Nieg.

Nieg might have made the ritual gestures of praise; he didn't remember if he had the time. He slapped a control on his belt control, and a storeroom door opened. The Ptercha'a leaped on the robot, sending it skidding across the hall into the storeroom.

A moment later the lights went out. Then they flickered back on, went off again, and stayed off. The emergency lights came up, nearly froze Nieg by flickering ominously, and finally steadied.

The fuse-damper had its own power source, and the emergency power system was working. Now to eliminate any mechanical fuses and make sure the control room stayed protected, because it was the only place where an attacker could disable primary and emergency systems.

Nieg had to persuade the Ptercha'a, feeling rather good about himself over his combat victory, not to tamper with the bomb. One of the ordnance experts was along in three minutes, waving a foam injector, carrying a slung toolkit, and bringing word that what fighting there was upstairs had moved outside.

"Friendly casualties?"

"Some, but I don't know any names."

Nieg realized that he could hardly ask about Major Shores without impairing confidence in his professionalism. In fact, his frustration at not knowing whether she was dead or alive was already over the edge into unprofessional conduct.

He took a few deep breaths and decided to make do with as much calm as they brought him. It would be enough to satisfy the control-center team, at least, and he had to start there. It was the place for reaching Banfi and Davidson—or failing that, taking over the coordination of the defense himself.

Linak'h:

The Marshal's study wasn't as secure as the basement, but Davidson had no intention of Banfi's risking himself in corridors that might hold ambushes to get down there. The study had adequate if not completely duplicate C-cubed facilities for the house and it was closer to the roof, if they had to evacuate by air.

Besides, right now the major communications problem was in the same room with them. Colonel Goerke wanted to follow up the repulse of the attack on the house by the arrest of all Ptercha'a on the premises.

"I know you don't have the authority to do that," Banfi was saying. His hands were at belt level, and Davidson could see the battered fingers twitching. The Marshal was carrying a sidearm; he obviously wished it were a solution to Goerke.

Right now, in fact, Goerke needed arrest much more than the Ptercha'a. Nine out of ten of the identified attackers so far had been human.

"I am the senior officer—" Goerke began again.

"Not outside the Zone. You don't have arrest authority over Ptercha'a around here. You can recommend to the Territorial constables that they arrest anyone you please, under their own laws, but—"

"With all due respect, Marshal, my duty to maintain the security of the Territory has been interpreted as overriding the legal agreements—"

"That was fifty years ago, and the precedent was specifically ruled out in the '74 Revision!" Davidson shouted. At least that got Goerke's attention, even if it also got him a glower from the Marshal.

"I am going to communicate with General Tanz on this matter," Goerke said.

"The link isn't secure," Davidson pointed out. "Even the threat of a breach of the Revision will have the Territorial Administration sharpening their claws for our balls!"

Goerke's reply was lost forever in a rumbling crash

that turned into a sound like a sheet of metal ripped apart by a giant. The door flew open, letting in a cloud of dust, and Davidson realized that his ears hadn't been fooled.

Somebody had slammed a small lifter straight down through the roof. It hung halfway into the hall outside, the pilot slumped over blood dripping controls behind a blood-spattered windshield. A belly hatch was open and clear, and humans of both sexes were jumping out of it.

To Davidson, they looked remarkably unlike a rescue party even before one of the women started shooting. He returned fire while diving for the floor; Banfi scrambled behind his desk while drawing his sidearm, then started shooting.

Only Goerke stayed on his feet. So he was the only one able to leap on the grenade when it came bouncing through the door. The blast flipped him head over heels, so that he slammed down on the desk, but his body and his vest absorbed most of the fragments and a useful amount of the blast.

Davidson took some fragments, but he also wore armor under his dress uniform, and ringing ears didn't spoil his shooting. A man holding another grenade toppled over the stair railing; his scream ended in a crunch, an explosion, more screams, and a burst of shooting. A few slugs climbed the stairwell and took out another lifter-borne attacker.

Then Major Shores bounded up the stairs at the head of a mixed force, humans of several organizations and Ptercha'a of the house guards. She held a carbine to fire from the hip and waved to Davidson in passing. He saw that one sleeve of her mess dress was ripped, and that the elegant arrangement of her closely trimmed dark hair was thoroughly disarranged.

"Minsky! Black Hunter!" She used the Ptercha'a term, again with a good accent. "Guard the Marshal!"

A *Shen* LI corporal and a black-furred Ptercha'a woman dashed into the study. "Get on the roof!" the Marshal yelled.

Davidson stared, and the Marshal cursed him in Toscana dialect. "Yes, you! I want an eyeball report!" Davidson turned as the communications displays lit up, reloading his sidearm on the run. As he fell in beside Shores, he heard the Marshal say:

"Good evening, General Tanz. I owe you an apology. We have a situation here that would not have arisen—"

Anything farther from the peasant curses of a moment before would have been hard to imagine. Davidson didn't hear the end of the speech or Tanz's reply, but as the door closed he saw the two guards removing Colonel Goerke's body from the Marshal's desk.

Linak'h:

"Somebody coming in over the roof," Juan Esteva said. The scrambler in his suit radio mangled his words; the scrambler in Jan Sklarinsky's helmet translated them back. "I don't think they look like friendlies," he added.

The laughter needed no scrambling. "Who paid you to think, Juanito? It looks like they're doing a pickup of the roof party."

Esteva wished that he could scan the frequencies and get some word on the situation inside the house, or at least if the Marshal was still alive. That ram-crash on the roof had to have been aimed at him, and at sucking into a firefight everybody who tried to defend him.

The defenders would win such a fight; Esteva didn't think the attackers were very good, and in any case the defenders were the best of the best, even the Ptercha'a security squad. But it wasn't written that all the defenders would survive the victory, or save Marshal Banfi before they won.

Esteva cursed, softly, so he wouldn't transmit. He wasn't going to scan anything or anybody until he'd finished here, as a mobile OP for three unarmored teams and Jan Sklarinsky with her sniper pulser. He had to be unagile, immobile, and hostile only against targets coming directly at him, so the sneakier unarmored people could do their job.

Jan at least was on top of hers—had been from the moment the shooting started. He wasn't keeping track of her kills, and the one time he'd asked her for a body count he got such a look that he wasn't going to ask again. But he saw her shift left, saw her security man shift right and deliver covering fire, and saw her shoot.

Two figures—humans—dropped off the edge of the roof. No, one dropped off, the other fell down out of sight behind a fringe of vine.

"Huntress to Outpost Green Two. Is that you hitting the roof?"

"Green Two to Huntress. Ah—did we hit—?"

"No, only bad guys. But we're coming up."

"Huntress, no way that's a good idea. We've got one—no, two—make that three lifters coming at the house. Don't know if it's a rescue or another pickup."

"Thanks, Green Two. We'll keep our heads down if you'll keep them off. This place can't stand too many ram-crashes."

"Tell me something I don't know," Esteva muttered, then remembered too late that Shores spoke fluent Hispanic. She was either too busy or too polite to notice the muttering, however.

"Green Four to Green Two, we have movement in the vehicle park. I say again, we have movement in the vehicle park."

Fire from the house, the tents, and the atrium made the three oncoming lifters circle. Huntress—Major Shores—came back on the air to authorize Green Four to investigate and engage hostile movement in the park. Esteva saw on his display that this would leave a path clear to the tents, and powered up his suit for movement.

He never got a chance to move. Green Four reported engaging hostiles in the park, then went off the air. At the same time a tremendous orange flash ripped the air from the direction of Green Four's last transmission. Esteva saw small trees, parts of lifters, and a few bodies tossed into the air.

"Yellow Outposts," Huntress shouted. "All Yellow Outposts, report." The four squads in the Yellow Sector reported in. One started on a description of the blast. Huntress cut the long-winded lady off.

"Yellow Outposts, move in on the vehicle park, immobilize all vehicles, and clear the area. Use nonlethals wherever possible."

Trust the major to keep her head. They'll be working right around our flank; if they really cut loose we could take friendly-fire casualties.

The Yellows had barely acknowledged when somebody came on the air to announce that the QR force had broken orbit ten minutes ago and had an ETA of something Esteva didn't catch, because somebody else transmitted right through it and the two signals garbled each other hopelessly. Esteva hoped they didn't unscramble each other as well, for the benefit of bad guys' EI gear.

Then he checked his suit's life support and made hasty adjustments. The temp control had *not* been fixed; the suit was ten degrees over normal and rising. A few more minutes and he would have been more scrambled than the signals, and Jan could have eaten him with a side order of *frijoles*!

Now he had two more lifters on both eyeball and sensors. One was lifting out of the park, and the advancing Yellows were spraying it with slugs. That made it a hostile.

The other one was coming in low from over the trees, and Esteva thought it was painted black. He knew it had something fastened to the roof, and he thought he saw a bulge with a barrel sticking out where a door ought to have been.

Then the roof of the newcomer spewed flame, and a moment later the fugitive from the Yellows blew up in the air. Its power pack discharged in a blue flash that would have dazzled Esteva if the faceplate hadn't automatically darkened. Fragments of lifter and flaming bodies rained down into the park.

More flames from the killer's roof, and one of the three lifters circling the house took a hit from what was now clearly an air-to-air rocket. Esteva wanted to cheer—the first reinforcements were on hand, and not a moment too soon—then saw the bulge in the doorway swivel. It did have a barrel sticking out, and that barrel was a cannon now spraying the park and the Yellow teams in it.

Reinforcements, my left ball!

"Green Two to all hands, I am taking the armed lifter under fire."

As Esteva spoke, he was selecting a round sequence for the suit's grenade launcher. Then he raised his left arm, in a gesture very much like the old fascist salute, and activated the launcher.

A solid slug ripped the lifter's hull open, an HE round took out one fan. Four wad rounds spread their liquid death from cockpit as far aft as the turret. The turret ceased fire, and the lifter swung toward Esteva. He had a horribly clear view of the mouth of its rocket launcher for a moment.

Then Jan Sklarinsky slammed a burst into the spread-out wad explosive, and the impact set it off. The explosion blew the turret out of its mounting. Some of its ammunition went off before it hit the ground, the rest when it struck. The lifter itself wobbled, unbalanced and losing lift, then abruptly came down with a crash.

Fire from half a dozen points converged on the wreck. Esteva didn't join in, because he and Jan both saw the same thing—the figures crawling out of the tent knocked down by the falling turret. Some of them were limping; at least one was on fire. Most of them were Ptercha'a.

He'd heard that you could tell how closely Ptercha'a were mated by how they helped each other in an emergency. Esteva didn't have time to note behavioral details; all he saw was people hurting and needing help.

Not much help he could give them now, except one form. He cut in the external speaker and yelled:

"From the tent! Ho! People from the tent! Over here! Get behind me and you'll be safe!"

Enough of the Ptercha'a understood Anglic to get the others moving. Then Huntress came back on; her orders stopped the firing and probably gave the trig-

ger-happy shooters heart palpitations. Colonel Davidson followed, relayed through to Esteva's external
speakers and using Ptercha'a.

By the time Esteva had his own circuits back, most
of the Ptercha'a were clear of danger. The crashed
killer was burned out, and Jan was alternately covering the search parties and giving first aid to the Ptercha'a. It took another dirty look from her to remind
Esteva that his suit too had a full medical kit for multispecies first aid, and he'd damned well better be less
ornamental and more useful starting *now*.

He pulled out the wound and burn sprays and the
scanner pack and went to work, even though he still
wondered where the three circling lifters over the
house had gone. If he knew the answer to that, he
might know a little more about who had been on what
side tonight, a matter that was maybe not quite as
trivial as Jan thought it was, considering how many
asses were on the line. . . .

Linak'h:

The rush of defenders upstairs, downstairs, and along
the halls to either side of the atrium quickly left Brian
Mahoney the senior officer in the hall. Or at least the
senior officer of the security detail—no one expected
Commodore Liddell to get into the down-and-dirty
fighting.

Mahoney briefly wished that nobody expected it of
him either. He'd had enough ground combat on Victoria to last him several incarnations, and he'd never
been fond of barroom brawls even when he regularly
visited bars. He wanted to find a nice quiet room

where he could have his choice of throwing up, getting drunk, or running in circles gibbering to himself.

Instead he posted warm bodies at the foot of the up staircase, the head of the down one, and any door that seemed to lead somewhere. He finished this while Brigitte Tachin maneuvered Liddell away from any direct lines of sight and as many windows as possible. Since the wall toward the atrium was half windows, this took some time.

In fact, Liddell was resisting the only solution—hiding behind a couch—when Mahoney heard the distinctive uproar of lifter-to-lifter combat. Then came the sound of a lifter's field generator dying, fans winding down, and a gruesome chorus of screams, bending metal, and sloshing water.

One of the atrium-wall windows shattered like glass, and everyone including Mahoney whirled or clapped hands over his face. Flying bits shredded curtains and upholstery but not, thank God, any friendly flesh.

Then Mahoney leaped for the sliding door into the atrium. It was locked; he stepped aside as Tachin tried to shoot it off. Sleepwads couldn't break metal; she finally had to hammer the latch apart with the butt of her Steurmann.

This took time, enough for the survivors of the lifter to be out, on their feet, and ready to prove they weren't friendlies. They also weren't using nonlethals. A Ptercha'a reeled, clutching a thigh, a couch caught fire, and several ornamental vases shattered into more fragment bursts.

Mahoney went flat and let off his first five rounds without bothering to aim. He was lucky enough to hit someone in the face, which could blind even with a sleepwad but also put the victim down more quickly than working through clothing.

He was even luckier in the man he hit. At least it looked like a man, and what he was carrying looked like a microwave-burst bomb. One of the big suitcase-sized ones could fry not only electronics but weapons and flesh all over the hall and clear the path to blocking the stairs and taking the people upstairs and down in the rear.

Instead the man toppled back into the pool with the microwaver under him. Apparently damaged, it went off with a low-order explosion that sent water surging out of the pool but harmed no one except the bearer. He floated lifeless in a spreading pool of blood, as his comrades scrambled out of the pool in all directions.

The ones who climbed out on the far side promptly went down, to well-aimed fire from the roof. Those who were only disabled found themselves being taken prisoner by the security in the wing beyond the atrium. This left three facing Mahoney and his companions.

The three wasted a few crucial seconds trying to pick off their enemies on the roof instead of the ones in front of them. Mahoney had reloaded and shot one in the face. Tachin found her Steurmann jammed, waited until one of the others turned to draw down on Mahoney, and slammed her weapon's butt into the man's belly. He grabbed the barrel and yanked. She let go of the gun, making him topple backward into the pool, then grabbed the handiest weapon, a beach chair, and slammed it down as hard as she could. It wrapped itself around the man's head and shoulders so that he was helpless even if conscious, a condition that Mahoney promptly remedied by wadding him in the neck.

This left the third attacker unaccounted for, and a chill clutched Mahoney as he thought of the—woman, he had the feeling—reaching the nearly helpless Commodore Liddell. At that moment another atrium window exploded, this time from the inside, and the woman in question sprawled on the atrium terrace in a mingling of blood, glass, outflung limbs, and straggling hair.

Mahoney and Tachin were so busy subduing her while watching their backs that Commodore Liddell had to tap Mahoney on the head with her sword scabbard to get his attention. He looked up, to see that his commander's dignity had survived intact, even if her uniform had not.

In her other hand she held the drawn sword. The tip was unmistakably red. Mahoney stared. Liddell nodded, then laughed. Mahoney hoped he only imagined a slightly shrill note in the laughter. He did not want to even think about Captain Rosie losing it.

"I had just enough training in bojitsu to use the scabbard," Liddell said. "That drew her attention, and of course nobody thinks of an officer's sword as a weapon these days. Or having a point," she added, and thrust hard at the nearest couch.

The point of the sword went in at least ten centimeters. Liddell drew the blade free, finished wiping it on the rug, then tore down a strip of curtain to dry it. From the steady rhythm of her movements, Mahoney knew she was trying to put her nerves in order and the nightmare battle behind her as much as he was.

Aides don't hug their flag officers in the aftermath of battle. Mahoney and Tachin were still closer to both Liddell and to each other than duty strictly required when Candice Shores came down the stairs.

"I've reported to the Marshal and Davidson. Colonel Goerke is dead, falling on a grenade."

"An accident?" Tachin said, then clapped a hand over her mouth as Shores jerked her head. As quickly as if Shores had been a three-star general, Liddell scurried up the stairs.

Shores sagged onto the skewered couch, ignoring the spilled food from untended plates on one end and the punctures from flying debris. Her uniform looked as if she'd been cleaning street shelters in it, and combat could maul even the close-cut, easily maintained LI haircut.

She still had two sidearms, neither now concealed, and a carbine slung over one shoulder—the one where the shoulderboard was half ripped off. She also had a distinct air of unapproachability.

Then a squad of armed caterer's men and Ptercha'a came double-timing down the hall, with a small neat Asian gentleman in coveralls in their rear. He also carried a slung carbine and at least one pistol and two knives that Mahoney could count before Shores jumped up from the couch at the sight of the man.

"Ah—" was all she could say. Or at least it was all she did say. Then she whirled on the man. Instead of drawing a weapon, he reached up and gripped her shoulder. Not what one would think of first as an intimate gesture, but Mahoney looked away. Now he knew who the Asian gentleman—the Asian officer—was.

When he turned back, it was just in time to join the others in staring at the spectacle of Colonel Nieg's departure. He was being propelled rapidly in the direction of the art gallery by Candice Shores, who had a firm grip on his right arm, which he in turn had thrown around her waist as far as it would go.

Twelve

In orbit around Linak'h:

Emt Desdai wished that he could split his vision as one split a display. One eye would watch *Nosavan* growing larger on the screen at the forward end of the shuttle's passenger cabin. The other would watch his fellow passengers, especially the Folk. (He was the only Hunter aboard; there were rumors that few had taken part in the attack on Banfi, so that few would have reason to flee. He wished he could leave with more than rumor for reassurance.)

Some matters were not rumors. The shuttle had been an hour late taking off, in the trail of the attack on Marshal Banfi's home. Operations at the Zone Port had been suspended, while both Hunter and human security examined the identification of passengers already aboard.

Then the shuttle had to fly escorted at an altitude and speed far below normal, to the Folk Territory, and find that two of the seven passengers expected to board there for *Nosavan* were not present. After delaying another hour, the pilot and the port leader agreed that the latecomers could find their own transportation up to *Nosavan,* if they still wished outpassage aboard her.

With the five Folk who had boarded for *Nosavan*, the two who had not come, the five who had boarded yesterday, and the one who had canceled his passage because of a hang-gliding accident, the thirteen Folk were either present or accounted for. All had booked passage before the attack; all seemed to have legitimate business, as did the three humans also boarding *Nosavan*.

It would be those who booked passage now, especially if they did so in haste and came with scant baggage, who would justify suspicion and even delaying departure. It therefore seemed unlikely to Desdai that there would be any such.

Those who had planned this raid would surely have given thought to not leaving a trail that would force even their friends to go in pursuit. Unless their friends were so powerful that the friendship bought immunity for claws dripping with fresh blood—and if so, Desdai and others were in the hands of Fortune.

None of the five Folk were saying much, so Desdai's personal recording devices were going to show nothing but faces that would be too familiar in a few days and casual chatter, all in the High Speech but with three different accents. Indeed, the silver-skinned old one was saying nothing at all; she seemed to be asleep.

Desdai hoped she had nothing to do with the bloodshed, and was not traveling alone. None of the others seemed to be paying her the attention they gave the drink dispenser, but she might have a traveling companion already aboard.

The other four Folk had the same air as the Space Security leader Payaral Na'an had met on Victoria. All were young, alert, clearly fit, dressed so of a pattern that they might have been in uniform, and seemingly concerned to show none of these qualities to the casual observer.

That was satisfactory to Desdai. Aboard *Nosavan* it would merely make others join him in suspecting the four; not all of their hosts would be casual observers, let alone friends.

Best be cautious about any monitoring of their cabins, however. They might be better trained at detecting such devices than he was at planting them, and as little as a complaint to Ship Leader Marder would be enough to expose him.

Then he would be trapped aboard *Nosavan* with enemies who knew no bounds of law in dealing with such as he. One did not court such a fate merely for the sake of fine tales to tell the children of one's children.

The screen blanked, and the shuttle pilot announced in a voice that seemed weary or angry:

"Your attention, please. We will be docking with our final ship, R.M.S. *Somtow Nosavan*, Victoria registry, bound for Peregrine, in approximately ten minutes. All passengers please strap in for our docking maneuver. We will remain docked for approximately two hours. Please check under your seats and in the forward and aft cabin racks for any carry-on baggage, and have all documents ready for inspection in the lock."

The announcement was repeated twice more, in Commercial Merishi and Ptercha'a, although everyone aboard seemed to understand Anglic and everyone remained seated.

Desdai had a crew pass and no carry-on baggage, so he was the first through the lock inspection. He made a special effort to be some distance from the lock when the robots started hauling the heavy baggage aboard. No one would suspect from even a detectable physical inspection of his baggage that it was anything more than a few entirely legal purchases of electronic gear for resale on Peregrine.

He was on his way to Ship Leader Marder's office to report for duty when two human crew passed him. One was the Boatswain Butkus who did not care for Hunters, but this time he did nothing worse than stick out an elbow too far for Desdai's comfort. The two humans vanished down the passage, still arguing.

"A goddam Scaleskin ship showing up now can't be a coincidence!" That was Butkus.

"Who says so? They've got a lot of ships. No reason one of them couldn't have been on its way here weeks ago."

"A warship?"

"Who told you it was a warship? Come on, don't hog all the gossip."

"Why the hell should I tell a fur-kisser the time of day?"

"Isn't there anybody you like, Chief?"

"When we've had five days to do ten days' work, no. I don't even like myself very much, let alone the Catmen or the Scaleskins!"

That made sense to Desdai. Butkus was not very likable even when he was not overworked.

It also now made sense to say nothing to the leader about whatever he might find it wise to do with the cabins of the suspicious folk. What she did not know, she could not forbid—nor be held guilty for, if Desdai went ahead and carried out the Confraternity's plans.

If. They and Payaral Na'an's House commanded equal but separate portions of his loyalty. He might wisely avoid a conflict between them, by assembling the components in his cabin into salable equipment, then giving the money to the Confraternity. His cabin would be a trifle crowded if he did, but better a crowded cabin aboard ship than the unconfined freedom of space without cabin, ship—or suit.

Linak'h:

Candice Shores would have given a small fortune to be able to wriggle and scratch, a large one to be able to strip and scrub. Instead she was strapped—one might almost say trapped—in the passenger compartment of the converted attacker that was carrying her and Colonel Nieg back to the Federation Zone.

At least they had privacy, for all the use they could make of it even if they wanted to—and she did not. It was not just post-combat adrenaline depletion, either. That sometimes led to soothing massages and in turn to soothing encounters.

Nieg had confirmed everything Colonel Davidson had said about the Bogatyr artist and recluse calling himself Oleg Govorov—and not a word more or less. He seemed to be less concerned about telling her the truth than about not telling her lies, and she supposed this was a good first step.

But if she thought that was enough to keep her from becoming suspicious—of him, of Oleg Govorov, of the Instrumentality and the High Hunter!—he was sadly mistaken.

"You can unstrap, people," came over the intercom. "We're going high and out to sea, then coming back to cruising altitude below radar horizon from the coast. That should force anyone who wants to shoot at us to show himself in the process."

The figures on the altimeter began climbing, as Nieg

unbuckled. Now that she could, Shores found that she had lost the impulse—or maybe the strength. That *was* adrenaline depletion.

The endless forest vanished from the screen as Nieg stood in front of it. She saw him putting something against his throat, something else into the player slot of the display controls. Then he sat down again, as the screen lit up with a color still.

It showed a tall man—a hair less than two meters in bare feet, more than that in the boots he wore—standing in front of a cabin made of well-shaped logs thoroughly weather-sealed in every chink and then painted green. He was holding the hand of a girl about six Standard years old, and beside him stood a woman—the Andromeda of the rescue picture—with a boy about two years younger than the girl standing in front of her.

The man wore military surplus trousers bloused into hiking boots, a shirt open all the way down a muscular chest, and a close-trimmed beard offset by shoulder-length hair. The woman and children wore similarly casual but clean assortments. The boy was barefoot.

"That's Oleg Govorov and his wife, Ursula Boll," Nieg said. "The girl's name is—"

Shores put a hand on the colonel's knee and stared at the display. "He's trimmed his beard," she said softly. "When he left it was halfway down his chest. My mother always said it made him look like a holy fool, or maybe just wholly foolish."

"Your mother had a sharp tongue, it seems," Nieg said. She sensed he wanted to say something useful, but feared silence too much to wait long for the right words to come.

"She *lied!*" Shores said. It was surprising how easy it was not to scream. The more surprising, when she really hadn't expected to find her father remarried, to a wife young enough to give him a family young enough to be her *own* bio-children.

Which is a point against you, not him. He was barely sixty when he left—

"When my mother drove him away," she said softly. She blinked.

"Oleg Govorov is my father, Nikolai Sergeyevich Komarov of Bogatyr. Am I under oath for this?"

"Yes. Major, what I'm about to tell you is classified Command Secret Red. You certainly are under oath."

"All right. I'll waive the warning about the penalties. What is there to tell?"

She listened with ears that no longer seemed closely linked with her brain to Nieg's story of recruiting Oleg Govorov as a double agent, to gain intelligence about the bandits operating in the Merishi Territory. He had long been a useful hand, ear, and eye, not to mention a sympathetic heart, for the humans settled in the Merishi Territory.

(By that point, Shores had a four-page list of strictly official questions she wanted to ask about those "humans settled in the Merishi territory." Well, maybe it would have been only three pages if one of those humans hadn't been her father.)

"But they don't know how high up in the Federation his connections go," Nieg continued.

"Who are 'they'?"

"Several different—entities."

"Classified BBA?"

"Or higher."

Nieg took a "Blabbers Boiled Alive" classification more seriously than he took any Higher Power. Shores knew an immovable obstacle when she saw it, and did not feel like testing herself as the irresistible force.

"He would be in danger if they did," Nieg concluded. "He might be naive enough to believe meeting his daughter wouldn't become known, or—"

"What the Hades do you mean, 'meeting his daughter'?"

"Where would you be going as soon as you got off duty, if you knew where Oleg Govorov lived?"

Candice Shores had never felt so entirely naked, even when she was. To do Nieg justice, he looked a little embarrassed himself, although she couldn't accuse him of forcing himself into the relationship that had given him the insights he was now using to strip her. She had stripped herself—and him—enthusiastically, and with mutually satisfactory results. At least until now.

"You're telling me I shouldn't."

"I am ordering you not to. You can't disobey my orders without being caught out twice—disobedience *and* breach of security. Twenty years in maximum security and the rest of your life in exile, at least."

"You don't need to remind me." At least she thought it had been a reminder, and not a threat. She would hold that belief as long as she could, if not as long as she might need it. She suspected that she would need it as long as she was on Linak'h—and how long that would be, the Creator alone knew. (Linak'h Command, she was sure, hadn't the remotest idea.)

"I'll try not to. And if there's anything I can do in return for your cooperation—because I want that, not just obedience, if we're going to be working together—"

"Working," in this case, is probably not a euphemism, although he hasn't lost any of his looks in the past two years.

"There is."

"What is it?"

"Warn *him* not to try contacting *me*."

"That's already on my list. But—"

"Bad news won't improve with age, Colonel."

"—I think your father's wife will have more to say about his actions than I will. *She* isn't naive. In fact, if he had been married to someone as impractical as he was—if they hadn't starved to death the first few years in the forest—"

"You wouldn't have recruited him?"

Silence gave Shores her answer, and let her thoughts echo in the hollow, almost infinite space that seemed to fill her head.

Ursula Boll wasn't naive, but Candice Nikolaevna Shores was. She had to be, to think that her—father's second wife—hadn't heard about how much her husband missed his Candy. He hadn't bothered to keep in touch with his daughter, of course, even as much as interstellar distances allowed, but he would certainly have felt sorry for himself and for his little Candy loudly enough for Ursula to hear it.

She would not be happy about having not-so-little Candy waltzing in from the stars to—divide her husband's allegiance, to put it politely. She would not have been happy, even without the additional, practical, compelling, life-and-death reason of security.

Shores was glad she was strapped in. Otherwise she would have put her head in her hands and cried.

Linak'h:

"Thank you," General Tanz said. "Screen off, displays on key command, security level One Red."

Lights chased one another around the consoles in Tanz's conference room, and the screen went dark.

Rose Liddell wriggled her toes inside her shoes and wished she could slip them off. The particular combination of lights also threatened to give her a headache, but if she closed her eyes she might fall asleep. Tanz was a remarkably easygoing specimen of two-star general, but might object if the Navy representative on even a highly informal council of war dropped off.

"We have a confirmed signature on that incoming ship. Merishi, neither *Fireflower*-class nor the mystery ship *Shenandoah* encountered on the way in. She's a standard *Ryn-Gath*-class heavy cruiser, in a hurry, but then who wouldn't be under the circumstances?"

The others at the table nodded. That was the way it had been in the last twelve hours, even before the last body was counted at Marshal Banfi's. (The brief pursuit hadn't turned up any more, or even any live terrorists. It was suspected that both humans and Ptercha'a had grounded and melted into the countryside.) New developments arose every few minutes, scraps of intelligence flew back and forth, everybody who had jurisdiction, troops, or both formed an opinion he pushed on everybody else—a festival of the lords of misrule that might have been comic if it had not threatened to get more people killed.

With fifty-some already dead, nobody laughed, and eventually order prevailed. Rubirosa and Tanz divided the responsibilities, Rubirosa taking the civilians and Tanz the soldiers. Since, unlike the baby in the tale about King Solomon, the responsibilities could be bisected without lasting damage, the return to some degree of order was swift. By the time Tanz sent a lifter to haul Liddell from her temporary quarters in the senior officers' apartment complex, it was possible to hold a meeting and get work done.

It wasn't possible to get everybody who really ought to have been there. Colonel Hogg had been pitch-forked straight into temporary command of Linak'h's Federation ground forces by Goerke's death. The chief of staff was temporarily commanding the Linak'h battalion, the chief of intelligence was in conference with either the Governor-General's staff, the local police, or some combination of them, and Bogdanov had to stay aboard *Shenandoah* in case that Merishi cruiser went from mystery to problem or even threat.

Marshal Banfi and Colonel Davidson were still at the estate, cleaning up. The rumor was that Banfi was prostrated by guilt over his role in the night's events. Liddell thought that anyone who believed that needed sedation and possibly a psychological evaluation, but also suspected it was being put about deliberately to disarm criticism. (Possibly also to let Banfi make a surprise "recovery" at a tactically convenient moment. He had used simulated illnesses of himself and key members of his staff as deceptive tactics in some of his less orthodox campaigns.)

So Tanz's conference room held the general himself, Colonel Nieg both representing and displaying Intelligence, Liddell holding the Navy's chair, and Major Shores to speak for the groundpounders. They couldn't make a binding decision even for Linak'h Command, but they could do a rough draft of a proposal for the Command to present to Rubirosa for a further coordinated presentation to the various political authorities who had to approve much of what needed to be done.

That was more than anybody could have done at the time of the breakfast Liddell hadn't eaten. It didn't do anything for the general frustration of having to deal with those political authorities at all. But that was a given; the alternative—unilaterally abrogating the Treaty of Administration and its subsequent revisions—was unthinkable, immoral, illegal, and impossible (choose as many as you wanted, in whatever order you wanted).

"That settles the Merishi, for the time being," Tanz said. "Their consul has met Rubirosa and delivered the usual official platitudes, although I heard he appeared genuinely shocked. Colonel, how is the evaluation of the pattern of the attack coming?"

"So far we have confirmation that our people conducted themselves very well—" Nieg began.

Tanz glowered. His square face didn't have enough spare flesh for a really effective glower, but he made up for it with bad intentions.

"I wasn't asking that. You know what I mean."

"It's still a hypothesis that there were two groups in the attack, one intended to be expended and the other to do the serious shooting. The second group's targets almost certainly included the first group, judging from the number of 'own goals' reported. The autopsies will be needed for a final division of the kills."

With fifty-some bodies, Liddell thought that would take a while. "What about the prisoners?" she asked.

"The Territorial Administration's Criminal Police Office has claimed joint custody of the able-bodied prisoners," Nieg said. "They are willing to leave physical custody to our MPs for the moment, however. Under the Optimum Treatment Clause of the '68 Revision, we have the other four in the hospital."

"Good," Tanz said. He tapped a message, got an acknowledgment in lights, and sighed. "The kitchen has promised to send up lunch. I doubt if I was the only one here who missed breakfast.''

Liddell thought the rumble of her stomach must have been heard outside the Zone. The only one who didn't smile was Nieg, but it was always easy to think of him as lacking normal human appetites.

Not now, though. The tension between him and Shores hung between them like a tropical ground mist on Dominion. Liddell hoped that it wasn't sexual tension, because that would mean two key people were being led by their hormones into creating professional problems for others. Frustration she could understand, being a veteran of it herself.

"Now, Colonel Goerke's dead. He will be missed . . ." And Liddell herself missed the rest of the tribute, as she recalled Tanz's real opinion of the late hero. He had been reliably reported to call Goerke "a Swabian's swine's arse," which both alliterated and exaggerated. Goerke was one of that vast pool of hardworking, technically competent, and totally unlikable officers whose absence would make the Forces much more pleasant—until they fell apart completely.

"The Linak'h BEU needs a new CO, particularly if we mobilize. It has been suggested that I take the radical solution of giving Major Shores a promotion to acting lieutenant colonel and turning the BEU over to her."

No one could mistake Candice Shores's reaction. She jumped as if she'd been slammed down on an impaling stake and managed to both flush and glare at the same time. When she had her voice under control, she said, "May I ask who suggested that?"

"You may ask," Tanz said blandly. Liddell decided that the legends of his psychological domination of chess opponents might be true. It would be interesting to play him sometime, although she suspected she would be mated in less than twenty moves.

"Do I have a choice?" Shores asked.

"It isn't an order," Tanz said.

"Then I'd advise against it. The BEU will need someone with more local knowledge, and more seniority to handle the mobilized Reserve units. Some of their COs were majors when I was a first lieutenant.

"I would suggest one thing, though. Make the date of Sergeant Sklarinsky's transfer to my company today rather than yesterday. That way the Linak'h battalion can take credit for her work last night. They've just lost their CO. I think it will help their morale."

Nieg couldn't meet Shores's eyes, which told Liddell exactly who had suggested the sudden spectacular promotion. Tanz was regarding the major with an avuncular affection, even though she had refused to help him with a major problem.

The BEU's XO had come down with an intestinal parasite two weeks before *Shenandoah* arrived. He was still recovering; it would be a month before he was fit for duty. The next senior officer was a very junior major, two other senior ones having been detached.

Candice Shores still had the right of it, and Liddell hoped Tanz's look meant he would concede the point without forcing Shores to complete her explanation. It would not help for Tanz to learn that *Shenandoah*'s LI company had a few holes in *its* cadre.

"I also have some seniority on you, Major. I still think it's a good idea." He cracked the knuckles of both hands, which were as thick and square as the rest of him. "Very well. Sophie Blum was going to move up to COS when Hayashida retired anyway, so I'll leave Giro with the battalion and Sophie on the staff.

But beware, Major Shores. You cannot do a good job where I notice it without some reward."

"I'll think about that, sir."

"Good. But wait until after you've had some sleep. I remember a saying, alleged to be Chinese: 'Be careful what you wish for. You may get it.' "

Lunch arrived, accompanied by Colonel Hayashida. Tanz waved him to a chair, pushed at him a covered tray and the stack of printouts the others had already digested, and told him to get to work.

Liddell tried to maneuver herself between Nieg and Shores, but they were too alert for her to do this without being noticed. In the end she decided that getting them both angry with her wouldn't make them less angry with each other, and that the best thing for her to do was eat.

Linak'h:

Colonel Nieg didn't find a chance for a private word with Major Shores until the conference broke up just before 1700. The sky was overcast except for the extreme western horizon, with clouds driving in from the sea and piling up against the mountains inland. No rain so far, but Nieg smelled it in the air.

"It was you who suggested the promotion, wasn't it?" Shores said. She didn't turn, glare, or shout at him. She almost whispered her question, with her straight back turned to him and her eyes on a rambler rose climbing the wall of Tanz's garden.

Nieg looked to make sure that the heavily manned sentry posts at either end of the wall were out of hearing. Then he nodded, realized she couldn't see him, and said, "Yes, it was."

He had to say it twice before he was sure she heard. "You can't bribe me to stay away from my father."

"Would I do anything—?"

She did whirl then, and Nieg took two steps backward, dropping into combat stance. Her response was to do the same. For a moment they stood there, with Nieg alert both for any moves by Shores and for any sign the sentries had noticed the confrontation. The disgrace of that was more likely to be fatal than anything Shores could do.

"It can never be a joke, Colonel."

"I wasn't joking, Major. I was asking you to believe that I am not an utter fool. It was a peace offering."

"Were we at war?"

"Let us say that negotiations had broken down."

"Yes, and you had issued an ultimatum."

"Had you accepted it?" Nieg hated having to ask the question, but ambiguity could be quite literally fatal here.

"I have now." She stepped back and let her arms fall to her sides. "I don't have to like it, do I?"

"I would question your judgment if you did."

"Again? You already doubted it once, with that offer. Where did you get the idea that anybody in my situation could do a good job with the Linak'h BEU?"

"I'm sure you're qualified."

"Technically, maybe. But the people side of running—oh, two thousand-odd troops who don't know me from Catherine the Great—Holy Creator, what were you thinking of?"

Nieg realized that he had been thinking of getting the best person for a job that needed doing, but conceded that his definition of "best" had been perhaps a trifle narrow. He had been in the Army since he was nineteen, and of those twenty-eight years he'd spent only three with line units. All the rest had been

Ranger or Intelligence assignments, where volunteers, elitism, and the small size of the units involved simply left many organizational problems outside one's mental horizon.

It was possible that Candice Shores's mental horizon was actually broader than his. Which meant, of course, that she certainly *could* command a battalion anytime one was available, but he was not going to insert his foot into his mouth so far and so firmly again.

"I believe it was a friend of yours who said that you would make a good Ranger, but that you might also make a fine general."

"A friend! That was Maddie Bloch!" Shores smiled for the first time since last night. "I don't know what you call someone who saved your life in a climbing accident."

"I try to avoid mountains unless I'm in a suitable vehicle," Nieg said. "If you challenge me to a rappelling contest, I'll concede without even putting on the belt and rope."

"All right. We'll make a spectacle of ourselves doing something else. How about an exhibition martial-arts bout?"

Nieg contemplated both Shores and the prospective bout with pleasure. If she was suggesting a friendly contest, that might be her peace offering. At least it suggested she no longer contemplated seriously attempting to demolish him in front of witnesses.

Although a full-contact bout might not be good for either of their healths; they both had a competitive streak, hers probably wider than his. But then he could find his father—and his grandfather, and about twelve siblings, cousins, aunts and uncles, and more distant kin by the score—for the price of a ticket to Pied Noir. (A respectable price, even on a colonel's salary, but it was only a problem in budgeting, not ten years' abandonment to lift off one's shoulders and mind.)

Who would have the edge? He was better and knew more different techniques. His eighteen extra years meant more experience; they might also have slowed him enough to compensate for that experience. She would definitely have the advantage in reach, height, weight, and possibly striking power and ability to take punishment.

Yes. An interesting possibility, particularly if the Pterchu'a could be persuaded to come to the bout, an easier proposition now that Goerke was dead. (In a year and a half on Linak'h, Nieg had sometimes thought of using a grenade on the colonel himself.)

Then from the clouds he heard thunder, and the first cold drops of rain spattered his cheek. He caught Shores's hand and they ran together down the garden, toward the conservatory.

Aboard R.M.S. *Somtow Nosavan*, off Linak'h:

In Joanna Marder's cabin, all screens were turned off. She had done that two minutes after she and Charlie entered the cabin, knowing that they had privacy for two whole hours. It had been nearly a week; it would be who could tell how long again.

Actually, anybody watching them enter the cabin could have guessed in thirty seconds what was coming. But the crew knew the basic facts and were polite about details. (Except for the navigator's trainee/assistant, and you couldn't tell from her questions which of them she wanted.) The passengers couldn't tap into the intercom. Charlie had made sure of that.

So could she and Charlie use the intercom, as a

backup remote control for certain systems they might want to keep—call it, under their hands?

"Charlie?"

"Umm?"

"Charlie. Are you there?"

"No, I'm here—and here."

She imprisoned one hand with both of hers, but it was imprisoned on her left breast and his other hand was free to roam where it would—where she would.

Marder wriggled happily but repeated Longman's name.

"Jo-oo-oo-oh!" he exclaimed, as she clamped her legs shut on his other hand and raised herself enough to bite his ear.

"Attention to orders," she whispered. "Can you fit the intercom with links to some of the security elements? The arms locker, to take a not entirely random example."

"Not by myself," Longman said promptly. A technical problem could always take his interest off sex, after the third or maybe fourth round. Before that, nothing short of the ship falling into a black hole could distract him, and total dissolution to the subatomic level seemed to Marder an unnecessarily drastic way of achieving *coitus interruptus*.

"What would you need?"

"About one watch, with somebody who's trustworthy and knows the computers."

"What about Emt Desdai?"

"Na'an planted him on us." Longman raised himself on his elbows, but somehow managed to keep one hand free to gently stroke the inside of Marder's left thigh. It was really remarkable how physically competent Charlie had become, at least in bed.

Then he frowned. "Although Na'an's got enough invested in this ship that he probably intends Desdai to protect us. Do you think that lopeared Hunter knows what he's supposed to protect us *from*?"

"He may be playing it by ear, lopped or otherwise," Marder said. Then she rolled over, so that she could see the exterior-view screen without craning her neck. Charlie had begun the evening by massaging it, then oiling it, then kissing it thoroughly. She didn't want to undo his work.

"So he might. But don't ask him for more than the help you need. If he volunteers information, though, make sure you're wired."

"And armed. Which goes for you too, dear Captain."

"You mean I am not best armed when I am least garbed? Where is your gallantry?"

"She wants anatomy lessons!" Longman growled. He started on them, so subtly that Marder had almost a minute to study the screen before she found the lessons too distracting.

The Merishi cruiser was a distant spark, barely showing a silhouette, and keeping her distance from all the other ships too. Nearer floated *Shenandoah*, a vast reassuring shape, like the door of home on a cold night—but she and Charlie were bound out into the night, not to be homeward bound for thirty Standard days at least.

Attackers clustered around *Shenandoah*'s bow and stern, like incandescent midges against black velvet. And there'd been another, larger ship in formation with *Shen* an hour ago, when they came in. Not a courier ship—that scout, and now she was gone.

Marder thought of interrogating the traffic-control net, but thought also that the scout's movements might be secret. Then she thought of her own movements, and when she had matched them to Charlie's she stopped thinking at all.

Thirteen

Victoria:

Commander Herman Franke knocked on Major Lucretia Morley's door. They kept separate bedrooms in the apartment they shared in the Victorian capital of Thorntonsburg, although they had been sharing a bed before the Victoria campaign ended. Lu was an early riser and a fresh-air fiend; Franke regarded less than eight hours' sleep as unnatural and liked his bedrooms almost at blood heat.

This morning, however, he was up first, even though it left him red-eyed. He had been up late putting the mission's files into their final order, long after Lu retired. So it was he who had received the midnight call from Sergeant Major Zimmer, and drawn the appropriate conclusions.

"What is it, Herman?"

The door opened and Major Lucretia Morley stood there in her favorite pink dressing gown.

"How fast can you pack an overnight kit?"

"How soon will you stop talking in riddles?"

Lu disliked cryptic talk so much that it was a wonder she had ever learned to use codes. "Sergeant Major Zimmer is coming in ten minutes, to take us to our breakfast with President Gist."

"I thought it was the Special Branch, in half an hour?" She looked at the clock. "It's only oh six thirty. And why the overnight bag? Is Gist throwing an orgy?"

"We may not be able to get back to the apartment, if Zimmer is right. He says he has evidence that the Special Branch security is compromised."

One thing out of many you could say for Lu: she was either asleep or awake. Her eyes narrowed, although Franke noticed no change in her creamy brown complexion.

"Hmm. Are we the targets, or is it the data?"

"It could be either," Franke said. "My guess is the data."

"We should have had better security," Morley said. "The Federation made no allowance for our turning up anything critical when they pulled their people off Victoria."

"That's hindsight," Franke pointed out. "It wasn't until three months ago that we were absolutely sure we were going to turn up anything. Trying to get Rift-well to reverse itself on that kind of notice is liking teaching pacifism to the Baernoi."

"Now who's using hindsight?" Lu said, but she was already stripping off the gown as she hurried to the bathroom. As she was awake or asleep, she was also either efficient or dead.

Franke already had his own bag and the files packed, so he spent the time while Morley dressed checking his sidearm and body armor. He didn't bother to check hers. It would be in perfect order, and anyway, her sidearm was a rather more sophisticated model than his, so he couldn't have told if anything was wrong anyway.

Franke had been a Navy line officer before his

hobby of intelligence led him astray. Morley was a professional MP as well as daughter of an old Monticello family that could probably arm a whole rifle company on the demand of any of its members.

Victoria:

Payaral Na'an reached his office early, as he had only to walk downstairs from the penthouse apartment. He preferred to spend even working evenings in his house outside Thorntonsburg, but the Victorian Ministry of Trade had presented its proposal concerning the charter of additional ships.

They probably expected a favorable answer. They might even receive one, if he could persuade his House that financing the Victorians' chartering of their own ships implemented rather than subverted the monopoly of Victoria's out-system trade.

They also deserved a swift answer. This they would not receive, for reasons that Na'an hoped he would not have to explain in detail. *Somtow Nosavan* had to profitably complete her first voyage before he would be able to refine his projections of the profitability of more ships.

That was at least thirty Victoria days away, if the ship had loaded and departed for Peregrine on schedule and encountered no delays or disruptions on any of the remaining three legs of her voyage. Meanwhile, however, an early start could be made on assembling all the other data needed for a response to the Ministry.

If he could not please them outright, he could at least avoid displeasing them by a mannerly show of zeal in their interests.

Victoria:

It would now be high summer in Hamilton State, Monticello, Lu Morley recalled. The thought made the chill wind of this "spring" day on Victoria seem even chillier. At least the smell of the sea partly redeemed the wind.

But it would be a warm wind back home, making the wheat fields ripple and the pecan trees toss their massive branches. Good weather for riding over to the Briggs estate, if you kept the horse to a walk; nobody trotted twenty kloms and nobody cantered or galloped a decent horse in an Eastern Slopes summer—

"Heads up," Raoul Zimmer said. The old Scout company sergeant major was grim-looking at the best of times, and if there were traitors in the Republican Police's Special Branch, these were not the best of times. He still looked ready for any emergency, and so did the wiry abo-descended corporal with him. (Rumor ran that Zimmer had found some trouble being accepted as an instructor in the Army of Victoria NCO School. He had won acceptance or at least ended rejection by challenging any three of the superpatriots to take him on in unarmed combat. There were various rumors as to how many he put in the hospital.)

The corporal looked at his watch. "Two minutes late, Top."

Zimmer nodded to Morley and Franke. "Stay back out of sight. If the car's being trailed, you jump in and Gullking will take you to Gist. I'll play rear guard with the cycle."

Morley considered the statistics about rear guards throughout history. They were not encouraging. But Zimmer probably knew them as well as she did. It was still outrageous that someone like Zimmer should lose his well-earned retirement to a warm vineyard on Pied Noir to a handful of hired thugs, but if he could live with the prospect so could she.

Two minutes turned into three, then four. Herman's solid bulk sharing the niche with her brought a touch of warmth, even with the wind blowing down the streets. She hoped that Zimmer's gamble on ground transport paid off. A well-handled lifter today would be a difficult target for air-to-air by anything less than a military machine.

It would also have to stay well clear of the rooftops, in the open sky where it would be a vulnerable target to a lurking missile team. A team that could, from the right roof, spot them almost anywhere in Thorntonsburg.

The most advanced mode of transport was not always the most tactically sound. This was one of those lessons hammered into her at the Kemali Academy, and she had once thought it intended to rationalize the hairy-chested Sulei preference for ground combat.

The years had grown no hair on her chest, and in any case Herman had enough for three or four people. They had taught her that high and fast may not take you high or fast enough, and that low and sneaky may take you past all the traps laid for anyone coming the other way.

Warmth brought her thoughts back to Monticello. She wasn't going back herself, though, not until she'd settled her future in the Army one way or the other by completing this mission. If it developed a whole new chapter on Linak'h, as rumor said it might be doing, both her oath and her common sense told her to see it through.

She also wanted to settle the question of taking Herman back with her. That wasn't entirely up to her, although her father would make only a negative contribution if he cared at all and her mother would approve if she learned in time.

Her grandmother, the Morley matriarch, would be the real deciding factor. Grandma Jean thought it would help if Lu married into one of the other old Afroam Monticello families, as convoluted as any Merishi House. Help what, Lu hadn't figured out yet, but maybe Grandma would come up with a straight answer when introduced to (don't say "confronted with" *yet;* remember due process) Herman—

The sound of two approaching ground cars and the sight of turning heads alerted the party. An Army car with a driver and guard in the front seat slid around the corner, followed by a civilian vehicle, also carrying two men.

At the same time, Corporal Gullking whirled and dropped to one knee. His carbine rose to firing position as three men ran out of an alley across the street.

Civilians, Morley thought. *Ragged civilians, like the Parrville mobs in the Rebellion.* Then she saw that their clothes were ripped by design rather than shredded by wear and neglect, and much too clean for men living in workers' dormitories or shelters.

She didn't need to see them reach inside their jackets to draw her own sidearm, and Gullking was even faster. His carbine droned a short half-magazine burst, and Morley's sidearm added three rounds.

Zimmer jumped in front of Franke and drew his pistol, but the men from the alley weren't the danger to him. The civilian car cut hard to the left, nearly losing control, and bounced as it hit the curb. It bounced straight into Zimmer, slamming him against the corner of the building. Then it crashed head on into the wall, flinging both men against their harnesses, before it crashed back in a cloud of smoke and a crackling of blue sparks.

It wasn't until then that Morley noticed that the passenger had a pistol in his hand, and that the driver's chest was a bloody ruin.

The Army car slithered and swerved wildly to a stop halfway down the street, then backed up. Morley was bending over Zimmer, ready to give first aid, when the driver of the Army car ran up to her.

"The Special Branch people were in on this," he gasped. "They tailed us. Then the driver must have got cold feet. He tried to drop back. I saw the other one draw. Did he—?"

"Yes," Franke's voice said behind her. Morley didn't hear the rest of his effort to calm the soldier, because she'd just discovered that Zimmer was dead. Nobody's brain could survive the kind of injuries he'd suffered long enough for any sort of regen. With no brain as a starting point, better doctors than any on this cursed mite-ball were helpless!

Candice Shores is going to hurt when she hears this. A jagged lump seemed to be stuck in Morley's own throat.

She rose, half lifted by Franke, who had plenty of muscle under the surplus ten kilos of fat, and saw the other soldier frantically trying to control the crowd. She owed what success she was having to there being only about a dozen people in sight.

But the firefight would have been heard halfway across town. People would be drawn like mites to open wounds, and not all of them the harmlessly curious. Two attempts meant that somebody out there certainly had people for a third.

Corporal Gullking shook himself like a wet dog and stared down at Zimmer's body. "We're not going to leave the top." He whirled at the driver, who jumped back at finding the carbine pointed toward his stomach. "You take these two to the President's house. Right now. Don't stop, don't ask or answer questions, and let them vouch for you. If you get them there alive, they will.

"Give me your number two. I've got a personal vehicle. We can take it, ditch the top's scooter, and hide his body until our friends can arrange for pickup and burial."

"Cremation," Morley said. "Cremate him and send the ashes back to Pied Noir."

"Whatever," Gullking said. "Are you with us?" His tone made it plain that the carbine's aim wasn't an accident. It also made it plain that he had learned well all the lessons Zimmer taught future NCOs.

If Gullking survived his involvement in this affair, he might be passing on those lessons some day. But first, she and Herman had to survive. Morley swore that would happen, if she had to blow the driver's head off at the level of the fifth rib.

Victoria:

Payaral Na'an heard from one early-riser on his staff that the mediacasts reported a shooting on the west side of Thorntonsburg. Either the 'cast had given no details or the woman had risen too early to be alert.

Na'an was prepared to sympathize with the last condition, although he doubted that it was only early rising that had nearly blunted his wit. The mass of detail he would have to absorb nearly justified recording it and using a sleep-teacher, if that could be done without a breach of security. It was plain that the Ministry of Trade on Victoria was one group of humans who knew as much as any of the Folk about the art of trade negotiations.

Na'an had no time to turn on the 'caster himself, but as the staff arrived he heard more. The shooting involved three unemployed day laborers, rather far from their usual Parrville territory, who had been killed. In the incident one Special Branch police officer had also been killed, and a second critically injured in the crash of their ground car after the death of the driver.

Two Federation military officers, part of the advisory mission to Victoria, were being sought as witnesses. One Ptercha'a robot servicer, who either had a different channel or a better imagination, claimed to have heard that the Federation officers were the targets of the shooting.

On this Na'an suspended his judgment until about 1030 that morning. By then, no fewer than five of his most reliable workers were absent, two with "urgent family business," one with a sudden attack of mite-sinusitis, and two simply gone with neither explanation, excuse, nor trail.

At that point Na'an decided that whatever became of the missing people, the office would be under security conditions until he was satisfied that there was no connection between the absent five and the shooting. This would mean guards at the doors and elevators, controlled and monitored access to the computers and key office spaces, and not least of all a bodyguard for Na'an himself.

One of the Ptercha'a, Na'an decided. He issued the necessary orders, then called up a file of assessments of the various security-trained Ptercha'a. Emt Desdai had enjoyed considerable input into this file; Na'an realized that once again he was trusting his life to Desdai's judgment, without the Hunter even being here!

He also realized that his bodyguard would need a high threshold of boredom, to endure watching his work today.

Victoria:

Franke and Morley did not eat breakfast at Gist's table or anywhere else. They were at the presidential residence within ten minutes. The driver was either on their side or too frightened of Gullking to misbehave. He also knew his car, the side streets of Thorntonsburg, and a few alleys as well. He knew them well enough to hit every crack and pothole, but delivered his charges to the presidential door with all their teeth and data intact.

They spent nearly as long before one of the Government Security Company—an Army unit, which Franke doubted was an accident—let them in. He envied Lu's ability to spend the nine minutes without shaking in her boots from imagining snipers locking laser beams on her nose from every window within six hundred meters.

Without calling for help, or even listening to the story beyond the moment of Zimmer's death, the sergeant stored them in a basement room. It was clearly secure from the outside, but also from the inside. The sergeant neglected to provide them with the codes for the lock.

The room irresistibly reminded Franke of picture he had seen of the chambers in which some of his ancestors had been gassed during the twentieth century.

The sergeant who'd locked them in didn't wear a black uniform, at least, and he hadn't made them strip naked and turn over their valuables. They still had the file, not to mention the access codes to the three places they'd dumped copies in case the one they were handcarrying didn't survive, and their sidearms and overnight bags.

Now, just as long as they weren't going to be here longer than overnight . . .

They were actually in the room until nearly 1600, but not alone past 1130. That was when President Jeremiah Gist of the Planetary Republic of Victoria appeared, complete with a robot carrying several insulated food containers. With him was Lieutenant General Alys Parkinson, commander-in-chief of the Republic's Defense Forces.

Getting Parkinson in from Fort Kornilov this fast probably meant breaches of security. Unless she had spent the night in Thorntonsburg, or even in Gist's bed, as rumor had it? Franke hadn't paid much attention to the rumors, as neither Gist nor Parkinson was indentured, underage, genetically unfit, or otherwise limited in what they could do in bed with whom.

Now, however, it might be to his and Lu's advantage to be able to deal with the top military *and* civil authorities on Victoria. Or at least deal with them as much as they were prepared to deal with Federation officers.

The Federation was recognized on Victoria as having done justice more often than not during the war, and having shed its own blood and treasure freely to fight the real crazies. But it was not loved, and there were always the surviving friends and relatives of the crazies and even the honorably dead to reckon with.

Victoria:

Na'an's eventual choice of bodyguard did not live in the trade mission compound. She had taken her chances at living in a small rented house outside town, sharing it with two tolerant humans and one of the Ptercha'a lifter pilots. When the lifter pilot did not bring his machine home, she rode the bus, and this morning the buses were all being passed through police roadblocks.

So she arrived very late, and reported for work not knowing if the police behavior affected her chief's security or not.

Na'an, fortunately, had other sources, obtained over the last two years at the cost of such a sum in bribes that his House might balk at the final figure. This was nearly unheard-of in Merishi Houses, but so was the sum Payaral Na'an had paid. For people hanging with the last claw of either hand to a precarious niche on a poor planet with a truly dreadful climate, the Victorians asked a remarkably high price for supplying reliable information.

If what came today was as reliable as it had been, the two Federation officers were Commander Franke and Major Morley. They had worked closely with Colonel Nieg, before his departure from Linak'h.

Also, an Emergence signal had been picked up, followed by a message in Federation Navy code indicating the arrival of a ship. Other data had not been deciphered, nor was it likely to be.

Na'an increasingly doubted that the shooting was a mere case of police versus vagrants. What it was could be the subject of many hypotheses, which he was prepared to analyze only if he had much more data and a powerful, secure computer.

Failing that, he would rely on the judgment of his organic mind, which held less data but was inherently secure. That was one superiority of the organic intellect over the electronic one that would survive, until some race evolved beyond the level of the Minds in the Sea and learned how to read others' thoughts, instead of merely projecting their own.

Victoria:

President Gist slashed a chunk off his third steak with his fork and chewed vigorously. If he'd been cutting or chewing natural beef instead of synthetics, he would have bent the fork or possibly choked to death. Lu Morley was prepared to contemplate that second possibility with equanimity, if she and Herman weren't likely to be arrested for assassinating the man.

At least Alys Parkinson would try to see that justice was done. "Somebody is going to pay for Zimmer," she'd said. "Gullking wasn't the only man he'd turned into the best sort of professional."

I'll pass that on to Candice Shores too, Morley swore.

Gist cleared his mouth with a swig of beer, wiped it roughly with a napkin, and belched. He had already eaten as much as the other three put together, but then he was two meters tall and a meter wide, and seemed able to ingest food without chewing.

"All right. You people have managed to stick your tools in the mincer, although I admit somebody turned it on when you weren't looking. Some of the damage is done, though. What's to do, to avoid more?"

Gist emptied the beer bottle, tossed it in the robot's trash bin, and stuck out his hand for another. Parkinson handed it to him with an air of genteel disapproval, whether of the drinking or of the delays in getting to a decision Morley couldn't tell.

Franke looked ready to speak. Morley shot him a look, warning that Gist was likely to answer his own question given time.

"We use the safe houses," Gist said finally.

"If Special Branch has been infiltrated—" Parkinson began.

"Not the regular one," Gist said. "Ours."

"Army security—"

"Had bloody well be better than police, or what are you doing to earn your salary?" Gist interrupted.

With mellifluous diction, Parkinson said, "Jere, put a sock in it." While Gist was digesting this command, the general went on.

"We compartmentalized the safe houses about a Standard and a half ago. The Army ones aren't known to anybody outside the Army, and not many inside. They don't even know about each other."

"Only two?" Franke inquired.

"We had rigid requirements. Working farms or outback factories, that we could staff entirely with trustworthy people without the neighbors noticing. Not just the staff, either—anybody who delivers milk or babies or spares has to be cleared, if not as high as the staff."

Morley and Franke exchanged looks. "That sounds like Colonel Nieg's work."

Now the others took their turn with "Should we tell them?" eyeball conversations. Then Parkinson nodded.

"Too bloody right it was that ballsy little bastard," Gist said. "And it looks as if Victoria and Linak'h are linking up after all. We've got word that they—

Linak'h—are sending us a scout. Not a courier, a scout that's coming all the way in.''

"That's a light cruiser hull with—'' Parkinson began helpfully, then flushed as Franke finished for her:

"—extra C-cubed and sensors in place of part of the weapons suite, an augmented power plant, and even more cramped accommodations than a regular light.''

"Sorry, Commander.''

"Anyway, the scout's coming in. About five days, and if we can keep you people alive until then, you can go out on the scout. I'd really advise you to take that trip. How much we can do to protect you is an open question—''

"Jere, let's be honest. We can do a great deal, at the risk of our own positions. We both have enemies within our own branches of the government; both could use our helping Feddie officers to escape the law as a club. What you decide depends on how valuable you think we are.''

"Or how valuable you think your superiors think we are,'' Gist put in.

Morley took a deep breath. Gist was about two seconds or one more stupid remark from being dissected by the sharp side of her tongue. Herman had more than once suggested she register it as a lethal weapon.

Parkinson put a hand on Gist's arm. "Jere,'' she said, softly but without pleading. Morley's eyebrows rose. If this was a hard-cop/soft-cop act, it was the best she'd ever seen. Of course, with Gist's style of charging head down and straight forward, maybe it wasn't an act.

"All right,'' Gist said. "I'll make it short. I can keep you safe until the scout comes. One of the safe houses, maybe something better or at least closer to the pickup point. Then I can get you on the scout. I can even make sure they're willing to take you."

"Federation laws would require pickup anyway, since other means of transportation seem to be unavailable," Franke said. "Also, they might have orders concerning us."

"Orders to use lethal force against the police of a friendly planet to free murder suspects?" Gist said.

Morley felt as if she'd been kicked in the stomach. She didn't notice until she felt Herman gripping her arm that she'd knocked her chair over backward and stood up, balanced ready to give the same kick to Gist. He hadn't moved, but Parkinson had her sidearm drawn.

Morley now wanted to do the same, but Herman's grip was firm. She used her eyes instead, lasering Parkinson until the general holstered her weapon and sat down.

"I think we're entitled to an explanation, at least," Franke said. "And keep it simple."

"You should say 'please' when you give a superior officer an order," Parkinson said, smiling. "Or have you picked up Major Morley's bad habits?"

"Alys, they've got a point," Gist said. "Time enough for jokes afterward if they agree." He looked at the remaining beer bottles, then folded his hands in his lap in almost a parody of piety.

"It's fairly simple. You've been accumulating a lot of intelligence about the Linak'h-Victoria connection. Some of that is bloody well certain to affect our security, and before the Feddies get around to telling us.

"Some more of it may affect our negotiations with the trade mission. There's bound to be something in the file that we can use against the Merishi."

"Blackmail?" Franke said, in an ostentatiously neutral voice.

"Call it negotiating from a position of superior knowledge," Gist replied, in the same tone.

"I see," Morley said. "You don't have to answer this, since it might be construed as self-incrimination, but what were you planning to do if we told you to stuff the whole idea?"

"Nothing. We'll simply let you out, where you can find a place to wait until you can arrange for a rendezvous with the scout on your own."

If "out" was out of the President's House, Gist was being both shrewd and ruthless. Shrewd, because he would have no legal responsibility for anything that happened afterward, and no possibility of being charged with holding hostages—something over which the Federation had been known to invade planets like Victoria.

Ruthless, because the chances of Morley and Franke staying free and alive for five or six days were too small to count on. Even if they stayed on the run until the scout ship was in orbit, the scout ship captain would be in an awkward position over taking them off if they had been meanwhile declared murder suspects and fugitives from justice.

Giving themselves up under the circumstances would be a death sentence; cop killers were never sure of justice on even the most civilized planets. It wouldn't have to be one of the turned Special Branch people responsible for their being "killed while trying to escape," either. Arrangements could be made to have the actual shooting done by more expendable pawns, who could then be publicly punished while the real criminals sifted through the data at leisure.

If Gist's offer was honest, it was worth taking. The alternatives were not only fatal to her and Herman, they did more damage to Federation interests than going along with Gist.

She was still going to break a knee, an elbow, and a random selection of fingers and toes of whoever was responsible for leaving her and Herman bare-assed in the matter of security on a planet suddenly turned hostile. However, that pleasure could be deferred.

"We agree, on a couple of conditions," she said. "One is that Herman and I get a few hours with a secure computer, to edit the file. What concerns Victoria you can have. What concerns anyplace else is off-limits."

"Now just a bloody minute—"

"I won't need a minute," Morley said. "Otherwise you can do as you damned well please. Did it occur to you that sacrificing us could mean the loss of our intelligence to the Federation? There will be witnesses to your role in our deaths, too.

"Even if the blame doesn't come home to you, the Victorian government as a whole will be responsible for a major intelligence loss, or maybe even leak. Then you won't get any help making better terms with the Merishi. The Federation can blockade this dusty dungheap of a planet with one light cruiser, and cut off *all* your trade."

Gist used the mechanical voice of a secretarial computer. "Memorandum to General Parkinson: Alys, see about negotiating for the lease of a battleship from the Merishi."

Then he smiled, for the first time in longer than Morley found it comfortable to think about. "I suppose that's fair enough. It would take guts on your part—"

"Do you want to bet your planet's good relations

with the Federation on our not having them?" Franke
shouted.

"Easy, Commander. In case you've got mites in
your ears, I've just agreed to the first condition.
What's the second, Lu?"

"I suggest that you don't let anybody know what
you've learned except Payaral Na'an. And don't tell
even him how you learned it. I'm not sure his mission
is entirely secure."

"I'd bet the last set of Alys's underwear on that,"
Gist said. "No problem."

Fourteen

Linak'h:

"Good morning, Captain Alva," Candice Shores said. "I am here on behalf of Intelligence, to secure the suspects from the terrorist attack."

"Ah—that is, thank you," the South Asian captain at the MP desk of the Zone Military Prison said. "Just a moment." She turned and pulled a security hood over her head as she bent to a screen.

Behind Shores, Sergeant Esteva looked around the office. It was actually a suite of three rooms, and so well furnished and sparkling that he wondered about the MPs' priorities in both duties and supplies. Appearances weren't everything, or even this much, and Linak'h Command had been on short rations until the squadron unloaded its cargo, which was certainly long after most of the work here had been done.

Maybe they thought they had to keep up appearances for the Ptercha'a, the way Goerke had always yattered about. They had to enjoy pretty good relations with the Territorial Police, or they wouldn't have had joint custody of the prisoners.

Esteva still had the feeling that he ought to watch his back here, and it was more his own kind who gave him the feeling than the Catmen. His eyes met Jan

Sklarinsky's, at the head of an LI squad, and he saw his own doubts reflected on her face.

Nice to know it isn't just my belief that all MPs matured in incubators and grew up in creches.

"Sorry to be so long," Alva said, pulling off the hood. It had been a good five minutes, but to Esteva she didn't sound sorry.

Then his attention was diverted by half a dozen MPs filing into the room, behind a sergeant who outweighed Esteva and Sklarinsky put together. It did not look as if much of his bulk was fat, either, or as if he had the easygoing temperament often found in very large men. Master Sergeant Dholso looked like the MPs' resident bully, and the people behind him like his gang.

Esteva was so focused on Dholso that he only heard snatches of the dialogue between Shores and Esteva. But he heard its ending clearly:

"—already at the pad, where the Merishi Territorial Security Guards will take custody of them. This is standard procedure, in cases where the Coordination has claimed custody of human prisoners. The Folk have acted as a neutral party. The prisoners will be well escorted, Major, so there is no need for you to concern yourself further about—"

"What?" Shores said. Then she looked at her watch, and from that to Captain Alva, with a face that would have stunned a Baernoi Death Commando. "You bitch! You delayed us deliberately. I'm reporting—"

"Hey?" came a voice in Esteva's ear. "How much for a bounce with your hotshot there?"

"Who do you mean?" Esteva said, pitching his voice just loud enough to reach Major Shores. He could tell from the swing of her shoulders that he'd succeeded.

Dholso wasn't familiar with the body-language code between Esteva and his CO. He prodded Esteva in the ribs. "Well, either one, actually. Or both together. I've heard the sniper peels off and goes for either—"

Esteva spun around. He wasn't going to permanently cure Dholso's interest in sexual partners. Not really. He was just planning to open the distance, get Jan at his back for security, and then see what developed.

What developed was Dholso's fist sailing out of the sky into Esteva's ribs, then the side of the man's hand into Esteva's neck. A little harder and the LI trooper would have landed on the rug with a broken neck.

As it was he landed at Sklarinsky's feet. She straddled him, then dropped into combat stance as two LI grubbed Esteva by the arms and unceremoniously dragged him to safety.

The other four LI had snapped into formation just ahead of Dholso's bullies. They were outnumbered seven to four until Esteva's rescuers had their hands free, but they were LI, they were ready, and they had the sense—as well as signals from Shores—not to go for weapons.

Shores had her hand on her sidearm, but as far as the half-conscious Esteva could tell had paralyzed Captain Alva by sheer force of personality. Alva was keeping her hands carefully in sight, and seemed to be trying to communicate something to Dholso.

He wasn't equipped to receive on her wavelength. Shores reached him, however. As Esteva sat up, cautiously fingering his jaw, Shores stepped up to the sergeant. He had a good ten centimeters on her in height and thirty kilos in weight, but seemed to shrink as she approached.

"Sergeant Dholso. I won't ask the reasons for your unprofessional conduct. I simply wish to remind you that there are several witnesses to your assault on Sergeant Esteva, including one of your superior officers." Esteva thought that a wink at Captain Alva was in there somewhere.

"Ma'am, he was going for—"

"If you think you have a case for self-defense, fine. Be ready to defend yourself against a few charges, like excessive force, brutality, and sexual harassment."

Shores knelt beside Esteva. "Juan, can you walk?"

"Ump," he said. His neck hurt too much to let him say more. He hoped his jaw wasn't broken. He had a feeling that being in fighting shape was suddenly about to be a lot more important, and Jan's nursing wouldn't console him. If she was off-duty enough to do it, that is, with both terrorists and *hijos de cabrón* like Dholso to be kept in line.

"Call an ambulance," Shores said. "Captain Alva, I want a line to your CO."

"He's at lunch."

"I am sure he will forgive indigestion more than my placing Sergeant Dholso under arrest, which are the two alternatives."

Captain Alva couldn't ask for the MP officers' mess fast enough. It took a while for her to get through, and in that time Esteva afterward remembered the whine of several lifters passing low overhead. He thought that was probably the prisoners on their way into Merishi hands, with all their intelligence lost to the Federation—and with it, a good chance to settle the score for the terrorist attack on Banfi's house.

The pain hadn't made Esteva want an anesthetic,

but now the frustration made him groan. Somebody pushed a spray against the unbruised side of his neck, and he floated off into pain-free contentment.

Victoria:

Payaral Na'an had not brought his bodyguard Seenkiranda because he expected to have to fight his way out of President Gist's residence. That would be futile as well as provocative.

He had brought her because it seemed that she and Emt Desdai were considering each other as pairmates. Therefore she would be extremely careful to do nothing that would provoke retaliation against him, such as cutting down one of the President's Guard Company, even if they shot her master before her eyes.

Na'an did not expect such a fate, in spite of the tone of Gist's message. Gist was incapable of most rituals of courtesy, even from his own race; the message was no exception. Na'an also did not expect the humans to bother Seenkiranda.

Humans, indeed, seemed to give Ptercha'a a greater measure of license than they did other sapient races. Even those who called the Servants "Catmen" usually did no worse than ignore them.

Was that the secret, the resemblance of the Ptercha'a to the human domestic pet known as the "cat"? Possibly. Payaral Na'an had heard that once the cat had been worshiped as a divine being, and cats had been carried aboard ships—sea or space, he could not remember—as totemic animals. From the behavior Na'an had observed in some humans toward their cats, he was not sure that the cult was entirely extinct.

"Come in," Gist called. The guards stepped aside and Na'an entered the President's office.

He found the President not alone. Indeed, the office was almost crowded, with Ground Security Leader Parkinson and Space Security Leaders Morley and Franke. He did not find this crowd encouraging, but saw no excuse in their presence for playing the coward.

"How may I serve you?" Na'an said. As far as he was concerned, they could conduct the whole meeting in Anglic. He would not appear to need a translator, either biological or electronic, when he knew the major human tongue as well as he did.

"By supporting our proposal to charter more ships," Gist said.

"Surely this is a matter for the negotiations already underway with your Ministry of Trade. Or has some reason compelled you to intervene personally?"

"Let's say that I've found a reason why my intervention would be to our mutual advantage."

He slapped a switch, and the large screen at the end of the office began scrolling data. Na'an watched for long enough to judge the data authentic, and for Gist's expression of triumph to become annoying. If he let the matter rest any longer, the initiative would fall even deeper into Gist's nest than it had been. Also, Na'an would begin to show anger.

"I begin to understand both your intervention and your definition of advantage," Na'an said. "May I inquire if anyone else can endorse the authenticity of this data?"

He was looking at Morley and Franke, even though it was Parkinson who nodded. After hesitation that even a newly nest-free clerk could have recognized, Franke also nodded.

Na'an decided that the precise source of the data could be ignored, if its authenticity was established and if he was allowed to assimilate it. "I ask one condition. I wish to put myself into assimilation mode, which requires privacy and also your word of honor that I will not be harmed."

"You have it," Parkinson said.

"Very good. It will be only—*hours*, I think—before we can discuss the matter of the chartering of more ships. The prosperity of my House and that of Victoria may not be in conflict after all. Also, both may well depend on developments on Linak'h."

Charlemagne:

The study group's workload was temporarily down, so Kuwahara was spending the last hour of his watch redesigning *Shenandoah* to his own specifications. Everyone who'd ever commanded a ship or flown his flag in one had a streak of naval architect in him, and Kuwahara wasn't going to let it be said that he was an exception.

He'd just finished the calculations that would allow a double-strength LI company when Captain Ropuski walked in. It was half an hour early for her watch.

"What's come up?"

"Courier message—terrorist incident on Linak'h. The outlaws tried to attack Marshal Banfi's reception for the squadron. Our casualties were light, theirs heavy, but from the tone of the message everybody seems to be somewhat on edge."

Kuwahara saved his data, cut off the graphics program, and nodded. News like this did nothing to improve his sleep or digestion either, and the people on Linak'h were under the gun.

On the other hand, they had the advantage of being on the spot. They did not need four Standard days to learn that a shot had been fired, or twelve to learn who had fired it and whom it had hit. They were at the right end of the interstellar-communications link, even if at the wrong end of the supply line.

"Circulate the message," Kuwahara said. "Everybody will learn it off the beervine soon enough anyway. Is there anything else?"

"The Army has come through with four people for the group," Ropuski said. She handed Kuwahara a combined electronic/print file. He slipped the electronic element into the terminal, watched it entered in the memory, and studied the paper.

Four officers, a major general, two colonels, and a major. Major Paymaran was a total stranger, Colonel Deere he knew by reputation—competent but slow. Colonel Vejtasa he knew better and liked, and the general he knew and liked very much.

He was Marcus Langston, who'd commanded the Victoria Brigade throughout the crisis there, as well as taking over the ground command after General Kornilov was assassinated. He'd been given a second star and a post as deputy CG of III Corps in Eleventh Army after the general reshuffling of senior commanders that followed Frieda Hentsch's promotion to Army command.

He was good, he was easy to work with (most of the time), and he and Kuwahara knew each other's ways. But since when had he been at Forces Command or even anywhere near Charlemagne?

"Langston's just in-system," Ropuski said. She looked at the calendar. "Not even in orbit yet."

"Courier ship?"

"Hardly. Even the Army has more respect for flag rank than that. There was a light cruiser, *Ehrbach*, I think, on her way past Agamemnon. They diverted her to bring him in."

That involved considerable expense for the Army, if not in money then in favors used up or now owed to the Navy. Was the Army going to such extreme lengths to demonstrate a cooperative attitude, suddenly? Or was Langston's assignment intended to be an extremely sophisticated bribe to Kuwahara?

The admiral told himself that it was the atmosphere of Forces Command that was making him paranoid. In command of a task force—any task force, not just the one off Linak'h—he would be ready to wait for the facts of the situation to develop.

So do the same here, you fool! he told himself.

"When is *Ehrbach* hitting orbit?" he asked.

"Two more days," Ropuski replied. "Shall we defer bringing the juniors on board until Langston arrives?"

"Yes. The Army's done us a favor. Let's return it with military courtesy, if we can't pay it any other way."

Also, seeing how Langston and his Army colleagues got along together would be a useful piece of data, even if it didn't smoke out any plots.

Victoria:

Councillor Payaral Na'an was back shortly after lunch, to Herman Franke's eyes half asleep. But that was only the appearance of any Merishi after spending several hours in assimilation mode. He was actually as alert as usual, and possibly even quicker to make decisions concerning the data he had just assimilated.

Since Na'an had had to enter mode on an empty stomach, the first order of business for him was food. He washed down a healthy lunch with plenty of apricot juice and soda water, then belched with more than ritual appreciation of the meal.

Accepting a meal counted as the equivalent of the half hour of polite chitchat the Merishi preferred before a business discussion. So the meeting was able to move straight into serious negotiations—and straight into the minefield Na'an had laid for Gist.

Afterward Franke realized that he had been close to bursting into half-hysterical laughter much of the time. It was a good thing he hadn't; Gist's temper might not have survived, and then the negotiations would have been equally dead.

But to see blackmail turned around to bite the blackmailer, and when you've been one of his victims only hours before—the gods had to have a sense of humor to allow that sort of thing to go on!

"I think we need to discuss other matters before the chartering of the ships," Na'an said. "You must appreciate that you have in your possession material that could injure my House. If my House is injured, I will be blamed, and therefore unable to participate in the negotiations or indeed continue with the trade mission."

Gist looked as if that would not be entirely bad news, Na'an continued, and the President's face changed. He was not, after all, as blunt-witted as he seemed.

"If I cannot protect my servants, of all three races, then I must ask you, who provoked my departure, to do so. I trust that is not asking too much?"

"That depends on what status they have. Also, a lot of them are nonhuman—"

"But entitled to the same protection rights as humans, by treaty," Na'an said.

Franke wanted to amplify that, but Lu kicked him in the shin before he could speak, and anyway Na'an could carry the ball well enough himself.

"It would be unfortunate for Victoria if the operations of the trade mission were disrupted at all. I believe that in such a case you would have no legal off-planet trade at all, until the agreement had been renegotiated from the beginning."

Something like a muffled "Hades!" escaped from Parkinson, and she nodded.

"Yes. I see the Ground Security leader understands clearly. Smugglers cannot supply all of a planet's needs for imports, and they are both unreliable and expensive.

"I think you are in a situation where you can only lose by continuing with this effort to influence the negotiations by ethically questionable methods. If you do, you will force me off Victoria, and then you will have two choices, both undesirable.

"You can protect my servants, and have your people asking why. They will ask loudly and often in the case of the Folk, who are not much loved on Victoria."

Sentimentality, it had often been said, was not in Merishi. Franke thought he had seldom imagined, let alone encountered, such a blatant demonstration of that fact.

"Or you can leave them at risk, from your own people, your own corrupt police, and anyone lurking in the shadows who is an enemy of all of us. Some will surely die, their deaths will raise questions, and when answers are not forthcoming from your government, the Federation may ask.

"The Federation will, after all, need the cooperation of the Folk to settle the matter of Linak'h, which seems to be much on its mind. I do not think it will be grateful to anyone who disrupts its efforts."

A Merishi genius for understatement was not listed in the standard references, so Franke concluded that this was probably personal to Payaral Na'an.

It seemed to have done the job, although Gist huffed and puffed and wondered out loud for some time about how many houses he could blow down before one of them fell on him. Franke held his tongue, and also held Lu's arm to keep her from unlimbering hers to slice Gist into manageable chunks for the office recycler.

"I think, Mr. President, that I can guarantee one ship, immediately and without any obligations on your part except discretion about what you have learned. After all, we of the Folk are prepared to take some risks.

"As to others—I think in fact that Linak'h is a good place to find others to charter. A considerable number of the ships of the Folk in that area stop at Linak'h for fresh supplies. Some are always in need of work."

Na'an managed carefully to look at everyone and no one at the same time. "I do not think the law allows me to give humans a legal empowerment in a matter of such value. However, I have reason to believe that humans will be traveling to Linak'h quite soon. May I ask you to carry such an empowerment to a trustworthy merchant of the Folk on Linak'h?"

Again he wasn't looking at anyone, but Franke and Morley didn't dare move their heads to exchange glances. The advantages of accepting were obvious, and if Na'an had already guessed as much as he had—

"I can't order you people," Parkinson said. "But if you have any feeling for Victoria—"

Franke's strongest feeling for Victoria at this point was an overwhelming desire to be fifty light-years from it, even if he had to ride in a courier or a Ptercha'a tramp. His next strongest feeling, his instinct for diplomacy, won.

"Of course. I believe that we can accommodate a message or even a messenger, unless our transportation arrangements fall through?" He looked at Gist, who merely nodded without raising his head.

Franke felt briefly sorry for the man, in whom power was bringing out a streak of bully that might soon make him too many enemies. Alys Parkinson would also go her way, and in that kind of loss Franke could feel for anyone.

Linak'h:

"Sergeant Dholso is being reassigned outside the Zone," Colonel Nieg said, as the cooker in his kitchen beeped for attention to its contents. He opened it and pulled out a casserole that to Candice Shores seemed to consist mostly of rice and smelled mostly of onions.

"Good," she said. "I wasn't joking about not being able to guarantee his safety. Unless he's got his bullies with him, the next time he meets anybody from the company, he's a medevac candidate."

"His squad is being broken up. I believe that was one of the conditions of the MP CO's not being relieved of his command by General Tanz. In return, it has been agreed that no charges will be brought against Captain Alva."

Shores knocked over her water glass. She caught it before it hit the floor, and nearly threw it at Nieg.

"She ought to be up on charges, damn her!"

"In theory, yes. In practice, charges against her would look like what Dholso and his superiors were trying to do to you through Esteva. Creating a situation where dropping charges can be traded for looking the other way."

"I was looking right at her. She was lying in her teeth."

"Probably. But she is indispensable to the MP CO, and he is not removable at the moment. His only possible replacement is a Reserve, who cannot be called up for duty in the Zone unless there is a state of emergency."

"Isn't Rubirosa going to declare one?"

"Tanz is discussing the matter with him," Nieg said. "But it may take a while, since it requires the consent of the Territorial Administration. Or would you rather have Captain Alva take over the MPs?"

Shores cringed dramatically and nearly knocked her loaded plate off the table. It had been filled while she wasn't looking, and even rice and onions now smelled tempting.

Between mouthfuls, Nieg disposed of the MPs. "The real problem is that the MP CO was a protégé of Goerke's. Either that, or the protégé of someone Goerke owes favors to. I have been trying to learn which, now that there is a serious problem with the MPs, but everyone is preserving the most impressive discretion. I would prefer not to bring questionable charges merely to intimidate probably innocent people into providing evidence of what may be nothing improper."

After she had sorted out that last sentence, Shores decided that she agreed with Nieg, and tucked into her meal. They were finishing off with tea and almond pudding when Nieg put down his cup.

"The matter of the prisoners turned over to the Merishi remains open, even if we cannot do anything to the MPs about it. I suggest that we consider a way to find more prisoners, who will be unquestionably under our jurisdiction."

"At least long enough to be interrogated by some reliable people who know the right questions to ask," Shores pointed out. "If the MPs hadn't sat around playing with themselves for nearly a week—"

"I agree. This means some effort to arrange an encounter with our—friends in the woods."

Shores waited, not knowing whether she wanted to hear her father mentioned or not. She couldn't put him out of her mind entirely, not when the distance to him was finally measured in kloms and not light-years. She could think of him in a reasonably detached manner when she was around Nieg. She believed that this was for professional reasons more than personal ones.

"Our friends are chronically short of supplies. Now, suppose a riverboat or a cargo lifter loaded with what they needed was to have a disabling accident?"

"Where?"

"In their territory or close to it."

"I see. I thought you were going to suck them across the border again."

"They may not be allowed to cross it, if their masters suspect that many of them would try to defect. After all, one can kill only so many of one's own soldiers before it leads to mutiny rather than intimidation."

"Are you in a philosophical mood tonight, Colonel?"

"An entirely practical one. Another raid into our territory would have the same results—a claim by the Merishi or the Coordination to the prisoners. But if we capture outlaws in the course of a hot-pursuit operation, they are *ours*."

Shores saw the picture more clearly now. Hot pursuit could be abused, but in this case it might not have to be, and the Merishi in any case were not in a very strong position to protest. If they raised too much suspicion of their motives in protecting arrested outlaws, they would be doing the Federation's work for it.

She also saw, as the final detail of the picture, who would most likely be doing the fighting. Her LI people were more secure, better trained and equipped, and more capable of hitting the raiders by surprise and carrying out the hot pursuit.

"I hope I don't smell another bribe," she said. She wanted to get this out before either wine, intimacy, or fatigue made Nieg question her judgment in saying it.

"I hope I do not smell paranoia in a fellow officer," Nieg said. "If it is a bribe, it is one to your Light Infantry. With a battle honor won in the sight of the whole Linak'h Command, they may be less eager to put Sergeant Dholso in the hospital."

Fifteen

Linak'h:

From the stream behind the house came laughter and cheerful shrieks, some of them female. Brokeh su-Irzim did not need to look to know what was going on. Lyka ihr Zeyem was continuing her fall from—however one wished to describe a state in which a woman did not swim nude with the Lidessouf twins.

Lyka was certainly a pleasant sight, su-Irzim admitted. She rather resembled his own former wife, although she was larger all around. (M'nila had been hardly heavier than the average Smalltooth; su-Irzim had easily been able to pick her up even though he was not a ritualist of the Lord of Strength.)

As to what else she did or left undone, it took a good deal to upset the twins, and a woman passing on from their embraces to somewhere else (or even someone else) would not be one of them. As he recalled Kalidessouf saying, "Women are like lifters. Wait long enough, and another one will fly by."

Although that remark probably did not apply here on Linak'h, where in the Territories one might wait for a lifter much longer than a normally endowed sapient wished to wait for a partner. . . .

Rahbad Sarlin stepped out of the house. He wore

only a towel around his waist and was streaming sweat from the bath. He started toward the stream, caught sight of su-Irzim, and fell into step beside him.

"Greetings and good faring, brother," Sarlin said, with mock solemnity. "We have word from the Scaleskin Territory."

"The prisoners."

"That may not be the best word for their status, but yes, they are the same men who were prisoners in the Federation Territory."

Su-Irzim wondered how long it had taken for the Merishi to decide that they should persuade the Coordination to work on their fellows in the Territorial Administration. He also wondered how much resistance the Administration had offered.

The Ptercha'a believed strongly in justice, but unlike the People believed that when it would shame someone it should be done privately. If it was done at all, the guilty party would be unlikely to commit further offenses. If it was left undone, shame alone had no power to alter behavior.

He wondered how they viewed the likely fate of the—call them activists—in Merishi hands. Indeed, both Ptercha'a opinion and the fate itself were somewhat important to the People's mission.

"Are we sending someone to Hufen?" su-Irzim asked.

Sarlin nodded. "The Merishi have asked. I think it would be best if it were you or Zhapso."

"You are the best at dealing with them," su-Irzim had to point out. "We do not propose to sit counting feathers while waiting for Behdan Zeg. Nor, I think, are we helpless to deal with him when he comes."

"Helpless, no. Less able to bring him on-planet without anybody noticing, yes. That is important. My mother's son has his moments of skill, and if he is having one of them, so much the better. We do not want to lose those skills because someone's mishandling him causes an uproar that our neighbors hear."

"You make him sound rather like a runaway roadhauler on ice."

"The comparison has been made, and in my hearing. It has lost the power to shame me."

It seemed to su-Irzim that Zeg himself had not lost the power to shame his half brother, even if rude remarks about him had. Once again su-Irzim thanked the Instrumentality for his good fortune in the matter of kin, if not of marriage. His five siblings and half siblings were scattered all over the Khudrigate, but none of them for reasons that brought shame. Even his father's choice of a second wife had been a respectable one.

"So, I speak various forms of Merishi better than su-Lal. I also need to know their Territory better."

"True. But our agent will not need High Merishi, unless he deals with some particularist who refuses to speak Commercial. Also, I need you here. Zeg can also shock and unsettle our friend su-Lal. He cannot do the same to you."

Ask Fleet Commander su-Weigho before you wager your tusks on that, my friend.

"You praise me to excess. Why not simplify matters by bringing the —humans in question—to us? We could claim to be neutral parties."

"We could. We would then have the work of keeping them and Zeg apart."

Su-Lal must have looked as bemused as he felt. Sarlin gouged the lawn as he stamped. "Zeg's wild ideas for the humans could set us at odds with every political body on Linak'h except the Wild Continent and the Alliance Territory!"

More quietly, Sarlin added, "Besides, moving them might be detected from orbit. *Gray Death* informed me that the humans have completed their satellite network. They could easily detect any unusual lifter movements, and bringing the humans in on the ground would be slow and dangerous."

"To whom?"

"You wish to see them dead?"

"Not before we learn as much as we can from them, and then who knows? There may be no case for their death at all."

Sarlin embraced su-Irzim with a vigor that the Fleet man found somewhat surprising. "Wisdom at last. The more time you spend in the field instead of at a console, the less blood you find it pleasant to shed. You still shed more of it, but as the toll mounts, so do your memories."

He lengthened his stride toward the stream, while su-Irzim turned back toward the house. It was nearly time for dinner, and he hoped the cooker had not ruined the uhrims. They grew only with difficulty on Linak'h, which raised the price of this staple of the People's diet to the luxury level—and the mission's budget did not allow for many luxuries.

Aboard R.M.S. *Somtow Nosavan,* the Peregrine system:

"Bridge warning to Captain. Twenty-five minutes to final maneuver for course to Peregrine." It was Boatswain Butkus.

"Any contacts?"

"Nothing, active or passive. Ah—we're keeping the active search down to the meteor-watch level."

"Good. This system hasn't any ghost ships that I've heard of, and if they think we need an escort they'll send one out."

"What do they think we are, anyway? A Catman clunker?"

Behind Joanna Marder, Charles Longman stifled laughter. She waited until the intercom was dead, then turned, trying to glare. She ended by laughing too.

"I suppose he could have said it without singeing the Ptercha'a in the process. But it is odd, how he's developing pride in this ship."

"It's a tribute to you, Jo," Longman said. "It is not beyond the bounds of natural law that you are a good captain."

"I have some good help, with the flattery and with other things."

Longman frowned. "Think Butkus could help with—ah, the other things?"

"If you're thinking of a three-way—" Marder began, then choked at the expression on Longman's face.

I think he is really developing the ability to be shocked at far-out sex, now that he's getting enough from one partner.

She did not dare say "a partner he cares for." She had thought it several times, but even the thought made her uncomfortable.

This trip was also the worst possible time to settle any major personal problem—or make minor ones worse by bad jokes.

"Sorry, Charlie. You know what I mean."

" 'When four people sit down to plan revolution, three are fools and one is a police spy.' Old Russian saying."

"Said by an old Russian?"

"Actually, by a young one, and female to boot, although she never was much for dominance and submission, so I never tried booting her. I tickled her all over with my toes once, but that's as close as we—"

"Charlie, seriously. I know I started it—but what about Butkus?"

Longman sat on the bunk. He definitely moved more gracefully now, clothes on or off. But she'd asked him to be serious; *take your own advice, Captain.*

"We could use a fourth, because three is the minimum for taking the ship through a Jump. If the intercom-bypass controls work, and nobody sabotages anything vital, we can lock down the whole ship and Jump to Linak'h with three people. With two, we'd risk being trapped in the Peregrine system—if that's when whatever we expect to happen happens."

"You think Desdai might be turned?"

"I don't understand Ptercha'a well enough to be sure one way or the other. All his motives that I understand lean toward keeping him faithful. But I was thinking more of casualties, even accidents. And—Jo, don't take this the wrong way—"

In what seemed like seconds, she conjured up a long and frightening list of what "this" might be. She conjured it up so fast that she had broken out in a sweat before Longman spoke again.

"—but I think we ought to agree in advance. We won't be hostages for each other. Somebody takes one of us prisoner, the other goes ahead the best he can. That makes it a lot harder for the bad guys, according to Karl Pocher, but it helps if you agree in advance. He thinks they might have done better aboard *Leon Brautigan* if they'd thought it over before."

Marder sat down on her bunk, weak-kneed with

relief. Then she patted Longman's knee. "You have the damnedest ways of saying you care for somebody!"

"Hunh. I haven't stopped being selfish, Jo. I've just stopped being stupid as well. But what do you think?"

"Good idea. Karl Pocher should know." Pocher and his crew had foiled a hijacking of the observatory tender *Leon Brautigan* off Victoria, but two of them had died in the process, at the hands of unbalanced human fanatics.

Aboard *Somtow Nosavan,* the menace seemed more likely to be Merishi, and how could you tell a stable professional Merishi from a bloodthirsty kill-crazy one? You probably couldn't, until it was too late.

"Twenty minutes more, and they'll want us on the Bridge," Longman said. He looked noncommittal about what to do with those twenty minutes.

Marder was glad he wasn't pushing it. A quickie had its points. Sitting quietly, bathing in the contentment of Charlies' newly intelligent affection, had more.

Victoria:

Herman Franke wasn't surprised when he stumbled around the last outcropping and saw a full-sized scout lying on the canyon floor. If this had been the first novelty of the last five days, he might have gaped. As it was, he was losing his power to be surprised.

He'd been surprised at the lifter crew that picked them up from a warehouse roof on the outskirts of Thorntonsburg, the night of Zimmer's death. They were Teresa DiVries and BoJo Johnson, a Freedom Legionary's widow and an adolescent boy.

"What's to be surprised about?" Johnson said, at Franke's look.

"Well . . ." Franke began. He didn't want to create a situation where a boy of sixteen would draw on him, but he didn't really know what to say.

"The Intel people got me a legal emancip," BoJo said. "And 'Reesa wants back at the people who got her husband killed. What could be simpler?"

Franke decided he didn't have the answer to that, and both their pilots had guns if he gave an answer they didn't like. So he climbed into the lifter and settled down, trying to sleep during the twelve-hour flight out to Blanchard Canyon.

He wasn't surprised it took that long, with a slow lifter, one recharging, and evasive routing. His back and kidneys were protesting when the lifter unloaded him and Lu at what he supposed was a "safe house."

Except that it wasn't any kind of house, let alone a farm. It was a survival shelter, so thoroughly hidden that if you weren't looking for it you could spend a week combing Blanchard Canyon for the few square meters of roof that jutted above the sand and gravel.

"Stay here," DiVries told them, "unless there's a flash flood. It's a little late in the year for them, though. You've got ten days' food and water, if you aren't greedy, and your personal weapons. Don't wander around, and the filters will take care of mites."

That was all they were told. The rest they had to piece together for themselves, in the five days they spent in the shelter. Five uninterrupted days in Lu's company wasn't quite as exciting as it would have been in the early stages of the relationship, when there was a lot of the obvious kinds of exploring to be done.

Now most of the exploring they did was outside. Franke preferred sailing to hiking, and wished Teresa

DiVries hadn't issued the warning about staying inside. To Lu, that was the same as leaving a fresh-killed carcass unattended in grumbler territory.

So Franke slogged along in his affiliate's wake, and got a good view of mite nests (the mites dormant at night, this early in the spring), exotic rock formations, and the marks carved by flash floods in past years. Some of them were a good fifteen meters above the level of the shelter. Franke wondered if the shelter had a flood-warning device, or if they were just supposed to rely on weather forecasts making it through Victoria's notoriously putrid radio reception.

They also found signs of recent human activity in the area, more recent than the war. That wasn't such a surprise, after the shelter. It had obviously been built during the war; just as obviously it had been visited for maintenance and resupply since. It could also accommodate a lot more than two people—and Lu was sure she spotted at least five more similar shelters on their rambles.

Since they roamed at night and Lu's fieldcraft was good, anybody in the shelters didn't notice the visitors. Even Lu at her most aggressive had the sense to stay out of the caves that showed signs of being used for storage.

"Booby traps trap boobies," she said. "But I wish I knew what all this activity is for."

"Somebody still has plans to play guerrilla," Franke said.

"The purpose of Intelligence is not to state the obvious," she said. "The real question is, who is going to be playing it against whom?"

"I don't know," Franke said testily. "You don't know. In fact, I wouldn't be surprised if the Victorians themselves don't know. At least most of them."

To his surprise, she agreed, and that was both their last discussion and their last ramble. The next night they received the alert signal, and now at dawn they'd slogged a good ten kloms down the canyon toward one of the side branches that sloped up onto the open desert at a relatively gentle angle.

That made sense, when he saw the grounded starship. It must have come in low, then dropped into the canyon branch and slipped all the way down out of any sort of easy visual contact. Other sorts of contact would be chancy, Victoria's satellite network having deteriorated even further since the war.

Their guides wore mite-protector masks, which also hid their faces as thoroughly as terrorists or Rangers could have wished. Franke was about ready to exchange these mystery guides for either of the others when the ground-access hatch in the ship opened. A figure seemed to float out of the shadows, then walked up to Franke and pulled up his mask.

"Commander Franke?"

Morley coughed at the breach of security, but the man seemed to be oblivious. His voice sounded familiar, but the face—

"Oh. No point in dawdling to kiss Intelligence asses." He waved at the ship. "Meet U.F.N. scout *Powell.* I'm Lieutenant Commander Gordon Uhlig, off *Shenandoah.* They wanted to send an officer they could spare who could fill you in on Linak'h."

"Not very flattering," Morley snapped.

"Remember what I said about no ass-kissing? But I'd advise moving yours. We want to be out of here before it gets light enough that we have to go supersonic in the canyon."

Franke shuddered at the thought of supersonic

shock waves hammering at the fragile geology of the canyon. Uhlig nodded.

"Yeah. Grab your baggage—"

"What baggage?" Morley said. "What our escorts are carrying is theirs."

"So come aboard Eden-clad, for all I care," Uhlig said. "But come aboard, and strap in the minute you get to your cabin. We want to be too fast for missile lock-on before we show up on anybody's radar."

Franke's naval training let him do the required mental calculations before they reached their cabin, which made the shelter look like a dance hall. Depending on the angle of climb, *Powell* might be reaching orbital velocity before it hit the Victorian stratosphere.

Somebody was in a hurry to have them on Linak'h, where they might be useful. Or at least off Victoria, where they had become useless and might become embarrassing.

Aboard R.M.S. *Somtow Nosavan*, in the Peregrine system:

"We are showing a disk on Peregrine. Repeat, we are showing a disk on Peregrine."

Longman grunted an acknowledgment. He was standing the Bridge watch alone except for Emt Desdai, since one of the last-minute crew additions was standing a hands-on watch in the Engineering spaces. (He and Jo didn't like them on duty alone, but couldn't juggle watch billets too much without it looking suspicious.)

There was always some amateur astronomer in every ship's crew, and the only way to keep him away from the Nav telescope when it wasn't in use was to heave him out an airlock. This stargazer at least was human—although was it really right to assume that the humans would be on the side of the angels (or at least the captain) when it came down hard?

Probably not, but Longman now knew the dangers of agitating himself into adrenaline depletion through worrying over decisions long since irrevocably made. Jo had taught him quite a lot besides sexual positions.

Humans assumed neutral unless clearly working with the Merishi—and hard to tell if they were. The one Ptercha'a—Emt Desdai—on their side (or they were most likely all in deep organics). Merishi basically suspect, except for that old woman and her traveling companion, a young lady who reminded Longman of a Merishi version of Candice Shores. (Big, muscular, graceful moves, and as far as he could judge Merishi standards, handsome.)

"Do you want me to relay the telescope image to the Bridge?" the stargazer asked.

Longman grunted again, this time something he hoped would be taken for "Yes." Why not indulge his curiosity? If Peregrine was just showing a disk on the ship's telescope, *Nosavan* was still invisible except by nonvisual means, and Peregrine wouldn't have much of those.

It was a nice planet, Peregrine, but it was the Hades of a long way from anywhere, and its total human population was still well under a million. It eked out a subsistence economy by acting as a depot and port-of-call for both Merishi and Baernoi, who had major planets closer than any Fed or Alliance human one, and (less formally) by catering to the needs of at least a dozen still more marginal or even outlaw colonies.

So far none of this had drawn the Federation's official notice, let alone official wrath. Things that the beervine was saying about Linak'h, however, suggested that this might be about to change.

Longman hoped that the precipitating incident wouldn't involve *Nosavan,* but knew that hope was all he could do. He and Jo both suspected that the Scaleskins had their ship targeted for something that wouldn't stand close examination, and only hoped it wasn't blowing *Nosavan* out of space the minute she unloaded her cargo.

But there had to be Merishi ships in orbit around Peregrine. They might be scanning deep into space now, with *Nosavan* showing up on their displays like a flare on a dark night—

The irritable whining of the detection alarm made Longman swivel in his chair, cutting off the alarm with one hand and punching on the intercom to Jo's cabin with the other. By the time the link was through, the sensor display was showing a large ship approaching them on an intercept course.

By the time Jo acknowledged, *Nosavan*'s sensor detector registered active scanning by the approaching ship. By the time the captain was on the Bridge and the ship was on Alert One, the approaching ship's drive was interfering with keeping a sensor lock on her.

"Somebody with a heavy hull, to be running that fast with shields down," Marder said. "Citizen Desdai, run a match with that ship's signature. See if we have her in our files."

Desdai was still running the match when the approaching ship came on the radio. *Nosavan* had neither a warship's file of signature data nor the computer speed to retrieve it quickly. They were beyond easy screen distance, but the voice was unmistakable. However fluent he might be in Anglic, the speaker was Merishi.

"Greetings, *Somtow Nosavan.* We are here to speed your unloading."

Longman and Marder looked at each other, for once glad for the lack of visuals. "We are still several hours from Peregrine orbit," Marder said politely. "I hope your assistance is not premature, or offered under the impression that we are in distress."

"Not at all," the reply came blandly. "But it is our plan that your return load will be mostly passengers for Linak'h. Possibly as many as two hundred, although—"

"Two hundred!" If there had been air between the ships, the other might have heard Marder without the radio. Butkus made an elaborate business of poking his ears clear with his little finger, and Longman shot a warning look at Marder. *No time to lose it, Jo.*

"Forgive me," Marder went on, trying to match the Merishi's blandness. "But *Somtow Nosavan* has cabin accommodations for a maximum of forty passengers. I believe that someone has been misinformed on this matter."

"We are acting on full information," the Merishi replied. "You will be provided with passenger modules for your hold, sufficient to accommodate more. In fact, we have four of them aboard now, ready to transship. . . ."

Marder let the Merishi ramble on in a long technical digression that seemed more intended to impress them with his knowledge of Anglic than anything else. However, Longman gave it more attention and began to build a coherent picture from the amount of information the Merishi was revealing.

The approaching ship had four sixty-passenger modules aboard and was prepared to transship and help install them on the way to Peregrine. The lighters in *Nosavan*'s hold took up too much space? Easily remedied. The Merishi could take them and their loads aboard and proceed directly to Peregrine, while *Nosavan*'s people finished installing the modules. This would diminish *Nosavan*'s profits? The charterers had already approved, and if there was any doubt, a trade would be acceptable. *Nosavan*'s crew could install the modules themselves, and that would be payment enough for hauling the lighters.

"Tell him yes," Longman whispered to Marder.

"Why?"

"I want a good long look at those people pods, without anybody from our visitor peering over my shoulder. They're sure to be Space Security, some of them at least."

Marder's mouth opened, then shut again. Longman could see that her calculations had brought her to the same point as himself. Nobody put a high-powered drive, a heavy hull, and sophisticated cargo-handling equipment into a ship intended to make a profit in the merchant service. *Nobody*.

What they had coming at them was a Space Security auxiliary ship, at least—and those ships not only had regular Security crews, they were usually armed. The Merishi had invested quite a lot in this ship, and then sent her to a miscreated back-of-beyond planet like Peregrine.

It didn't add up. Or rather, it added up to even more reason to be paranoid.

Linak'h:

Rahbad Sarlin awoke at the knock on his door.

It was Brokeh su-Irzim, with a sheaf of messages held between thumb and midfinger, rather as one might hold a dead and decayed skrin on the way to the garbage bin.

"Our comrade has met with the Scaleskin's Service of Justice representative," Sarlin said, after reading the message. "He seems to take a great many words to—"

"Read it again."

Sarlin did not like su-Irzim's tone, but obeyed. "Lord Most Holy!"

"Yes. Apparently the—humans—are presently being claimed by the Coordination of Linak'h. The Furfolk accuse them of crimes against the peace and unity of the planet."

"The peace and *unity*?"

"Do not blame me if the Ptercha'a cannot read a map."

"I wish it was only that."

Su-Irzim seemed to want an explanation, but Sarlin's string of curses came out first. The Inquirer waited with elaborate patience until the Special Projects commander had exhausted his breath.

"Behdan Zeg is three days out, and about to leap into the middle of this like the Great Khudr into the midst of his father's betrayers."

"I wish he might have the same effect on our enemies."

"Do not waste your prayers for that. Rather, thank the Lord of Gifts how he is coming. F'Mita ihr Sular knows this work almost as well as any Fleet commander. If she had charge of the loading of *Perfumed*

Wind, I suspect we will be receiving many things more useful than Behdan Zeg."

He did not add his suspicion, that *Perfumed Wind* and a cargo that would finally leave the mission adequately equipped might well be a bribe to distract them from Behdan Zeg. Sarlin would leave a final judgment until he saw who accompanied Zeg. No reinforcements for the mission were mentioned, but that might reflect security considerations rather than their absence.

Sarlin dismissed su-Irzim as swiftly and politely as he could, followed his own advice about thanks to the Lord of Gifts, and went back to bed.

Sixteen

Linak'h:

Halfway to full dawn, a hundred kloms west of the Braigh'n River.

"Rangers would be perfect for this job," Candice Shores told her team. "But they need the job done today, not perfectly. Let's show them that LI Regulars can do it both ways."

Somebody muttered an indelicate play on the last two words. Shores grinned. After days of frustration and stress followed by days of planning, with the mission off and on and then off again, it was not only on, it was mission day. By full dawn on the Braigh'n, she and her people would be in action—and somebody (she would not call them "Merishi" yet) would be getting a sharp reminder that there was no risk-free way to play games with the Federation.

"All right. We have time for a two-minute backbrief from everybody. Yariv, you're at the end of the alphabet, so you're at the beginning of the brief-back."

The communications sergeant took a deep breath. "Our priorities are first to establish a sensor net on the east bank of the Braigh'n, covering the ten kloms closest to the river; second to detect any hostile heavy weapons in the area; third to draw their fire, permitting their detection and destruction by our aerial or orbital fire support—"

With only sixteen people (this *was* a Ranger-sized mission, but power suits had their uses as force-economizers) the backbriefs took barely half an hour. There was time for a hot cup and a high-energy bite, then a visit to the latrines before suiting up. (Power suits were designed to deal with natural functions on long missions, but were not infallible.)

On the way back from the latrines, Shores met Brigitte Tachin, part of the ground party sent dirtside to support the mission. Nobody was keeping track of who was aboard *Shenandoah;* if a dozen officers and men suddenly vanished from her mess decks, nobody on the ground would know. Nor would they know that the dozen were handpicked veterans of the Victoria dirtside fighting.

" 'Allo, Candy," Tachin said. "We are all keeping our fingers crossed or knocking wood." She tapped her forehead.

"That's the spirit. Sure you don't want to transfer to the Army? The gunners need good people."

"Candy, have you taken lessons from Maddie Bloch in—ah, *seducing* people—into changing their branch of Forces?"

"I admit to keeping bad company."

"Ah, that is the first criticism I have heard of Colonel Nieg. I had thought him a paragon."

"Well, I saw you were getting warm for him, so I had to turn you off somehow."

The Brigitte Tachin of even two years ago would have flushed at that remark. Shores remembered having to keep her rather salty tongue under control, except when she was alone with Elayne Zheng, who sometimes managed to shock *her*.

The Improved Mark II Brigitte Tachin merely made a vulgar gesture. "As long as you don't turn him off you," she said, and trotted off on her business.

The Mark II Tachin might wear stars someday. A pity there was no Mark II Brian Mahoney about whom the same could be said. There was a relationship which might not survive one being a natural admiral and the other a natural commander.

Settle your own affairs first, Candy, then start handing out the advice. Father first, then Nieg—but before either one, the hash of those SOBs across the river. Whoever they are.

Linak'h:

Full dawn on the Braigh'n, and the sound of low-speed engines rolling across the half-klom of dark green water, as a blunt bow clove both the water and the mist hanging over it.

Colonel Davidson stretched his long legs almost to the railing on the foc's'le of the *Old South*. The riverboat's deck vibrated gently, as her aft propellers drove her steadily up the Braigh'n River.

They were making good time, although the reason for this might not help today's mission. The river was as low as anybody could remember it in the last generation, although for a river the size of the Braigh'n that still meant plenty of room for a vessel the size of the *Old South*.

A hundred meters long and twenty wide, she had spent thirty years plying up and down the river, handling bulk cargoes to and from all settlements and passengers and package freight to smaller ones and sometimes isolated steadings. Merishi, Ptercha'a, and human had shared her passenger cabins, and both Ptercha'a and humans served in her crew today.

She could make a good twelve knots against a current like this, which made her an almost stationary target for sophisticated weapons. That of course explained her role as bait. She was not expected to face sophisticated weapons.

Her cargo of goods useful in isolated communities would also be invaluable to the lurkers across the river. They had no sophisticated arsenal—at least not under their direct control. (The same people who had killed the would-be defectors at Marshal Banfi's, Davidson suspected, also controlled the heavy firepower. It would certainly make a ruthless kind of sense.)

So the people ought to come out. Then Candice Shores's LI would drop in behind them, to cut off their retreat, detect and suppress their fire support, and collect as many prisoners as came to hand.

The bait crews would have the main job of taking prisoners, though. One crew on the *Old South*, another on a heavy cargo lifter equipped with an elaborate passive sensor suite and also loaded with a tempting cargo. Both were armed largely with nonlethals, to increase the prisoner count, and aboard the boat, to avoid endangering her civilian crew.

The whole operation was skating along the edge of half a dozen laws and regulations and most if not all of the treaties and revisions governing relations among the Territories on Linak'h. It also risked forcing the Coordination to take a stand—which was not a bad idea, if they were (as Davidson and Banfi at least suspected) canoodling with the backers of the terrs.

But Tanz was like Banfi; neither of them believed

in waiting for either Forces Command or the enemy to control the situation. They would move—and it might be the right move, if it caught the Merishi red-handed backing something far more illegal than any of today's responses.

Davidson decided it was time to stretch his legs. He rose and walked aft, skirting the hatches that had already gouged his shins three times. No running aboard the *Old South,* but three or four laps around her obstacle-course deck was a good unkinker for legs, aside from the risk of slipping on the decorative planking (and what explained that, other than men who floated on the water when they could fly over it being inherently mad?).

It would also help the mission's cover. If one of the prime targets of the opposition was spotted from the bank (where unseen eyes had to be watching) blithely walking the decks, the word might reach key leaders.

It also might reach a sniper with orders to put key Federation officers down without ceremony, delay, or warning. But that was a soldier's chance Davidson was taking.

Like fighters since the days of caveman raids, he spent a few of the prebattle moments wondering if he'd said the right thing when he said his goodbyes. He'd nearly said a proper (or as the Wee Free Kirkers would call it, improper) farewell to Olga, but the brooding presence of Marshal Banfi inhibited both of them.

Banfi had the dead from his party on his mind, no doubt about that. It hadn't paralyzed him, but his habit of going off into a brown study and then coming out of it with a long monologue had increased.

Most of the time, he talked about his wars. Most of the time he talked about them, he talked about the times he'd led combined Ptercha'a and human forces, sometimes against entirely human forces and almost always successfully. (It was a tribute to the human tolerance for the Ptercha'a that Banfi had received his baton in spite of this. So was the number of humans in the Territory, living confidently and more or less happily under Ptercha'a notions of law and justice. Davidson and Banfi both prayed that nothing would come of this crisis to alter that.)

Banfi. An old man rambling, or an old soldier recalling experience that might apply to new wars? Davidson hoped it was the second. He also hoped Linak'h Command and Carlos Rubirosa would recognize it if it was.

He finished his fourth turn around the decks and decided to go below for a cup of tea. Breakfast was long since over and the galley closed, but the second cook was one of his people, a Ptercha'a security guard who'd been briefed, then sequestered five days ago. (His human opposite number had not been briefed, but he had been sequestered. He would stay that way, in more comfort and much less danger than his replacement, until the mission was completed.)

The horn blatted, a gross noise like a giant with some intestinal disorder. Signaling for the turn coming up, no doubt. With the water low, a sandspit ran a hundred meters out into the river. The *Old South* would have to pass barely fifty meters away, to stay in the deep channel.

Then from the bank, where it had been screened by the sandspit, half a dozen skateboats darted. At the same time the bushes along the bank spewed running figures, some dashing onto the sandspit, others stopping and setting up what looked like heavy weapons.

Davidson didn't need the horn sounding again, the

alarm screaming, the signal rockets, or the shouts from both sides to know that the trap was sprung. He needed and had a few seconds to get flat on the deck on the port side, before a sleet of rifle rounds whistled overhead.

Linak'h:

"Arapaho, Arapaho, Arapaho!"

The code word for the riverboat being under attack seemed to echo in Candice Shores's ears. She checked her suit displays, gave the lifter pilot a thumbs-up, then switched to the command frequency.

"Heads up, people!"

As the ground dropped away, she heard:

"Beastmaster to Huntress. Confirm liftoff?"

"This is Huntress. We're on the way. Your status?"

"Beastmaster" was Nieg, aboard the big lifter that was the other bait. He and Davidson were both risking major intelligence coups for the other side to sweeten the bait. Nieg also knew that he would have the best possible real-time intelligence from the sensor suite aboard the lifter.

Eight lifters wobbled out of the clearing. Four could have carried the armored LI people, but with no margin for ECM gear, self-defense weaponry, or the rest of what would be needed. They had moved from the base to an isolated clearing less than thirty kloms from the river, flying just above the treetops on evasive routing and (everyone hoped) remaining undetected.

At least there'd be no detectable sensor scanning, even with all the detectors tuned for maximum sensitivity. But the Mark I Eyeball attached to a clear head and that head equipped with a radio was still one of

the most formidable sensors of all. Fifty kloms upstream and three thousand meters above Shore's altitude, Nieg would certainly be listening for any radio
signals from along the lifters' route.

The lifters were running at maximum power, which
with this load would shorten their range. That didn't
matter; they didn't have to go far, and an attacker
was dedicated to drop down and recharge any with
critical problems.

Shores wished they'd been going in by attackers
themselves. But an actual overflight by even two attackers had been vetoed; Rubirosa said it was "too
provocative." It was lifters or nothing for the LI, and
in the end they decided lifters were much better than
nothing.

Shores watched the distance registering, and asked
for a slight course change. "Eighty will bring us in
right over the fight. Try seventy-eight."

"Can do." The lifter pilots seemed to be enjoying
working with a better grade of LI than Linak'h Command had provided until now. Or maybe it was their
being handpicked for the mission, and intensively
trained after being picked.

The whole mission had been set up on extremely
short notice, using available assets and praying that
the opponent's unwillingness to believe that the Federation would do this would substitute for inevitably
leaky security. It was a gamble, of a sort that you
could only justify by success, and now that they were
committed Shores knew that all she and the other fifteen LI could do was succeed or die trying.

Ten kilometers to the river. Eight. Five, four, three,
two—

They shot out over the water, and at the same time
began climbing. The lifters were carrying solid-fuel

boosters for extra vertical acceleration, and the G-loads rapidly mounted.

Shores saw the landscape spreading out below, with the river winding through it, the trees and double shadows blurring its banks. A patch of mist and a boat aground—no, that was the battle around the *Old South*—altitude two thousand two hundred meters, pulling seven Gs—

"Coming up on the drop point—"

"Beastmaster to Huntress—good luck!"

The flight of lifters split into two, each subflight with two LI carriers and two supporters. The supporters began launching their decoys, turning up their jammers—Shores winced as radio communication blanked out with an ear-torturing howl. Smoke trails and flare bursts blanked out the landscape nearly as thoroughly.

"Go, go, go!"

The lifters reared up on their tails. The rear hatches opened. Gravity did the rest.

Candice Shores and the other three aboard her lifter fell out into the smoky sky. Then she took a position check, did a visual orientation, and fired her rocket pack.

In the sky around her, fifteen other smoke trails ignited as the other LI did the same. They soared above the scattering lifter flight, above the layer of smoke left by the flares, decoys, and other countermeasures, into the sky of Linak'h.

Shores recalled the classic remark about rocket-riding a power suit:

"I'd give up sex for life to do this once a week."

If the ancient gods had ever existed, they must have felt like this as they flew over the earth.

Then more smoke rose from the earth below—trails crossing the trees, and bursts along the riverbank.

A clamor on the radio, cutting through the jamming, all variations of "What the Hades—?" but not all in Anglic.

Shores took a reading on the largest source of the smoke trails, double-checked the position, and sent it both to her people and to Nieg.

Or rather, she tried to send it. Somebody else was jamming now, as hard as the lifters. And something was trailing smoke up from the forest, heading toward the lifters, ignoring all the countermeasures—

Warning came too late. The lifter blew apart in mid-air as the missile detonated its remaining ammunition. A second lifter flipped like a playing card from the shock wave, tumbled out of control for a thousand meters, and regained stability just above the river.

"Hot pursuit," it seemed, was going to be hotter than anybody had reckoned on. Who had trapped whom seemed to be in question too.

But the mission of LI was and always had been to engage enemy heavy weapons, C-cubed centers, and transport. The more of that the bad guys had brought up, and the more they used it, no matter on whom, the more targets.

"Huntress to Archer Team—power dive. Stop at five hundred meters."

A dive with the rocket packs thrusting rather than braking was the hairiest of all LI maneuvers. Anything else would leave her team falling free, even at terminal velocity vulnerable targets for more missiles, lasers, or even ground marksmen.

Shores saw her teammates flip over and dive. More missiles came up, but the smoke seemed to be baffling lasers. The sudden dive baffled the missiles; their onboard guidance apparently couldn't track targets the size of power suits or was suffering from the saturation jamming, and the smoke baffled eyeball aiming from the ground.

The missiles swerved and went chasing off after the retreating lifters. More smoke trails smeared the sky. Then more explosions erupted—not the missiles catching the lifters this time, but the backup attackers coming into laser range. From well inside the Federation Territory, the attackers could still reach out with their lasers to pop missiles silhouetted against the sky.

Shores murmured thanks, not caring if it got through the jamming. She had one more job before she could ride her own pack down to join her team. Fix the position of the enemy heavy weapons—it looked like mostly rocket launchers, for now—and give that position to her teammates.

They weren't carrying the heaviest LI weapons load to improve their looks.

Linak'h:

"*Liebchen*, listen."

Oleg Govorov was always ready to listen to his wife. Or almost always. Not now. He was trying to translate the line of her thigh into the line he wanted on Diana the Huntress—

"Oleg!"

"Don't break the pose. I can't—"

Ursula stamped over to him and snatched the applicator from his hand. He raised one hand to protect his face, and waved the other, not quite sure what to do with it. Ursula certainly looked angry enough to slap him, with the children in their rooms as they were supposed to be when she was posing nude.

"What is it, Ursul?"

"Can't you hear?"

He listened, and heard a noise like ripping fiber-cloth somewhere off to the west. Not too far, either—but he didn't see any clouds that could have brought that kind of weather.

"Yes. What is it?"

"A battle! I knew I should have warned the—"

"Not so loud, Ursula. The children."

"The children, the children, the children! If they don't know what the Federation is by now, they're too witless to be yours!" Her hand flew to her mouth. "Oh, *Gott,* forgive me, Oleg—"

He hugged her. "All right, Ursl. You have a point. It must be the Merishi trying to stop the refugees from crossing the river. Or maybe the Federation is trying to help the refugees. I heard rumors that they were going to do something like that."

"You *heard*?" For a moment he thought Ursula would faint.

"Oh, Healer Kinkuhn was by two nights ago. He said that the refugees were only going to feint an attack, and then surrender. Is that the right term—'feint'?"

"Why didn't you tell me?" She looked as if she wanted to scream and then slap him.

"Because then you would have argued with me about sending it to the Federation. The Merishi would not have stopped because the Federation knew. They would just have come for us, along with the refugees."

It was the old argument, even if today might take it to new heights. She was the orphaned daughter of parents who had ridden the Merishi star trail from an outlaw colony beyond Peregrine, because it was that or die on the world they could not call home. She wanted to push his neutrality to the limit, or even break it in favor of the Federation.

He did not. He resisted her with all the force he should have used on Catherine Shores, and if he had he might still be able to hold his Candy in his arms—

No. That picture of her in the week-old mediaprint reminded him that she was a grown woman now. Tough, too, like her mother—and had it only been soldiering that made her that way?

"Very well," Ursula said. "I admit that as long as we stay here, we cannot risk the children. But why must we stay here?"

"Examine your conscience, Ursula, and think of who else could do as well what we are doing here. With help from Kinkunh, I admit, and others too. But they need us."

"And I need you, and you need me," Ursula said, trying to pout but ending with a smile. "You would never keep the radio working, you would burn the food, you would be seduced by all your models and have angry fathers and husbands chasing you through the forest—"

"What do you think I am, a satyr?"

"When you look at me that way—"

"When you look that way—"

She patted his cheek. "Very well, *Liebchen*, let me get us some beer, then we can go back to being fuzzy and artistic. The Federation certainly knows everything they need to by now, that is certain."

Linak'h:

Colonel Davidson had nothing but his sidearm for long enough to become nervous. However, with nothing that would let him hit back he had time to observe the attack more closely. This occupied his mind, which helped the nerves.

The skateboats swung wide around *South*'s bow, making a ninety-degree turn in a ragged formation. They bounced over each other's wakes, and one rider lost his grip on the controls. His boat went one way, he went another, both vanished in clouds of spray, and another skateboat ran over the upturned hull of the first. The second didn't overturn or spill its rider, but came to an abrupt stop as its power died. Its rider was the first casualty, as a sniper posted in the port wing of the bridge picked him off.

The rest of the skateboat riders opened a ragged fire, mostly aimed backward over their shoulders. Davidson found that his safe place on the port side was suddenly highly unsafe, or would have been if the riders had been aiming. Their fire was not only ragged, it was uniformly high. If they were going to hit anything, it was likely to be their comrades to starboard of *South*.

The skateboats raced for the west bank of the Braigh'n as Davidson shifted position. Somebody crawled up to him with a carbine; he took it without seeing who, checked the magazine, and searched for a target.

The skateboats offered none. They drifted untended in the current, as their riders waded ashore and vanished into the undergrowth. Davidson rolled to free his belt comp and called the bridge, to warn them of the river-crossers. The boat's main radio could then pass on the warning to the reserve lifters, ready to drop automatic sensors in a semicircle around any bridgehead and follow up the sensor drop with troops.

The colonel was so busy studying the weapons of

the skateboat riders (he wanted to spot any portable AD missiles) that it was a while before he realized that the attack on the starboard side was remarkably quiet. His first thought was treachery—his people overpowered by *South*'s crew in Merishi or Coordination pay!

Then he thought he ought to eyeball the situation before panicking about it. He low-crawled across the deck, to find himself practically face to face with a woman in a faded and sodden coverall, crawling over the railing. Her weapon, an ordinary sporting rifle, was still slung, and the knife on her belt was still snapped into its sheath.

Davidson looked past the woman, without moving his carbine muzzle. All along the bank, people in light (almost featherweight) infantry combat gear were pouring out of cover. There had to be at least a hundred, few of them firing and most of those aiming toward the flanks rather than the boat. Davidson saw one man aiming at the bridge knocked down into the water by a man and a woman, who disarmed him, then held his head underwater until he went limp.

The defense team aboard *South* had already reached the same conclusion as Davidson: this was another mass defection. Today there were no commissars with gunships to shoot down the defectors, and few of them were making a serious attempt to fight before they gave themselves up. The defenders were mostly lined up along the starboard side, with snipers keeping an eye on the trees.

Except for the snipers, they were also making good targets of themselves. The sudden transformation of a suicidal charge into a mass surrender could confuse even good troops, but not everybody from the bank might be coming over tamely—

The warning Davidson had been ready to shout

came from elsewhere. A sniper fired three times from the bank. The woman Davidson had faced threw up her hands and plummeted into the river. Three or four of her comrades still standing waist-deep whirled and raked the bushes with fire.

Then from astern, and from *both* banks, SSWs slammed solid rounds into the fugitive soldiers. They either had no armor or had removed it for ease in swimming. The solid rounds penetrated even torsos, and blood mixed with spray.

The *Old South*'s own SSW went into action from the stern, mixing grenades and slugs. On the bow, the launcher crew locked, loaded, and elevated their tube, and started pumping out 100mm rounds loaded with 22mm submunitions on ranges called in from the bridge.

The SSW fire slackened, but there were too many bodies floating and too many wounded thrashing and screaming in a river turning from green to red. The lucky fugitives found helping hands at the *Old South*'s railings. The boat wasn't under fire yet, and with no targets the defender had the sense not to shoot wildly into the trees.

The unlucky ones floundered back to the bank. The unluckiest made it all the way into the tree line, just before the sky split apart and a rocket barrage descended.

At least it seemed to be mostly rockets, some standard HE or frag warheads, some with clustered submunitions. The smoke, flames, and crash of explosions and falling trees made Davidson fearfully aware of how noisy a battlefield could be. Energy weapons, electronics, and silent, sneaky kills by Rangers or their like on the ground hadn't eliminated things that banged, whizzed, or crashed, using technology that would have been comprehensible to Napoleon or Rommel.

The rockets were coming in at a rate that suggested

to Davidson lifters equipped with rotary launchers and large-capacity magazines. Not the sort of thing guerrilla bands or even the Ptercha'a militia the Merishi allowed were likely to carry around.

Davidson reached that conclusion as he reached the bridge. Hoberman, the sergeant and Victoria veteran leading boat's LI squad, waved a greeting.

"We're on the horn to both the ground and air CPs," he said. "That SSW on the west bank is in Fed territory, so even if none of the rockets cross the river—"

At that moment conversation went from difficult to impossible. Rockets, lifters, decoys, AD missiles, and what looked like Candice Shores's people in their suits suddenly filled the sky, both to the naked eye and on the sensor display. Half a score of different kinds and colors of fireballs, smoke clouds, and smoke trails joined the general chaos. It made any All-Union Tattoo look pathetic.

In all the uproar, Davidson became aware that Hoberman was looking to him for orders. "Permission to shut down transmitting for a bit, sir? We're getting some high-powered jamming. If the bad guys can jam that hard they can listen too."

Davidson nodded, saving his voice for some time in the next millennium when he wouldn't have to scream over this din. The Federation—using the term loosely—still had a number of unpleasant surprises in store for the opposition, if they could remain surprises.

Linak'h:

Candice Shores didn't jet down. She'd used up too much of her rocket pack in a high-altitude hover, collecting and transmitting target data. At least she hoped she'd transmitted it; the jamming was getting both heavy and sophisticated.

If the teams were safe on the ground with the data, the jamming wouldn't matter. At this point even fully armored LI went over to visual targeting as much as possible, which it would be today from ground level. Smoke here and there, and trees everywhere, but anyone who got a clear sight line to a rocket launcher could hit it.

Clear sight lines worked both ways, as a climbing missile abruptly reminded Shores. She tried to launch a decoy, discovered that she'd used up her supply, and activated the "Disconnect" and "Time Fuse" commands on her rocket pack. It soared up as she dropped, then exploded. The missile chased one of the fragments and exploded on a proximity detonation that totally erased the fragment and buffeted Shores with shock wave and debris. Smoke swirled around her; for a moment she was disoriented and she was afraid vertigo and then a tumble would be next.

She closed her eyes, relying on the inner-ear stability that hadn't let her down since her first soccer game. It came through; when she opened her eyes she was in the dereve position, plummeting through the smoke-fogged sky, already passing a thousand meters. The forest below was turning from a green carpet into an array of individual trees, with lightly thatched upswellings of ground here and there.

Shores called up a position display, and decided that she really did see four coherent sets of position indicators, indicating that the four squads were on the ground. No way to learn more, not with the jamming or without popping her chute early and making herself an easy target. She'd be down into the trajectory of those enemy rockets soon, if she wasn't already, and friendly fire would be coming the other way just as soon, if *it* wasn't already.

At five hundred meters Shores decided it was chute time. The parawing deployed smoothly, easing her from terminal velocity into a controlled descent toward the best available piece of clear ground. It was at least a klom from anything she remembered as an enemy position; half that from one of her squads. It would have to do.

Time for a weapons check. Eye-in-the-sky time was over, or at least the job was now over to somebody else (Beastmaster, likely enough). Now she could get to the down-and-dirty, and make this a bad day for those rocket rattlers.

Seventeen

Aboard R.M.S. *Somtow Nosavan*,
the Peregrine system:

Four days, seventeen hours, twenty-six minutes out of
Peregrine—Joanna Marder wasn't counting the seconds. Less than four hours to Jump—and thank the
Creator that Linak'h was only one Jump. She shuddered at the thought of *Nosavan* spending hours in
some uninhabited system or extrasystemic patch of
space, setting up for another Jump, while plots rip-
ened aboard her.

She wasn't entirely happy at the thought of returning to Linak'h, either. She would have preferred
someplace that was close to the Navy and far from all
Merishi. But if she couldn't have just the first, she'd
take a place that had both. Besides, if the whole idea
of somebody having nefarious schemes for *Nosavan*
wasn't her imagination and Charlie's, then shifting the
Jump destination might trigger the bad guys' move.

She stretched, wishing that the command chair was
a bed, and not necessarily one shared with Charlie.
She had reached an intermediate stage of adrenaline
depletion. She wondered if the real plot of their enemies was to wait until she and Charlie had reached

an acute stage. Then there was Emt Desdai—and did Ptercha'a suffer from adrenaline depletion?

She decided to call up material on Ptercha'a physiology. It would focus her mind on something else besides danger vs. no danger, and all the calculations for the Jump were made anyway. Made, stored, and being updated automatically as the telescope (now slaved to the computer, and stargazers *hands off*) recorded benchmarks—

The Bridge door chime sounded. Charlie jumped half a meter but didn't take his eyes off the Engineering board. She nodded to him.

"On screen, please. We are approaching our Jump point," he said.

The screen lit up as the visitors stepped into range of it. One of the Merishi, one of the Engineering humans, and Boatswain Butkus.

"Excuse me, gentlemen," Longman said. "Passengers are not allowed on the Bridge except in planetary orbit. We are—"

Butkus made a slow turn. Now they could see the wristlocks on him. Also the plastic scattergun the human was holding on him, and the large-bore slugthrower in the Merishi's belt.

"You are not wishing that harm come to Mr. Butkus," the Merishi said. His Anglic was accented but intelligible. Was the formality of manner due to the alien language, etiquette, or a military background?

Jo, don't be absurd. Her conscience no longer spoke in Paul Leray's voice, which made it easier to listen to.

She looked at Charlie. They'd agreed about not letting each other be used as hostages. But the boatswain was an innocent bystander—probably as innocent as the 196 Peregrine passengers ("the Peregrinations," Charlie called them) in the people pods.

No point in risking him until we've got a clearer picture, Marder thought. She tried to signal this to Charlie with eyes and hands. He nodded absently. Most of his attention seemed to be on his displays.

As far as she could read them, Engineering was now under local control, from the Aft Sphere. Charlie's board wasn't worth its weight in used tea leaves, and Emt Desdai was nowhere to be seen.

Marder refused to contemplate the possibility of his being dead or treacherous. The situation was depressing enough as it was.

She signaled the tech on the computer panel to keep his hands still and in sight, and hit the switch for opening the Bridge door.

Linuk'h:

Candice Shores took three jumps to cover the distance to a stream, cutting the last jump short when she saw that it would take her into a meadow. She could have covered the distance in a single jump, and been a slow-moving target above the treetops while she did.

A lot of people still had the image of LI or Rangers in power suits striding godlike across the landscape in long lines, sweeping all before them. People like her, who had spent many hours in intimate (there was no other term) relations with the suits, had other notions.

The purpose of suits was not to create a target-rich environment for the other side. It was to find where the other side offered such environments, mark them, and stand back while less vulnerable or more potent systems came down hard. It was the venerable quartet of find, fix, fight, and finish, but with LI's main job the first two.

Both electronic and eyeball data showed the other three people in her squad also on the edge of the meadow. She did an all-frequencies scan, hoping if nothing else to learn more about the jamming.

All she heard was squeals and static. Captain Liddell had been much more imaginative after *Shen* nuked the terrs' HQ on Victoria. *She* had played "A Life on the Ocean Wave" to swamp everybody else's talktalk.

Now for an audio check. Shores turned the suit's external pickups to maximum gain, and for almost thirty seconds distant explosions and rocket screeches didn't drown out natural sounds like wind, water, and trees rustling. Not necessarily good news, that—if the reserves had crossed the river in force, there'd be more noise.

Probably "political factors" (better known as "Governor-General Rubirosa getting cold feet") had intervened, and she and her people were going to have to reach the pickup point on their own. Not impossible, just unreasonable and dangerous, about what—

"Lifters approaching!"

They had come in so low over the trees that the LI had no way of detecting them until they were in hearing. At slow speed, that was just before they came in sight, to flare for a landing.

That slow speed also made them beautiful targets. Shores's mental prayer was that someone in one of the lifters would panic and open fire, proving that they were the other side. The lifters were Merishi design, but that didn't provide the evidence she would need at her court-martial if she massacred friendlies.

Then somebody popped a hatch, stood silhouetted

in it for long enough to prove that he was Merishi, and jumped to the ground. As he landed he must have seen one of the suits. His eyes grew as round as a Merishi's could, and he leaped wildly, missing by several meters the skids of a lifter whose pilot had also seen lurking enemies and was climbing out as fast as he could.

Then two other lifters also started climbing, but from sideports Merishi slugthrowers laid down bursts. All four LI opened up at once.

Shores had only five rounds left in the integral launcher, and took out both fans on the near side of the middle lifter with them. She unslung the SSW, checked the magazine, and chopped turf to one side of the grounded Merishi. LI orders were to avoid causing personnel casualties if possible, but destroy equipment and supplies to prevent interference with the defectors, fugitives, refugees, or whatever else you wanted to call them.

Four LI against three armed lifters could not be bloodless, however. The Merishi on the ground took Shores's hint and ran across the meadow toward the stream. One of the lifters lurched away in the same direction, ceasing fire. But Shores's target could no longer steer, and from the open side door of the other lifter somebody shot fast and furiously.

A severed branch clanged off Shores's helmet, making her ears ring and overloading the audio pickup so that it went temporarily dead. Then one of her squadmates put a grenade into the open lifter door, and the sky split apart.

Shores found herself slammed back against a tree so hard that her head hit the inside of her helmet. Padding and harness prevented concussion or fracture, but not moments of confusion. She saw dimly fragments of lifter spray the landscape, with big ones hitting hard enough to chop down trees. She saw the other lifter flipped completely over and slammed to the ground before the pilot could regain control.

The Merishi in it were tough, though. Three of them came out, not fighting but in shape to carry a fourth. A fifth hobbled along after the other until one of them noticed him, turned back, and half-dragged, half-carried him out of sight. A curl of foam in the stream Shores thought must be the first Merishi on the ground, swimming for his life.

He was welcome to it. Another branch had cracked across her left knee, and the joint didn't feel completely reliable. The servos whined and whimpered when she put her weight on it, but the joint didn't give or lock up. Good news, balanced by the fact that the same branch had also bent her SSW hopelessly out of firing shape.

Then she heard, "Alpha Three to Huntress. Come in, Huntress. Alpha Two's down. We're cutting him out of his suit now."

Shores slapped her metal thigh. LI armor had built-in diagnostic and first-aid equipment that made it almost as good as a walk-in roboclinic. If they were taking Yariv—Alpha Two—out of his suit, either the suit was completely wrecked or he needed more help than it could give—which was probably the result of damage to the suit.

Every LI leader's nightmare: a small, isolated team in hostile territory, with somebody so badly hurt they had to ditch his/her suit. That meant a carry—LI didn't leave wounded or dead behind, and not even suits if they had a choice.

This time they had no choice about the suit. "How

is he?" Shores asked, as she angled through the brush toward the others.

"Not great. How far to the pickup point?"

"Six two." Six point two kloms to the coordinates they'd been given, at any rate. If the assigned pickup lifters hadn't been among the casualties, or Rubirosa's nerves shot down the whole idea of pickup, or—

To Hades with the possibilities. Stick to certainties, which started with standard tactical formations, as in:

"Three, take point. Four, sling Two as soon as he's stabilized and monitored. I'll take trail and keep a listening watch. As soon as we've cleared this area, I'll call in the clans."

This would put all four teams on the march, general direction north. Toward pickup, away from the Merishi forces they'd perhaps mauled enough to give them pause, and out from under any supporting fires that might be on the way in spite of the Governor-General or other malign influences.

Aboard R.M.S. *Somtow Nosavan*, the Peregrine system:

The two hijackers said nothing for the first ten minutes after they entered the Bridge. If this was *Nervenkrieg,* Marder decided that it was not wholly unsuccessful. The tech at least was openly sweating, and Marder felt even sorrier for the man than she did for Butkus.

Being the center of the hijackers' attention had a perverse sort of dignity. But sitting to one side, with as much control over your fate as a mushroom in a cave, had none.

After doing an imitation of a temple image for another few minutes, the Merishi finally spoke. "We have control of both the Bridge and the engines now, do we not?" He was addressing his human colleague.

"Yes. Unless somebody does something crazy." The man displayed his scattergun to emphasize how futile that would be.

As he did, he turned so that his body shielded Butkus's back from the Merishi's view. Marder thought she saw him move after that, and even some movement of Butkus's head. Her mind screamed at her body not to show that she'd noticed anything, but she'd imagined it all, and that hope was as crazy as action.

The body listened; it slumped into the command chair as if satiated or completely drained of adrenaline. *Which would not be an act in another few minutes.*

If they were alive that long. She wondered if the ship was going to be redirected or destroyed. The odds, she decided, were in favor of destruction. The Merishi weren't idiots; they had to know how many suspicions they'd aroused already, with the visit to Peregrine topping things off. The time and money they'd thrown away to speed up the unloading of the cargo and the loading of the passengers—the *condemned* passengers—not to mention the expensive equipment their Navy had provided—

Nosavan was dead, but some of her people still hadn't lain down yet. For the sake of the 196 below— the Merishi's primary targets—she and Charlie would have to take the faintest chance of changing the outcome.

What the Hades! All she could lose was her life.

Then the technician sat up straight. Something had changed, in the pattern of lights on his console. The screen over the door was wavering, too. The Merishi noticed the reactions and set his back firmly against the most solid bulkhead he could find.

"What is going on?" he said. The muzzle of his weapon swung toward the tech. "You are the most frightened. I think you will tell me first."

The muzzle steadied on the tech, who was bathed in sweat and looked incapable of saying a coherent word. The muzzle was also now completely turned away from either Butkus or the human hijacker.

The Merishi's eyes were good, his reflexes not quite good enough. Butkus came at him from one side, the wristlock swinging from one hand, while the human tried to get a shot from the other side. The Merishi got off two shots before Butkus's hundred kilos slammed into him. Then Butkus had one hand around the Merishi's thick wrist, and the other trying to get a similar grip on the other arm.

The Merishi had a backup weapon somewhere. That was obvious. Just as obvious was the fact that the human had switched sides, and was trying to get a safe shot at his former leader. Marder decided it was time to risk intervention herself. She was stronger and possibly faster than Charlie, even if he was unhurt—and where the Hades had the two rounds gone anyway?

She came out of the command chair with a gymnast's leap and roll that she knew she could barely have managed as a teenager. Adrenaline or sheer desperation, whichever it was—wonderful things.

She crashed into the tangled pair, human and Merishi, and Butkus gasped something obscene and complimentary. She punched the Merishi hard in the groin—the sexual anatomy of the two races was sufficiently similar to make this a useful point of attack. Her free hand groped up and down the thick legs, finally coming to a pouch with something even more solid than scale-sheathed muscle inside it.

She didn't know how to use the weapon she found—it looked like a miniature cricket bat with a light bulb running the length of the flat end—but it was so heavy that she didn't need to. It made a good club, and the Merishi made a solid thump when he sprawled facedown on the deck.

He was not quite unconscious, so Butkus efficiently used the wristlock on him. It was a tight fit on the Merishi's thicker wrists, but nobody seemed terribly concerned for the hijacker's comfort.

Then Marder needed to hold on to her chair to go on standing. She even closed her eyes briefly, which was asking a lot of the human hijacker before he'd even explained himself, but if she saw the Bridge waltzing around her for one second longer—

When she opened her eyes, she thought the hallucinations were worse. The human hijacker was squatting on the floor, with his scattergun now in the hands of Emt Desdai, who wore shorts and a broad grin. His tail, however, was fluffed up, a sure sign of recent anger or sexual arousal in a Ptercha'a. Somehow, Marder doubted that Emt Desdai had found a sexual partner.

"I'm sorry I had to go along with them until now," the hijacker began urgently. "I couldn't even talk to the other two, once I overheard what they were going to do. They're going to rig the ship to blow, after they're taken off by a Merishi ship."

Longman nodded. "Somebody's fiddling with the matter/antimatter feed controls. I can read that much, even though I can't override."

"Forgive my failure—" Desdai began, but Longman waved him to silence. He winced as he waved, and for the first time Marder saw that the left side of his shirt was soaked with blood.

"Oh, one of those nasty little micropellet slugs shattered on the arm of the chair," he said. "Better than the arm of me, or I wouldn't be waving at you. But is there any way we can get down to Engineering Local and clobber those people?"

"If you don't mind me and Butkus doing the job—" the hijacker began.

Marder juggled factors, knowing how little she knew and that she had even less time than she had knowledge. "No. We need Butkus to suit up and keep an eye on the people pods. If the Merishi are after the passengers, they might try to sabotage their life support."

This could no longer be done by remote control; Emt Desdai's cutouts should have taken care of that. But if the remaining hijackers had numbers and nerve, one of them could suit up, climb into the holds, and dispose of 196 human beings (Creator, save the babies!) with a beltful of demo charges or a few twists on key valves.

Butkus was big, tough, had plenty of suit time, and was a qualified marksman. He was also more trustworthy out of her sight than the hijacker. Not as trustworthy as Charlie, but Charlie was in no shape to suit up and go climbing around the holds.

Marder stood up. "Citizen Desdai, take your old post."

"Yes, Ship Leader." He bared his teeth at the tech, who slid out of the chair in a faint. "The *z'dok*!"

It said a lot about Butkus, that he didn't raise an eyebrow at a "Catman" calling a human that.

"How many are there down aft?"

"One of the Folk is here. Another is disabled. I do

not know if I killed him. A third is trapped in his cabin, like the rest of the passengers.

"The two humans and the last of the Folk are at Engineering Local. Also, they have with them the *k'rrint* of the Folk leader. You know her, the large companion to the old woman?"

The word implied a sexual relationship contrary to law, custom, taboo, good taste, and the advice of all the partners' friends. It was vaguely consoling to know that sexual folly knew no bounds of species.

Then Longman stood up. "Jo, slap a sealer on my ribs and keep an eye on the Jump board. Emt, before you sit down, can you go and use this"—he held out a multitool—"on the left rear corner panel in the Bridge head?"

"Charlie—"

"Jo—Captain, ma'am. We don't have time to argue. I can't take this ship through the Jump if Helpful Harry here changes sides again. You can, as long as I give you back the engines."

"What should I seek?" Desdai asked. His ears quivered faintly with anticipation. Too bad he couldn't go down to Engineering, but Charlie was right—a Jump-capable team had to be on the Bridge.

"A bag. With a few souvenirs from some Navy friends."

Charlemagne:

The Flag Officers' Club at Forces Command was one of the few social centers in the Federation Forces that had a substantial official maintenance allowance. This was justified on the grounds that it was frequently the location for official receptions, etc., valuable to nonmilitary personnel—at least among the Federation elite.

Since Forces Command also attracted a disproportionate number of flag officers with private incomes, this allowance was almost superfluous. It was still appropriated, however, and some of it was actually used, to give the club extra luxuries.

One of these was a suite of conference rooms of varying sizes. They had every possible convenience, and so much privacy that it was possible to not only deliver a proposition but act on its acceptance without fear of interruption or even being recorded in sound or video.

Kuwahara's dining companion tonight was ineligible for a proposition from him. He was Major General Marcus Langston, a week on duty with the study group and just surfaced after three days' total immersion in its files.

Kuwahara took a medium-strength Scotch from the robot (a full-strength one on an empty stomach usually brought on migraines) and sipped it. Langston did the same with a very weak Briggs Commercial Bourbon and water.

"So. What do you make of this stew we've been told to cook without a recipe?" Kuwahara asked.

"I am reminded that duty is duty," Langston said. He took a somewhat larger sip of his drink.

"Anything else?"

"Do you really want me to speak *ex cathedra* after three days' cursory examination of maybe five percent of the data bearing on the situation? Sorry, you haven't been that sloppy," he added, as he saw Kuwahara frown. "Also, I don't suppose you're in the mood for jokes."

"Not really. I can face premature retirement, but I

don't have to laugh at the ridiculous angle of the dagger sticking out of my back."

"All right. Call it a hunch?"

"Fine. You played some potent—hunches—on Victoria."

"The caliber of the opposition helped," Langston said. He took a healthy swig of his drink. "And I think that's what's going to happen here."

Kuwahara knew a man who was going to go on without prompting when he heard one. He was silent.

"The biggest mistake would be focusing on the Merishi. They're not working up to a break with us unless we alienate the Ptercha'a first. That automatically gives the Merishi ground forces almost as good as ours or the Baernoi's, plus a network of planets in strategically awkward spots. Awkward for us, anyway."

Kuwahara nodded. The estimates of the military potential of the Ptercha'a seemed to need revision upward every two Standard years now. When he joined the Navy, it had been every five years.

"If the Merishi can swing the whole race of Catmen to their side, they automatically become a desirable partner for the Tuskers. Then we face the Big Brawl"—service slang for a coalition of the three space-traveling nonhuman races—"and correspondingly big trouble.

"The Merishi are going to have some problems getting to this happy moment, however. One of them is their own ineptness at large-scale military organization. Sometimes the cultural analysts get one right. I think they did so there, and my feeling is that the Ptercha'a know it even better than our academics."

Considering that the Ptercha'a had several centuries more experience dealing with the Merishi than the human race did, this seemed likely enough. Individually the Merishi were as formidable in war as one could wish. However, they seemed to lack the ability to organize as well for war as they did for trade.

"Another is something I don't think we realize either," Langston said. He took a large swig. "Maybe it's my ancestry talking—even though these days, you need to get very mystical to talk about 'Afroam memory of slavery.' Nonetheless . . .

"The Ptercha'a had the fortune, good or bad, to be contacted from the stars when they were still preindustrial. It's easy to put a culture like that into a sort of stasis that suits your needs.

"It's hard to recognize when the culture starts breaking out of that stasis," Langston added. "Damned hard. I think the first other race to recognize where the Ptercha'a are now, where they want to go—it will be a while before the Catmen call them enemies."

Langston was right. This was not an occasion for jokes. Or if the future relations of three whole sapient races was humorous, then it was the kind of black comedy that only gods with a malicious wit could appreciate.

Being only an admiral, Sho Kuwahara put down his drink. He suddenly preferred to face the evening sober in both mind and body.

Linak'h:

The odometer on Candice Shores's suit registered 6.7 kilometers before they reached the planned pickup. A slight detour to rendezvous with the last squad accounted for the difference.

Of the sixteen dropped LI, they had one KIA (suit ditched and demo'd, body packed by Gamma Two), one wounded out of suit (Alpha Two), and two wounded in suits (Gamma One and Beta Three). No MIA, which made for a pride that Candice Shores could feel radiating from the others and reinforcing her own, and a lot of damage inflicted on Merishi C-cubed, rocket launchers (big rotary ones on lifters), and supply vehicles. (Not so much pride there; they all knew that Merishi parents didn't like getting condolence 'grams any more than human ones, but at least nobody had seen Ptercha'a corpses, let alone made any.)

They also had no pickup. Shores put another kilometer on the odometer beating the bushes, and being beaten by some of the springier ones. She had green smears on the front of her armor to match the black ones on the rear when she came back to report a negative haul of pickup, messages, or anything else.

"Okay. This is not the best news I ever heard, people. However, we can get in that route march we missed on Schneeheim."

The laughter was somewhat hollow, but an all-hands power check made the notion look feasible. Just barely. Shores was tempted to declare an E&E situation, which meant ditching the suits and exfiltrating unpowered, if necessary unclothed, and if possible undetected, but not unarmed.

However, they had four casualties, a body, a man who couldn't walk, and two people who would be slower out of armor than in it. Not to mention that suits were faster if more detectable, and Yariv might not last overnight without medical care.

They'd go out in suits, and in formation, too. Major Merishi forces could find them whether they split up or not, with airborne sensors, and kill them with heavy weapons. Small detachments might be intimidated by fourteen LI suits in battle array, and could be suppressed if they weren't intimidated. (At least once, anyway. Ammunition was a lot shorter than power.)

Shores divided the team into two wings of seven, with one of the suited wounded in each one, took the right wing herself, and led her people north.

Aboard R.M.S. *Somtow Nosavan*, the Peregrine system:

Engineering Local was strictly a backup to Bridge Engineering. Ships the size of *Nosavan* could run with completely unmanned Stern Spheres, and the two watchstanders normal for her were there mostly to visually monitor life-support equipment. That, after all, had most of the moving parts, and if one of them started moving the wrong way it could be fixed without the fixer being reduced to rarefied gas in nanoseconds.

That was a fate that still might overtake him and the whole ship, Longman realized. However, having established that he was expendable, he was determined not to be expended unless necessary, and to have some say as to the necessity.

He would know about the necessity in a few seconds. The hijacker—Longman now knew him as Hank—knocked on the hatch of Engineering Local. Longman stepped forward, so that he was in sight of the peephole—no screen pickup here, although one was scheduled if they had the stellars after the voyage.

"How goes it?" The voice was human, and pleasantly drawling.

"Brought a souvenir."

"So I see. We don't either of us go that way."

"Reinie, be serious. It was splitting them up I was after."

Longman tried to look pitiful, and remembered Marder's warning about not indulging his streak of ham. He held his wristlocked hands at waist height, and took comfort from their invisible looseness and the weight of the bag at his hip.

He would have taken more comfort at Emt Desdai or Butkus at his back. But they both had jobs somewhere else, and Jo at least was safe. He could even go in his pants, both fore and aft, and she wouldn't be here to see it!

The thought almost created the urge, and must have made his appearance incredibly realistic. The hatch popped, then swung open.

Longman waited just long enough to orient himself. The Merishi—Security, he had to be—in a chair. The two hijackers at the console—and the displays showed that yes, they had cut off Engineering Local from the Bridge, but praise Buddha, not started the last lethal step!—and the Merishi woman more or less draped over another chair. She was reading a small viewbook.

Longman decided she didn't remind him nearly as much as before of Candice Shores. He could imagine bouncing with Candy—had imagined it, in delightful if ultimately frustrating detail, several times. He could not imagine her being the bounce-slave of any male (or female, or other organic or electronic entity either).

Why wait? Every second gave Hank more time to change his mind.

"Freeze!" Hank shouted, drawing his scattergun. Everybody froze, including Longman, with his wristlock dangling and one hand reaching for his bag.

The hand popped out with his strictly nonissue snub

pulser at the same time as the Merishi hijacker came out of his chair. He blocked the shot of the two human hijackers, although they were turning and drawing fast.

He didn't block Hank's shot, or his own. The Merishi's shot hit Hank in the stomach. Hank's hit the Merishi in the arm, hurting but not stopping. The Merishi crashed into Longman, whose gouged rib cage and loss of blood slowed his draw.

Instead Longman used knees and fists. Merishi internal organs were deeper inside and cased in a tougher skin; he slowed the Merishi without hurting him. The Merishi gripped Longman's wrist and without serious effort squeezed until the human officer screamed.

At that point Hank fired again. Two scatterslugs ripped up into the Merishi's torso from below, making an appalling mess all over the deck, Hank, and Longman. The Merishi was too dead to care, and a moment later so was Hank.

As the Merishi Security officer died, the Merishi woman flung the view book at one human hijacker. Propelled with all the strength of an arm inherently stronger than a human's, it ruined his face and flung him back against the console. His mate was drawing when Longman shot him—not fatally, but enough to spoil his aim.

That gave the Merishi woman time to jump, wheel, and kick. Her feet were bare, and her nonvestigial claws added to the kinetic energy of the blow did horrendous damage to the other hijacker's groin. Longman had never even imagined such a scream, and finally got rid of his lunch.

The dry-heaving was beginning to hurt his ribs when

the Merishi woman pulled him upright and looked at him. He hoped she was looking at him anxiously.

"Thank you," he said. It seemed inadequate. It also looked as if it was futile. Her reply was a blank stare.

Oh well, you don't need a common language to know when somebody is settling the score for a lack of bedroom manners.

Longman shuddered at the sight of the Merishi hijacker's corpse. He had come close to such a fate a few times himself. Then he looked back at the Merishi woman.

Come to think of it, I can *imagine Candy settling accounts like that.*

He mentally drank a toast to the strong women of all races while he studied the displays. Everything was either giving totally erroneous readings or almost nominal. He ran a two-minute series of diagnostics and was glad to discover that it was the second.

Then he restored control of the engines to the bridge and motioned the Merishi woman out into the passageway. He closed, locked, and double-sealed the hatch, then squeezed a long string of firewad into the hinges, lock, and everywhere else it would penetrate.

The Merishi woman watched the blaze when the firewad blew with open eyes. Longman remembered that Merish had a higher level of illumination than Earth. She also seemed unbothered by the waves of heat pulsing from the hatch as the firewad fused it into a shipyard repair job to open.

It would have been more permanent to wreck the console itself, but dammit, this was *his* ship!

"Charlie?"

The voice on the intercom was Jo's. Sweet merciful High Powers, he hadn't said a bouncing word since he left the Bridge! He quickly summarized the fight, ending with the description of the Merishi woman and her invaluable help.

"I don't know why she did it. Maybe she's a secret agent for good Merishi?"

"The *Somtow Nosavan* Spies' Convention can wait, Mr. Longman. Right now, you and your Merishi lady friend are wanted on the Bridge."

"The passengers—"

"Are alive, Butkus says. He's spoken with people in all four pods. They're scared but all right.

"However, we have an approaching ship on the passive sensors. ETA about forty minutes. I want to Jump in fifteen. Even if the other's Merishi and she's carrying a Follow Me, that will help. We'll Jump to Linak'h, set up for a micro-Jump even if we're on a direct course, then shout for help."

Jumping from this deep in a stellar gravity field was risky for anything except a fully equipped warship. *Shenandoah* could have done it easily.

However, the approaching ship was most likely the Merishi pickup. When its captain discovered that all was not in order (or according to his orders) aboard *Somtow Nosavan,* she would either have to imitate a warship or be turned into that gas cloud that had been so much in Longman's mind.

He put his hand on the Merishi woman's arm to guide her along the passageway. She looked at him, then plucked his hand off with an unmistakable gesture. He yelped with pain and rubbed his wrist—it was the same one that her late unlamented lover had nearly broken, or maybe not so nearly.

Jump first, X-rays afterward, Charlie.

Eighteen

Aboard U.F.S. *Powell*, the Linak'h system:

Herman Franke was in the captain's cabin of the scout for the second time since leaving Victoria, and the first time since the Jump to Linak'h. He did not expect to be there even as long as he had the first time, which was a perfunctory twenty minutes of polite platitudes and fine coffee.

He didn't mind, and not only because he finally was fifty light-years from Victoria. (Forty-eight, actually, as Lu pointed out; he called her a pedant and she glared at him.) For one thing, the cabin was cramped. Scouts were basically light cruisers, and light cruisers were notoriously the least comfortable ships in any navy.

The other thing was, if it took more than five minutes for the captain to make up his mind to answer the call they'd received, there was going to be trouble. For the captain eventually, but probably for other people first.

"There seems to be a lot of chasing and being chased going around," the captain said.

Gordon Uhlig shrugged. "I would have been skeptical myself. But Franke and Morley are certainly on the run. Why not *Somtow Nosavan?*"

"That message they sent—"

Lu Morley lost her patience, in spite of Franke's hand on her shoulder. "They sent it, you mite-brained sandturd, because they really were being chased! They were scared they were going to be overtaken, and wanted the news—"

"The accusation," Commander Bronstein corrected, his voice politer than his face.

Franke decided that matters aboard *Powell* were escalating about as fast as they apparently were on Linak'h. He swore to deal with Lu later, over her tendency to put his foot in other people's mouths (at least it felt like his, even if she was the better dancer by far), and glared at Bronstein. (It was a glare modeled after Lu's, allowing for the fact that his face was cherubic and hers was normally stern.)

"Commander Bronstein, there is probably a priceless load of intelligence aboard *Somtow Nosavan*, including the answer to what's happening on Linak'h."

"There's also a priceless load aboard this ship," the captain replied.

"Ah—strictly speaking, this is classified Command Secret, but—there are three dumps of our data on Victoria."

"Secure?"

"Yes, and all with different access codes. Commander, Lu and I are now expendable. *Somtow Nosavan* is not."

"Nobody said *Powell* was, either."

Franke suddenly found himself as ready to call Bronstein a whiner as any four-star Blue & Gold worshiper (Charles Longman's Aunt Di came to mind). His glare was a sufficiently good imitation of Lu's to make Bronstein wince.

"Commander, I am one point seven years senior to

you as to date of rank. Although I have worked largely in Intelligence, I do have a line commission and an underway command rating." (They were just barely current, but would stand up at the now apparently inevitable court-martial.)

"I can therefore give you two choices: proceed to a rendezvous with *Somtow Nosavan* or be relieved of your command." He hoped Lu had her hand close to her sidearm but not actually on it. "Lieutenant Commander Uhlig will provide any assistance I may require. I hope that your officers will be—"

"Oh, shut up, Herman," Lu said. Her hands were in her lap. Nobody but Franke would have noticed that they were shaking slightly. "You don't have to kick a man when he's down."

Bronstein now looked more befuddled than threatened. "Ah—I admit that you may have a clearer notion of the priorities in this situation than I do. Only next time, give me a little background before you wade into me!"

"I'm sorry I didn't, and if I can in the future I will. Fair enough?" Franke said, in a "This is my final offer" tone.

"Fine."

They shook hands all around, and Franke followed his affiliate out into the passage. Not for the first time, he wondered if Intelligence would ever get out of its classic dilemma: too little security, and vital material leaks; too much, and good men look stupid because they don't have the facts at hand.

They hurried back to their cabin and strapped in; Lu swallowed her antidisorientation medicine. She was slightly prone to Jump-sickness, and micro-Jumps were worse than star-Jumps in bringing that on.

Aboard U.F.S. *Shenandoah*, off Linak'h:

Commodore Liddell contemplated the repeater display in Flag Quarters from the perfect position on the mat in front of her desk. She normally did not combine yoga and tactical planning sessions, since the tactical planning worked against the proper mental state. However, right now her mental state was past praying for; she would have to make do with what the yoga did for her muscles and joints.

The display showed light cruiser *Weilitsch,* one of the Victoria veterans, on her way out of orbit. She was bound for a position at Jump distance over the north pole of the Yellow Father, with a courier ship piggybacking with her. Once in position, *Weilitsch* would act as an in-system relay, security for the courier ship at the Linak'h end of her Jumps, and if necessary the bearer of bad news to the rest of the Federation. Liddell didn't like giving up a combat ship, but the light cruiser/courier ship combination was not only doctrine in this kind of situation, it made sense.

How to avoid the last and worst mission for *Weilitsch*? Liddell decided that the Federation commanders (herself included) had probably been overoptimistic in accepting General Tanz's scenario for the confrontation with the Merishi Territory. They still had a good part of the law on their side (as well as a good part of their LI on the Merishi side of the river, a less agreeable thought).

But "law, schmaw, *abigezunt,*" as her Ancient Languages professor at Thatcher College often put it. No law had prohibited or altered the fact of a double crisis—confrontation on Linak'h, which needed all the orbital firepower the Federation could muster, and confrontation in space.

If *Somtow Nosavan* was half as hot as the message relayed through *Powell* said she was. Liddell decided that they could wait for confirmation, which meant waiting about six or eight more hours for the rendezvous of the two ships at the fringes of the system.

It would be simpler once they had confirmation; incredibly simple if they had confirmation that *Nosavan* was being chased. The only ship able to handle any threat to *Nosavan* and also take off her passengers if necessary was *Shen* herself. The transports had the capacity but not the speed, protection, or armament to fight. The light craft could either fight or evade most threats, but it would take all of them together to hold *Nosavan*'s two hundred people and/or intelligence sources. (She wished Herman Franke had emphasized the "people" a little more than the "source" aspect, but she suspected that Major Morley would be removing appropriate amounts of skin over that on the way to the rendezvous.)

The question left was the best use of the ships remaining behind. Thank God for one favor: Captain Moneghan, the senior cruiser captain, was another old Vic, and his ship, *Cavour,* was just out of Riftwell Dockyard with a miniature flag C-cubed suite. More oriented toward low-orbit and ground-support work, but right now that was exactly what the Mad Irishman would need . . .

The division of forces was now simple enough to do in her head. Two more cruisers for Moneghan, so he could both protect the transports (moved into the safest possible orbit) and help the groundpounders. Also most of the 879th Squadron.

For *Shen,* a light cruiser, a scout, six attackers, and

three shuttles. (Ideally, anyway; four and two would be enough in a pinch.) Also off-load at least half the buses, with a weapons mix that would give Moneghan some strategic firepower as well as ground-support capabilities. "Flag to Communications. Signal, Security One Red: All ships to be at thirty minutes' notice for getting underway for an in-system operation as soon as possible. Any ship not able to be ready in less than two hours, notify the Flag immediately."

"Aye, aye, Commodore." It sounded like Brian Mahoney, who had qualified for Communications OOW last year. "Alert status?"

"No change."

"Aye aye." Her display showed the signal being composed, coded, and transmitted. She stood up and pulled on her robe. The squadron was already at Alert Two, the highest that could be sustained indefinitely. There'd be enough trouble getting everything stowed, sealed, and checked with the people who could be spared from that grade. Alert One would make the squadron temporarily impregnable, and in the longer term less mobile and more tired.

She switched channels.

"Pavel. Can you meet me in Flag Quarters in about ten minutes? I want to run a battle plan past you."

"Certainly, Commodore. Your tea or mine?"

Linak'h and its system:

Candice Shores led her battered but still effective LI troopers on a slog through the shadows of Linak'h's nighttime north temperate forests. She thought that the tint of yellow from the Yellow Father below the horizon gave the ruddy light from the Red Child a bilious quality. It certainly made Yariv's complexion look even worse than the medical sensors said his condition justified.

Powell came out of her micro-Jump and swept across the outer fringes of the Linak'h system's asteroid belt, on the way to her rendezvous with *Nosavan*. An hour after the Jump she began calling the refugee ship; it was a nerve-racking half hour on the scout's bridge before they received an answer.

Colonel Nieg climbed down into Lieutenant Nalyvkina's gunship as it dangled on a trapeze from the big cargo lifter where the Intelligence officer had spent the last eighteen hours. The little lieutenant checked her passenger's harness, activated the rear-cockpit displays for his entertainment, then cut her machine loose.

Just above the treetops, it skimmed toward a clearing where an IR beacon glowed. Nalyvkina flared it out, dropped into the clearing with the tail brushing the outer branches of snowleafs, and landed.

Nieg was unstrapping even before his pilot popped the canopy. As she helped him out, she asked, "Are we going across the river again?"

The tone of eagerness was unmistakable. So was the almost hungry look in her eyes as she stared at the light attacker waiting in the center of the clearing, lift generator already warmed up and canopy open. The pilot waved urgently to Nieg.

"Satellite pass in another five minutes, Colonel. Move it if you don't want them to read the number on it."

Nieg shook his head. "I don't know." He couldn't have told her if he had known, but it was really too soon to tell if his proposed follow-up was feasible.

If all the key people endorsed it, the Federation

would not only be crossing the river again, the lieutenant would get to fly in combat or something very close to it. But that depended on cooperation from Linak'h Command to begin with, and then from Marshal Banfi.

It all really came down to one question: how seriously did Linak'h Command and the Ptercha'a take Banfi's commission as "Warband leader first rank"? Not the honorific titles; the actual legal commission that made him the third-ranking Ptercha'a officer in the Territories even though he was a human Marshal of the Federation.

"Legal fictions" were the source of endless amounts of what Nieg never thought was very good comedy. There were too many unhumorous problems to face, when lives depended on turning those legal fictions into realities.

Nieg scrambled into the rear cockpit of the light attacker. The engine was whining even before the canopy closed, and they took off under both lift and thrust. Again staying low, they accelerated to Mach One and then began to climb as they reached the radar shadow of the Rustsand Hills.

Nieg tried to relax, in spite of the cramped seat, noise, vibration, and flight suit (more comfortable than a suit of armor, if not as versatile). He didn't expect to get much sleep or spend more than a few hours out of his flight suit the next day or two. After that it was even odds whether he would be a corpse, a POW, under arrest, or a victor heaped with laurels.

He admitted that he would prefer the last. He even thought, old-fashioned as it might be, that a nice laurel could be a hug from Candice Shores. He could even return, since she would be another of the victors.

Linak'h:

"One light cruiser, apparently *Weilitsch*, is on its way toward the stellar north pole," Zhapso su-Lal said—or rather intoned. He was in officiating-priest mode, Brokeh su-Irzim thought. It would take a while to complete the briefing at this rate.

However, he was prepared to be tolerant. Just back from Hufen, which hardly deserved the name of "city," he had totally failed to gain access to the humans. In fact, they were now being guarded by Ptercha'a as well as Merishi, and both races seemed to be hostile to any curiosity about their charges, no matter from whom or for what reason.

He had also seen so many movements of weapons and equipment, all Merishi-crewed, that for a time he had wondered if he would be allowed to return to the People's Territory, let alone to the mission. However, the Scaleskins had in due course let him go, and the People's Territorial Governor could not have pushed him onto the homeward-bound lifter faster. (Perhaps he felt that assassins of three different races might be stalking su-Lal, and did not wish blood shed upon the tiled floor of his goldtusk's palace.)

"All other ships of the squadron are clearly preparing to depart orbit. The four transports have already moved into a low equatorial orbit. Buses are being unloaded from *Shenandoah*, and shuttles are bringing down the remaining supplies and nonessential personnel from the transports."

The display showed the orbit the Federation transports now followed. It was easy to tell its main objective—to keep them out of easy range of the Merishi Territory or the Coordination. They would be below the radar horizon of everything except the Southern Ter-

ritory, which had no military bases, and the southern-
most inhabited part of the Wild Continent, which had
very little of anything.

They would also probably be under escort from any
light cruisers not committed to support of Federation
ground forces—or whoever else ended up with the job
of sorting out the crisis along the Braigh'n River. Su-
Irzim did not envy any warrior of any race that particular task, although he was anticipating an ingenious,
possibly even effective solution, given the demon-
strated record of the humans involved.

Considering the aesthetics of tactical originality
could wait. Su-Lal was still speaking.

"We have reports that the Merishi heavy cruiser
Dan-Gyon is also preparing to get underway. The
communications watch has reported much Emergence
activity in various locations. Some of it appears to
be micro-Jumps by unidentified ships. Also there is a
substantial volume of Merishi communications going
off-planet."

Su-Lal did something more than sit down, less than
collapse, and held out his mug for more uys. Beer and
ale, it appeared, were not strong enough. Or perhaps
it was simply having to spend time among the Merishi
with their vile *okugh* that had given him a thirst.

Su-Irzim did the pouring. Rahbad Sarlin gave every
appearance of having taken root on his couch. One
almost expected to see lichen on his tusks and green
tendrils sprouting from his thumbs.

Then he grunted and opened one eye.

"So the Merishi committed their own warriors to
this—situation?"

"I somehow doubt," su-Lal said with extreme precision, "that all of their vehicles exchanged Merishi
crews for Ptercha'a ones before going into action."

"In that case a few estimates about Merishi and ground combat need changing. Ours, the humans', and the Ptercha'a's."

"I am ecstatic," su-Lal said. He raised his freshly refilled mug but sipped rather than gulped. "Does that mean we can ask for ground reinforcements?"

"We can ask," Sarlin said.

Su-Irzim heard the note in Sarlin's voice that told of a wish to close off the topic. He wondered, though, if that was wise. Or was Sarlin merely wishing to discuss it without su-Lal present?

Su-Lal was Syrodhi, of an old family, and it was not impossible that he was passing on material gained in his Inquiry work to the Syrodh Amalgamation or some other fraternal body of the old rulers of the Khudrigate. This had happened before, and although a breach of both law and custom it was seldom punished by worse than discreet retirement to private life (where a good job usually awaited the retiree).

Perhaps it was the uys, the tension, or the ease of moving from one hypothesis to another once one had started speculating. But the idea flared like a missile warhead self-detonating in su-Irzim's mind.

Behdan Zeg had many vices, but also many skills, some rare among the People—such as a fluent knowledge of the Ptercha'a True Speech. He had also trained irregular ground forces, among the People to be sure, but several times over a period of years.

Could the mission find its reinforcements among the Ptercha'a? The People had never found reason to join the other elder races in the habit of using Ptercha'a as hired warriors, but new circumstances might create those reasons. Also, if there was some prejudice against the idea on Petzas or Baer, they were far away and the mission was far from the Governor.

Su-Irzim sipped his own beer and speared a sausage with the point of his field knife. He would need to speak with Rahbad Sarlin about this, once he had organized his own thoughts a trifle more. If nothing else, it would be better than waiting for the humans and Merishi to decide for or against war, and praying that *Perfumed Wind* would pass safely through any space battles that might erupt.

Although if the ship was caught—

No He had some regard for F'Mita ihr Sular and the rest of the crew of *Wind*. The mission badly needed the ship's load of supplies. And finally, it displeased the Lords to ill-wish a comrade's blood kin, whatever the comrade might say about the kin!

Aboard R.M.S. *Somtow Nosavan*, the Linak'h system:

Joanna Marder watched the bulky figure of Commander Franke and the more graceful one of Lucretia Morley march onto the Bridge, and rose to greet them.

"Welcome aboard," she said. "It's more of a pleasure for me to see you than the other way around, I'm sure."

Franke shrugged. "So far, we haven't risked as much as you have."

From the Engineering board came something that sounded suspiciously like one of Charles Longman's more adolescent snorts. Dr. Ibrahim al-Raufi, bending over Longman, clucked in his best imitation of a mother hen.

"Do not excite yourself, please, Mr. Longman," he said. Marder wondered how far his tongue was thrust into his cheek when he put on that manner and the accent that went with it. He was a singularly appealing mixture of standup comedian and superb doctor, and had done invaluable work for both the minds and bodies of the refugees. It wasn't over yet, either.

"Who's excited?" Longman said. "I just remember fairly clearly that you were both on Victoria when *Nosavan* spaced out. I assume you didn't walk from there to here."

Morley started looking daggers at Longman. Marder decided that it was time to tighten a few seals. Federation Intelligence might have led Franke to think he had golden balls and Morley that she was the Great Goddess incarnate, and neither of their opinions mattered much on the Bridge of her own ship.

She looked around to make sure that she had everyone's attention. "Security lock on Bridge," she said, then faced the two boarders.

"Charlie, I, Computer Technician Emt Desdai, Dr. al-Raufi, Boatswain Butkus, and—I suppose you can call her Special Agent—Ezzaryi-ahd—"

"Merishi?"

"Yes. She—well, let's start from the beginning. All of these people at least are going to have to be cleared for all the discussions we have about what to do with *Nosavan*."

She wasn't sure if it was Alliance vs. Federation, Merchant Marine vs. Navy, Navy vs. Intelligence, or just ship's captain vs. interlopers that made her tongue even sharper than usual. No, it was all of those, plus stress, fatigue, and wishing that the scout was at least a heavy cruiser, able to fight anything the Merishi were likely to have on their trail *and* take the old, young, and sick aboard.

Wishing wouldn't turn a scout into anything, and

bad manners might turn the Intelligence people unco-operative. Marder was about to ask for their agreement on clearances more politely when they heard the ear-torturing squall of Ptercha'a mating cries outside the Bridge.

The screen flashed on, showing Ezzaryi-ahd backed against a bulkhead, trying to keep out of the way of two Ptercha'a who were embracing in a fashion that made Marder flush. She now knew what those who described her and Charlie as "looking ready to strip off and go at it right then and there" meant.

She waited, and fortunately Ezzaryi-ahd did too, until the Ptercha'a squalls had subsided to cooings and running claws through each other's neck fur—which was really about as intimate as the Ptercha'a ever allowed themselves to be, at least in human presence. One of them was Emt Desdai, the other was a Ptercha'a woman wearing cut-down Federation Navy coveralls.

"Who is she?" Marder asked.

"That's Seenkiranda, in the service of Payaral Na'an," Morley said. "Surely you must have seen her around the trade mission."

"Can't say that I have," Marder replied. She sat down on the end of her command chair. "People, I have a ship to run, we both have a lot of information to exchange, and only the Creator knows who's on our trail. Commander Franke?"

"We have recorded two Emergences," Franke admitted. "No contacts, active or passive, though. Or at least nothing that isn't an asteroid—or disguised as one," he added.

He looked at Morley. "I'm willing to waive the security regs if you are. In fact, I'll make it official if you like."

"I don't care. But She Who Must Be Obeyed might

have a few things to say, if the family name has to stand between me and a court-martial."

This confirmed Marder's long-standing suspicion, that Major Morley was one of the Monticello Morleys, and had set her hat for Herman Franke. Not nearly as odd a match as she and Charlie, and even if it was she wished them well.

"Very well," Franke said. He assumed the most dignified stance his rumpled clothes allowed and intoned solemnly, "As senior Navy and Intelligence officer present, I authorize discussion of Command Secret matter at this meeting. Do all present waive the reading of the penalties for unlawful disclosure of said material?"

Everybody did, including Emt Desdai when he came in. (Seenkiranda had gone down to his cabin, to unpack.) After the hurdles of bureaucracy were cleared, matters went more smoothly. It was less than an hour before they had swapped all the information anybody thought worth passing on, and in another half hour they had a situation report that Franke hoped could be coded and securely squirted to *Shenandoah*.

"They can relay it to Linak'h Command," he said. "Right now I want Commodore Liddell between me and General Tanz. I don't want him between me and Commodore Liddell."

Nobody seemed to disagree with that proposition. "I suggest that the two ships stay in company, but that we have copies of all intelligence aboard both. That way if worst comes to worst, we can squirt final updates either way and separate, to give a pursuer two targets.

"I also suggest that Seenkiranda and I transfer to *Nosavan* and ride her in. Seenkiranda because she can help with security and also because Citizen Desdai probably won't let her out of his sight again."

"You see clearly, Commander," the Ptercha'a said.

"I'm qualified for command, even though I haven't actually done it, and I do know one end of a ship from the other after a little familiarization. I have the feeling that a little help there would be useful too."

Marder had felt for days that someone had pushed sand behind her eyeballs. Now a different stinging came, and she blinked.

"Yes, that would be—fine."

"Good. Now—Dr. al-Raufi, would any of your friends in the passenger modules object to testifying to how they got here? If there's a secure intercom link —"

"Remember Desdai's work?" Marder said.

Franke slapped his forehead. "Forgive me, Citizen. I can use it, and your friends won't have to suit up."

The doctor's face lost its good humor. "I am quite sure that many of my fellow passengers will have much to say that you will find worth hearing," he said, and each word was as sharp and crystalline as a glass knife thrusting into a Merishi body.

Linak'h:

Candice Shores closed her faceplate and checked the seals, as the smell of her own long-enclosed body enveloped her again. A breath of fresh air had been a lifesaver, but they were approaching contact with a large unidentified body of troops. It might all come down again at any moment, and by now power, ammunition, and the spirits of the people inside the suits were all running short.

At least they'd all had that good night's sleep and a high-energy breakfast the day before. Some of them had managed catnaps at night, although she thought that if South Asian adepts had invented power armor they would not have bothered with beds of nails. Ration bars sustained life, and as long as there was life (and movement, and preferably no superior enemy in sight) there was hope.

But it now wasn't just the mixture of yellow and red sunlight that was making her people look a little bilious. The scouts were coming back—no, only one, and she hadn't heard firing. It was Sklarinsky. Automatically Shores did an external sight check on the sniper's suit, checking for damage or camouflage disruption. No problems, as she'd expected. (Jan Sklarinsky could have done this mission better with a coat of camouflage cream and a plastic knife, but the suit's sensors and recording gear had their uses.)

"Where's Gur?"

"I left him in contact with the—well, I think they're friendlies. They're Ptercha'a, but most of them look like civilians, with pickup weapons. There's a security detail, with regular weapons and at least one SSW, but also some old folks, and quite a lot of children."

"Vehicles?" It had taken a lot of self-restraint for Shores to stay silent that long. Then she had to consider the possibility of exhaustion producing hallucinations.

"A few three-wheelers for the baggage, and some trailers for the ones who can't walk. I think I heard a trail cycle, but most of the ones I saw were on foot."

"Did any of them—" Shores began, then stopped.

She had to go see this for herself. It was unlikely that Sklarinsky would mistake Ptercha'a children for anything else, and improbable in the extreme that the Ptercha'a would be using their kids as bait for ambushing the LI detachment.

Apart from that, anything was possible.

Nineteen

Linak'h:

"Malcolm, age is overtaking me at last."

Colonel Davidson turned from the telescope, which had survived the attack on Marshal Banfi's house, to face the Marshal.

"Sorry, Marshal. I was just watching *Shenandoah* leave."

"How did she look?"

"Bright and shiny." He didn't want to be drawn into a discussion of what he'd really thought. It was always hard to tell when Banfi would tolerate a poetic streak and when he would be as brutal toward it as any farmer's-daughter drill sergeant.

"Is that all?"

Davidson remembered films taken of *Shenandoah* breaking out of Victoria orbit after the end of the war there—or what they had thought was the end of the war. Someone had said that she blazed like a flaming sword of justice.

Now she made Davidson think more of a Blue Death on the hunt.

"Ah. Private, I see. Never mind. I just found that I needed to refresh my memory. Are you a betting man?"

"It depends on the race."

"Read this."

It was decoded Ptercha'a, and Davidson found his eyebrows trying to hide themselves in his hair as he read it. "What's the bet?"

"That we'll have a visit from Colonel Nieg before lunch."

"I don't bet on sure things, Marshal. What about betting that his first proposal is—has to be spaded onto the garden?"

"You spent too much time around the Wee Free Kirkers, Malcolm. They corrupted a naturally plain tongue into delicacy. Ah, well, none of us are perfect, and some of us are old enough to accept the fact. What about the bet?"

"Ten stellars?"

"No odds?"

"Even or nothing. Nieg drives hard bargains, but you're a Marshal and he's not a fool."

"If he is, there are going to be a lot of dead Ptercha'a before long."

Chimes rang from the telescope monitor. Davidson scanned the displays. "The Merishi are also getting underway. Both *Don-Gyon* and that converted transport of theirs."

"Does the transport have any combat capability?"

"Not that I know of. Just legs and capacity."

The chimes rang again, but this time it was only the light cruiser flagship *Cavour*, making a routine evasive adjustment to her orbit. The remaining Federation ships were staying either low or out of danger or both, the transports in fact below the horizon from this far north.

There were plenty of explanations and even much justification for *Shenandoah*'s priority. Davidson hadn't heard more than rumors of what *Somtow Nosavan* was bringing in, but if half of them were true she might bring an end to the crisis right now.

But the Federation's big gun going out on the retrieval mission might also leave Linak'h Command— the Marshal was right, be plain-spoken and call it "bare-arsed." Then only a little more of the hasty temper the Merishi had already shown could make the crisis twice as big in half the time.

Linak'h:

Sergeant Sklarinsky had told the exact and entire truth, as far as Shores could tell. Trailing out for nearly half a klom was a whole—clan, was one translation—of Ptercha'a, armed and equipped as Sklarinsky said.

Except that it looked more like five hundred–plus than three hundred. Also, these weren't Ptercha'a who'd crossed the stars straight from tribal villages back in the Gus'hn Mountains. These were townies, trekking across country with a lot less preparation than they really needed.

A lot less preparation, and therefore a lot more desperation. Although better check—

"I do not have the True Speech," Shores said, using a memorized phrase. "I would hope we need not use Shopspeak." Again, she used Ptercha'a, and a term which she had been told was vaguely derogatory (except by those who said it was very derogatory, and if any Merishi were in hearing then bounce them!).

This produced a lot of shouting back and forth, including some wails of frightened children, who seemed to sound alike no matter what race they belonged to.

Shores was in a mood to terminate with total loathing whoever had driven these people out into the forest. First human refugees, then Ptercha'a. What next, a village of Antahali Baernoi? There probably wasn't one within twenty light-years, but with madness abroad on Linak'h the way it had been on Victoria, why should that stop—

"Pardon me," said a Ptercha'a voice in Anglic. Shores looked down—farther down than usual, when she was in armor and the speaker was Ptercha'a. She saw a gray-furred Ptercha'a female—the gray seemed to be her natural color rather than the result of age, for she looked unwrinkled about the neck and muzzle—with a child just short of Ptercha'a adolescence. The child was gaping up at Shores's armor with the obvious fascination military hardware generated in the young of all races.

"I listen with pleasure," Shores said.

"I am Pelyah, pair-mate to Healer Kinkuhn. He has gone ahead with our scouts to the—" She groped for a single word, and finally came out with "—the Place of the Man Who Is a Friend to All, to warn him of our coming. He did this, after asking the scouts who stayed behind to watch your warriors and the rest of us to await your coming."

So the LI had been under observation by the refugees' militia, without detecting it? Shores was annoyed with herself and her people, but wasn't going to take it out on this woman.

Besides, some of the legends about Ptercha'a prowess held more than a grain of truth. One of the ones that did was that they could hide, stalk, and if necessary ambush better than anybody human except Rangers.

"I am grateful that you did not think us enemies. But we are—"

"Oh, it was very certain that you were not enemies. You were fighting those who made us flee our towns. Now we hope that you will march with us to the Place. The Scaled Folk"—that was only mildly insulting—"and their Slaves"—very insulting, for Ptercha'a who served dishonorable masters—"will not dare attack us when you are with us, to fight them or see the dying. They will also not dare attack you while you are with us, for the number of old and children who would die. The Slaves at least would fear blood feud."

Shores managed to sort all this out quickly enough not to look stupid. The Ptercha'a were refugees because the Merishi and their Ptercha'a mercenaries were beginning a crackdown on civilians in the Territory. They figured that the LI could fight off attacks on the way, or at least bear witness to any massacre. At the same time, the bad guys wouldn't dare carpet-bomb the LI, for fear of exactly such a massacre.

Well, Intelligence had said that there were tribal-level Ptercha'a among the inhabitants of the Merishi Territory. The Scaleskins seemed to prefer to have a supply of that sort around, in fact.

Pardon me, Folk, if I don't think that is much to your credit.

Aloud, Shores said, "I see no reason that we cannot do as you suggest. How far is it to the Place?"

Pelyah had to ask, but the answer finally arrived.

"About ten kloms."

"And you say this Place—the man there—will not inform the Scaled Folk?"

"In times past, he would have told them. But he will never allow them on his land. He is truly a Friend to All."

Something too vague to be called a suspicion hov-

ered at the fringes of Shores's mind. "How does he
live? Is he a farmer?"

Pelyah smiled. "Oh, no. His pair-mate might do
that, but he has not the sense. He makes pictures, and
statues, and carvings, and—"

Now it deserved the name of suspicion. "Ah—does
he have a name?"

This time Pelyah Kunkuhn didn't have to ask. "My
pair-mate says he uses the name Oleg Govorov, which
is not his real name. I cannot believe that he is a
criminal, so—"

Suspicion hardened into certainty, both delightful
and horrible. In spite of Nieg's best efforts to keep
them apart, she was about to meet her father. She
was about to meet her father in the process of dump-
ing several hundred Ptercha'a refugees on him, and
probably destroying his neutrality, home, and peace
of mind for good.

She gripped a tree limb, forgetting the power of her
servo-augmented arm and hand, and felt wood crum-
ble and snap.

"Are you all right, Major?" Sklarinsky asked, helmet-
to-helmet so that they wouldn't be overheard.

"I—no, I'm quite sure I'm Napoleon Bonaparte,"
Shores said, with a laugh that she hoped didn't sound
hysterical to either race. "Back there's Russia"—she
pointed south—"but there lies the road to France"—
with a wave toward the north. "*En avant, mes enfants!*"

The last came out loudly enough to draw a few
looks. Sklarinsky glared and the lookers turned away.
Shores felt the frustration of being unable to shake
herself awake in a suit.

Then she picked up the branch she'd ripped off and
whirled, holding it like a swagger stick.

"All right, people. We have a civilian-protection mission added on top of everything else."

"Them?" somebody said. Shores didn't like the tone of voice.

"The Ptercha'a," she said. "There's a neutral area about ten kloms ahead. We're going to escort them there, and then arrange for pickup for all hands."

The faces around her showed that they'd heard the blessed word "pickup" most clearly. She hoped they wouldn't let their minds run ahead of their feet!

Linak'h:

Colonel Nieg rode out from the Zone the same way he'd come, in a light attacker. The wind was up, though, and the pilot made three passes looking for the right place to change over to lift and land. The Marshal's battered estate still had numerous trees and gardens that the old man would not care to have singed with jet exhaust.

If the pilot had made a fourth pass, Nieg was ready to open his canopy and go over the side for a low-altitude jump. At barely a hundred meters he would have to deploy the chute immediately, but it would be faster than waiting for a nervous pilot to reconcile respect for the Marshal's property with the orders of his colonel passenger.

The jet did kick up some debris on landing, and pleading foreign-matter ingestion, the pilot took off almost immediately. Nieg decided not to make an issue of it. If his approach to the Marshal was successful, they would have all the lift assets they could use, and if it was not—

He refused to think about that, and not because it

was too frightening. He had not faced the prospect of a lover's death in combat before, but he had been as close to members of his old Ranger team in all other ways as he was to Major Shores. He had walked on after their deaths; he would walk on after hers.

What threatened him was laughter. All his efforts to keep Candice and her father apart had been futile. In fact, the success of his plan could easily depend on their getting together and cooperating.

It would be justice, although of a dangerous sort, if the warlike major and her artistic father were hopelessly incompatible. Then the plan would depend heavily on the good sense of Ursula Boll—

"Good morning, sir," Sergeant Major Kinski said. He nearly blocked the door, since half of it was boarded up pending repairs. "How can I help you?"

"I'm Colonel Nieg. The Marshal knows I'm coming."

"I never heard anything about it, sir."

"Oh. Security considerations, I suppose."

"Nothing at all, sir. If you'll wait here, I'll go and see if the Marshal is available."

"This is urgent, Sergeant Major."

"I'm sure it is, sir. But you'll have to wait until I've talked to the Marshal, at least on the intercom. Security considerations, you know."

Nieg managed not to address his next remark to the door just closed in his face. He swore in his ancestral tongue and in Ptercha'a, which he found more satisfying than Anglic. He was considering switching to Merishi when the door opened again.

"The Marshal says you can come in and wait. He'll be down in about twenty minutes."

Nieg's anger crackled in his voice. "What's he doing, playing with Lieutenant Nalyvkina?"

Kinski seemed to grow even taller and wider. Nieg

noted with professional detachment that the sergeant major appeared both psychologically ready and physically able to manhandle him.

"Forgive me," Nieg said. "I'm short of sleep, and my tongue and temper ran away with me. That was an offensive remark, and I apologize for it."

"No problem, sir. Just remember that I've got a daughter about Olga's age, so don't spout off about her."

"Yes, Sergeant Major." Nieg wondered if he ought to salute, but Kinski was leading him into the battered hall and to a reasonably intact chair.

A robot brought him a sandwich—it was closer to lunchtime than to breakfast, he realized—and a drink, after more than the promised twenty minutes. It was nearly half an hour and a second sandwich before Colonel Davidson came down, in camouflage battle dress, to lead him upstairs.

Nieg's first glance showed him one thing: part of his mission was no surprise to Banfi, message or not. The Marshal stood beside his war-scarred desk, wearing camouflage battle dress without insignia. He also wore a broad leather belt, and his baton was thrust into it. By regulation that was all the uniform or insignia a Marshal had to wear. He could appear in mess dress, civilian clothes, or nude, but as long as he had the baton he was entitled to all the privileges of his rank, from salutes on up.

He could even wear the insignia of a Ptercha'a legion leader, the three red swords on a gold field on each shoulder, which Banfi displayed on his battle dress. For an extra flourish, he was wearing both his Ptercha'a Stalker (their Ranger equivalent) and Federation LI badges, and his holster was Ptercha'a work even if his sidearm was human-made.

Nieg decided that he did not want to know if the sidearm was regulation. It would be appropriate if it was not. This whole situation mocked "regulations," more even than Nieg enjoyed.

His discomfort, he knew, would provide much amusement for a good many old comrades and superiors, several of both long dead, many of the rest retired. "Cowboy" was one of the politer terms (in Anglic at least) always used for him in his Ranger days, and now he was being out-cowboyed by a Marshal of the Federation.

At least he'd been defeated by an honorable opponent.

"To what do I owe the pleasure of this visit?" Banfi said.

"Circumstances with which you are doubtless familiar, in general if not in detail."

" 'God is in the details,' " Banfi quoted. "Assume I wish to play God."

The request was reasonable if the phrasing was not. Nieg ran through the Territorial Administration's accession to the request from the Merishi Territory for no more Federation military operations on the east bank of the Baigh'n, and its authorization for "humanitarian assistance requested through diplomatic channels." (Nieg wasn't the only Federation soldier who'd been up all night; Army and Navy together had put in several hundred hours' work loading food, medicine, air-droppable shelters, Ptercha'a and human clothing, and lightweight ground vehicles aboard several more heavy lifters. They had also loaded most of Linak'h Command's supply of nonlethals aboard eight of the 879th Squadron's attackers.)

"All of this means—?" Davidson prompted discreetly.

"It means that we can help anyone who wants to come out if we do it in a way that can be accomplished by Ptercha'a forces. They do not have to be Territorial, just not Federation. They can even be humans resident in the Territory."

"Splitting hairs," Banfi mused. "But not out of reason. I imagine the Merishi are really trying to buy time, so there won't be another clash with their heavy weapons under our gun. They can't afford that, if Major Shores and her people did their job properly."

"As far as I know, they have. We believe they are in close proximity to one band of refugees that has been identified from orbit."

"One led by a Healer Kunkuhn?"

Nieg's chair banged on the floor. "How did you know?"

"He told me," Banfi said, and handed Nieg a printed message. Nieg read it, then picked up his chair. He would have sat on the floor if there had been no chair available.

"He is Confraternity, it seems," Nieg said quietly. "I presume you know Federation policy on dealing with them."

"So does Kunkuhn," Banfi replied. "He knows the number of both Merishi and Ptercha'a who would be hostile or at least embarrassed. He respects us for knowing the facts of life.

"However, he is afraid that the Merishi planned a general massacre of his community, a Confraternity stronghold. So he is leading them out." Banfi activated his terminal. "This map is based on incomplete data, but I suspect he may well run into Major Shores on the way north—"

"To her father," Nieg said softly.

Davidson looked so bemused that Nieg had to explain in some detail. Then he looked so relieved that Nieg wondered if he had a rival for Major Shores's—

no, not bed-friendship. More than that, if possibly less than marriage.

However, Major Shores, if she survived, would make her own decision on that. Nieg refused to worry about matters whose outcome he could not influence. This battle was not one of them.

It was, however, going to be more precarious than he had thought. Banfi could have taken "command" of a band of refugees, with a little stiffening from both human and Ptercha'a militia and some "volunteers" from the Federation forces. He could not take command of refugees who were avowed Confraternity, without forcing both Federation and Territory into something like the prohibited degree of relations with the Ptercha'a nationalist organization.

"I suggest that we compromise," Banfi said. "We wait for confirmation that the refugees are in the neutral zone you've described. Then we move in the supplies and a few armed volunteers fast, before night if possible.

"Every lifter that goes in comes out with a load of refugees. We can say that we didn't have time to check their politics, we were so concerned to avoid incidents, if anybody asks.

"I don't think the Territory will. They have a strong faction of Confraternity sympathizers. The Merishi are probably going to concentrate on sealing off the river, and may not have much left over after that, at least their own people."

This made sense to Nieg. It also made sense to ask Banfi why, when he seemed so well informed on the basis of a network he had not shared with Nieg, they didn't pool their intelligence a trifle more carefully.

Nieg wanted badly to ask this. He knew that he would be the pot calling the kettle black, however.

He had dashed in here on no notice (and why, he wondered—equipment failure, somebody at Command HQ forgetting, or—even in his mind he whispered the word—*sabotage*?), expecting Banfi to go along with a plan using him but not made with his support or input.

Truce with the Marshal, for now and perhaps for good. (It could not hurt Candice to have the favorable notice of a Marshal of the Federation.) And a planning session—

"May I feed this into your terminal?"

Five minutes with graphics got more done than the previous half hour. Five minutes more on scrambled channels finished the job.

"Now, I think we can offer you better than a sandwich while we're waiting to hear from the other side of the river," Banfi said. "If you can cope with Sergeant Major Kinski again—"

Nieg had the feeling that his entire encounter with the majordomo had been monitored, but decided it would be one degree too embarrassing to have it confirmed.

Linak'h:

Oleg Govorov lay nude on his stomach on a blanket in the sun. He could hear lifters in the distance, but so far in the distance that he had a clear conscience about taking a sunbath.

Healer Kunkuhn had come in, with his scouts. They now guarded the area as well as any twenty Ptercha'a could do, which was probably well enough. Other scouts were patrolling—he thought that was the correct term—between the neutral area and the rapidly approaching refugees. The children were already playing with some of the younger scouts—no tales of Ptercha'a eating naughty children for his little ones!—and Ursula was at the radio, listening for when the refugees broke radio silence.

There was nothing for him to do except not wander in the woods as he often did to settle a question in his mind, about an idea or even a work already in progress. Swimming also involved going too far, so sunbathing in the backyard was all that was left.

Diana. The goddess of the hunt. How to tell Ursula that she was not his vision of Diana? There was too much flesh on her, even though it was layered over muscle—and he loved having both the flesh and the muscle in his arms, but it would not work as a painting.

He could use her as the model and then rework the painting closer to his image. But how would she take that? Possibly no better than being told she was the wrong model from the first. It had, perhaps, been a mistake to use her as Andromeda, even—the princess had been unmarried, so perhaps no more than fifteen.

Ptercha'a shouts echoed across the clearing, and sentries on top of the house presented arms. Two of the scouts came running back, with several newcomers plodding behind. One of the newcomers was Pelyah Kunkuhn.

Behind her strode two Federation Light Infantrymen in combat-battered power armor. The nameplate on one said "Sklarinsky," the other was too smudged and smeared with plant sap to read from here.

Govorov decorously wrapped the blanket around his waist, reached for his shirt, and stopped with it dangling from one hand. Armor-suit faceplates didn't let you see through very well from the outside, even when they were polarized for two-way vision. But the long face and the large dark eyes—even though the face was lined and dirty in a way he'd never seen it except after a soccer game—

He walked up to the armored figure and started rubbing the plant sap off the nameplate.

SHORES

"*Slava Bogu,*" Oleg Govorov said softly.

The faceplate swung open. Then the Light Infantry-man named Sklarinsky helped Candy unseal, unlock, and remove her helmet.

The hair was darker, and she'd never worn it that short.

While they were a family, she'd never done a lot of things she had done since the last time he saw her.

Ten years.

Candy shook her head. "F-father," she said. Her voice wavered back and forth across the boundaries of steadiness.

Oleg Govorov wanted to fall on his knees and wrap his arms around her waist. He had just sense enough to realize that this was a public place, in which he would make a grotesque spectacle of himself. Only a giant's arms could go around the waist of a suit of LI power armor.

He reached up—that he could manage—and gripped her by both shoulders. "I am *not* going to hug even my daughter in one of those clanking monstrosities," he said firmly. "Go and change."

"Yes, Father," she said, and then shifted to Russian. "Only you do not want to hug somebody who has spent two days in power armor until she has taken a bath as well, and I am not going to take that bath until my team have bathed first."

Twenty

Aboard R.M.S. *Somtow Nosavan*, the Linak'h system:

Joanna Marder flexed her knees and floated up to the airlock hatch. As much as she enjoyed the walkaround inspection of *Nosavan*, the confinement of the suit almost made up for the view of space overhead. Even that was limited by the bulk of the ship's hull and the swell of the asteroid's horizon, in this minuscule gravity almost literally a stone's throw away.

The airlock cycled; she stepped through into the EVA equipment bay and started stripping off the suit. It was a short-duration model; she didn't need to be assembled and disassembled like an LI in armor. It also left her on intimate terms with her body exhalations, and after even an hour of that she felt she needed a bath.

It could wait, though. Water rationing was tight enough that even the captain had to wait her turn. The original supply had been adequate, and the recyclers were working fine. The Merishi had even reloaded the tanks at Peregrine—anything else would have sounded alarms at once, and given Marder a perfect excuse not to leave.

But *Nosavan*'s life support was a freighter's, not a

liner's and there were leaky pipes in two of the people pods. Also people damp outside and getting dry inside, as the water supply slowly shrank.

Powell had transferred every ton of water she could spare, through an improvised rig that had lost a good ton or two into space and finally frozen up. Marder hoped that the Navy people would be a little better at laying out the antenna net so that the ships could receive and transmit without moving.

Snugged down on the asteroid, they were hard to detect even visually, almost impossible to detect electronically except from such close range that *Powell*'s passive sensors would give warning. Moving, they would be a shout in a cave—possibly hard to locate precisely, but known to be there.

The Bridge was empty except for Herman Franke, who was not so much standing watch as keeping an eye on the master display by the command chair. The other eye and most of his attention seemed to be on the recorder he was playing, with an earplug for listening and a throat mike for editing.

He unplugged and stood up as Marder entered. "All quiet, Captain. The antenna party reports they're about done. Butkus says they've worked hard, for Christless Navy pukes. He didn't know I was listening when he said that."

"Don't do anything to him, please."

"Do I look like a four-star Blue & Gold fanatic?"

He didn't. In fact, he looked rather like a uniformed (barely) teddy bear, with hair right out at regulation length and shaggy at the ends. Oddly pleasant, too. Marder had always liked the intensity that seemed to come with a man's being lean (and hungry?), but she felt an intensity of his own kind in Franke.

"Anything else?"

Marder saw that the drink dispenser was empty except for water. She poured herself a cup; fluid loss from EVA had to be replaced whether you liked the warm, recycled water or not.

"Al-Raufi has a couple of problems. There's a girl in Pod Three with what he calls a spinal parasite. I asked him for details and origin, and he gave me the details but not the origin."

"Probably an outlaw colony."

"Almost certainly. He says he's seen cases like this before—not where, though. It's not infectious over the short run, but if it lasts more than another ten days they'll have to quarantine the refugees. Also, the girl may be paralyzed."

Marder put her head in her hands. With an unknown infection aboard, the refugees would be quarantined regardless—one more ordeal for them, after so many. Probably *Nosavan*'s people too, and Charlie's wrist wasn't improving as it ought to; he needed an orthopedic exam—

"Why don't you lie down, Captain?"

"When I want medical advice—"

"What about friendly advice? Or is that Charlie Longman's prerogative?"

He was steering her to one of the chairs as he spoke, lowering the back, raising the feet, and arranging her on it. For a moment she thought he was going to kiss her on the forehead. But he only arranged one of the first-aid blankets over her, and went back to editing the recording. As she drifted off to sleep, she saw him keying in the com gear, to transmit the latest batch of intelligence over to *Powell* and Major Morley.

Aboard U.F.S. *Shenandoah*, the Linak'h system:

The repeater screen in Communications showed Brian Mahoney the same view of stars that he'd seen there on his last watch, and the watch before that, back to *Shenandoah*'s departure from Linak'h orbit four days before. Once it had showed the Yellow Father slightly off-center, but that was just before the Jump.

Every few minutes the screen linked with the scanner telescope, and then the view was also the same. The Merishi heavy cruiser *Don-Gyon* and her transport consort were squarely in the middle of the view, riding in *Shen*'s wake as if both formations were on a single set of rails across the Linak'h system. The distance displayed under the picture was always the same, too. Ninety thousand kilometers, give or take a couple thousand.

Lieutenant Commander Rosza, Mahoney's relief, came up to stand behind Mahoney's chair. Rosza had mellowed in the last two years, possibly because of Mahoney's increasingly solid skills as Communications OOW, possibly because Rosza was leaving the Navy at the end of this commission. Teaching, he said, although Mahoney couldn't believe Rosza as a teacher of anything except developmentally limited teenage boys. They might respond to his manner, and if they didn't he could punch them out with a clear conscience.

"How's the signature recorder?" Rosza asked.

"Top line," Mahoney replied. "If we were in atmosphere, we'd know it every time they flushed a toilet aboard her."

"Good." Rosza lowered his voice. "I've heard the beervine. Commodore Rosie thinks the Scaleskins may have Follow Me's aboard those two ships."

"The transport, too?"

"Not necessarily. It came through right on the cruiser's tail. It's how the cruiser came through on our tail, nearly half an hour behind us, that's got people worried."

"Um." The Follow Me was one of the "Flying Dutchmen" of space navies, a possibly legendary Merishi sensor that allowed a ship to detect the Jump interface of another ship after nearly half an hour (instead of the usual five to ten minutes) and follow the other with a Jump that would land the two ships in the same part of the same system and possibly within firing distance if the Follow Me operators were good.

And if the device existed. It was supposed to have been perfected in the final years of the Third Hive War, when the Merishi were human allies but all parties were exhausted and interstellar communications had broken down. No one knew for certain if the device had been used in combat before the war ended, and there were few confirmed reports of its use since.

"I've heard of the beast," Mahoney said. "But what I want to know is, why haven't they flown it more often, if it's a century or more old? I would think it might be handy."

"It might not be so handy, if we'd had a century to study it and work out countertactics," Rosza pointed out. "Or it could be expensive, cranky, and space-consuming, usable only on large warships. There could be lots of good reasons."

"Then what's the good reason for their springing it now?"

"That Linak'h is a hell of a lot more important to the Scaleskins than we've been led to believe?"

"Give the man a half-stellar aromatic! Keep on this way, Mahoney, and you'll make a Navy man yet!"

Rosza was right, as long as "Navy man" and "warrior" weren't synonymous. If it came to a fight, he might want to stay off watch, or the sound of his knees knocking and teeth chattering would drown out the voice links. And he wouldn't stop thanking God that Brigitte was down on Linak'h, supporting the Army's convoluted scheme for evacuating refugees from the Merishi Territory without fighting the Merishi except by proxy.

There was something to be said for combat on the ground, after all. You could zig, zag, or dig, and have at least the illusion of control over your own fate!

Linak'h:

Being in a sauna was an odd place to find oneself in the middle of a campaign if not actually on the battlefield, and that could change at any moment. However, Candice Shores wasn't going to complain. This was the second bath she'd had since she suited up, the morning of the battle for *Old South*. It was her first since she came into the "neutral zone" three days ago.

Fortunately her role in the evacuation had been down (as in "down on the ground") but not dirty. After the first security detachment—the first Ptercha'a platoon she had ever seen commanded by a Federation Marshal—arrived, her LI team stood down, except for one section on picket duty to the south (the evaluated area of the greatest threat and the expected route of most of the refugees). The refugees themselves took care of pitching shelters, digging latrines, unpacking and distributing food and clothing, and generally maintaining discipline and organization with a minimum of outside assistance.

Then two more LI officers and forty more armored troopers flew in as "volunteers," and Shores's job became an office one. Not under all circumstances, and definitely not nine to five, but she'd have a little warning before she needed to suit up and move out.

Hence the sauna, which she now shared with Colonel Nieg. Two alone meant only a short stay, just enough to work up a good pore-scouring sweat; the rest of the job would have to be done in the pool, with biodegradable soap and a brush they'd take turns wielding on each other's back. (Which was as far as they'd gone toward resuming their previous relationship. Shores wondered if her father's presence was inhibiting Nieg, until he had formally spoken to the man. If so, she intended to apply some heavy-caliber disinhibitors at the earliest convenient moment.)

A heavy lifter whined overhead, coming in for a landing. Shores heard the note of the fans change as they swiveled for flareout and landing.

"If we don't get any more major groups coming in, we should be out of here in another day," Shores said.

Nieg smiled. "*If* is an ill-omened word in this type of situation, Major."

"We've been taking in ten an hour and shipping out fifty for a day and a half. The secondary camp's almost empty, or was the last time I inspected the pickets. What more can you ask?"

"What you are asking is more forbearance than the Merishi are likely to show indefinitely. Also, that the human inhabitants of the Federation Territory won't think we're taking more risks for Ptercha'a refugees than we were for human ones."

Shores felt as if she'd smelled something too long dead. "How far has that gone?"

"If it goes much farther, there will be questions asked about what kind of Ptercha'a the refugees are."

Shores thought several obscene words and said a couple under her breath. Nieg shrugged. "Human— no, call that sapient—nature. At least we have the Ptercha'a refugees well away from human settlement."

"Where?"

"The big lifter we were going to use as alternate bait—it dumped its load at a preselected site. We've been unloading the refugees there. That way we don't have to either buy supplies for them locally or take lift off the evacuation for a few more days. Also, some of the—scouts—are experienced hunters. As long as they don't poach anybody's turkeys or fish ponds—"

A knock on the door.

"Colonel Davidson. Am I interrupting anything?"

"Nothing that need continue," Nieg said. Shores mouthed a promise to pluck his pubic hairs one at a time at the first opportunity and loosened the door bolt. (No remotes in most of her father's buildings, and one that would stand up in a sauna was probably unobtainable locally at any price. Her father took the bucolic existence seriously; she thanked the Creator that he, his wife—the term "stepmother" didn't come easily to her—and the children had all been healthy so far.)

Davidson opened the door. The moisture in the air promptly condensed into a cloud of steam; his battle dress started to wilt but he was made of sterner stuff. "Sorry to bother you, but there's a major refugee band that we've spotted coming in. I thought the colonel might be needed for an ID, and Major Shores to lead an escort."

Nieg muttered something that sounded like skepticism about Davidson's mental processes deserving the name of thinking. Shores resolved to learn at least the basic terms (of endearment and insult both) in his ancestral language.

"Why us?" she asked. She had a chilly feeling that came from suspicion and not from the open door, although she wanted to ask Davidson to shut it. Nudity lacked dignity when covered with gooseflesh.

"There are at least four Merishi-type lifters flying over the refugees," Davidson said. "No hostile action that we can see so far, but we also don't have radio contact with the people on the ground. We're putting a radar picket up to give low-altitude coverage and alerting flights of heavy and light attackers. The Navy's also promised a light cruiser."

"Nonlethals, I hope?" Nieg said.

Shores reached for a bucket, to draw cold water for a quick sluicedown. Bathtime was definitely over, if the Merishi had finally run out of patience.

Aboard R.M.S. *Somtow Nosavan*, the Linak'h system:

"Bridge, this is Butkus. I'm in the lock. Locking and sealing now."

"Good," Charles Longman said. "Get up here fast. We've picked up a signal on that line you just laid. *Shen*'s inbound. She has our location, but she also has a tail. ETA two hours, twenty-four minutes."

"Bounce the tail!"

"It's probably Merishi. Sure you want to?"

"Not unless it's as good as—urrkkk?"

"Butkus, you there?"

A moment's silence was followed by the sound of

Merishi laughter, and a human grunt. "Still here. That strongarm lady didn't get the joke."

"Maybe she didn't think it was a joke," Marder said over Longman's shoulder. "She understands a lot more Anglic than we thought."

"Nobody tells me anything," Butkus said, sounding aggrieved.

"I'm telling you something," Marder said. "Move it!"

"Aye aye, Skipper."

The intercom went off. "Ezzaryi-ahd's a little on edge," Marder said. "Her mistress hasn't been feeling very well. Al-Raufi said he would diagnose her as a stomach ulcer, if she was human."

"And the nearest multispecies facility is on Li-nak'h," Longman said. He wanted to groan. "What if she gets really sick?"

"Then we're really in trouble," Herman Franke said blithely, from the fold-down chair by the bridge entrance. "The lady hasn't said much about herself, and her companion's said even less. But I suspect that she's a high-level traveling representative of one of the big Merishi Houses. 'Companion' to her is a good cover for someone like Ezzaryi-ahd."

"Private intelligence services?" Longman said.

"When did you take your Basic Officer's—?" Franke began.

Longman glared. "They made me an officer for buggering my instructors," he snarled. "Any other questions?" Then he saw Jo's hurt look, about to change into that of a wrathful goddess, and sighed.

"Sorry. My wrist's kicking up bad." It was, but he was also scared half out of common sense, if not out of his wits. *Join the Navy and see the bulkheads. Leave the Navy and see more combat in your first merchant-*

marine cruise than the average blue-suiter sees in ten years.

The Bridge door opened and Butkus entered, sketching a salute. "External tie-downs all released, Captain, except one that's rigged to blow from Mr. Longman's panel. Switch ninety-two. Security's set, with all the guards ready to hit a couch if we maneuver. Ezzaryiahd went back to the old lady's cabin, said something about a sedative."

Her and me both, Longman thought.

"She really would be a hell of a fine woman, if she didn't have scales," Butkus added. Longman saw Jo fighting laughter.

"Boatswain, explore your sexual fantasies—"

"Extent to Labyrinth," came Commander Bronstein's voice from *Powell.* Longman wished he knew who had come up with those code words. He would buy them a drink dirtside, well charged with laxative.

"Labyrinth here," Marder said. "We are ready to get underway on your signal."

"Very good. Ah, we have a complaint about your boatswain's conduct, when our party wanted to try retrieving some of the antenna components."

Marder looked to Franke for a lead, which wasn't quite the way a captain was supposed to behave, strictly speaking, but right now part of her job was diplomacy and Franke a necessary adviser. He made a circle with thumb and forefinger, then thrust the middle finger of his other hand through the circle.

"We can handle the complaint at some more convenient time," Marder said. "I appreciate your concern for equipment, though."

Before Bronstein could reply, they all heard alarms and the voices of several people who would have been shouting if discipline and tradition allowed it. Then Bronstein again, sounding slightly out of breath.

"Just picked up a strong, close Emergence signal. Also, we've got a multiple-source active sensor scan coming in. I think it's a Merishi drone flight."

"Got a location?" Longman snapped, forgetting to let Marder lead. She ignored the blunder.

"Not this soon, without going to active mode ourselves."

"Crap," Longman said, with feeling.

Marder took over. "We can wait for the bad news, Extent."

"My feeling too, Labyrinth. But be sure your power's up to getting underway on about minus ten minutes' notice!"

Longman looked at the Engineering displays. "We're there already, Extent."

"Good. Hold on, Labyrinth, we're almost home."

Longman would have been more touched by Bronstein's faith if he hadn't heard the anticipation in the other captain's voice. He realized that he was thinking like a merchant officer, with the classic complaint against the Navy:

Bastards always want to wade into the enemy instead of keeping us safe.

Aboard U.F.S. *Shenandoah*, the Linak'h system:

Shenandoah and her escorts went to Alert One the minute *Powell* reported the Merishi decoy net. Liddell abandoned dignity and sprinted to the Auxiliary Combat Center. Its chief during combat was Commander Charbon, but distributing flag officer and CO to different CCs was another strict regulation that out-weighed any personality factors.

Liddell watched the squadron snapping into combat readiness with a curious sense of detachment. She did not have a ship of her own to worry about. Each ship of the squadron was a module of a complex combat system, with her brain a separate module plugged into (or separated from) each one equally.

Right now she was staying separate. Pavel, the light cruiser and scout captains, and the pilots of the four attackers and two shuttles riding launchers didn't need her looking over their shoulders. Neither did the department heads, from Commander Zhubova readying buses to follow the six manned vehicles and Fujita keeping his plant on line for any demands the battle might make down to the newest and most junior rating sweating out her first real damage-control situation.

What they needed was intelligent output from the Commodore Liddell module.

What the Commodore Liddell module needed was for the two ships they were coming to rescue to stay together, detected or not. As long as *Powell* and *No-savan* were essentially one target, they were also a fairly invulnerable one. Deliberately firing on a Federation warship like *Powell* was an act of war. (*Shen*'s Merishi companions had enjoyed their immunity for the same reason, as tempting as it had been to simplify the tactical situation by converting them into debris fields.)

Bronstein was a good man for routine work; Liddell knew she would have sent someone else if she'd realized how unroutine *Powell*'s mission would become. She said a short prayer for his rising to the occasion and made a solemn vow that he would be a civilian on the spot if he really messed it and survived.

Marder she trusted—good head, good background (the Alliance Navy didn't give three stripes to idiots often enough to notice), and good help from Herman Franke and (unlikely as it seemed) Longman. *Charlie's family of admirals is going to have to rethink the man after this.*

If *Powell* gave her half a chance, Marder would keep *Nosavan* alive through anything short of Merishi willingness to start a war.

"Message from *Powell*," Charbon said. "They're getting unusual signatures from the drones."

"Have they been detected yet?"

"No positive lock, but the signals are getting stronger. They think the drones have targeting radars, though."

Which didn't necessarily mean they were also carrying weapons, but why not? Merishi tactical doctrine had a reputation for inflexibility, but Liddell knew too many cases in which such a reputation had been a comforting myth put about by an opponent to avoid the need for rethinking his own tactics.

Also, a hit by a drone-launched missile was less provocative. "Accidental launches" happened often enough for one or two more at critical times to have some credibility, particularly with those who wanted to give an opponent the benefit of the doubt. (There would be a lot of humans with that attitude toward the Merishi, and a good many of them with sound motives. They might even be right.)

Liddell studied the signal again, and hastily ran her tactical plans through yet another revision. She hadn't noticed the number of drones in the flight. Signature data on the ship coming in from the Emergence point said light cruiser or something about the same size. Either way, much too small to carry that many drones.

So—one Merishi ship coming in from out-system.

The two on *Shenandoah*'s trail. And a third one, with carrying capacity if nothing else, lurking undetected somewhere not too far from the two Federation ships.

Scratch the plan of sending one of her own light cruisers ahead, to test the drones' responses and weapons load, and blast them as "menaces to navigation" if they let fly. The drones and mystery ship (she was beginning to hate mystery ships) together might be too much for a light cruiser, even if the Merishi were only trying to stage an "accident."

No buses, either. They weren't faster than the ships over long ranges and lacked the shields you needed in an asteroid belt.

"Signal to *Powell* and *Nosavan:* 'If forced to take evasive action, maintain minimum-interval formation to limits of drive-interaction tolerance.' "

The two ships couldn't piggyback; *Nosavan* wasn't equipped to handle anything as large as *Powell*. But if they could keep their drive fields only a few hundred meters clear of each other, there would be no quick way of dealing with one ship without endangering the other. Also, an order to stop and be boarded was only serious if there were lethal-force methods of enforcing it.

As for tricks like disabling the drive—or in this case, breaching the cargo hold and the people pods inside—they were much harder to do in space than in mediacasts. They could also be easily interpreted as piracy—and piracy was something the Merishi would have to repudiate, if *Shenandoah* left anything to repudiate.

ETA was down to an hour and thirty-four minutes. Liddell now prayed for an asteroid density around the two ships great enough to confuse the drones, for clear space ahead of *Shenandoah*, and for mercy for a commodore obliged to use brute-force tactics.

Linak'h:

"We have that satellite scan of the refugee area coming in," Colonel Davidson said.

Candice Shores put her helmet down and bent over the display. She was otherwise fully suited-up, and beginning to sweat. Banfi's field HQ in one of the outbuildings was poorly ventilated, and the suit life support didn't cut in fully until she was sealed up.

And she still had to lock on the new rocket pack! She could never have got through the door wearing it, but there was another ten minutes before she'd be combat-ready.

The display came up; the refugee column showed in green, Federation air cover layered above them in blue, and the Merishi in red. There'd been a change since the last verbal description of the tactical situation, too.

"The Merishi aren't flying close above the refugees any more. Looks like they've pulled their lift back to just above what they've got on the ground. Is that lift or ground?"

"Hard to tell. They're staying under cover, and nonvisual signatures—"

"—don't let you tell a rocket launcher from an ambulance," Shores said. She realized too late that she'd interrupted Marshal Banfi.

The Marshal's head turned like a lifter gun turret, then he nodded brusquely. "I remember Flight Six on Victoria too. Let us hope the Merishi have also heard of it."

Shores watched the display remain static for another two minutes. "Any identification on the refugees?" she asked, more to make conversation than anything else.

"Biosensors say Ptercha'a," Davidson replied. "They're still maintaining radio silence."

Nieg frowned. His frown asked "Confraternity?" as loudly as a shout. Shores looked at him. Could she ask without words, "Do humans have more trouble with Confraternity Ptercha'a than with any other kind?"

Whatever she'd asked, he answered it with a squeeze of her hand. She saluted, then turned and lumbered up the stairs to the dark backyard.

"Candy?" It was her father.

"I've got to get my pack on, Father."

"I thought it was something like that. Does *Vaya con Dios* still mean anything to you?"

She hugged him, awkward out of the need to be gentle with her servo-boosted embrace. For the first time, it struck her as a wonder of human nature that what parents seeing their children going off to war felt hadn't long since led to universal peace.

But then, there'd been a lot of different standards of parenting through the ages, too. And there was the old saying Captain Moneghan quoted so often:

"You can refuse a man a drink or a loan. But when he wants to fight, you have to oblige him."

Edit to "you can find it hard *not* to oblige him," chalk up another eternal truth, and get moving!

Twenty-one

Aboard R.M.S. *Somtow Nosavan*, the Linak'h system:

Herman Franke sat on the folding seat and dictated into his recorder.

"*Shenandoah* ETA, seventeen minutes. We are all using that as the measurement of time now. We hope Liddell and we are talking about the same point in space for the arrival, but we can't ask. We are now under total blackdown, and will be until *Shen* arrives or we are positively sensor-locked.

"Butkus has just come up to report. Within the limits of blackdown conditions, he and two refugees with suit experience have been rigging our final line of defense. Number Two Hatch has been loaded with debris and rigged to blow on command from the Bridge. This would simulate a major hit and perhaps give us a few minutes' grace.

"We won't use it except as a last resort. The blast could lead to air loss for the entire hold. If any of the people pods had lost integrity by then, it would be a death sentence for everyone in them. 'Reckless endangerment' is the mildest charge we could expect; 'multiple homicide' is more likely.

"Just overheard, Butkus to Marder: the bodies of

the dead from the attempted hijacking have been used as part of the debris. I suspect Mr. Longman of this bit of verisimilitude for an otherwise bald and unconvincing narrative.

"Just convince the bastards for five minutes. That's all we need.

"I shouldn't put this down, but I will. If I'm going out, this is a damned good company to go out in. And Lu—whether you read this or not, I love you."

Franke thought of erasing the last paragraph. He even had his thumb poised to do so, then heard:

"ETA for *Shen*, fourteen minutes, and we have registered positive sensor lock, Merishi Type 231M-4 targeting suite. Prepare to get underway."

It was something of a relief to Franke, the Intelligence operative, that Bronstein, the professional spacefarer, also sounded a little tense.

Aboard U.F.S. *Shenandoah*, the Linak'h system:

With the ETA down to twelve minutes, Rose Liddell switched her squadron from fast and forceful to slow and sneaky.

"All ships, blackdown—now!" The order not only killed drives, shields, and all other avoidable emissions, it put the cruiser and the scout onto preplanned courses that diverged farther and farther from the flagship's.

As their distance increased, it became harder for any opponent who detected one ship to draw reliable conclusions about the positions of the others. Liddell wished she'd dared to risk stopping the whole squadron and letting the Merishi trailer risk overshooting; collision risk in that case was negligible.

But the Merishi astern was most likely only a reserve, or even a diversion. The one certain and one hypothetical ship ahead, along with the drones, were a real menace, one that had to be blocked as quickly as possible.

Silent and dark, *Shenandoah* raced toward her goal.

At ETA ten minutes, she began launching her manned vehicles. This could not have been done in blackdown condition without the new launchers; as it was, all four attackers were out in three minutes, and the shuttles two minutes after that. Like the larger vessels, the attackers went to blackdown mode and let their intervals of departure put them on diverging courses.

Now it was increasingly likely that more than one of *Shenandoah*'s squadron would detect an enemy, giving a quicker position fix for laser illumination or attack. Lasers are instantaneous, at normal battle ranges. They are also narrow, if they are expected to illuminate a ship at battle ranges, let alone damage an armored hull. Lasering without precise targeting in advance is an even better way than active sensor scans to reveal yourself to an opponent.

The two shuttles, on the other hand, made no attempt to be quiet, slow, or invisible. They accelerated rapidly toward the estimated position of *Powell* and *Nosavan*, and as they did they broadcast loudly that they were on a humanitarian mission, rescuing a disabled refugee ship. Interference with them violated the Kirov Agreement and every other statute for the Safety of Life in Space that the major spacefaring races had ratified.

This was perfectly true. Each shuttle carried a medi-

cal team of four and two crew, all volunteers, as well
as portable tanks of water and oxygen. One had a
portable operating room installed. (*Shenandoah*'s medical department under Commander Francesca Mori was
determined not to wait until their ship started taking
damage before they pulled their weight.)

As the shuttles began broadcasting, Rose Liddell
personally broke radio silence with a message to the
Merishi ships astern. She reminded them that *Shenandoah* would enforce the laws about interference with
humanitarian missions, and that she hoped they would
maintain a safe interval in the event her squadron was
obliged to use lethal force.

It was a temptation to work off some of her tension
on the Merishi captain, but one Liddell could control.
If the whole affair ended ten minutes from now in
an anticlimactic rendezvous with the two Federation
ships, she would not care to have an insulted Merishi
Space Security captain waiting in the wings for the
next round.

Linak'h:

Candice Shores led forty-one suited LI into action.
They dropped in two north-south lines, a klom apart,
one on either side of the oncoming refugees.

The western line, including Shores, jetted in from
the now sadly misnamed "neutral" area. Their mission
was to contact, disarm if necessary, and screen the
withdrawal of the refugees.

The eastern line was closer to the Merishi. Their
job was to contact the Merishi, warn them off, use
their organic nonlethals to restrain the Merishi if nec-

essary, and if that didn't work call in more nonlethal aerial fire support.

In this close-quarters situation, there was no substitute for armored Federation LI, even if the operation was nominally under Territorial Militia command. Armed refugees could kill an unarmored trooper through accident or panic. Nonlethals intended for lifters were not so harmless against unarmored troops. (Webheads threw out metallic tapes, to tangle fans or jam jet intakes. The tapes flew out at the speed of a bullet, were razor-edged, and weighed several kilos apiece.)

Shores watched the two lines settle into place on her display, which combined data from her own suit sensors and that fed from a heavy attacker overhead. Some EWOs had a distinctive "touch" in data feeds; Shores thought she recognized Elayne Zheng's.

The western line reported contact with Ptercha'a, mostly armed and mostly male in sight for now. Shores and Sklarinsky, doing bodyguard, used bounding overwatch to advance three hundred meters toward the refugees.

They'd just confirmed the observers' reports visually when from the refugee lines somebody opened fire with a Merishi-style SSW. They were shooting toward the east, and the second burst of fire touched off a major secondary explosion.

Shores's first thought was that some dumb son-of-a-Catwoman had blown away one of her own people. Before she could complete that thought, the eastern line started checking in. They'd seen the blast, but it hadn't been one of them.

Shores and Sklarinsky trotted forward, while the rest of the eastern line went to bounding overwatch and joined the advance. It was a little hard to bound through

Ptercha'a sometimes eight and ten abreast, with three-wheelers, scooters, and even some pack animals.

As she advanced, Shores saw that most of the Ptercha'a were even more heavily armed than she'd thought. Where she hoped it would work, she pointed at the weapons, then at the ground, then shouted the Ptercha'a word for "friend" as loudly as she could.

Where the Catman looked too hotheaded to be trusted with a weapon, she simply grabbed it and tucked it under her arm. By the time they'd reached the other side of the refugee formation, Sklarinsky was carrying so many confiscated weapons that she couldn't have drawn her own.

"Dump and demo," Shores decided. Their arsenal was mostly nonlethals, but a few grenades and demo charges in a firefight were like a contraceptive implant—you never needed them as much as when you didn't have them.

She had to hand signal her orders to Sklarinsky. As the sniper sergeant piled the weapons on top of the command-detonated charge, a psywar lifter came floating down. Loudspeakers and radio blasted the forest night with urgings to the Ptercha'a to lay down their weapons and proceed west, where they would find friends, food, shelter, and a safe passage out of dangerous territory.

From the number of refugees who started looking west and even heading that way, Shores guessed the message was getting through.

"Hope they move it, though," Sklarinsky said. "When I was out on picket before Fatherset, I saw a Ptercha'a work gang loading your father's studio equipment into a lifter. I don't think the neutral zone's going to be around much longer."

"Wonder who got to Father?" Shores said.

"Maybe the little colonel promised to make an honest woman of—hey, I was only joking."

"Next time, think before you—"

Another SSW opened up. It was Merishi like the first one, but this time it came from the forest to the east, well beyond the LI's most advanced pickets.

Shores went to the all-hands circuit. "Front line, Huntress Volunteers, ground and freeze. Second line, back one hundred meters. Flank squads, beacons at . . ." She looked at the map display and called out two sets of coordinates. Beyond the line between those two points, she signaled to the flyboys to start laying down their nonlethals.

"Do not fire unless you are fired upon by an identifiably hostile target," she added, for her own people. "Stay cool, everybody, and we'll have the edge, because the bad guys are losing it."

She didn't put a name to "the bad guys," and not just because she knew some Merishi who knew Anglic might be listening. If the Ptercha'a did not drop their weapons or at least hold their fire, there would be two sets of bad guys in the forest tonight, with her LI caught in the middle.

Then the reassuring whistle and thump of nonlethals being laid down drowned out even the blatting of the psywar lifter. They were aimed at different targets, but she hoped that both would be equally effective where they hit!

Aboard R.M.S. *Somtow Nosavan*, the Linak'h system:

They stopped counting down toward *Shenandoah*'s ETA when the two ships lifted off from the asteroid.

It didn't matter that much anymore, with the ships moving and the shuttles not only on the way but telling everybody that they were.

Charles Longman listened to the radio with a throat that was so dry it hurt almost as much as his wrist. Only part of it was fear; they'd turned down the air humidification to save water. He was starting a sinus headache, too, and not a mite for light-years!

"Mainbase, this is Crimson Three. We have a visual on a drone. No visible armament. Merishi Type O8X, with some nonstandard modifications. Recording—"

"Azure One to Mainbase. We have radar and IR signatures on a large mobile target, bearing 270-210-280 relative. Estimated speed twelve km/s; repeat one two kloms per second. Course—"

Longman looked at the display, and saw that he wasn't the only one.

"Christ." It neither prayer nor curse, simply a statement of disbelief.

"I thought there were too many drones to come from that cruiser," Marder said. They listened to Azure One describe the rest of the contact's characteristics, and Longman felt even worse.

"The Scaleskins have a bouncing *battleship* in the system!"

"Maybe," Marder said. She'd heard the note of panic in his voice; her look told him that. Herman Franke frowned.

"I wonder why they're sending in clear?"

Marder bared her teeth at him, telling Longman as well that she saw through his ploy. But Longman knew he had to prove that he could speak calmly.

"They wish the Merishi to overhear," Emt Desdai said, before Longman could speak. "It is as with the shuttles. They hope that displaying knowledge will produce fear, or at least wisdom, in the Folk."

Longman muttered something about Folk wisdom being a byword for ignorance, but before he had the nerve to say it out loud, Azure One was back.

"Target is accelerating. Velocity now nineteen km/s. One nine km/s. Active sensor probing in all modes from the target. They have active sensor lock. We are going to maneuver to test their ability to hold—"

"Extent to Labyrinth. We have an asteroid dead ahead. Hold formation on us. We are going to pass beyond it, then back down into its cover. Shuttles, do you copy?"

"Labyrinth to Extent, we copy—"

"Mainbase to Azure One, break!"

"Crimson Two to all hands. Missile launch from a drone bearing—"

"Azure One to Mainbase. We have laser lock. Maneuvering—!"

The last message ended in what Longman would have sworn was a scream, followed by a roar of static.

Aboard U.F.S. *Shenandoah*, the Linak'h system:

Brian Mahoney learned that day how true it was that after days or weeks of crossing billions of miles or hundreds of light-years, space battles often lasted only minutes.

It was not a surprise, when one thought it over. The limited supply of weapons and the ruggedness of the targets (at least while they had shield and drive power) meant that if you wanted to fight at all, you tried to get to close range. The largest starship still occupies a small fraction of the amount of space that can be scanned by an opponent's sensors and reached by her weapons. But if those weapons strike anywhere else but in the right small fraction, they might as well have stayed at home—which is where the replacements will have to be found, if you fire your entire weapons load without hitting anything. Good intentions don't count in space combat, only good shooting.

The miracle is not that space battles are so few. The miracle is that there are so many, when one considers that they require even more mutual consent than most forms of sex.

From the firing on Azure One to the end of the battle, it was exactly thirteen minutes.

Azure One died from an unambiguously hostile laser beam, fired from a now unambiguously hostile if still unidentified large spaceship. Crimson Two reported the loss, then engaged and destroyed the drone-launched missile without waiting for Mainbase authorization or identification of the missile's target.

The shuttles promptly took evasive action, breaking down below the asteroid from which *Powell* and *Nosavan* had just departed. They also unloaded decoys, whose jammers considerably added to the radio noise.

The ship approaching from out-system accelerated rapidly, sending a radio command to the drones. Some of them launched missiles before they self-destructed. *Powell* promptly opened fire on the missiles with her self-defense lasers. They were not the heaviest of their kind, but the drones' weapons load was small; their missiles were not hardened or maneuverable. *Nosavan*'s Bridge crew watched the missiles turn into globules of sparkling debris, then the new asteroid cut off their view.

Powell had to remain in open space to engage the

missiles, and so gave the large hostile ship a clear target. She illuminated with lasers and launched missiles. *Powell* broke laser lock with minimal damage, but the missiles were already on their way, with her signature locked in their memories.

They were also being scanned by every ship in the Federation squadron, from *Shenandoah* on down. As the blasts of the dying drones and their missiles faded away, lasers and countermissiles began probing the enemy ship's salvo.

The salvo was recorded at eighteen missiles. Two were never accounted for. One hit the asteroid sheltering the two Federation ships. It didn't shatter the rock, but it knocked off major chunks. *Powell,* not yet closed up, escaped damage, but a piece the size of a small house wrecked *Nosavan*'s Number Three Hatch and another flying boulder nearly set off the deception charges at Number Two.

Aboard *Nosavan,* the Bridge crew held on and prayed for no more space-junk hits. Any more lost hatches would decompress the hold. A missile hit would be a quicker way of dying for everybody.

None of the remaining fifteen missiles came near *Nosavan.* They ran into the Federation counterbarrage, with lasers, particle beams, frag and fuser/EMP warheads, and dirty socks all blasting away.

The missiles that didn't disintegrate lost guidance and wandered off, giving one shuttle crew a severe fright but doing no other harm. Through the fading cloud of debris and particles from the missiles and the battered asteroid, *Shenandoah* swept at nearly her maximum speed.

Using your own space junk as a screen for attacking required superb shiphandling (read: Pavel Bogdanov), a stout hull (but *Shenandoah* had three meters of steel and ceramics between vacuum and vitals; a shield was useful but not always necessary), and a flag officer determined to come to grips with a proven enemy.

Rose Liddell launched buses as her ship cleared the debris, and at the same time gave for the first time in her life the order:

"Full power, main laser battery."

Lights, gravity, and displays all flickered from a power surge even *Shen*'s sophisticated computers could not entirely handle, as Fujita fed power to the big lasers in the ship's belly. They were the standard four, and their beams focused into a single thrust of shipkilling light well before they reached the target.

Shields are transparent to light, and the other ship had no time to lay a dust screen or to drop shields and maneuver. The laser boiled off chunks of the outer hull, sent disruptive shock waves through the inner one, crippled sensors, equipment, and crew, and made the subsequent missile hits superfluous.

There were still five of them, however. Two of the buses had been launched on self-targeting mode, using their onboard sensors to load their missiles. They launched between them twelve missiles, and it was a measure of the other ship's toughness and weaponry that she took out six of the eleven that functioned properly.

The other five hit and exploded so close that fratricide (debris, EMP, or both) took out three warheads completely and reduced a fourth to a low-order explosion. The fifth yielded its planned twenty megatons, and that was the end of the target as a fighting ship.

Four other buses, each carrying a similar load, turned and slaved themselves to the light cruiser's control. They were intended as backup in case *Shenan-*

doah herself lost C-cubed, or for chasing the second ship, if that was possible.

In Communications, Mahoney monitored the dialogue that ended the battle.

Merishi captain: "The damaged ship may also require humanitarian assistance. Do I have permission to approach and board?"

Liddell: "Wait. The warning about approaching the other Federation ships, however, is still valid."

A short exchange with Extent and Labyrinth, scrambled at both ends. It was amazing how cool Charlie Longman could sound. Mahoney wondered how he would sound if he had to make talktalk instead of just monitoring other people's.

Then he could hear the frustration in the commodore's voice as she replied:

"Our own mission is urgent. You are authorized under the appropriate conventions to assist the other ship to the limits of your ability."

"Thank you." If the Merishi captain felt any triumph, his voice didn't show it. Did he realize that Liddell was letting him deny the Federation a major intelligence coup, not to mention covering his tracks, if everybody's suspicions about the dead ship were right?

But then, if we're right, he'll be picking up his own people, fried, fragged, radiated, and otherwise massacred. No reason he should look forward to that.

Mahoney looked at his watch, as he listened to the report of the shuttles rendezvousing with the two ships they'd come to rescue. The whole battle had come and gone in fourteen minutes. He doubted if he'd suspended his natural functions for that long, but he really couldn't remember having breathed.

It took another six minutes before *Weilitsch* reported that the other ship, which she and the buses had been chasing, had Jumped. In another two, the shuttles were both docked with *Nosavan* and Charlie Longman went off the air, to be replaced by somebody named Herman Franke, whom Mahoney had thought was on Victoria.

But then the plan of campaign for Linak'h hadn't even survived to the point of contact with the enemy, so why not more surprises at every turn?

Linak'h:

Candice Shores waited until the barrier of nonlethals was thoroughly down (or up, depending on what kind of round you were talking about) before ordering another advance. Even then, she took only Sklarinsky and eight troopers. The rest fell back, to form security for the medevac lifters who were now landing protected medics with multispecies kits.

The stuff they'd been laying down wasn't supposed to kill any of the four races represented on Linak'h. However, Shores had buried a few people who were "supposed" to be alive, or at least attended their funeral. Also, with some of it, metabolic-stimulator injections (and pray to all the various Higher Powers that the medics remembered which shape of injector held which race's) and treatment of fragment wounds (nonlethals did explode out of containers solid enough to stand firing and ballistic trajectories, after all) helped speed recovery.

Few Ptercha'a had been caught in the barrage, and a good many had prudently speeded their departure by dropping heavy or obsolete weapons. The medics caught up with her point team about the time they began to run into Merishi casualties. Shores and her people kept out ahead, able at least to tell Merishi who were breathing from those who weren't or needed help to go on.

They'd completely run out of Merishi when they reached a clearing about five kloms beyond the OECZ. Not quite a clearing—the trees provided a screen overhead, and nets were slung from one to another to thicken up the cover.

Under that cover, Shores counted twelve lifters. From the way they were sunk into the ground, she judged they'd landed heavily loaded. She also saw that most of them had roof guns, open-mounts but still lethal if manned.

One squad lay back, on watch, with orders to hit the first gunner who reached for an actuator. The second squad followed Shores and Sklarinsky to the first lifter, and formed a security circle around them as Shores strode up to the bow.

The cabin was sealed, but inside Shores saw two Ptercha'a. The nearer one, in the pilot's seat, wore an earring, and the farther one had a Merishi pulser across his lap and tribal dyemarks on his ruff and ears. He was also conscious enough to go for his weapon.

Feeling more like a bully than a soldier, Shores punched her left fist through the nearest window and tossed an itch gas grenade in with the other. The two Ptercha'a promptly opened the opposite door, leaped out, and ran off, scratching vigorously. One of them began shedding clothes as he ran, and was nearly nude before he vanished among the other lifters.

The lifter-to-lifter search took a good twenty minutes, with Shores expecting a booby trap or a shot in the back every second. (Neither might have done her much harm in her suit, but dammit, she didn't want to kill anybody else tonight! The people who'd given the orders for the various messed-up Merishi games were out of her reach.)

The final score was ten lifter loads full of ammunition, one of assorted supplies, and one empty, as well as nine conscious and four unconscious Ptercha'a prisoners. Since two of them were pilots, Shores loaded them all in the empty lifter, had them memorize a safe-conduct code that she then passed on to the air watch, and saw them lift out and head east.

"What happens if the Merishi are trigger-happy?" Sklarinsky asked, as the lifter's lights faded over the treetops.

"Sergeant, as a field-grade officer I can finally give master sergeants advice. My first piece of advice is: that's their problem."

"Yes, ma'am. What's the second?"

"The second—no, make that an order. The next order is to time-fuse all our demo charges and blow up those lifters. Ten loads must be a good part of their reserve ammo on Linak'h. I don't know what kind it is, but it's sure as Hades going to be nonlethal once we get through with it."

That was almost overoptimistic. The blast as the ammo dump went up tumbled several of the LI rear guard and nearly knocked a medevac lifter out of the sky. Shores thought of sending somebody back with a chemanalysis kit to see if there was some new explosive involved, but she and the troopers were all too tired and ready to lift out for home.

Besides, Intelligence would probably discover that the new superexplosive was a commercial demolition compound developed before the First Hive War. "There is nothing new under the sun" sometimes seemed to hold true, no matter how strange or far the sun was.

The Yellow Father had risen with the Red Child creeping across its face, when Shores returned to her father's house. There was nothing of his left now, nothing of him. The only sapient presence in the cleared land was the military, Ptercha'a and human. The last of the refugees were already across the river.

Shores popped her faceplate and walked down to the pool, where she and Nieg would have gone after the sauna. Already windblown dead grass and leaves floated on the green water.

"It will come back, Father," she said, wiping her face where the morning breeze couldn't reach it. "We didn't use much, and most of it won't hurt the forest life."

"Candice?"

She turned, to see Nieg looking even shorter than usual. She felt no loss of dignity on either side as she bent to kiss him, and he rose on tiptoe to receive the kiss.

"It's time to go. Unless you want to be in the history books as the last human out of the Merishi Territory on Operation—whatever we decide to call it."

"No name? The historians will never forgive you!" Then something about his phrasing struck her.

"The last human?"

"Some of the Ptercha'a wanted to walk out, for reasons that satisfied Marshal Banfi. I defer to his judgment in matters concerning Ptercha'a."

"I see."

"I hope so. Marshal Banfi has been placed in a much more influential position than we anticipated at the beginning of the whole Linak'h situation. But then, I suppose that a master of maneuver like that can also use his skill against his own people, if they stand between him and some valued goal."

They talked about Marshal Banfi's possible goals all the way back to the lifter, when they had to be quiet because Colonel Davidson was also part of the last lift out.

Twenty-two

Charlemagne:

Speaking literally, it was Admiral Baumann on the carpet. She strode up and down the deep red rug of her office, hands behind her back, pausing between apparently deep thoughts every few seconds to glare at the three officers sitting on the phalanx-hide couch.

In the traditional sense of the term, they were on the carpet. Baumann had been quite explicit, even at the height of her imperial wrath half an hour ago.

"I really hope that you are all officers who take your oaths seriously. I do not want to learn that any of you sent to Linak'h any orders that could reasonably be interpreted as permission to start a war."

They'd all flatly denied it, and Ropuski invited Baumann to examine a copy of the communications log she'd prudently brought along. That somewhat mollified the Empress, and the passage of time and adrenaline finished the work. She still had the spring-legged stride that reminded Kuwahara of Major Shores, and which in Baumann was not a sign of vitality and good spirits but of the wrath to come.

"Very good," Baumann said. She slid into an armchair and stretched out her long legs. "I believe you are telling the truth. I hope you can convince all the committees, the Ministries of Trade, Space, War, Foreign Relations, Justice, and Cultural Affairs—have I left any out?"

"Not to my knowledge, Admiral," Kuwahara said. "But then, I've only seen the mediacasts. You might have more recent information."

"Such as the Coordination invading the Territory?" Baumann snapped.

Kuwahara decided that soothing phrases would be wasted on Baumann, and in fact he suspected that in her situation he would be quite as irritable. The situation that the local commanders—yes, including Rose Liddell—had allowed to develop was not a good one. It did not reflect well on them, even though major-damage control had already been put into effect. (If Liddell had helped allow the situation to arise, she had also done the most dangerous part of the cleanup so far.)

What had turned an incident into a potential—no, make that actual—crisis was an additional message that arrived twelve hours later. The Coordination had informed the Territorial Administration and the Federation Governor-General that citizens wanted for criminal and terrorist activity against the Coordination and friendly institutions were being harbored illegally by the Territory. Both humans and Ptercha'a were responsible for this situation.

If the criminals and terrorists were not turned over to the Consolidation or other mutually agreeable authorities within thirty Linak'h days, the Coordination would feel itself free to take such action as seemed appropriate under the circumstances.

The Merishi hadn't endorsed the ultimatum, not even their Territorial governance, but an ultimatum it was. If anybody in the Federation doubted it, the media would make it their business to persuade them, probably well before the thirty days expired.

Not that Kuwahara disagreed. He thought that the Coordination had potentially painted itself into a corner, going ahead without more assurances of Merishi support. But then they might have wondered what other tricks the Federation had up its sleeve, beyond letting Marshal Banfi go on active duty as a Ptercha'a general.

Or they might have had assurances no Fed on Charlemagne or even Linak'h knew about. The media would not hesitate to speculate aloud and at length on that, nor would Intelligence, and again Kuwahara thought they were both right.

In fact, it was hard to see that the Federation's response had many more advantages than its having been a *response*, rather than simply sitting around and waiting for the other side to act. If the end was strained relations with the Ptercha'a, even that advantage might have cost too much.

At the far end of the couch, General Langston's eyes met Kuwahara's.

Aboard U.F.S. *Shenandoah*, off Linak'h:

On the screen in her cabin, Rose Liddell saw a shuttle undock from *Somtow Nosavan*. It wavered, then hung in space only a few hundred meters from the battered cargo ship.

A moment later the reason for the hesitation came on screen. Four attackers of the 879th, bound up from the planet now that Linak'h Command had released them back to the Navy's control. Liddell heard the intercom proclaim that all hands should be alert for taking attackers aboard.

She was as alert as her fatigue allowed, and could maintain that degree of alertness as long as she didn't actually have to get out of her chair. They all needed a duty-free day or half-day, but the Coordination's ultimatum had blown that one out the lock. A duty-free minute would be the most they could manage.

Yes. A customized duty-free minute for each of the crew. She'd promise that in her all-hands address later today. It should at least be good for the right kind of laugh.

Liddell slipped out of her robe and started the sun salute. The Federation and its friends wouldn't have to watch their backs in space, thanks to *Shenandoah,* and that was something.

More than something—the ships *Shen* had fought had been doing something so blatantly out of line that even the Merishi would have to repudiate it or be branded sponsors of piracy, terrorism, hijacking, and defacing public rest rooms. In the process, the squadron had also staged a major intelligence coup that would benefit more planets than Linak'h, starting but not ending with Victoria. That dusty planet was going to cast a long shadow over *Shenandoah* and her people.

One thing Liddell vowed, as she slipped into lotus position and began casting around for an appropriate mantra. None of *Shenandoah*'s people were going to suffer because nobody in Linak'h Command had found the courage to tell Marshal Banfi, "No, you can't hold your damned party!"

Linak'h:

Candice Shores's father and his wife were still waving when the lifter cleared the treetops and Nieg swung it toward the south. Shores leaned back in the copilot's seat, twisted her neck and shoulders as much as the harness allowed, found the kinks disappearing—then suddenly felt tears streaming down her face.

Nieg climbed until it was safe to use the autopilot, then took her hand. She could see that he wanted to do more, which was a little bit of a relief. Fine. He could listen.

"I was just thinking—the first time I see my father in ten years, and what do I do? I barge into his home and drive him out of it, wife and children, paintings and pets."

"I didn't see any pets."

"Ursula has a cat. Big black tom. I think they got him away safely."

"I hope so." He was silent for a moment. "You were on a mission, you know."

"Obeying orders is an old, bad excuse."

"It's also not the same thing. You weren't ordered to wreck his home. If you did, which I doubt."

Nieg shrugged. "I was considering—Banfi was, too—pulling him out within a few more weeks anyway. The situation in the Merishi Territory was going to erupt regardless of who held what kind of parties. Too many people were taking to the woods for one reason or another, and most of those reasons led to trying to shoot someone.

"As it is, he came out with his family, his artwork and supplies, and hundreds of new Ptercha'a and human friends. Kunkuhn will give both him and Ursula jobs at the camp, unless the Territorial Administration sends in somebody to take charge."

"That would be stupid."

"I agree. I have recommended that the refugees be treated as a self-governing community. This is a rather complex status, legally, but it means that Kunkuhn would have more or less a free hand."

Shores said nothing. To the west, the Yellow Father had dipped so low on the horizon that the haze had turned it almost the same color as the Red Child, still in the blue-green evening sky higher up.

"I hope you won't consider this a bribe," Nieg said. "But—"

"What is it?" She realized it had not come out the way she wanted it to sound.

Nieg stiffened. "It is going to be hard for us to work together if you suspect my motives for every courtesy and consideration."

"I'm sorry. But—oh, Hades. You couldn't help notice that I was wallowing in guilt. I thought you might be proposing something to soothe me." She wiped her eyes with the back of her hand, and noticed blisters and calluses on the palms that hadn't been there on Schmecheim.

"So stop feeling guilty. Start considering who you want for a quick-reaction force cadre. It will have the LI, the Ranger detachment we're expecting, one Regular rifle company, a Reserve unit for local knowledge, and possibly some attached Ptercha'a scouts. Also extra transport, an SFO team, and so on. You're going to command it, with the rank of lieutenant colonel."

"Acting or local?"

"Both."

Shores looked at the altimeter. "We're not high enough for oxygen starvation to be affecting my hearing."

"It isn't." Nieg carefully avoided looking at her. "I did not recommend that it be both. However, you are now one of the Hentschmen. General Tanz meant what he said when he promised to reward you. And Marshal Banfi favored both promotions. So did Colonel Davidson."

"The woman tempts him?"

"Who is 'him'?"

"The colonel who is not here."

"The colonel who is here is also tempted. Will he have an opportunity to yield to temptation?"

Shores slid a hand behind Nieg, as far as the harnesses would allow, and squeezed those wonderful neck and shoulder muscles. His eyes grew heavy-lidded and turned to slits, for a moment rather like her stepmother's cat.

The opportunity wouldn't come by chance, she knew. There was a Baernoi ship in orbit that Nieg had to evaluate, even visit. There was a mass of intelligence for him to sort, from the refugees and defectors. They both had to go to the party Franke and Morley were throwing in memory of Top Zimmer—and she would have tears to spare for him.

But she and Nieg had reached the point of making time for each other, even at the dawn of a war.

The Yellow Father dipped below the horizon and they flew south in twilight.